CRIME
YELLOW

Gollancz New Crimes 1

CRIME YELLOW

YELLOW

Gollancz New Crimes 1

Edited by
Maxim Jakubowski

VICTOR GOLLANCZ
LONDON

First published in Great Britain 1994
by Victor Gollancz
A Division of the Cassell group
Villiers House, 41/47 Strand, London WC2N 5JE

Typeset at The Spartan Press Ltd,
Lymington, Hampshire
Printed in Great Britain by St Edmundsbury Press Ltd,
Bury St Edmunds, Suffolk

CONTENTS

INTRODUCTION

Welcome to another year in the life (or should it be the death?) of crime, this time under a new hospitable roof at Gollancz, a publishing house whose credentials in the crime and mystery fields are already impressive: past home of luminaries as diverse as Dorothy L. Sayers, John le Carré, Sara Paretsky, Lionel Davidson and so many other major names long associated with the genre.

The yellow covers and spines of past Gollancz mystery titles were once a traditional element of identification with quality in crime writing. It is with great pleasure that this anthology series renews that visual tradition, still dear to the hearts of many fans and readers.

The *New Crimes* series was launched in 1989 at Robinson Publishing before moving, in its fourth year, to its distributors at Constable. Under its new yellow guise, this is effectively the sixth volume of the series and it is an association we greet with enthusiasm, as we join one of the great publishing names in crime fiction.

Our aim has always been to present the best new stories available from both British and American mystery writers, whether they occupy the hardboiled left centre of the genre or its opposite cozy domain. Crime fiction can be both realistic and entertaining. As a category, it offers its authors a wide range of possibilities ranging from sheer escapism to literary endeavour. All elements have always been welcome in *New Crimes*, whether from new or established writers. Last year's volume garnered three of the six nominations for the prestigious Crime Writers' Association Short Story Gold Dagger (including the eventual winner, Julian Rathbone), while in previous years material first published in the series enjoyed two Edgar nominations. Achievements we hope we can repeat, and improve on, in the future.

Our assorted contributors again offer a varied criminous cocktail, blending well-known talents, rising stars, new writers, all supplying wondrously entertaining stories guaranteed to cheer and disturb you in equal measure, as all good mystery writing should.

On our first yellow menu, we have:

ED GORMAN is a *New Crimes* veteran and Edgar nominee. The editor of the indispensable *Mystery Scene* magazine and prolific crime, western and horror author, Ed lives in Iowa. His stories are sparse but powerful and 'One of Those Days, One of Those Nights' is no exception, with its acute psychological insights into jealousy that might ring a worrisome bell with some.

Sherlock Holmes' appeal never fades, despite the passing of the years. The ultimate paradigm of the great detective, he continues to inspire the metaphorical grandchildren of Conan Doyle. Past Chairman of the Crime Writers' Association ROBERT RICHARDSON offers a new Sherlockian tale in the grand old tradition, which originally appeared at Christmas 1993 in a truncated version in the *Independent*. This is the first publication of the full text.

SUSAN KELLY, author of the popular Nick Trevelyan and Alison Hope series, shows us a murky but delightful peek behind the scenes of a well-known Shakespeare play, recently in the public eye following its film version by Kenneth Branagh. The story will no doubt send you back to the play or the movie to appreciate its ingenuity and irony. Susan has recently published her first mainstream crime novel, *The Seventh Victim*.

JO BANNISTER is another British mystery writer whose star is in the ascendant following impressive reviews for her novel *A Bleeding of Innocents*, which has since been followed by the equally powerful *Sins of the Heart*.

MAT COWARD's first ever mystery story in last year's *New Crimes* was shortlisted for the Gold Dagger Award. He has since sold another half a dozen stories to other collections and magazines, and we are pleased to see him return to the fold with a witty tale of realism and retribution.

Following a two-year sabbatical of sorts in sunny Spanish climes, LESLEY GRANT-ADAMSON is now back in London's Islington (with forays to Nottingham as writer in residence at the university). Her new novel, an international thriller, *Dangerous Games*, has just appeared, and is a sequel to her popular *A Life of Adventure*.

MARTIN EDWARDS works as a solicitor in Liverpool, and his novels feature the detection and exploits of Harry Devlin, a Liverpool solicitor. Draw your own conclusions! The fourth and latest in the series is *Yesterday's Papers* (named like the previous three after a pop song). He has also written several Harry Devlin short stories, one of which appears here for the first time.

Newcastle-based CHAZ BRENCHLEY's story is particularly dark and gritty, and an excellent example of a new school of realism that is emerging among younger British mystery writers. His latest novel, *Paradise*, borders on horror and is heartily recommended, unless you have a weak heart, that is . . .

University librarian at New Orleans' Xavier University, ROBERT E. SKINNER is the acknowledged expert on the works of Chester Himes, about whom he has written a study, *Two Guns from Harlem*, and whose posthumous novel, *Plan B*, he edited. His fiction has appeared in *Ellipsis* and *Hardboiled*.

JOHN MALCOLM is the current Chairman of the Crime Writers' Association. He is the author of ten art mysteries featuring his popular sleuth Tim Simpson, the latest of which is *The Burning Ground*. He works in the export trade and lives in Sussex.

RUSSELL JAMES' tale of evil doings in the English countryside proves once and for all that crime in country retreats is not what it used to be in the glory days of Agatha Christie. A marketing consultant who lives in Cheltenham, Russell is part of the new wave of neo-realist British crime practitioners and has been compared by some to a British David Goodis for his pervasive noir atmosphere and downbeat but powerful novels.

American author MICHAEL Z. LEWIN has lived in Somerset so long that he qualifies as an honorary Brit. Creator of the popular Leroy Powder Minneapolis novels, he is also a prolific short story writer and contributor to past volumes of this series, as well as a specialist of mystery radio plays. His latest novel is *Underdog* and he co-edits (with Liza Cody and Peter Lovesey) the annual *CWA Culprit* anthology, with whom we entertain a most pleasant rivalry (they have no shame: they even publish one of my stories in the 1994 volume!).

HOWARD DOUGLAS is our newcomer this time around. It is a pseudonym for a British writer, mainly interested in television, who lives in France. There is nothing particularly confidential about his identity, but he shares his real name with another crime writer already active on the scene, which could create some confusion. The last time this occurred was in America when there were two John MacDonald's; both John and Ross became famous none the less, so we shall keep our eyes peeled for further developments.

JANWILLEM VAN DE WETERING is Dutch but has for some time written in English and lives in Maine in America. He is well known for his Amsterdam cop mysteries featuring

Detectives Grijpstra and de Gier. After a hiatus of five years or so working on film scripts, he has recently published a sequel to his famous *The Maine Massacre*.

Few American authors can write about police procedure with the accuracy of O'NEIL DE NOUX. He turned to mystery writing after a lengthy spell on the front lines with the New Orleans police and his novels have all featured LaStanza, an intrepid Big Easy cop, as does his new story. Back in the Crescent city after a sojourn in Oregon, O'Neil is presently enjoying a stint as motoring correspondent for *The Times Picayune*.

MARK TIMLIN is a regular fixture in my anthologies, and justice was duly served when his contribution to the previous volume was nominated for the Gold Dagger. He didn't win, but then Mark's South London sleuth Nick Sharman is anything but an establishment figure. Once again here Sharman comes to the help of friends, and navigates shady waters with his customary rakish charm. Mark, once a regular on the music scene, is another writer whose titles owe much to rock music. His new Nick Sharman novel is *Pretend We're Dead*.

Enjoy, and remember that, from now onwards, crime is yellow . . .

Maxim Jakubowski

ONE OF THOSE DAYS, ONE OF THOSE NIGHTS

Ed Gorman

The thing you have to understand is that I found it by accident. I was looking for a place to hide the birthday gift I'd bought Laura – a string of pearls she'd been wanting to wear with the new black dress she'd bought for herself – and all I was going to do was lay the gift-wrapped box in the second drawer of her bureau . . .

. . . and there it was.

A plain number ten envelope with her name written across the middle in a big manly scrawl and a canceled Elvis Presley stamp up in the corner. Postmarked two days ago.

Just as I spotted it, Laura called from the living room, 'Bye, honey, see you at six.' The last two years we've been saving to buy a house so we have only the one car. Laura goes an hour earlier than I do, so she rides with a woman who lives a few blocks over. Then I pick her up at six after somebody relieves me at the computer store where I work. For what it's worth, I have an MA in English Literature but with the economy being what it is, it hasn't done me much good.

I saw a sci-fi movie once where a guy could set something on fire simply by staring at it intently enough. That's what I was trying to do with this letter my wife got. Burn it so that I wouldn't have to read what it said inside and get my heart broken.

I closed the drawer.

Could be completely harmless. Her fifteenth high school

reunion was coming up this spring. Maybe it was from one of her old classmates. And maybe the manly scrawl wasn't so manly after all. Maybe it was from a woman who wrote in a rolling dramatic hand.

Laura always said that I was the jealous type and this was certainly proof. A harmless letter tucked harmlessly in a bureau drawer. And here my heart was pounding, and fine cold sweat slicked my face, and my fingers were trembling.

God, wasn't I a pitiful guy? Shouldn't I be ashamed of myself?

I went into the bathroom and lathered up and did my usual relentless fifteen-minute morning regimen of shaving, showering and shining up my apple-cheeked Irish face and my thinning Irish hair, if hair follicles can have a nationality, that is.

Then I went back into our bedroom and took down a white shirt, blue necktie, navy blazer and tan slacks. All dressed, I looked just like seventy or eighty million other men getting ready for work this particular sunny April morning.

Then I stood very still in the middle of the bedroom and stared at Laura's bureau. Maybe I wasn't simply going to set the letter on fire. Maybe I was going to ignite the entire bureau.

The grandfather clock in the living room tolled eight-thirty. If I didn't leave now I would be late, and if you were late you inevitably got a chewing out from Ms Sandstrom, the boss. Anybody who believes that women would run a more benign world than men needs only to spend five minutes with Ms Sandstrom. Hitler would have used her as a pin-up girl.

The bureau. The letter. The manly scrawl.

What was I going to do?

Only one thing I could think of, since I hadn't made a decision about reading the letter or not. I'd simply take it with me to work. If I decided to read it, I'd give it a quick scan over my lunch hour.

But probably I wouldn't read it at all. I had a lot of faith where Laura was concerned. And I didn't like to think of myself as the sort of possessive guy who snuck around reading his wife's mail.

I reached into the bureau drawer.

My fingers touched the letter.

I was almost certain I wasn't going to read it. Hell, I'd probably get so busy at work that I'd forget all about it.

But just in case I decided to . . .

I grabbed the letter and stuffed it into my blazer pocket, and closed the drawer. In the kitchen I had a final cup of coffee and read my newspaper horoscope. Bad news, as always. I should never read the damn things . . . Then I hurried out of the apartment to the little Toyota parked at the kerb.

Six blocks away, it stalled. Our friendly mechanic said that moisture seemed to get in the fuel pump a lot. He's not sure why. We've run it in three times but it still stalls several times a week.

Around ten o'clock, hurrying into a sales meeting that Ms Sandstrom had decided to call, I dropped my pen. And when I bent over to pick it up, my glasses fell out of my pocket and when I moved to pick them up, I took one step too many and put all 175 pounds of my body directly on to them. I heard something snap.

By the time I retrieved both pen and glasses, Ms Sandstrom was closing the door and calling the meeting to order. I hurried down the hall trying to see how much damage I'd done. I held the glasses up to the light. A major fissure snaked down the center of the right lens. I slipped them on. The crack was even more difficult to see through than I'd thought.

Ms Sandstrom, a very attractive fiftyish woman given to sleek gray suits and burning blue gazes, warned us as usual that if sales of our computers didn't pick up, two or three people in this room would likely be looking for jobs. Soon. And just as she finished saying this, her eyes met mine. 'For instance, Donaldson, what kind of month are you having?'

'What kind of month am I having?'

'Do I hear a parrot in here?' Ms Sandstrom said, and several of the salespeople laughed.

'I'm not having too bad a month.'

Ms Sandstrom nodded wearily and looked around the room. 'Do we have to ask Donaldson here any more questions? Isn't he telling us everything we need to know when he says "I'm not having too bad a month"? What're we hearing when Donaldson says that?'

I hadn't noticed till this morning how much Ms Sandstrom reminded me of Miss Hutchison, my fourth grade teacher. Her favorite weapon had also been humiliation.

Dick Weybright raised his hand. Dick Weybright always raises his hand, especially when he gets to help Ms Sandstrom humiliate somebody.

'We hear defeatism, when he says that,' Dick said. 'We hear defeatism and a serious lack of self-esteem.'

Twice a week, Ms Sandstrom made us listen to motivational tapes. You know, 'I upped my income, Up yours,' that sort of thing. And nobody took those tapes more seriously than Dick Weybright.

'Very good, Dick,' Ms Sandstrom said. 'Defeatism and lack of self-esteem. That tells us all we need to know about Donaldson here. Just as the fact that he's got a crack in his glasses tells us something else about him, doesn't it?'

Dick Weybright waggled his hand again. 'Lack of self-respect.'

'Exactly,' Ms Sandstrom said, smiling coldly at me. 'Lack of self-respect.'

She didn't address me again until I was leaving the sales room. I'd knocked some of my papers on the floor. By the time I got them picked up, I was alone with Ms Sandstrom. I heard her come up behind me as I pointed myself toward the door.

'You missed something, Donaldson.'

I turned. 'Oh?'

She waved Laura's envelope in the air. Then her blue eyes showed curiosity as they read the name on the envelope. 'You're not one of those, are you, Donaldson?'

'One of those?'

'Men who read their wives' mail?'

'Oh. One of those. I see.'

'Are you?'

'No.'

'Then what're you doing with this?'

'What am I doing with that?'

'That parrot's in here again.'

'I must've picked it up off the table by mistake.'

'The table?'

'The little Edwardian table under the mirror in the foyer. Where we always set the mail.'

She shook her head again. She shook her head a lot. 'You are one of those, aren't you, Donaldson? So were my first three husbands, the bastards.'

She handed me the envelope, brushed past me and disappeared down the hall.

There's a park near the river where I usually eat lunch when I'm downtown for the day. I spend most of the time feeding the pigeons.

Today I spent most of my time staring at the envelope laid next to me on the park bench. There was a warm spring breeze and I half-hoped it would lift up the envelope and carry it away.

Now I wished I'd left the number ten with the manly scrawl right where I'd found it because it was getting harder and harder to resist lifting the letter from inside and giving it a quick read.

I checked my watch. Twenty minutes to go before I needed to be back at work. Twenty minutes to stare at the letter. Twenty minutes to resist temptation.

Twenty minutes – and how's this for cheap symbolism? – during which the sky went from cloudless blue to dark and ominous.

By now, I'd pretty much decided that the letter had to be from a man. Otherwise, why would Laura have hidden it in her drawer? I'd also decided that it must contain something pretty incriminating.

Had she been having an affair with somebody? Was she thinking of running away with somebody?

On the way back to the office, I carefully slipped the letter from the envelope and read it. Read it four times as a matter of fact. And felt worse every time I did.

So Chris Tomlin, her ridiculously handsome, ridiculously wealthy, ridiculously slick college boyfriend was back in her life.

I can't tell you much about the rest of the afternoon. It's all very vague: voices spoke to me, phones rang at me, computer printers spat things at me – but I didn't respond. I felt as if I were scuttling across the floor of an ocean so deep that neither light nor sound could penetrate it.

Chris Tomlin. My God.

I kept reading the letter, stopping only when I'd memorized it entirely and could keep rerunning it in my mind without any visual aid.

Dear Laura,

I still haven't forgotten you – or forgiven you for choosing you-know-who over me.

I'm going to be in your fair city this Friday. How about meeting me at the Fairmont right at noon for lunch?

Of course, you could contact me the evening before if you're interested. I'll be staying at the Wallingham. I did a little checking and found that you work nearby.

I can't wait to see you.

Love,

Chris Tomlin.

Not even good old Ms Sandstrom could penetrate my stupor. I know she charged into my office a few times and made some nasty threats – something about my not returning the call of one of our most important customers – but I honestly couldn't tell you who she wanted me to call or what she wanted me to say.

About all I can remember is that it got very dark and cold suddenly. The lights blinked on and off a few times. We were having a terrible rainstorm. Somebody came in soaked and said that the storm sewers were backing up and that downtown was a mess.

Not that I paid this information any particular heed.

I was wondering if she'd call him Thursday night. I took it as a foregone conclusion that she would have lunch with him on Friday. But how about Thursday night?

Would she visit him in his hotel room?

And come to think of it, why *had* she chosen me over Chris Tomlin? I mean, while I may not be a nerd, I'm not exactly a movie star, either. And with Chris Tomlin, there wouldn't have been any penny-pinching for a down payment on a house, either.

With his Daddy's millions in pharmaceuticals, good ole Chris would have bought her a manse as a wedding present.

The workday ended. The usual number of people peeked into my office to say the usual number of good nights. The usual cleaning crew, high school kids in gray uniforms, appeared to start hauling out trash and run roaring vacuum cleaners. And I went through my usual process of staying at my desk until it was time to pick up Laura.

I was just about to walk out the front door when I noticed in the gloom that Ms Sandstrom's light was still on.

She had good ears. Even above the vacuum cleaner roaring its way down the hall to her left, she heard me leaving and looked up.

She waved me into her office.

When I reached her desk, she handed me a slip of paper with some typing on it.

'How does that read to you, Donaldson?'

'Uh, what is it?'

'A Help Wanted ad I may be running tomorrow.'

That was another thing Miss Hutchison, my fourth grade teacher, had been good at – indirect torture.

Ms Sandstrom wanted me to read the ad she'd be running for my replacement.

I scanned it and handed it back.

'Nice.'

'Is that all you have to say? Nice?'

'I guess so.'

'You realize that this means I'm going to fire you?'

'That's what I took it to mean.'

'What the hell's wrong with you, Donaldson? Usually you'd be groveling and sniveling by now.'

'I've got some – personal problems.'

A smirk. 'That's what you get for reading your wife's mail.' Then a scowl. 'When you come in tomorrow morning, you come straight to my office, you understand?'

I nodded. 'All right.'

'And be prepared to do some groveling and sniveling. You're going to need it.'

Why don't I just make a list of the things I found wrong with my Toyota after I slammed the door and belted myself in.

A) The motor wouldn't turn over. Remember what I said about moisture and the fuel pump?

B) The roof had sprung a new leak. This was different from the old leak, which dribbled rain down on to the passenger seat. The new one dribbled rain down on to the driver's seat.

C) The turn signal arm had come loose again and was hanging down from naked wires like a half-amputated limb. Apparently after finding the letter this morning, I was in so much of a fog I hadn't noticed that it was broken again.

I can't tell you how dark and cold and lonely I felt just then. Bereft of wife. Bereft of automobile. Bereft of – dare I say it? – self-esteem and self-respect. And, on top of it, I was a disciple of defeatism. Just ask my co-worker Dick Weybright.

The goddamned car finally started and I drove off to pick up my goddamned wife.

The city was a mess.

Lashing winds and lashing rains – both of which were still lashing merrily along – had uprooted trees in the park, smashed out store windows here and there, and had apparently caused a power outage that shut down all the automatic traffic signals.

I wanted to be home and I wanted to be dry and I wanted to be in my jammies. But most of all I wanted to be loved by the one woman I had ever really and truly loved.

If only I hadn't opened her bureau drawer to hide her pearls . . .

She was standing behind the glass door in the entrance to the art deco building where she works as a market researcher for a mutual fund company. When I saw her, I felt all sorts of things at once – love, anger, shame, terror – and all I wanted to do was park the car and run up to her and take her in my arms and give her the tenderest kiss I was capable of.

But then I remembered the letter and . . .

Well, I'm sure I don't have to tell you about jealousy. There's nothing worse to carry around in your stony little heart. All that rage and self-righteousness and self-pity. It begins to smother you and . . .

By the time Laura climbed into the car, it was smothering me. She smelled of rain and perfume and her sweet tender body.

'Hi,' she said. 'I was worried about you.'

'Yeah. I'll bet.'

Then, closing the door, she gave me a long, long look. 'Are you all right?'

'Fine.'

'Then why did you say, "Yeah. I'll bet"?'

'Just being funny.'

She gave me another stare. I tried to look regular and normal. You know, not on the verge of whipping the letter out and shoving it in her face.

'Oh, God,' she said, 'you're not starting your period already are you?'

The period thing is one of our little jokes. A few months after we got married, she came home cranky one day and I laid the blame for her mood on her period. She said I was being sexist. I said I was only making an observation. I wrote down the date. For the next four months, on or around the same time each month, she came home crabby. I pointed this out to her. She said, 'All right. But men have periods, too.'

'They do?' 'You're damned right they do.' And so now, whenever I seem inexplicably grouchy, she asks me if my period is starting.

'Maybe so,' I said, swinging from outrage to a strange kind of whipped exhaustion.

'Boy, this is really leaking,' Laura said.

I just drove. There was a burly traffic cop out in the middle of a busy intersection directing traffic with two flashlights in the rain and gloom.

'Did you hear me, Rich? I said this is really leaking.'

'I know it's really leaking.'

'What's up with you, anyway? What're you so mad about? Did Sandstrom give you a hard time today?'

'No – other than telling me that she may fire me.'

'You're kidding.'

'No.'

'But why?'

Because while I was going through your bureau, I found a letter from your ex-lover and I know all about the tryst you're planning to set up.

That's what I wanted to say.

What I said was: 'I guess I wasn't paying proper attention during another one of her goddamned sales meetings.'

'But, Rich, if you get fired —'

She didn't have to finish her sentence. If I got fired, we'd never get the house we'd been saving for.

'She told me that when I came in tomorrow morning, I should be prepared to grovel and snivel. And she wasn't kidding.'

'She actually said that?'

'She actually said that.'

'What a bitch.'

'Boss's daughter. You know how this city is. The last frontier for hard-core nepotism.'

We drove on several more blocks, stopping every quarter block or so to pull out around somebody whose car had stalled in the dirty water backing up from the sewers.

'So is that why you're so down?'

'Yeah,' I said, 'Isn't that reason enough?'

'Usually, about Sandstrom, I mean, you get mad. You don't get depressed.'

'Well, Sandstrom chews me out but she doesn't usually threaten to fire me.'

'That's true. But —'

'But what?'

'It just seems that there's – something else.' Then, 'Where're you going?'

My mind had been on the letter tucked inside my blazer. In the mean time, the Toyota had been guiding itself into the most violent neighborhood in the city. Not even the cops wanted to to come here.

'God, can you turn around?' Laura said. 'I'd sure hate to get stuck here.'

'We'll be all right. I'll hang a left at the next corner and then we'll drive back to Marymount Avenue.'

'I wondered where you were going. I should have said something.' She leaned over and kissed me on the cheek.

That boil of feelings, of profound tenderness and profound rage, churned up inside of me again.

'Things'll work out with Sandstrom,' she said, and then smiled. 'Maybe she's just starting her period.'

And I couldn't help it. The rage was gone, replaced by pure and total love. This was my friend, my bride, my lover. There had to be a reasonable and innocent explanation for the letter. There had to.

I started hanging the left and that's when it happened. The fuel pump. Rain.

The Toyota stopped dead.

'Oh, no,' she said, glancing out the windshield at the forbidding blocks of falling-down houses and dark, condemned buildings.

Beyond the wind, beyond the rain, you could hear sirens. There were always sirens in neighborhoods like these.

'Maybe I can fix it,' I said.

'But, honey, you don't know anything about cars.'

'Well, I watched him make that adjustment last time.'

'I don't know,' she said skeptically. 'Besides, you'll just get wet.'

'I'll be fine.'

I knew why I was doing this, of course. In addition to being rich, powerful and handsome, Chris Tomlin was also one of those men who could fix practically anything. I remembered her telling me how he'd fixed a refrigerator at an old cabin they'd once stayed in.

I opened the door. A wave of rain washed over me. But I was determined to act like the kind of guy who could walk through a meteor storm and laugh it off. Maybe that's why Laura was considering a rendezvous with Chris. Maybe she was sick of my whining. A macho man, I'm not.

'Just be careful,' she said.

'Be right back.'

I eased out of the car and then realized I hadn't used the hood latch inside. I leaned in and popped the latch and gave Laura a quick smile.

And then I went back outside into the storm.

I was soaked completely in less than a minute, my shoes soggy, my clothes drenched and cold and clinging. Even my raincoat.

But I figured this would help my image as a take-charge sort of guy. I even gave Laura a little half-salute before I raised the hood. She smiled at me. God, I wanted to forget all about the letter and be happily in love again.

Any vague hopes I'd had of starting the car were soon forgotten as I gaped at the motor and realized that I had absolutely no idea what I was looking at.

The mechanic in the shop had made it look very simple. You raised the hood, you leaned in and snatched off the oil filter and then did a couple of quick things to it and put it back. And *voilà*, your car was running again.

I got the hood open all right, and I leaned in just fine, and I even took the oil filter off with no problem.

But when it came to doing a couple of quick things to it, my brain was as dead as the motor. That was the part I hadn't picked up from the mechanic. Those couple of quick things.

I started shaking the oil filter. Don't ask me why. I had it under the protection of the hood to keep it dry and shook it left and shook it right and shook it high and shook it low. I figured that maybe some kind of invisible cosmic forces would come into play here and the engine would start as soon as I gave the ignition key a little turn.

I closed the hood and ran back through the slashing rain, opened the door and crawled inside.

'God, it's incredible out there.'

Only then did I get a real good look at Laura and only then did I see that she looked sick, like the time we both picked up a slight case of ptomaine poisoning at her friend Susan's wedding.

Except now she looked a lot sicker.

And then I saw the guy.

In the back seat.

'Who the hell are you?'

But he had questions of his own. 'Your wife won't tell me if you've got an ATM card.'

So it had finally happened. Our little city turned violent about fifteen years ago, during which time most honest working folks had to take their turns getting mugged, sort of like a rite of passage. But as time wore on, the muggers weren't satisfied with simply robbing their victims. Now they beat them up. And sometimes, for no reason at all, they killed them.

This guy was white, chunky, with a ragged scar on his left cheek, stupid dark eyes, a dark turtleneck sweater and a large and formidable gun. He smelled of sweat, cigarette smoke, beer and a high sweet unclean tang.

'How much can you get with your card?'

'Couple hundred.'

'Yeah. Right.'

'Couple hundred. I mean, we're not exactly rich people. Look at this car.'

He turned to Laura. 'How much can he get, babe?'

'He told you. A couple of hundred.' She sounded surprisingly calm.

'One more time.' He had turned back to me. 'How much can you get with that card of yours?'

'I told you,' I said.

You know how movie thugs are always slugging people with gun butts? Well, let me tell you something. It hurts. He hit me hard enough to draw blood, hard enough to fill my sight with darkness and blinking stars, like a planetarium ceiling, and hard enough to lay my forehead against the steering wheel.

Laura didn't scream.

She just leaned over and touched my head with her long, gentle fingers. And you know what? Even then, even suffering from what might be a concussion, I had this image of Laura's fingers touching Chris Tomlin's head this way. Ain't jealousy grand?

'Now,' said the voice in the back seat, 'let's talk.'

Neither of us paid him much attention for a minute or so. Laura helped me sit back in the seat. She took her handkerchief and daubed it against the back of my head.

'You didn't have to hit him.'

'Now maybe he'll tell me the truth.'

'Four or five hundred,' she said. 'That's how much we can get. And don't hit him again. Don't lay a finger on him.'

'The mama lion fights for her little cub. That's nice.' He leaned forward and put the end of the gun directly against my ear. 'You're gonna have to go back out in that nasty ole rain. There's an ATM machine down at the west end of this block and around the corner. You go down there and get me five hundred dollars and then you haul your ass right back. I'll be waiting right here with your exceedingly good-looking wife. And with my gun.'

'Where did you ever learn a word like exceedingly?' I said.

'What the hell's that supposed to mean?'

'I was just curious.'

'If it's any of your goddamned business, my cell-mate had one of them improve your vocabulary books.'

I glanced at Laura. She still looked scared but she also looked a little bit angry. For us, five hundred dollars was a lot of money.

And now a robber who used the word 'exceedingly' was going to take every last dime of it.

'Go get it,' he said.

I reached over to touch Laura's hand as reassuringly as possible, and that was when I noticed it.

The white number ten envelope.

The one Chris had sent her.

I stared at it a long moment and then raised my eyes to meet hers.

'I was going to tell you about it.'

I shook my head. 'I shouldn't have looked in your drawer.'

'No, you shouldn't have. But I still owe you an explanation.'

'What the hell are you two talking about?'

'Nothing that's exceedingly interesting,' I said, and opened the door, and dangled a leg out and then had the rest of my body follow the leg.

'You got five minutes, you understand?' the man said.

I nodded and glanced at Laura. 'I love you.'

'I'm sorry about the letter.'

'You know the funny thing? I was hiding your present, that's how I found it. I was going to tuck it in your underwear drawer and have you find them. You know, the pearls.'

'You got me the pearl necklace?'

'Uh-huh.'

'Oh, honey, that's so sweet.'

'Go get the goddamned money,' the man said, 'and get it fast.'

'I'll be right back,' I said to Laura and blew her a little kiss.

If I hadn't been sodden before, I certainly was now.

There were two brick buildings facing each other across a narrow alley. Most people drove up to this particular ATM machine because it was housed in a deep indentation that faced the alley. It could also accommodate foot traffic.

What it didn't do was give you much protection from the storm.

By now, I was sneezing and feeling a scratchiness in my throat. Bad sinuses. My whole family.

I walked up to the oasis of light and technology in this ancient and wild neighborhood, took out my wallet and inserted my ATM card.

It was all very casual, especially considering the fact that Laura was being held hostage.

The card would go in. The money would come out. The thief would get his loot. Laura and I would dash to the nearest phone and call the police.

Except I couldn't remember my secret pin number.

If I had to estimate how many times I'd used this card, I'd put it at probably a thousand or so.

So how, after all those times, could I now forget the pin number?

Panic. That's what was wrong. I was so scared that Laura would be hurt that I couldn't think clearly.

Deep breaths. There.

Now. Think. Clearly.

Just relax and your pin number will come back to you. No problem.

That was when I noticed the slight black man in the rain parka standing just to the left of me. In the rain. With a gun in his hand.

'You wanna die?'

'Oh, shit. You've got to be kidding. You're a goddamned thief?'

'Yes, and I ain't ashamed of it either, man.'

I thought of explaining it to him, explaining that another thief already had first dibs on the proceeds of my bank account – that is, if I could ever remember the pin number – but he didn't seem to be the understanding type at all. In fact, he looked even more desperate and crazy than the man who was holding Laura.

'How much can you take out?'

'I can't give it to you.'

'You see this gun, man?'

'Yeah. I see it.'

'You know what happens if you don't crank some serious money out for me?'

I had to explain after all. ' . . . so, you see, I can't give it to you.'

'What the hell's that supposed to mean?'

'Somebody's already got dibs on it.'

'Dibs? What the hell does "dibs" mean?'

'It means another robber has already spoken for this money.'

He looked at me carefully. 'You're crazy, man. You really are. But that don't mean I won't shoot you.'

'And there's one more thing.'

'What?'

'I can't remember my pin number.'

'Bullshit.'

'It's true. That's why I've been standing here. My mind's a blank.'

'You gotta relax, man.'

'I know that. But it's kind've hard. You've got a gun and so does the other guy.'

'There's really some other dude holdin' your old lady?'

'Right.'

He grinned with exceedingly bad teeth. 'You got yourself a real problem, dude.'

I closed my eyes.

I must have spent my five minutes already.

Would he really kill Laura?

'You tried deep breathin'?'

'Yeah.'

'And that didn't work?'

'Huh-uh.'

'You tried makin' your mind go blank for a little bit?'

'That didn't work, either.'

He pushed the gun right into my face. 'I ain't got much time, man.'

'I can't give you the money, anyway.'

'You ain't gonna be much use to your old lady if you got six or seven bullet holes in you.'

'God!'

'What's wrong?'

My pin number had popped into my head.

Nothing like a gun in your face to jog your memory.

I dove for the ATM machine.

And started punching buttons.

The right buttons.

'Listen,' I said as I cranked away, 'I really can't give you this money.'

'Right.'

'I mean, I would if I could but the guy would never believe me if I told him some other crook had taken it. No offense, "crook" I mean.'

'Here it comes.'

'I'm serious. You can't have it.'

'Pretty, pretty Yankee dollars. Praise the Lord.'

The plastic cover opened and the machine began spitting out green Yankee dollars.

And that's when he slugged me on the back of the head.

The guy back in the car had hit me but it had been nothing like this.

This time, the field of black floating in front of my eyes didn't even have stars. This time, hot shooting pain traveled from the point of impact near the top of my skull all the way down into my neck and shoulders. This time, my knees gave out immediately.

Pavement. Hard. Wet. Smelling of cold rain. And still the darkness. Total darkness. I had a moment of panic. Had I been blinded for life? I wanted to be angry but I was too disoriented. Pain. Cold. Darkness.

And then I felt his hands tearing the money from mine.

I had to hold on to it. Had to. Otherwise Laura would be injured. Or killed.

The kick landed hard just above my sternum. Stars suddenly appeared in the field of black. His foot seemed to have jarred them loose.

More pain. But now there was anger. I blindly lashed out and grabbed his trouser leg, clung to it, forcing him to drag me down the sidewalk as he tried to get away. I don't know how many names I called him, some of them probably didn't even make sense, I just clung to his leg, exulting in his rage, in his inability to get rid of me.

Then he leaned down and grabbed a handful of my hair and pulled so hard I screamed. And inadvertently let go of his leg.

And then I heard his footsteps, retreating, retreating, and felt the rain start slashing at me again. He had dragged me out from beneath the protection of the ATM overhang.

I struggled to get up. It wasn't easy. I still couldn't see. And every time I tried to stand, I was overcome by dizziness and a faint nausea.

But I kept thinking of Laura. And kept pushing myself to my feet, no matter how much pain pounded in my head, no matter how I started to pitch forward and collapse again.

By the time I got to my feet, and fell against the rough brick of the building for support, my eyesight was back. Funny how much you take it for granted. It's terrifying when it's gone.

I looked at the oasis of light in the gloom. At the foot of the ATM was my bank card. I wobbled over and picked it up. I knew that I'd taken out my allotted amount for the day but I decided to try and see if the cosmic forces were with me for once.

They weren't.

The only thing I got from the machine was a snotty little note saying that I'd have to contact my personal banker if I wanted to receive more money.

A) I had no idea who this personal banker was, and

B) I doubted if he would be happy if I called him at home on such a rainy night even if I did have his name and number.

Then I did what any red-blooded American would do. I started kicking the machine. Kicking hard. Kicking obsessively. Until my toes started to hurt.

I stood for a long moment in the rain, letting it pour down on me, feeling as if I were melting like a wax statue in the hot sun. I became one with the drumming and thrumming and pounding of it all.

There was only one thing I could do now.

I took off running back to the car. To Laura. And the man with the gun.

I broke into a crazy grin when I saw the car. I could see Laura's profile in the gloom. She was still alive.

I reached the driver's door, opened it up and pitched myself inside.

'My God, what happened to you?' Laura said. 'Did some-body beat you up?'

The man with the gun was a little less sympathetic. 'Where the hell's the money?'

I decided to answer both questions at once. 'I couldn't remember my pin number so I had to stand there for a while. And then this guy – this black guy – he came out of nowhere and he had a gun and then he made me give him the money.' I looked back at the man with the gun. 'I couldn't help it. I told him that you had first dibs on the money but he didn't care.'

'You expect me to believe that crap?'

'Honest to God. That's what happened.'

He looked at me and smiled. And then put the gun right up against Laura's head. 'You want me to show you what's gonna happen here if you're not back in five minutes with the money?'

I looked at Laura. 'God, honey, I'm telling the truth. About the guy with the gun.'

'I know.'

'I'm sorry.' I glanced forlornly out the window at the rain filling the kerbs. 'I'll get the money. Somehow.'

I opened the door again. And then noticed the white envelope still sitting on her lap. 'I'm sorry I didn't trust you, sweetheart.'

She was scared, that was easy enough to see, but she forced herself to focus and smile at me. 'I love you, honey.'

'Get the hell out of here and get that money,' said the man with the gun.

'I knew you wouldn't believe me.'

'You heard what I said. Get going.'

I reached over and took Laura's hand gently. 'I'll get the money, sweetheart. I promise.'

I got out of the car and started walking again. Then trotting. Then flat out running. My head was still pounding with pain but I didn't care. I had to get the money. Somehow. Somewhere.

I didn't even know where I was going. I was just – running. It was better than standing still and contemplating what the guy with gun might do.

I reached the corner and looked down the block where the ATM was located.

A car came from behind me, its headlights stabbing through the silver sheets of night rain. It moved on past me. When it came even with the lights of the ATM machine, it turned an abrupt left and headed for the machine.

Guy inside his car. Nice and warm and dry. Inserts his card, gets all the money he wants, and then drives on to do a lot of fun things with his nice and wam and dry evening.

While I stood out here in the soaking rain and —

Of course, I thought.

Of course.

There was only one thing I could do.

I started running, really running, splashing through puddles and tripping and nearly falling down. But nothing could stop me.

The bald man had parked too far away from the ATM to do his banking from the car. He backed up and gave it another try. He was concentrating on backing up so I didn't have much trouble opening the passenger door and slipping in.

'What the—' he started to say as he became aware of me.

'Stick up.'

'What?'

'I'm robbing you.'

'Oh, man, that's all I need. I've had a really crummy day

today, mister,' he said. 'I knew I never should've come in
this neighborhood but I was in a hurry and—'

'You want to hear about my bad day, mister? Huh?'

I raised the coat of my raincoat, hoping that he would
think that I was pointing a gun at him.

He looked down at my coat-draped fist and said, 'You
can't get a whole hell of a lot a money out of these ATM
machines.'

'You can get three hundred and that's good enough.'

'What if I don't have three hundred?'

'New car. Nice new suit. Maybe twenty CDs in that box
there. You've got three hundred. Easy.'

'I work hard for my money.'

'So do I.'

'What if I told you I don't believe you've got a gun in
there?'

'Then I'd say fine. And then I'd kill you.'

'You don't look like a stick-up guy.'

'And you don't look like a guy who's stupid enough to get
himself shot over three hundred dollars.'

'I have to back up again. So I can get close.'

'Back up. But go easy.'

'Some goddamned birthday this is.'

'It's your birthday?'

'Yeah. Ain't that a bitch?'

He backed up, pulled forward again, got right up next to
the ATM, pulled out his card and went to work.

The money came out with no problem. He handed it over
to me.

'You have a pencil and paper?'

'What?'

'Something you can write with?'

'Oh. Yeah. Why?'

'I want you to write down your name and address.'

'For what?'

'Because tomorrow morning I'm going to put three
hundred dollars in an envelope and mail it to you.'

'Are you some kind of crazy drug addict or what?'

'Just write down your name and address.'

He shook his head. 'Not only do I get robbed, I get robbed by some goddamned fruitcake.'

But he wrote down his name and address, probably thinking I'd shoot him if he didn't.

'I appreciate the loan,' I said, getting out of his car.

'Loan? You tell the cops it was a "loan" and see what they say.'

'Hope the rest of your day goes better,' I said, and slammed the door.

And I hope the rest of my day goes better, too, I thought.

'Good thing you got back here when you did,' the man with the gun said. 'I was just about to waste her.'

'Spare me the macho crap, all right?' I said. I was getting cranky. The rain. The cold. The fear. And then having to commit a felony to get the cash I needed – and putting fear into a perfectly decent citizen who'd been having a very bad day himself.

I handed the money over to him. 'Now you can go,' I said.

He counted it in hard, harsh grunts, like a pig rutting in the mud.

'Three goddamned hundred. It was supposed to be four. Or five.'

'I guess you'll just have to shoot us, then, huh?'

Laura gave me a frantic look and then dug her nails into my hands. Obviously, like the man I'd just left at the ATM, she thought I had lost what little of my senses I had left.

'I wouldn't push it, punk,' the man with the gun said. 'Because I just might shoot you yet.'

He leaned forward from the back seat and said, 'Lemme see your purse, babe.'

Laura looked at me. I nodded. She handed him her purse.

More rutting sounds as he went through it.

'Twenty-six bucks?'

'I'm sorry,' Laura said.

'Where're your credit cards?'

'We don't have credit cards. It's too tempting to use them. We're saving for a house.'

'Ain't that sweet!'

He pitched the purse over the front seat and opened the back door.

Chill. Fog. Rain.

'You got a jerk for a husband, babe, I mean, just in case you haven't figured that out already.'

Then he slammed the door and was gone.

'You were really going to tear it up?'

'Or let you tear it up. Whichever you preferred. I mean, I know you think I still have this thing for Chris but I really don't. I was going to prove it to you by showing you the letter tonight and letting you do whatever you wanted with it.'

We were in bed, three hours after getting our car towed to a station, the tow truck giving us a ride home.

The rain had quit an hour ago. Now there were just icy winds. But it was snug and warm in the bed of my one true love and icy winds didn't bother me at all.

'I'm sorry', I said, 'about being so jealous.'

'And I'm sorry about hiding the letter. It made you think I was going to take him up on his offer. But I really don't have any desire to see him at all.'

Then we kind of just laid back and listened to the wind for a time.

And she started getting affectionate, her foot rubbing my foot, her hand taking my hand.

And then in the darkness, she said, 'Would you like to make love?'

'Would I?' I laughed. 'Would I?'

And then I rolled over and we began kissing and then I began running my fingers through her long dark hair and then I suddenly realized that—

'What's wrong?' she said, as I rolled away from her, flat on my back, staring at the ceiling.

'Let's just go to sleep.'

'God, honey, I want to know what's going on. Here we are making out and then all of a sudden you stop.'

'Oh God,' I said. 'What a day this has been.' I sighed and prepared myself for the ultimate in manly humiliation. 'Remember that time when Rick's sister got married?'

'Uh-huh.'

'And I got real drunk?'

'Uh-huh.'

'And that night we tried – well, we tried to make love but I couldn't?'

'Uh-huh.' She was silent a long moment. Then, 'Oh, God, you mean, the same thing happened to you just now?'

'Uh-huh,' I said.

'Oh, honey, I'm sorry.'

'The perfect ending to the perfect day,' I said.

'First you find that letter from Chris—'

And then I can't concentrate on my job—'

'And then Ms Sandstrom threatens to fire you—'

'And then a man sticks us up—'

'And then you have to stick up another man—'

'And then we come home and go to bed and—' I sighed. 'I think I'll just roll over and go to sleep.'

'Good idea, honey. That's what we both need. A good night's sleep.'

'I love you, sweetheart,' I said. 'I'm sorry I wasn't able to . . . well, you know.'

'It's fine, sweetie. It happens to every man once in a while.'

'It's just one of those days,' I said.

'And one of those nights,' she said.

But you know what? Some time later, the grandfather clock in the living room woke me as it tolled twelve midnight, and when I rolled over to see how Laura was doing, she was wide awake and took me in her sweet warm arms, and I didn't have any trouble at all showing her how grateful I was.

It was a brand-new day . . . and when I finally got around to breakfast, the first thing I did was lift the horoscope section from the paper . . . and drop it, unread, into the wastebasket.

No more snooping in drawers . . . and no more bad-luck horoscopes.

THE WOMAN OF GOODWILL

Robert Richardson

It snowed heavily on Christmas Eve, 1889, the year of my marriage. When we rose on Christmas morning, London was muffled in white, familiar landmarks unidentifiable as presents wrapped in thick paper, stillness and silence the more pronounced in thoroughfares that normally clattered with the ceaseless activity of the city. We entertained no company, and, after exchanging gifts, enjoyed our first Christmas luncheon together. As we finished, Mary's kindly mind turned to one she knew was alone that day.

'I still regret Mr Holmes would not join us,' she said. 'I find it depressing to think of him on his own in those gloomy rooms.'

'He will be perfectly content,' I replied. 'He will read his books, smoke and play the violin. His only irritation will be the inertia of a day when even criminals may observe goodwill to men.'

'So you have told me,' she replied. 'But will he eat?'

'He will certainly not starve.'

'That is not good enough,' she said, rising from her seat. 'I insist that you take him some cold goose and mince pies. I shall ask cook to prepare them immediately.'

'Go to Baker Street in this weather?' I protested. 'There can be no cabs operating.'

'It is now a fine, sunny day,' she replied. 'The snow is not so deep that you cannot walk half a mile.'

I protested no further. Her consideration was Christian and sincere and it would have been churlish to refuse my role

in fulfilling it. Holmes would be indifferent as to whether I
visited or not, and a walk after such an abundant meal was
not a displeasing prospect.

The snow, while deep, was not impassable and there were
others abroad with whom I exchanged seasonal greetings as I
trudged my journey. I turned out of Marylebone Road into
Baker Street, where I followed another's footprints before
they crossed to the other side. I knew that Mrs Hudson was
visiting relatives and, on knocking, expected to have to wait
some moments until Holmes descended. In fact, I heard him
hurry down the stairs and he opened the front door with
alacrity.

'You, Watson?' he said in evident surprise. 'I was
expecting . . .' He stepped out and looked up and down the
street. 'Have you seen anybody?'

'Not in Baker Street. Are you expecting a visitor?'

'Yes. She will approach from that direction . . .' he pointed
to the north, '. . . once she has decided . . .' Abruptly, he
became aware of his lack of greeting. 'Watson, I treat you
without ceremony. Come in, my dear fellow. What brings
you?'

'My wife's insistence.' I held up the canvas bag I was
carrying. 'She is concerned lest you go hungry on Christmas
day.'

He laughed as he ushered me inside. 'Your wife is too
kind, Watson – as are you for coming. A very merry
Christmas. We will drink to the festive day.'

I followed him into the familiar rooms and he poured tots
of whisky for each of us as I removed my greatcoat.

'Who is your expected visitor?' I inquired.

'A young woman of good sense and comfortable means
who lives within a mile of here. She is in the greatest distress,
but is tormented by uncertainty. She is spending time on her
own while she considers how best to present her problem to
me.'

'What is her name?'

'I don't know,' he replied as he handed me the glass. 'I
didn't see her.'

'You didn't see her? Then how can you know?'

He appeared amused. 'You have lunched – or perhaps wined – too well, Watson. The explanation is clearly visible in Baker Street.'

'I told you I saw nobody.'

'But as you walked up from Marylebone Road, didn't you observe footprints preceding you?'

'I did, but they crossed to the other side and I took no further notice.'

'You should have done. They were very informative.' He moved to the window overlooking the street and beckoned me to join him. 'About half an hour ago, I came to stand here and noticed those footprints directly opposite, crossing to this door. Unaware of anyone having knocked, I went outside to investigate.

'The footprints begin out of Marylebone Road on the correct side for this address. However, outside the first house where the number is visible, she realized and crossed to the other side. She stood opposite for a few minutes – there are clear indications of her stamping her feet to keep them warm – then summoned up courage to approach. She paused on the step and at one point lifted the knocker – the snow that had settled on it was disturbed. She then withdrew and continued up the street.'

'Very well,' I agreed. 'I cannot dispute the pattern of movement. But how is it a woman? And the other details?'

'The prints were made by new boots sold by Thomson and Weekes. Such footwear is not cheap and is bought by sensible young women who place more importance on quality than fashion. She would not venture out to see me in such weather on Christmas day unless there was a serious reason, and I would suggest that a mile is the furthest she could walk in such conditions.'

'And she is now thinking the matter over?'

'Of course. At the end of Baker Street towards which she has walked lies Regent's Park, an ideal spot to be alone for meditation.'

'But will she return?'

'I hope so. She is clearly in urgent need of help, but I can only give it if she overcomes her reservations . . . ah.' He stepped back from the window, drawing me with him. 'This must be she, and her face reveals she has made her resolution. Admit her when she knocks. The presence of a respectable professional man may help to ease her misgivings.'

As he spoke, the knocker was struck with some timidity. 'Quickly, Watson, or she may flee again!'

I hurried downstairs, mentally composing myself; so nervous a caller needed to be greeted with calm. She was some twenty-three years of age, dressed in an ankle-length tweed coat, the boots Holmes had identified, a smart but practical bonnet and sensible, fur-lined leather mittens. Her striking grey eyes were troubled as she saw me.

'Mr Holmes?' she inquired hesitantly.

'No, I am his colleague, Dr John Watson,' I said. 'However, if you will step inside, he is at home.'

She shook her head as though regretting what she had managed to accomplish. 'I have no appointment and Mr Holmes is not expecting me.'

'He is,' I replied, 'and is anxious to meet you.' I stepped forward and took her arm. 'You are in great distress and have come to the best man in England for assistance.'

Clearly bewildered, but responding to my assurance, she allowed me to lead her into the house and back up the stairs. Holmes had prepared a third whisky, smaller than those he had poured for us.

'You must be very cold after so long in the park,' he said as she entered. 'This will warm you. It has been diluted with water.'

'In the park? How can you . . .?' Despite her agitated state, she smiled slightly. 'But of course, you are Sherlock Holmes.'

'You have not come here to pay me compliments,' my friend replied. 'I suggest you first sit by the fire and compose yourself.'

'Thank you.' She took the offered chair, removing her bonnet to reveal long fine hair, the colour of wheat, coiled into a bun. For a few minutes we waited in silence until Holmes spoke again.

'You clearly have some familiarity with my methods, so will accept that from the evidence in the snow of your earlier visit I know this is a matter of urgency. When you are ready, please tell us what it is as briefly as you are able. We might begin with your name.'

Our visitor had obviously calmed herself, for she proceeded without further delay. 'My name is Anne Fortescue and I am the only daughter of the Reverend Alfred Fortescue, vicar of St Andrew's church in St John's Wood. Do you know it?'

'A baroque building in the style of St Martin-in-the-Fields,' Holmes commented. 'I have frequently passed it, but never had occasion to enter. Pray continue.'

'My father received the living more than fifteen years ago after a short curacy in East London,' Miss Fortescue went on. 'Apart from our cook and maid, we live alone, my mother having died when I was less than a year old.'

She placed the glass, its contents unfinished, on a table beside her, before she contined. 'Our lives are, and always have been, unremarkable and I can think of nothing in the past that could be of any relevance to what occurred last night.'

'When your father would have been occupied with his clerical duties.'

'Indeed, and it was at the last – a special midnight service – that something utterly inexplicable happened.'

'Not inexplicable,' Holmes corrected. 'Extraordinary, perhaps. To you, frightening. But, like all things in this mortal world, it can be explained. That is my business. The details, if you please, and my compliments on the conciseness of your narrative.'

'Thank you . . . the service began at eleven-thirty and was to be a series of lessons and carols with my father conducting the choir. There were some fifty people in the congregation, the numbers being reduced by the weather. The service proceeded without incident until the fifth lesson, which my

father was to read. He climbed the steps to the pulpit – I was
in the pew directly in front of him, but paying no particular
attention – but instead of speaking he looked straight ahead.'

Miss Fortescue paused, as though the moment she was
describing was so vivid in her mind that it still shook her. She
raised her face to Holmes with a look of remembered terror.

'He said nothing! There was just a long silence. To relate it
sounds prosaic, but it was totally unnatural. I feared he was
taken suddenly ill and rose to go to him. Then he shouted
"No! No! No!" Three times it rang through the church. Then
he almost fell back down the pulpit steps and ran – he is not a
young man, Mr Holmes, but he ran – towards the vestry. We
were all so startled that for a moment we just stared in
disbelief, then I ran myself, followed by others sitting near
me.

'The other door of the vestry leading into the churchyard
was open, and as I reached it I saw him racing through the
falling snow. I cried after him and pursued him out and
along the road until I lost him in the darkness. No one has
seen him since.'

Holmes looked at his watch. 'And this was nearly fifteen
hours ago. Have you consulted the police?'

'One of our local officers was in the congregation and
raised the alarm, but in the darkness of a winter's night a
man may vanish in London without difficulty. They are
searching even now, but I can give them no help as to where
he might have fled or what has driven him there. They
counsel patience, but remaining in the vicarage unable to do
anything was intolerable! Like so many, Mr Holmes, I have
heard of you, but never thought that one day I might come to
you myself.'

'You were right to do so now,' Holmes told her. 'But why
did you hesitate when you first arrived?'

'As I walked here, it seemed to me so bizarre an occurrence
– with no suggestion of a crime – that I feared you would
resent being disturbed on such a matter on such a day. When
I first reached your door, my misgivings overcame me. I
nearly returned home without seeing you.'

'You were right to change your mind,' Holmes told her. 'As you say, there is no apparent criminality, but the confounding may also concern me, especially when it causes the innocent such distress. At this stage, I have only one question. You mentioned that your father is not a young man. How old is he?'

Miss Fortescue seemed puzzled. 'He will be sixty-eight in February.'

'Yet he was appointed vicar of St Andrew's some fifteen years ago, after what you describe as a brief curacy. He must have taken holy orders late in life. What was his profession previously?'

'He was a doctor, Mr Holmes. A general practitioner.'

'And where did he practise?'

'In Liverpool . . . is there any relevance in this?'

'I cannot imagine so,' Holmes said dismissively. 'The point merely intrigued me. However, we can accomplish nothing here. Watson, you will want to return home, but we are for St John's Wood.'

'I have no commitments,' I said. 'If this lady has no objection, I should like to accompany you.'

'As you wish,' Holmes said. 'But we leave immediately. The afternoon light will quickly fade. Miss Fortescue, will you be so kind as to wait in the hall downstairs while I attire myself?'

'Of course. I am very grateful to you, Mr Holmes.'

He nodded his thanks, and as our visitor left the room moved swiftly to where he kept his collection of newspaper clippings. They covered, I knew, many years and included narratives of the most recondite events that had caught his attention; on more than one occasion their contents had provided some invaluable fragment of information. He picked up the first volume and turned its pages before pausing and reading for a moment. Then he closed the book and glanced at me.

'Has it ever struck you, Watson, how our existence is constantly governed by chance?'

'What do you mean?'

'You and I first met at a haphazard point when our lives touched. Years of unrelated movements brought our paths together at that moment. Today is an occasion when such a random pattern has the additional spark of the incredible, what we call a coincidence.'

'Then you knew of this matter even before Miss Fortescue arrived?'

'Only in part. Her name did not immediately strike me, but as she spoke a faint memory returned. Having established part of her father's history, I am certain her visit must be connected with something that happened more than twenty years ago, and had remained half-forgotten in my mind. Now, because some bishop offered an obscure curate a living relatively near this house, his daughter has approached me and brought it to my attention again.'

'And what was the original occurrence?'

'There is no time to explain now,' he replied. 'We must not keep Miss Fortescue waiting. Do not reveal that I know anything and I will afford you the details when we have the opportunity. Fate, as some men call it, has delivered me a most unexpected Christmas present. I pray that it will not prove a tragic one.'

Public-spirited citizens having made efforts to clear the pavements outside their homes, our journey was accomplished more speedily than would otherwise have been the case. St Andrew's stood back from the road, surrounded by its churchyard with the vicarage behind from which Miss Fortescue collected the key while we waited in the portico beneath the Ionic columns of soot-smeared white Portland stone. Inside, it was a handsome square building with a gallery supported by iron pillars round three sides of the nave, the section facing the altar bearing the organ and rows of box pews. At the chancel steps, Holmes looked back down the flagstones of the central aisle covered in a deep blue runner.

'How tall is your father, Miss Fortescue?'

'How tall? I really cannot understand how—'

'People are often puzzled when they see my methods in action,' he interrupted. 'Be so good as to indulge my questions. There is always a purpose to them.'

'As you wish . . . about Dr Watson's height.'

'Very well. Now, your father's exact movements from the moment the service began. I presume he entered from the vestry, which is where?'

'Over there, to your left. He walked to the chancel steps, bowed to the altar, then crossed to the choir stalls to conduct them for the first carol.'

'For which the congregation rose? Thank you. And then?'

'He sat on a chair by the choir as the lessons were read and—'

'And remained in that position, except for leading the choir in further carols, until he entered the pulpit to read the lesson,' Holmes concluded. 'That is perfectly clear. Let us first see if the vestry affords any clues.'

The room contained a high cupboard in which the choir's surplices were stored, a desk and chair and a large padlocked chest for the safe-keeping of church plate. Holmes opened the outer door and looked across the gravestones for a moment, then remarked on a pair of rubber overshoes just inside the threshold.

'They are my father's,' Miss Fortescue explained. 'He wore them as he walked from the vicarage.'

'And clearly fled without them,' Holmes commented. 'Watson, will you wait here with Miss Fortescue for a moment, then enter the church and imitate her father's movements . . . Incidentally, I noticed a pool of water near the altar. Take care you don't slip.'

After he left us, I assured Miss Fortescue that Holmes would not request such a pantomime without good reason before I followed his instructions. There was no sign of him as we re-entered the church, but I heard his voice call me from some part of the building.

'First to the choir stalls, then enter the pulpit.'

I did as he bade me, finally climbing the nine steps that curved round the oak pulpit and standing before the Bible set on the outspread wings of a carved eagle. I gazed across the ranks of dark deal pews and saw Holmes sitting in one of them towards the back.

'Oh, there you are,' I remarked.

'Yes, Watson . . . where you could not see me until now.' He rose and unfastened the brass catch securing the gate at the end of the pew and stode down the aisle. 'During the first part of the service, Miss Fortescue, your father would only have been able to see part of his congregation. Even when they rose to sing, his attention would have been directed to the choir. Only when he entered the pulpit and instinctively raised his eyes would everyone have been visible.'

'But whom did he see?' she asked.

'That we must discover. You said there were some fifty people in the congregation. Were there any strangers?'

'Not to my knowledge, but latecomers may have arrived after I took my place.'

'Is it the habit of this church to greet worshippers at the door?'

'Yes. My father's curate, David Sinclair, does it.'

'Then we must speak to him. Where may he be found?'

'In the curate's cottage in the adjacent road. It is but a short distance.'

The 'cottage' was imaginatively named, being in fact the end house of a short terrace. Miss Fortescue knocked, and the door was speedily opened by an upright, black-haired young man in clerical garb. His face transmuted into instant relief and his dark eyes lit with affection and concern as he saw our companion.

'Anne!' he cried. 'Where have you been? I spent an hour at the vicarage waiting for you to return.'

'I have been to seek help, David,' she replied. 'This is Mr Sherlock Holmes and his companion, Dr Watson. Mr Holmes wishes to talk to you.'

'Of course. Gentlemen, this way please.'

As we stepped inside, Sinclair placed his hand on Miss Fortescue's arm with such natural familiarity that it was clear their relationship was deeper than that of a young man showing courtesy to his vicar's daughter. In the front room, he set her on a comfortable chair before turning to Holmes.

'Clearly you are aware of what has occurred, sir,' he said. 'I do not know how I can assist, but if there is anything in my power I shall do it.'

'I wish to ascertain if anyone unknown to you attended last night's service. I assume you recognized most of the congregation.'

'Yes. Except for a young man and woman who arrived just before the service began.'

'Did you speak to them?'

'Hardly at all. With the service about to commence, I wished to take my own seat. I welcomed them and handed them each a service sheet.'

'Where did they sit?'

'In a vacant pew near the back. I noticed because I followed them as I went to my own place at the front.'

'Did you see them again?'

'No. As you may imagine, there was great confusion after the incident with Mr Fortescue. I was too shocked by what had happened to even remember the strangers. It is only now that you have recalled them to my mind. Are they of importance?'

'Almost certainly,' Holmes replied. 'They appear to have been the only unusual feature present during the service. A connection between their presence and the vicar's strange behaviour seems irrefutable.'

Sinclair turned to Miss Fortescue with a look of anguish. 'Forgive me for not paying attention to them! Had I done so, perhaps—'

'No blame attaches to you,' Holmes interrupted. 'Many churches are attended by strangers at Christmastime. You were not to know that this man and woman were anything other than seasonal visitors to the parish.'

'But now they have disappeared!'

'In this weather, they are not likely to have travelled far. It may be possible to locate them.'

'My concern is locating my father,' Miss Fortescue said.

'We share your anxiety,' Holmes said. 'And it is possible that the police's activities may have yielded results. If so, they will seek you at the vicarage. Mr Sinclair may escort you home and leave you in the care of the household staff. We will return to the church.'

The possibility, however faint, of the best of news awaiting her at home roused Miss Fortescue to action and we left the curate's house. We separated in the churchyard, with Sinclair assuring us that he would find us if the vicar had returned or the police afforded information. The late December light was dying as we passed between the gravestones amid attendant elms and yews, and fresh flakes of snow drifted about us.

'An explanation first, Watson,' Holmes said after we had lit several gas mantles in the nave. 'I told you earlier that this matter contains echoes of an old story.'

We sat in one of the pews, the mantles throwing light and shadow about us as he related his narrative.

'Alfred Fortescue was the son of a distinguished Scottish surgeon. By the eighteen-sixties, he was established as a general practitioner in Liverpool. The neighbourhood was one of well-to-do merchants, but he also held a weekly surgery in the dockside area of the city, asking of his patients no more than they could afford, which in many cases was nothing. He married Emily Dawson, the daughter of a shipowner and a woman of volatile temperament who lacked neither ambition nor pride. His comfortable private income was insufficient to satisfy her. She complained about the time he spent attending impoverished patients when he could have been attracting high fees from others; she grumbled at what she saw as the paucity of her wardrobe; she resented the modesty of their lifestyle. In short, she became a scold.

'Fortescue refused to abandon the underprivileged and the couple quarrelled frequently. The arrival of a daughter – the young woman we have met today – might have reconciled their differences, but in fact had the opposite effect. The wife irrationally complained that if her child was to be raised like a ragamuffin, she would have nothing to do with her, and from the time of the birth Fortescue was obliged to employ a nurse. He appointed a woman called Jane Smith, whose arrival aggravated the mother's behaviour to the extent that she became unbalanced in her mind.

'Tragedy struck when the child was six months old. Emily Fortescue had started to wander the house at night, now weeping, now laughing. When they heard her, the staff or Fortescue himself would return her to her room and she would be given a sedative. On the Christmas Eve of 1867 the household was awoken by screaming followed by the sound of breaking glass coming from the nursery. Hastening to the room, they found a terrible scene. Jane Smith, whose bedroom was adjacent, was clutching the baby and Fortescue was standing by the shattered sash window staring at the ground below, where his wife lay dead from a broken neck.

'The doctor appeared too shaken to speak, but Smith was totally calm. She handed the infant to the cook and asked the butler to summon the police. When they arrived, she confessed to responsibility for Emily Fortescue's death. She said she had heard sounds from the nursery and on entering had seen a figure standing near the cradle. Afraid for the safety of her charge and not recognizing the intruder in the darkness, she had run across the room and pushed her violently away. The woman had staggered backwards through the window. Moments later, Fortescue had burst in, followed by the staff. It was a story she never altered, and she was subsequently imprisoned for manslaughter. After her trial, Fortescue left Liverpool with his daughter and was never heard of again.

'The matter attracted scant attention in the London papers, but the provincial press reported it in detail and an acquaintance of mine in the city sent me the cuttings as he felt they would be of interest.'

'In what way?' I inquired. 'It was a tragedy, but no mystery is apparent.'

'It was to my perceptive correspondent,' Holmes replied. 'He pointed out that Jane Smith had been one of the doctor's dockside patients, the very class of person his wife had so resented. Fortescue's behaviour marked him as a sympathetic man, so why did he employ someone likely to cause his wife such offence? The question intrigued me also, but other cases drove it from my mind.

'Some ten years later, however, I had been engaged on an inquiry in Lancashire and I made a detour to Liverpool before leaving the county. The practice was in the hands of a newcomer, but many people remembered Fortescue, including his former butler whom I was able to trace. He said that immediately prior to the screaming he had heard raised voices, although he could not be certain from which part of the house they came.

'He rose and left his room which was on the floor above the nursery. At the foot of the stairs, he heard the scream and the breaking glass and at that moment could see the door of the nursery at the far end of the corridor. He hurried to the room and could recollect no sign of Fortescue until he entered the nursery himself. In other words, Watson, the doctor was in the room at the moment his wife went through the window, a completely different account to that given by Smith.'

'Did he give evidence at Smith's trial?' I asked.

'Yes, but made no mention of what he told me. He said that Smith was so adamant of her version of events – a version that condemned her – that he felt he could have been mistaken in the confusion. But, even so, many years later he wondered if he had really been in error.

'I used my influence with Scotland Yard to secure an interview with Smith in Holloway Prison. She greeted me courteously, but expressed surprise at my interest. Her story was unchanged. I put to her an alternative narrative but, rightly suspecting that I had no firm evidence, she denied it. When I left, she asked that I should not approach her again, a request I have honoured.'

Holmes stared thoughtfully at the pulpit at the far end of the church. 'So is the truth now within my grasp?'

'What was the alternative story you put to Smith?'

'A bow at a venture, Watson, and fatally lacking a reason.

It seemed clear that . . .' He broke off as the creak of the west door opening behind us sounded through the silent church. 'Who is there?'

As we turned in our seats, Sinclair and Miss Fortescue entered, accompanied by a young man, his hat held respectfully in his hands.

'Mr Holmes,' Sinclair said. 'This is one of the strangers who attended the Christmas Eve service. The lady with him was his wife. He came to the vicarage to inquire about Mr Fortescue.'

'Indeed?' said Holmes, as we rose and joined them. 'And where is your wife?'

'She is unable to come, sir,' the man replied. 'But she was concerned and I said I would make inquiries. I'm told he has not returned.'

'No, but your interest does you credit,' Holmes said as his keen eyes examined the stranger in the light of the gas mantle. 'What is a newly married left-handed ledger clerk from Manchester doing in St John's Wood?'

'Do you know me, sir?' the man demanded in amazement.

'No, but your accent is unmistakable, the new ring on your wedding finger visible and it is the elbow of the right sleeve of your jacket that has required repair. That is the one you must lean on your desk while writing with the opposite hand. What is your name?'

'Michael Chester. My wife and I are visiting relatives of hers in London for Christmas.'

'And what brought you to St Andrew's last night?'

'We wished to attend a service. This was the nearest church.'

'And you've never been here before?'

'This is the first time either us have visited London.'

'Then it is difficult to see how the presence of yourself and your wife has any bearing on the Reverend Fortescue's disappearance.' Holmes thought for a moment. 'Do you have any connection with Liverpool?'

'My wife's grandmother was born there.'

'And your own family?'

'I was raised in an orphanage in the city of Chester, from which I was given my name. I know nothing of my parents.'

'For one so disadvantaged, you appear to have advanced yourself.'

'I had a benefactor, the wife of an alderman who supported the orphanage. When I showed skill in letters and numbers, she arranged additional education for me and later helped me secure a position with my present employer.'

'Most commendable,' Holmes commented. 'I'm obliged to you for answering my questions. Your attendance last night was clearly irrelevant to what has happened. Thank your wife for her concern. When Mr Fortescue returns we will let you know. Where are you staying?'

Chester gave an address nearby and turned to go after Holmes assured him we would contact him.

'One final question,' Holmes added. 'When were you born?'

'Eighteen sixty-two,' he replied. 'Why do you wish to know?'

'It's of no consequence. We will contact you when there is news.'

Chester closed the west door behind him and Holmes stared at it for a moment until Miss Fortescue spoke.

'You indicated to that young man that my father will return. Are you certain?'

'As I know where he is, yes.'

She cried and grasped the lapels of his greatcoat. 'In pity's name, take me to him!'

'You have my assurance he is safe.' He unclasped her trembling fingers. 'I must insist that for the moment you leave this in my hands. You and your father will soon be reunited. In the meantime, return to the rectory and await my arrival. Mr Sinclair will accompany you.'

'You are a cruel man, Mr Holmes!' she protested.

'That is how it may appear,' he agreed. 'But you must trust me.'

'Come, Anne,' said Sinclair. 'I am certain we can have faith in Mr Holmes.'

With reluctant obedience, she allowed the curate to lead her out through the west door again. I observed a look of misgiving on Holmes' face as he watched them depart, then he stood for several minutes absorbed in thought.

'Paths again, Watson,' he said finally. 'After many strange turnings, those that crossed once may cross again. I now know what Fortescue saw when he mounted that pulpit.'

'What was it?'

'He saw himself on the night of his wife's death. And now he must face a terrible truth.'

Holmes was silent for a long time and I was not moved to question him. In the sombre light of the nave, his face appeared grave with concern as much as occupied by thought.

'The unravelling of this will cause pain, Watson,' he said finally. 'But unravelled it must be, even after so long. I am sure I must have the answer, and you will be privy to it. But anything you learn must be treated with the confidence of the confessional.'

'Of course,' I agreed. 'But where is Fortescue and why did you refuse to take his daughter to him?'

'Because she must never know the story,' he replied. 'Meanwhile, he should be allowed to reappear when he chooses. As to where he is, it was nearly midnight when he fled. Had he gone to the home of one of his parishioners, they would in charity have advised his daughter. A hotel would have been suspicious at the appearance of an elderly vicar arriving in some distress and without luggage and alerted the police. Similarly had he collapsed and been taken to a hospital dead or alive. No public transport is running, so he has not left the area.

'It is obvious that he can only have returned to this church after everyone had left. He entered through the vestry and prayed. When I asked you to imitate his movements during the service, I drew your attention to the pool of water near the altar, the result of snow melting from his shoes.'

'But why has he still not revealed himself?'

'He is greatly troubled in his mind and—' Holmes stopped abruptly as we heard the sudden clang of a bell, muffled inside the building but clearly audible in the silence. The note was followed by another, then a third, fainter this time. Holmes whirled on his heel, features alert and apprehensive.

'In God's name!' he cried. 'Where is the ringing chamber?'

'I'm not certain,' I replied. 'But I know a similar church which has an entrance by the organ. If we tried the stairs from the lobby . . .'

But Holmes was gone, racing like a man possessed. I hastened after him up the stairs I had suggested. We emerged on the gallery by the organ, next to which was an iron spiral staircase.

'This way!' Holmes cried, and leapt up the steps with the speed of a cat. By the time I reached the door at the top, he was already in the chamber. Suspended from one of the bell ropes was a figure in a long gold and silver chasuble; Holmes had grasped his legs and was lifting the body as best he could to reduce the deadly pressure on the neck.

'The chair, Watson!' he shouted. 'Get him down! Quickly!'

I snatched up the chair, then stood on it and began to tug at the simple noose into which the rope had been tied, but the crude knot had tightened. Instinctively I fumbled in my pocket for the sturdy Army knife I invariably carried out of old habit, snapped open the blade and cut the rope.

'I have him!' Holmes cried, and let the vicar's body slide through his arms until he could lift it like a child's and carry him to a wooden bench alongside the wall. I felt for a pulse; the beat beneath the skin of the wrist was as faint and irregular as the flutter of a butterfly's wing and the flesh around his thin lips was livid blue.

'He is not long for this world,' I said. 'He is bitterly cold, and now this . . .'

'Then may Heaven forgive me!' Holmes exclaimed. 'I had assumed he would have found warmth as well as shelter.'

He undid the knot and gently lifted the rope clear, then removed his coat and wrapped it around the vicar.

Fortescue's grey eyes opened and his lips moved as he croaked an attempt at speech.

'Rest yourself,' Holmes told him. 'You may talk later.'

'He has very little time left in which to speak,' I said. 'Perhaps it will be better if he does so while he can.'

'Yes,' Fortescue whispered. 'Mr Holmes, you must be my confessor.'

'I can grant no absolution.'

'Then your understanding will be the best I can hope for. How much do you know, sir?'

'Much, but there are gaps in my knowledge. Can you answer my questions?' Fortescue nodded. 'How much did you hear of our conversations in the church?'

'Not all, but enough. When I heard voices, I crept into the organ loft, still lacking the courage to return. You must know that until I heard what you said this had been no more than an insane nightmare. When you said I had to face a terrible truth, I knew what it must be.'

'But I am still uncertain of parts of that truth,' Holmes told him. 'Where did you meet Jane Smith?'

Fortescue's face darkened, but he looked Holmes straight in the eyes. 'On the Liverpool dockside. She was standing alone beneath a riverside lamp. I knew what she was because I was seeking one. A young man is taught to temper his desires, but it is not always possible. After that first encounter, I visited her regularly, during which time I began to have affection for her, although our relationship could never be more than what it was. Then she left Liverpool without explanation and I neither saw nor heard of her again for some two years.

'She returned as a patient at my dockside surgery shortly after I had married. I was dismayed that she still followed the same sordid profession, but she pointed out she had no choice. While intelligent, she was poor, ill-educated and without advantages. Her only skill she said was that of tending to young children; as the eldest daughter of a large family, she had been obliged to undertake the care of younger brothers and sisters.

'When my wife refused to accept Anne, I realized I could offer Jane respectable employment. You must believe me when I tell you there was no impropriety while she was under my roof.'

'But her appointment offended your wife,' Holmes remarked.

'I paid no regard to that. Emily had proved a bad wife and would be a worse mother; she would have resented whomsoever I had engaged. Jane was excellent at her duties, attentive and gentle to my daughter. That was all that mattered to me.'

'And the night your wife died,' Holmes said. 'Tell me if the theory Jane Smith rejected when I put it to her was correct. Your wife had become dangerously unbalanced. That night she entered the nursery and in some manner threatened her child. Awakened by the disturbance, you went into the room and saw what was happening. Having ensured your daughter's safety, you attempted to calm your wife, but she was too agitated. In the struggle she fell through the window to her death.'

Fortescue shook his head. 'You are too charitable, Mr Holmes. I deliberately forced my wife through that window. She had threatened to kill our child. Before the police arrived, Jane spoke to me. She said the truth would leave Anne parentless and insisted she must take the blame. If I supported her story that Emily's death was a tragedy caused by her protecting Anne, there was a chance she would not hang. To save myself, I placed her life in peril. Although she escaped the executioner, I have never been able to flee my conscience. I entered the church as a form of penance.'

Holmes looked at me. 'You understand now why I said certain things must never be revealed, especially to Miss Fortescue.'

'Indeed,' I said, then turned to the vicar. 'But why did you attempt to take your life?'

'Mr Holmes knows that,' he replied.

'Yes,' my friend agreed. 'Had I realized you were listening, there were things I would not have said. It was very stupid of me.'

'It does not matter now. I . . .' the vicar's breath caught painfully in his throat and I felt for the pulse again then shook my head at Holmes' inquiring and anxious glance.

'You must . . .' Fortescue's voice was fading. 'Protect her as you have promised, Mr Holmes. I lied for the wrong reasons, but you must do so for the right ones. Condemn me only in your secret heart and let God . . .' He was gone, and Holmes looked at him with a great sadness.

'There were three principals in this tragedy, Watson,' he said. 'A wealthy doctor, a proud woman and a common prostitute. And the meanest of them was the noblest.'

'She is to be admired for taking the blame,' I admitted. 'And one hardly expects self-sacrifice from a woman of the streets.'

'You display the prejudices of our age, Watson. Can't you see the full extent of her sacrifice?'

'I acknowledge she sacrificed her freedom and . . .'

'Damn it, man!' Holmes cried. 'She did infinitely more than that. She sacrificed her child!'

'What do you mean? I don't understand.'

'You rarely do!' Holmes whirled away and spoke again with his back to me. 'Forgive me, Watson. Your long loyalty deserves better from me, but this is a wretched business. Michael Chester is Jane Smith's son. The son who has grown to manhood while his mother has been incarcerated for a crime she did not commit. And when I saw the greyness in his eyes that is echoed in those of Anne Fortescue, I knew who his father must be.'

'You mean . . .?'

'Yes. The vicar of St Andrew's, whose flock would condemn Jane Smith as shameful. He didn't know because she never told him. But on Christmas Eve, the anniversary of the tragedy he can never have forgotten, he looked across the pews of this church and saw a face so like his own as a younger man that he fled in terror. Then he overheard my conversation with Michael Chester and began to guess the

truth; he knew it when Chester told me when he had been
born – the period during which Jane Smith was away from
Liverpool. At that moment he recognized how much she had
sacrificed, and a lifetime of remorse became too much to
bear.'

'And what will you tell Miss Fortescue – and Michael
Chester?'

'Michael Chester and his wife need know nothing, least of
all that their chance attendance at this church led to his
father's death. We shall tell them that the vicar perished in
the cold and his actions are inexplicable. They will leave
London none the wiser and continue with their lives. As for
Miss Fortescue . . . is it possible an inquest might not detect
that a rope has been about her father's neck?'

I stooped and pulled the high embroidered collar of the
chasuble away from the flesh; there were faint marks, but the
thick material had protected him and he had been hanging
but a few moments.

'Unless a doctor was looking for them, they would probably be overlooked,' I said.

'Then better some think I have failed than the truth be
known,' Holmes said. 'Help me take him into the churchyard, where it may be supposed that he died from the cold.'

Darkness had fallen and there was no danger of us being
seen as we carried our burden. We lay him between two
rows of gravestones, then hastened to the vicarage and said
we had found him. Miss Fortescue was too distraught to pay
any attention when Holmes expressed regret at being mistaken in all his reasonings, and we left her in the care of
Sinclair and her staff. On leaving the vicarage we visited the
house where Michael Chester and his wife were staying; they
were dismayed and saddened at what we told them and we
left them in happy ignorance.

'There is one final matter,' Holmes said as we returned to
Baker Street. 'I shall write to Jane Smith and request that she
will see me again. She is the only person who can answer
what questions are left.'

*

I accompanied Holmes for the encounter at Holloway. Jane Smith bore the marks of long imprisonment, but retained the looks of a striking woman. When the wardress who escorted her to us had left, she reached into the pocket of her prison gown and produced Holmes' letter.

'Is my son a good man, Mr Holmes?' she asked.

'That was my impression. And with a kind-hearted wife.'

'I am pleased. When you visited me some years ago, I refused to answer your questions but am prepared to do so now.'

Holmes nodded his appreciation. 'Why did you protect Alfred Fortescue?' he began.

'For the same reason any woman would protect a man, whatever he had done. Because I loved him.' She saw the expression on my face and smiled. 'Yes, Dr Watson. Such feelings are not expected among women of my profession, but they are possible. After we first met, he was kind and considerate and had our situations been different we might have married. But we both knew that was impossible.

'It was through me that he learnt of the deprivations my sort of people suffer and it was because of what I told him that he opened his charitable surgery. Our relationship continued – for true affection, Doctor – until I knew I was with child. I could have demanded that he support me, but knew that if the truth ever emerged he would be ruined. I left Liverpool, bore my son and placed him in an orphanage as I was unable to raise him myself. When I returned to the city, Alfred had married and later employed me.

'His wife was intolerable, and on the night of her death entered the nursery and threatened to kill her own daughter. When Alfred murdered her, I immediately knew what I had to do. He protested, but he was always a man I could persuade.' She looked down at the letter again. 'You say you have protected Anne from the truth of this, for which I am grateful. She was not in my care for long, but I loved her.'

'I understand from the governor that you will be released soon,' Holmes said. 'I could assist you to find your son.'

Jane Smith shook her head. 'I abandoned him, Mr Holmes. I have no right to reappear in his life after so long.'

'What will you do?'

She smiled at both of us grimly. 'I shall return to the streets, Mr Holmes. Apart from the few months I was Anne Fortescue's nurse, that is all society holds me worthy of.'

'I cannot allow that,' Holmes protested. 'Dr Watson and I have influential friends who would assist you.'

'Many of your friends, sir, are the sort of men who will have only one interest in me,' she replied. 'I know a side of their respectable lives of which you gentlemen are ignorant.'

'None the less, you must approach me on your release.'

'Thank you, but I doubt that I shall.' She rose from the wooden chair on which she had been sitting. 'I must now return to my cell.'

Holmes had stood up with her. 'I deem it an honour to have met you, Miss Smith,' he said.

She bowed her head in acknowledgement and was led away.

'You cannot add this case to your chronicles, Watson,' Holmes remarked. 'Fortescue's crime must remain unpublished for his daughter's sake – and of course your polite readers wold be grossly offended at being asked to admire one they are taught to despise. But it is a pity that so remarkable a woman should be forgotten.'

As I write, I am an old man and our society is much changed, now for the worse, now for the better. Later in this twentieth century, Holmes's admiration may be accepted and shared. Anne Fortescue married David Sinclair, who became an archdeacon; she recently died an honoured and beloved woman in the diocese. Jane Smith was beaten to death in an alleyway in Cheapside and Holmes counted it one of his greatest regrets that he was never able to identify her murderer. At his expense, she was buried in a Sussex churchyard. He and I were her only mourners.

MUCH ADO ABOUT SOMETHING

Susan Kelly

Messina
First of May

Dearest Mama,

Well, there's been a to-do here this last week and no mistake.
I don't really know what to make of it so I shall set it all down
exactly as I remember it and see what you think. Only what
you might call the official version is all wrong, as far as I can
see; it holds water the way a length of butter muslin does.

It all started when the Prince of Arragon, that's Don Pedro,
came back from the wars after a mighty victory, with nobody
important being killed at all. My master, Signior Leonato,
met him at the gates and welcomed him and said he must
stay with us as long as he wanted. Well, the prince thanked
him and said he'd stay at least a month. You should have
seen the master's jaw drop! It's one thing to offer unlimited
hospitality and quite another to have it accepted like that.
Still, he bit the bullet and gave orders for rooms to be
prepared and banquets set out and we didn't stop in the
servants' hall that night until gone midnight and Sarah, the
housekeeper, said she'd never known anything like it, the
gentlefolk all drinking and carousing till dawn.

The prince brought such a lot of people with him, you see,
that the house was full to overflowing. There was his

brother, Don John, that they call John the Bastard, which always seems a bit disrespectful to me but apparently it's all right to have natural sons when you're a prince, not like with the rest of us. He's a proud sort of man, though, with a nasty sneering way about him, much higher and mightier than Don Pedro himself.

Then there's Signior Benedick. You know, Mama, I've mentioned him before, the one that's always pinching the maids' bottoms and trying to put his hand up our skirts and down our bodices. He hasn't changed. You may remember how I told you a couple of years back that there was a bit of a thing between him and Miss Beatrice but how it all came to nothing in the end and now they haven't a civil word to say to each other. Sarah says they're still sweet together underneath it all but he called Miss Bea 'Lady Disdain' in front of the whole household and asked if she was not dead yet, and if that's love, Mama, then you can keep it.

If ever there was a man with his eye on the main chance, I should say it's Signior Benedick.

Then there was this Signior Claudio, that we'd heard so much about. It seems the prince has taken a fancy to him and loaded him down with money and lands and titles which not everyone is thrilled about, I suspect. He's little more than a boy, really, but old enough to be making sheep's eyes at Miss Hero all the same. He looked at her like he'd never seen a woman before although she is lovely, if I say so myself, all little and dainty and that mass of black hair that looks like a fine mist when it's brushed out in the morning. And she knew he was looking at her, all right, blushing away, which looked right pretty against her porcelain skin and I said to Sarah that we'd be laying out a wedding feast before Don Pedro went away again and she said that that was as maybe and meantime I could get on with stoking the fire.

I was right, though. Within three days Signior Claudio had secured Miss Hero's hand; or rather he got the prince to do it for him which is not my idea of wooing, but then the gentry is different to us as you've told me a thousand times, Mama. And as for Signior Benedick and Miss Bea – well Sarah wasn't wrong, she seldom is. I was on my way to the wash-house with the bedclothes and I saw them sitting behind a hedge, all furtive, so I thought, 'Two can play at that game,' I thought, and I hid behind the other side of the hedge and listened and he was saying to her, 'I love nothing in the wide world so well as thee,' which I thought was very pretty and it made me a bit misty-eyed for a minute but it didn't stop him goosing me when he passed me in the passage on the way to dinner that night. I nearly dropped my tray and it wouldn't be him that got the rough edge of Sarah's tongue if I had done, would it?

So there we were, working non-stop at preparing the wedding feast for Miss Hero, and the ladies all excited with cloth of gold and jewels and veils and presents. I enjoyed the work and was whirling around singing that fine new song I told you of – 'Sing no more ladies, for men were seducers ever,' it goes – until Sarah told me she could not stand any more of my warbling. Then the wedding day dawned and that was when the real excitement began.

There was an odd thing happened that morning, though, which I'd better tell you about first. Sarah said that I might as well go and give Don John's room a good turn out as he had upped and left at first light without a word to anyone and left his room like a pigsty to boot with wine spilt everywhere and other things I'd not like to examine too closely. So I did. And I was coming downstairs again into the front hall with my mop and bucket and there was a rat-a-tat-tat at the door and the master himself came rushing to open it, so I made myself small against the staircase since I knew I shouldn't have come down the main stairs but it was the nearest way and we were that busy.

It was those two men from the Watch I told you about, Dogberry and Verges, that no one can ever understand a word they say. And they were going on and on to the master about two men they'd arrested during the night they said were out-and-out villains and arrant knaves and the master kept looking at his pocket watch and wishing they would get to the point. Then the big one, Dogberry, said something about treason and slander and the master said rather abruptly that he had got a very busy day in front of him and could his two 'kind neighbours' come back later when he would have the leisure to decipher them. And he shooed them away without further ceremony.

Then he turned round muttering something like 'Too early,' or 'Too soon,' and saw me standing in the shadows and said, 'Maria!' like he was very shocked to see me there. I curtsied and he said, 'Well, well. This is a great day for the house, Maria. Here's for you to celebrate Miss Hero's good fortune,' and gave me a coin which I put into my pocket without looking, thinking it to be a brass penny. So I thanked him and curtsied again and ran off with my bucket and mop back below stairs, but when I remembered to look at the coin, what do you think it was, Mama? A silver ducat!

The wedding was fixed for late morning to be followed by a feast going on all day and far into the night. Miss Hero looked so lovely in her white gown and veil, standing there waiting for her new lord. It's not just that she's beautiful either, Mama, she's so good and kind and not at all hoity toity the way Miss Bea can be when the mood takes her.

Only then, when the friar asked Signior Claudio if he took Hero for his wife he went and said, 'No!' – just straight out like that. Then he called her a wanton and a common stale (excuse me, Mama, but I'm just repeating what I heard, however shocking) and said he had seen her with another man the night before, with her clothes all ruffled and her virtue gone and not for the first time either and the prince backed him up and said he'd seen it too. Miss Hero fell to the ground in a dead faint and I thought the master would have died of shame, wailing out that he wished he had never got a daughter and that it would be a kindness were somebody to stab him through the heart.

Signior Claudio, meanwhile, he turned on his heel and marched out saying there would be no wedding today, leaving the master and Miss Bea and Signior Benedick to carry Miss Hero away senseless. We were all dismissed, of course, since the master didn't want the whole world to witness his disgrace. Later, we were told that Miss Hero was dead indeed and that Signior Benedick had challenged Signior Claudio to a duel to the death. That would be Miss Bea making him, I think. I can't see him doing it of his own idea. Claudio and the prince sat there looking all grave, but obviously thinking that dying was the only thing My Lady could decently do in the circumstances.

I could hardly get on with my work what with crying over Miss Hero and the shame that had fallen on the household and Sarah told me if I didn't pull myself together, there'd be trouble. It seems it's only the gentry that's allowed any sensibility. After all, it's not as if someone like me would be able literally to *die* of shame like Miss Hero did.

Only then, late that afternoon, I was up in the apple loft sorting out some good ones from last year for baking, and that Dogberry and Verges turn up in the yard below, with two men in chains this time, men in the uniform of Don Pedro's army, and they tell the master and the prince and young Master Claudio that the whole thing was a put-up job – that what the prince and Claudio had witnessed the previous night had been him – this man, I mean, in chains – with Mistress Margaret, Miss Hero's lady's maid – her I've always said was no better than she should be; well, haven't I? – and he calling her by Hero's name and her looking just like Miss Hero in the night, being small and dark-haired. He said that Don John had put him up to it because he hated Claudio because Don Pedro liked him better than his own brother and had given him all that money and stuff.

Well, Claudio was distrort (I do not think I have spelt that aright, Mama, but you will know what I mean). He talked of throwing himself on his sword and I wanted to run down and offer to hold it for him in case he should otherwise miss it, which I thought likely. Although after he'd got over that, he said something along the lines of 'Anyone can make a mistake'. But the master just smiled kindly and said he could make amends by marrying his niece instead. First I thought he meant Miss Bea and I thought, 'Here, hang on a minute', but he went on to say that he had another niece, the daughter of his brother Antonio, who looked just exactly like Mistress Hero.

Well, this was news to me. I remembered something I'd heard from one of the grooms, though, soon after I came to work here. He said as how the master had a natural daughter he'd got on a serving maid nigh on twenty years ago and who was the spit and image of Miss Hero only not quite right in the head. He said they kept her lodged in the village where she was looked after kindly enough but not allowed out to be seen and talked about. When I mentioned this to Sarah at the time she flew right off the handle at me and told me it was not my place to go spreading gossip and slander and that she'd take the kitchen poker to me if I did it again. So I didn't talk about it any more and it went right out of my mind, until then.

The next thing is that someone turns up saying they've captured Don John who was behind all this deceit and they bring him in still all haughty and arrogant and sneering and the master looked, I have to say it, a bit put-about. Don Pedro is all for dealing with him right away and Don John looks very hard at Signior Leonato with that grim smile of his and the master says quickly not to spoil the wedding festivities and that he will deal with Don John after the prince has gone back to his old wars.

So, the next morning, Signior Claudio and the prince turned up again in their dress uniforms and spurs just like before and they led a woman out, all veiled in white, and Claudio swore to marry her. Then they lifted the veil and he staggered back and started moaning, 'Hero, my Hero. It is you. You're not dead after all,' and stuff like that, except, Mama, the thing is it *wasn't* Miss Hero although I admit it looked very like her, and perhaps it wasn't so very surprising that he should make such a mistake since he didn't really know Miss Hero at all well.

So they were married without further ado, her all smirking with lips which looked like Miss Hero's lips but weren't, and staring at him with what might have been eyes of rapturous love but just looked empty to me. Then Signior Benedick and

Miss Bea were married too and they all stood around congratulating each other and looking mightily pleased with themselves and it was hardly my place to say anything, was it, Mama?

Do you ever get the feeling there's some secret which everybody knows except for you?

Anyway, the prince had to go back to the wars earlier than he thought so the next morning they set off, with the whole household turning out to do them honour and Claudio's bride still smirking and simpering fit to bust and him looking perhaps just a little bit less full of himself than he had the day before, like he suspected there was something up but couldn't quite put his finger on it. Signior Benedick reckoned he had to stay behind – something about a lamed horse – and would catch up with them later.

So, I was standing there in my best apron like all the rest, waving, when I happened to glance up, and saw Miss Hero draw quickly away from a second-floor window where she'd been watching. I know it was her, but I said nothing. As soon as the prince and his retinue were out of sight, they all burst out laughing, even Sarah. The master was rubbing his hands with glee, and embracing Signior Benedick and saying it was a good day's work all told. 'You'll not find me ungrateful, signior,' says he, 'nor his lordship.' Then he put his arm round Mistress Margaret too and told her she had done well instead of telling her to pack her things and be gone without a character or reference as I would have done, the trollop.

After supper one of the grooms comes into the kitchen and says that Don John has escaped. I'd like to know how since I'd have thought the dungeons here were impregnable but he's a cunning one, that bastard, and may have a pact with the D— for all I know. He'll be miles away by now, having taken Signior Benedick's best horse, which has apparently recovered from its lameness. Lucio, the groom, says he doesn't think we will see Don Pedro alive again. Nor Signior Upstart Claudio for that matter, or if he does survive he 'won't dare show his face round here again with his idiot bastard of a wife. Then he says that Miss Hero will be the

prettiest princess of Arragon that ever was when she marries
Don John. Of course, I asked him what he meant and he just
laughed and said that Don John is the rising star now, and
Sarah told him to hush up if he knew what was good for him
and nodded her head in my direction rather meaningfully.

I went to the master's room last thing with some hot water
for his ewer and he came in while I was still there. I said, 'A
neat day's work, sir, by my troth,' and he looked at me funny
like and said, 'You're a good girl, Maria, and a loyal one too,
I'm sure, that knows what side her bread's buttered.' Then
he gave me *another* silver ducat and I went off back to my
room and thought I would write you all about it while it was
fresh in my mind and see what you—

What disturbed me there was a knock at the door. It was
Sarah and she had a little silver tray with a goblet of the
master's best fortified wine that he saves for special occasions.

'The master thought you might be wakeful after all the
excitement of the day, Maria,' says she, 'and sent me with
some of his wine to help you sleep.'

You told me, Mama, when I was lucky enough to get this
place, that I must be honest and loyal to my employer and
then he would be good to me and you see how right you
were.

Sarah saw the pen and paper on my night table and said,
'Writing to your mama again, Maria?' and I said I was and
she said I was a good, dutiful daughter but that it was late
now, my tallow was almost burnt down and that I should
drink my wine and get myself to bed.

'You can finish your letter in the morning,' said she.

So that is what I shall do.

LAST OF KIN

Jo Bannister

At the mention of the words 'sweet little old lady', everyone
who knew her immediately thought of Mrs Nancy Budgens.
Even people who didn't know her got a mind's eye view of
someone very *like* Nancy: someone of about seventy with a
soft powdery complexion, fluffy peach-white hair, faded but
still warm blue eyes, no great height and nothing you could
call a waist without setting off a lie detector. They pictured the
way she smiled, the blue eyes disappearing in a mass of
crinkles pushed up by the apple cheeks, and the way she
walked, with a slight roll like a deep-sea sailor. They knew her
wardrobe consisted almost entirely of flower-printed cotton
dresses.

Asked to speculate further, they would have attributed to
this archetypal Little Old Lady a large close-knit family of
equally apple-cheeked husband, children, grandchildren and
quite possibly great-grandchildren as well. It seemed somehow part of the package, that such a plainly maternal figure
should come with all the trimmings.

But in fact Nancy Budgens did not have the perfect family
life which would have completed the picture. Mr Budgens,
branch manager of a local bank for twenty years, died at his
desk just weeks short of retirement. Their daughter Sandra
never married, though she did raise a child. A dull woman,
prematurely middle aged, she seemed content in her undemanding job as an assistant librarian; until one morning she
was found hanging from a length of picture cord attached to
the specially high shelf for books of a certain artistic nature.

Which reduced the already small family to just two: Nancy and her grandson Trevor. When anyone asked she would put on that brave smile patented by little old ladies and say, 'Trevor's all I have left.' Then: 'And I'm all he has.'

This led some of her friends to suppose the relationship closer than in fact it was. Although alone, Sandra Budgens had managed to provide a home and a decent upbringing for her son without recourse to her parents. Young Trevor saw as much of his grandma and grandad as most boys – occasional holidays, birthdays, Christmas – and no more. There was an element of wishful thinking in what Nancy said. Though they were indeed next of kin after Sandra's sad meaningless departure, she and Trevor remained more amiable than close.

For one thing, Trevor wasn't Reliable. As the widow of a bank manager Nancy put a lot of stock in Reliability, which she judged by such things as having a Proper Job and a Nice Home and Nice Friends. Trevor disappointed on every count. He was an actor. He said he was quite a good one and made a decent living. All Nancy knew was that he visited her at times when people with Proper Jobs would be working, and he wore clothes she wouldn't have let Mr Budgens put in their own dustbin. He shared a run-down Victorian house with several other Thespians of both traditional sexes and one or two others.

In spite of that, he seemed a kind young man. He brought her chocolates on her birthday, and flowers for no particular reason, and phoned her at intervals to check that she was keeping well.

And she was keeping well; but she was aware of the passing of time and the need to make proper provision for her old age. The family home, which had never felt a burden until recently, seemed to be getting bigger, the stairs steeper, the bathroom further down the landing with every month that passed. Once it had been her ambition to die in this house; now that seemed less a hope than a sentence. She thought there must be easier ways for an old lady with a little money to spend her last years.

She asked Trevor round to discuss the situation. He came willingly enough but puzzled, as if she'd asked for his advice on gerbils. All he knew about money was that if you didn't pay what you owed people came after you with pick-axe handles.

'I'm not a wealthy woman,' Nancy began coyly. 'Your grandfather, God bless him, left me comfortable, but that's getting to be a long time ago. Running this house has eaten into what he left. Then there was the inflation, and the recession . . . ' She smiled apologetically.

Trevor glanced around him. It wasn't a big house but it was a considerable asset. He couldn't believe she was desperate enough to be asking him for money. 'Grandma, of course I'd help if I could. But – '

But when Trevor said he was successful he meant he could live on what he earned as an actor, and didn't have to work in kitchens when he was 'resting'. It did not mean he had a numbered account in Switzerland that the Inland Revenue knew nothing about. His mother's estate had boiled down to a few thousand pounds in a building society, which he considered his insurance against destitution if the roles he specialized in – petty criminals, undesirable boyfriends and assorted Shakespearian gravediggers and sword-carriers whose first names were always Second – dried up. His only other assets were an elderly van – his ability to transport scenery had won him several parts – and a fifth share in a house that grew mushrooms.

Oh yes: and an elderly grandmother with a much nicer house of her own and no other relatives.

Nancy patted his hand absently. 'Would you, dear? Bless you. But that's not quite what I had in mind.

'You and I are one another's only family, Trevor. When I die, what I have will naturally be yours. I've always hoped it would be enough to provide you with a little security.

'But if I do what I have in mind there won't be as much left as I'd like. I'm an old lady now, but I could live another twenty years. And nice residential accommodation doesn't come cheap. I'd have to sell this house and buy an annuity.

On the credit side' – Nancy wasn't a bank manager's widow for nothing – 'I'd never be a burden to you. On the debit side, there mightn't be much left for *your* old age. Before I burn any boats I'd like to know how you feel about that. Would it be a major blow?'

Trevor had never given it much thought. He knew he was his grandmother's only heir, and anticipated benefiting at some point, but he'd never worked out how much he could expect let alone how to use it. He thought about it now.

She was seventy-one: no great age by today's standards. She was fit, she had no history of illness – she might live to be a hundred. He'd be in his fifties then. There were an awful lot of fifty-year-old actors for whom 'resting' had become a permanent state of affairs. Whatever the house was worth, whatever she got for the antiques that furnished it and whatever remained from his grandfather's investments, it would all be gone by then. Even if she didn't live to be a hundred; even if she only lived another ten years, say, which was nothing. Every week she would reduce his expectations by hundreds of pounds.

The mere fact that he wasn't able to brush it off unconsidered, with a gallant smile and a casual 'Grandma, it's your money, use it how you want', told Nancy that however well he was doing in his own terms her grandson did not have the kind of financial reserves beside which her own paled to insignificance.

'Oh dear,' she said anxiously, reaching for his hand, 'it *would*, wouldn't it? You've been counting on it. You're a good boy, you've never asked me for money, even when you couldn't possibly have had enough. And now I'm proposing to spend your inheritance. No, it really won't do – I shall have to think again.'

Trevor got a belated grip on his expression and clasped her hand in return. 'Don't be silly, Grandma,' he said. 'It's your money – Grandad made it and he'd want you to use it in your best interests. Spend it and enjoy it. I've some money of my own: not a fortune but enough to see me through the odd sticky patch. Mum left me nearly ten thousand, and I've

added a bit to it since I've been working. And hell, I'm only
twenty-five: if I can't put together a comfortable stake over the
next forty years I should have been a greengrocer instead!
Now, tell me about your plans. Is there somewhere you've got
your eye on?'

Nancy's face lit up with pleasure. If it was true that Sandra
had never fulfilled the highest potential as a daughter, that
she and her mother had in fact found it hard to like one
another, she had at least raised a son to be proud of. 'Trevor,
you're a lovely lad.' Nancy got up and bustled over to her
bureau, coming back with a sheaf of envelopes made of
expensively grained paper. 'Yes, I have. I've been doing a bit
of research, and there's a couple of wonderful places.'

She spread the brochures in front of him, pointing out the
lifts, the en-suite bathroms, the extensive gardens with the
enthusiasm of a child comparing holiday camps.

'I think Rosedale's the one I shall go for. Look at those *lovely*
flowerbeds! And if you pay a little more for a room on this side
of the house' – she tapped the illustration with a fingernail –
'there's a view of the river. Oh, I did used to love the river
when we were younger! I really think it would be worth
finding a little more to be able to enjoy it again.'

'What's this one?' asked Trevor, holding up a well-thumbed
prospectus with a lot of gold-leaf on the cover.

Nancy's voice went schoolgirl breathy. 'The Beeches. The
Rolls-Royce of residential provision for the elderly – the sort of
place you only get sent to if the family feel really guilty about
the way they've treated you. I wish someone had treated *me*
that badly! Even by selling this place I couldn't meet the fees at
The Beeches.' She smiled cheerily. 'Still, it's nice to dream.'

''Course it is, Gran,' Trevor said bravely, well aware that
her dreams were putting the boot into his. Even if he'd never
thought of it in those terms, this house had been his insurance
against having to play comic footmen in pantomime in
Huddersfield. When it was gone he was on his own. Her news
had given him much to think about.

As his had given Nancy. But they parted on the doorstep
with their customary brief hug as if all was well.

'You are a *nice* boy, Trevor,' his grandmother said again. 'I've been quite worried, I don't mind saying. I'm glad we've had this talk.'

'There's nothing to worry about,' Trevor said firmly. 'Like you always say, all we've got is each other. If we don't look out for one another, who else will?'

Normally they met every month or so. But there were practicalities to discuss so there was nothing odd about them going for a drive in Trevor's van just three days later. The inquest heard that it was Trevor's suggestion but that Nancy jumped at the idea.

They drove down to the river and parked where they could just see the roofs of the Rosedale Retirement Home across the municipal playing fields. 'It's a nice area,' said Trevor.

'Yes, it is pretty,' agreed Nancy. 'Not that I'll be able to walk this far, but it'll be nice to look at from the bedroom window. That's the advantage with The Beeches, you see.' She turned and indicated the butter-coloured stone of a large house surrounded by tree-studded lawns that rolled down to the water's edge a quarter of a mile upstream. 'No walking – it's an actual riverside property.'

'I'd have thought that was a drawback for a retirement home. Don't the old dears keep sliding in?'

Nancy smiled. 'There's a chicken-wire fence to catch them. I don't think they lose many.'

Trevor grinned. 'You and Grandad had a boat on the river, didn't you?' She nodded. 'Mum used to try and make me come out with you sometimes: she said the fresh air would do me good. But I never did like being that close to water.'

'I remember,' murmured Nancy. 'When your grandad tried teaching you to swim you screamed so much he had to give up. Such a pity.'

Trevor shrugged. 'There are worse handicaps for an actor. The only time it gives me a problem is in *The Tempest*.'

Nancy chuckled. 'You must favour your father's side. I can't think how a grandson of mine could *not* love the river. It's *beautiful*.'

A man walking his dog along the far bank saw what

happened next. The van doors opened and a young man and an elderly lady got out and strolled along the bank a few feet from the water, a brown torrent swollen by months of rain. As they walked the woman gestured up and down stream as if pointing out items of interest. Then they turned back to the van.

In doing so the old lady lost her footing on the rain-softened bank and fell with a startled squawk first to her knees and then, as she struggled to get up, down the muddy slope into the river. At once the young man threw himself full length on the bank in an effort to reach her. But her hand remained tantalizingly beyond his grasp. After only a brief hesitation he kicked off his shoes and slithered down the muddy bank into the water.

The witness was unable to say quite what followed. Poor Mr Budgens reached his struggling grandmother and grasped her hand. But then either he lost his footing, or in her panic she unbalanced him, and he disappeared under the roiling flood. He surfaced yards out into the river, where even in normal weather there was depth enough for quite big boats, and yelled and waved his arms over his head until he disappeared again. Twice more he floundered to the surface, further from the bank each time, while the witness watched in helpless horror. After that he did not see him again.

By then help had reached Mrs Budgens. Strong arms pulled her up the bank, wrapped coats and car-rugs around her, chafed her trembling hands. All she could say was, 'Trevor. Where's Trevor? Where's Trevor?'

The inquest was a formality. Death by misadventure, and an eloquent tribute from the coroner for a courageous young man who braved an element he feared deeply in an attempt to rescue a frail old lady. It was the stuff of tabloid headlines, and Nancy Budgens was touched by the kindness paid by so many people who never knew him to poor Trevor's memory.

When it was all done, no one was surprised that Nancy sold her house and used the proceeds to move into residential accommodation. There were a few raised eyebrows that she chose a home so close to the scene of the tragedy. But as she pointed out, she had always loved the river; and in a sort of a way, there was something of Trevor in it now. Perhaps it was odd of her. Bereaved elderly ladies of seventy-one were entitled to be odd.

So she moved into The Beeches. It was worth every penny it cost. With poor Trevor gone there was no one left to consider but herself, so she spent the money with a clear conscience. Together, the proceeds of her house and Trevor's building society bought an annuity that would keep her in the state to which she meant to become accustomed for as long as she lived. It was, after all, what Trevor would have wished.

Trevor had been her last surviving blood-relation, her only heir. And she had been his.

DO THE WORLD A FAVOUR

Mat Coward

I'd been planning to take my flask of coffee into the station and sit on a bench on the up platform for a while, watching it all go by. I like watching railway stations. I'm not a train-spotter, I just like watching stations. The people, the journeys, the swirls of litter and pigeons.

But when a block-shaped, middle-aged woman in a bad hat levered her scowl into the back seat of the mini-cab and shouted *'Driver!'* I took such an instant, deep dislike to her that I thought: well, why not? Could be a nice day for a drive.

'Where to, love?' I said, weaving the taxi out of the car park on to the main road.

'The Pier Hotel. Do you know it?'

'Of course I know it,' I lied. 'I'm a taxi driver.'

She sniffed. 'On your break, were you?' she asked.

'No, that's all right. Just stretching my legs.'

'It is not all right, thank you very much,' she said, turning her face a fraction to the left so that she could look out of the window instead of at the back of my head. 'You don't think, perhaps, that this country might be just a little more competitive if people spent less time on breaks, and more time working?'

'Why don't you', I replied, not loudly but clearly, 'hurry up and die and do the whole world a favour?'

She was already sitting upright, she obviously wasn't one to slouch, but now she sat even uprighter. 'I beg your pardon?' Ridiculous expression: it means *you* must beg *my* pardon.

We were passing along the seafront, going in the wrong direction for the hotels, though she was too paralytic with anger to have noticed yet. I pulled into the kerb, stopped the car and got out.

The old bag banged about the backseat for a bit, before re-establishing her centre of gravity. 'What on earth do you think you're doing?'

Two kids – teens, I suppose, early twenties – sat slumped against the beach railing, a plastic Co-op bag spread on the ground between them. I looked at them, looked at their bag: at a rough calculation, it contained about fifty pence. I groped a fiver out of my shirt pocket, and stuck it in the girl's hand. The kids looked at me, for the first time.

'Cheers, mate,' said the boy, with a shuffling movement of his mouth, that might have been a smile when he first got it, several birthdays ago. It made his upper lip split and bleed a little.

The girl was still staring at the money, trying to remember what she was supposed to do with it, and it wasn't until I'd got back into the cab, just before I closed the door, that I heard her say, 'Yeah, cheers, mate.'

I clunked my seat-belt, and looked in the rearview mirror. 'Sorry to keep you, love. Just on my break.'

The old bitch selected an unamused smile from her armoury, deployed it, and said, 'You won't be expecting a tip, then.'

'What, not even so close to Christmas?'

'There would seem little point in my giving you my money only for you to pass it on to beggars.'

'True,' I said. 'I take your point. You could give it to them yourself, couldn't you, cut out the middleman?'

She redistributed her buttocks, huffily. 'I do not give to beggars.'

'Never?'

'Not under any circumstances. Begging is not an activity I wish to encourage.' I could sense her nodding in the back there, congratulating herself on her good judgement.

'Still,' I said – and then paused. Thing is, I'm a quiet chap generally. My ex-wife says I'm the sort who only talks when I haven't got anything to say. But this conversation interested me. 'Still: homeless people, eh? I mean, you can't just walk on by, can you? Can't pretend they're not there.'

She leant forward. 'There didn't used to be any *homeless people* in this town. *Homeless people'* (a phrase she pronounced with a mixture of disdain and disbelief) 'used to stay in the cities. I just don't know what went wrong with this country.'

I could tell by the tone of her sigh that she really didn't know. Incredible. 'Well, I'm only guessing, madam, but could it perhaps have something to do with a complete absence of compassion on the part of the better-off?'

She found another humourless chuckle; this one, a sort of swallowed woof. 'Compassion!'

'You're familiar with the term.'

'I'm familiar with the disease, certainly. But I'm glad to say it is not one from which I have ever suffered. I reward prudence and punish improvidence. I do not waste my energy on compassion. Why don't these people get a cloth and a bucket and knock on a few doors?'

'If they came to your door, unwashed and tatty and clutching a smelly rag and a bucket of dirty water, you'd pay them to clean your windows?'

'Don't be ridiculous! Where are we going?' She was looking past me, through the windscreen, where town was giving way to country.

'Nowhere you'll enjoy,' I replied, and then, quickly, before she could digest my words: 'Those kids looked like they should be worrying about puberty, not where their next meal's coming from.'

It worked. 'I don't appreciate sexual language, thank you,' she said, sitting back in the seat.

'You got a husband?'

'Of course.'

'Poor bastard.'

The old bitch crossed her legs and lounged, almost happily. 'So, your compassion extends to my husband? You don't hate him the way you hate me.'

Mat Coward

Ah, she wasn't stupid, then. Good: the really stupid feel no fear. 'Most fascists are women,' I explained. 'Women of your class never have to earn a living, so they spend their entire lives sitting around polishing their ignorance. At least their husbands see a tiny bit of the world, get their hard edges knocked off a bit.'

'That's how you imagine me spending my days – eating caviar and truffles, scolding the maid and reading detective stories? How very old-fashioned!'

'Disillusion me.'

'Not that it's any of your business, but as it happens I am a district councillor and a magistrate.'

I should have guessed. 'Well, well. Prejudice combined with power. You really are the complete item, aren't you?'

She shook herself, sat forward again. 'I asked you where we were going.'

'And I answered.'

'This is not the way to the Pier Hotel. Don't try to cheat me, driver. Better men than you have tried that, and lived to regret it. Now, where do you think you are taking me?'

'I told you, love: you're going somewhere you don't want to go.'

'*Where?*'

I adjusted the rearview mirror. I wanted to be sure she could see my face properly. 'Death, death, death,' I said, grinning with all my teeth. 'Death, death, death. You get it? You're going to die.'

She stared for a moment (not in fear yet, more in silent repetition of her family motto: 'I just don't know what went wrong with this country'), and then, predictably, began to rattle at the door handles.

'No good,' I said. 'You can't open them. They can only be opened by the driver, you see, to guard against fare dodgers.'

With outrage gouged from her soul, she snarled, 'Do I look like a fare dodger?'

I gave her an appraising once-over. 'No, to be honest you don't. What you look like, since you're asking, is an evil old bag who deserves to die.' And after that she didn't say anything for quite a while. In fact, she went dead quiet, that is, after the screaming.

'Why?'

I let her have a come-on-girl-don't-be-coy look, via the mirror. 'Why do you think? I'm a serial killer. I pick up evil old bags in my mini-cab, drive them out to remote spots, and rip 'em. You must have heard, it's been in all the papers.'

A little later, she said, 'There wasn't anything in my paper.'

'*Daily Mail*?' I said. She nodded. 'There you are, then. I don't approve of the *Daily Mail*, left them off the press release list.'

She started to nod again, then changed her mind and shook her head instead. 'You're no serial killer.'

'No? What am I then?'

'You're just an absurd little man who feels sorry for scroungers, and resentful of success. Like all your sort. You are a little man who is about to lose his job.'

I took the next corner at a speed that sent all the dashboard clutter into orbit. Crumpled tissues, Fox's Glacier Mints and evil old bitches flew about the taxi's interior like confetti in a crematorium chimney. As she climbed back on to her seat, I turned right round in mine and stared at her for three, four, five, carelessly suicidal seconds.

'And you, my lovely, are a fat lady who is about to lose her innards.'

You don't have to travel far round here in search of a lay-by or quiet country track, the sort where you can conduct private business uninterrupted and unobserved. Indeed, the one I eventually chose, or happened upon, might have been designed specifically for the purpose. I half expected to see one of those signs, you know, like the one that says 'P on Verge Only,' except this one would have said: 'Area Designated for Torturing Fascist Bitches to Death. Please Leave this Facility as You Would Wish to Find It.'

I found it by instinct. I used to drive round those roads all the time in the old days, roads that are only between somewhere and somewhere else unless you're a vet, or a tenant farmer, or some kind of tradesman.

I saw a turning, confidently swung the cab into it, and within seconds we were hidden from the entire known universe. The tractor tracks beneath us were hard and dry and antique-looking. The hedges either side of us almost met at the top.

I was invisible. To everyone except her.

'You can keep the hat,' I said.

'The hat?' She shivered. 'Why the hat?'

'Because you look like shit in it.'

At first, when I'd got her out of the car and told her to take all her clothes off – take them off and burn them – she'd still been a magistrate coping calmly with a difficult journey. 'And how do you think you are going to persuade me to do that?' she'd asked.

'With this,' I said, and smacked the baseball bat down on the car, leaving a dent in the roof.

Her hand went to her mouth, slowly. 'My God. You really are a serial killer.'

I had to laugh at that. 'Christ alive, I was right: you wouldn't know real life if it tore your tits off and fed them to you. Which it's about to do, as it happens.' I hefted the bat. 'Every taxi driver carries one of these, these days. Even in a content little town like yours.'

Now, fifteen minutes further into eternity, she stood there trembling, truly terrified at last, and wearing nothing but her stupid hat.

I left her there for a moment, while I sat in the driver's seat, with the door open, and smoked half a cigarette. I knew she wouldn't try to get away: lady magistrates in seaside towns don't run away from serial killers, dressed only in crappy hats. They just don't.

I crushed the cigarette out against my shoe and flung it into the bushes, walked up to the old bitch and said, 'Move.'

'What do you mean?'

'You're in the way,' I told her. I got back into the car,

closed the door, and started the engine. I rolled the window all the way down. 'You're in the way, I can't get the car out with you standing there. Move.'

She dropped to her knees, holding her wrists together by her belly-button as if they were tied. Which they weren't. She was shaking violently, and dryly crying. 'What do you mean?' she said.

'Look I'm sorry,' I said. 'I just can't do it. Just haven't got the backbone, I suppose. Must be your lucky day.'

'What do you *mean*?' she howled.

I beckoned. 'Here – come here. That's right. It's a cold day, but I'm not going to kill you. I am a serial killer, you see, but I'm on my break. Here. Take this.' I still had my flask, untouched, so I poured her cups of coffee, one after the other until the flask was empty, and stood over her while she drank them.

Irrelevant, I suppose, but I couldn't help noticing that she didn't say thank you. That kind have no manners.

It was all lies, of course. All of it, all lies. I'm not a serial killer. Me? You're joking! I don't even use slug pellets. Or didn't, when I still had a garden, still had a house of my own. I'm squeamish, that's the truth.

It was all lies about the taxi, too. It was a taxi, yes, but it wasn't my taxi. I'm not a taxi driver; used to be an electrician. Now I'm – well, I'm just me.

As I said, I'd been planning to sit in the station, sip my coffee slowly, but then she slammed into the back seat, shouting *'Driver!'* And I glanced at the open driver's door, saw the keys hanging from the ignition – I'd seen the driver jump out a few seconds earlier, to use the loo, perhaps, or get a sandwich from the kiosk – and I thought, why not?

So; all lies. The taxi, me being a serial killer. It was even a lie when I told her I wasn't going to kill her. I have killed her. I gave her all my coffee.

Well, why not? I still have the flask. I've plenty of pills back at the bedsit, plenty more coffee, I could always make up another batch tomorrow, go back to the station, sit for a while watching the trains and the pigeons and the people rushing around.

I wonder how far she walked before she died?

TWO BIRDS, ONE STONE

Lesley Grant-Adamson

'Don't look now,' said Rain Morgan, under cover of reading the menu, 'but that woman over there . . . '

'Yes?' Holly Chase, Rain's leggy black deputy on the *Daily Post* gossip column, looked.

'Well, I used to know her.'

'Italian?'

'American by now, I should think.'

Holly crunched a stick of *grissini*. The woman was well-dressed without being extravagant, and handsome in a way that suggested she had once been girlishly pretty. The type, thought Holly, to ripen early and be matronly when she reached forty. Her companion might have been rather older but all Holly could see of him was the back view of a thickset man with iron grey hair. 'Aren't you going to speak to her?'

Rain shook her head. 'I'd hardly know what to say. You see . . . '

'Yes?'

But the waiter had come for their order. Parma ham and melon for both of them, a bowl of pasta, some fish. When he had gone Rain said brightly: 'What I find encouraging about this place is that it's used by Italians. Not every Italian restaurant in London can claim that.'

Holly reprimanded her with a wag of the *grissini*. 'Don't change the subject. I want to hear about the mysterious dark-eyed beauty over there and what happened between you.'

Rain gave a wry smile. 'I'm afraid she took my advice.'

Holly pealed with laughter and people turned to watch her. 'So it was bad advice and you're scared she'll confront you with it!'

'It was perfectly sensible advice. I just didn't appreciate how she'd use it.'

And she told Holly about that summer in Sicily, when she was supposed to be studying baroque architecture in Palermo but let herself stray from the city's humidity to a weekend of fresh air on a friend's hill farm.

It was late summer, a time when stunted vines bowed with their burden of full grapes, when olives were young and firm and fields blazed gold with melons. The sun was no longer at its most vicious, the rains and the greening of the island were yet to come. This was the space between seasons. A beautiful time, a busy one. Busy especially for Rain's friend, Maria, who led one existence in Palermo and a separate 'weekend' one in the country. A writer, Maria was a cautious feminist who mocked the rift between her ideals and the reality of being a wife and mother of five children on a Mediterranean island.

Driving out to the farm, through villages where brilliant bracts of bougainvillaea cascaded from stone walls, Maria warned Rain: 'We're a dying breed, an old family loosening its grasp on the remnants of its country estates. I'll be embarrassed when you see how feudal this part of my life is.'

Maria meant the peasant families who, generation after generation, were obliged to work for her husband's family, particularly at harvest times. She was still explaining the intricate system of loyalties and responsibilities which bound the country people when they reached the farm.

The house sagged with the slant of the land. Yellow swallow-tailed butterflies toyed with a delicate jasmine on the courtyard wall and a medlar tree threw a little shadow. In the vineyard below the house, stooped figures were slashing at the vines with quick knives. Men, women, children – entire families were crouching and reaching for the clusters of grapes. Every living thing seemed cowed by the power of the sun.

Rain intended to help but there was a knack to be learned in the cruel twist of the sickle-bladed knife, the *runcuneddu*, and there was no shade in which to learn it. She offered to skivvy instead and went into the farmhouse where, Maria said, a meal was being prepared. The harvesters had been combing the rows of vines since sunrise. They had eaten a breakfast of salads mid-morning and were soon to be given lunch. When work stopped at sundown, they would be fed pasta.

'Feudal.' Maria had repeated her word. 'But that's the way it's always been done at the *vendemmia* here and, while my mother-in-law lives, that's the way it must go on. One day we'll get up to date and they'll bring their own snacks as people do on other farms.'

In the kitchen Rain met Rosalia, a girl with glowing skin and tumbling black hair. After the figures humbled among the vines, she appeared particularly vivacious. Rosalia loved to talk.

An aubergine stew was cooking on a stove. The girl occasionally stirred it. Rain cut up flat loaves of good yellowish bread. Rosalia sliced melons, holding them against her breast, hacking away one end of the fruit with a single blow of her knife and checking for ripeness. Then she sliced lengthwise on to a platter, breaking her rhythm only to scoop out seeds that she saved in a bowl. Juice dribbled over her hands, down her dress and scented the day.

Rosalia talked. Of her longing to go to America where her friend's family had emigrated, of her father's recent death, of her sisters' marriages and many children, and of her brother's eagerness to marry her off.

'He's old-fashioned,' she objected. 'He fears the responsibility of an unmarried sister who might bring disgrace on the family.'

'Might you?' Rain frowned above the bread knife.

'No. I tell him my virginity is as important to me as it is to him, but he won't listen. He thinks I'll let myself be seduced, that women are weak in that way.' She lifted another melon and her knife was an arc of golden light. 'There are two men who want to marry me. One's my brother's friend, Stefano, who's also our cousin. The other's the son of a small farmer beyond the village. My brother would like me to marry Stefano but he says he wouldn't mind if I chose Giuseppe because he'll inherit a farm. Stefano won't inherit land.'

She cast seeds into the bowl and continued slicing. Her voice was firm. 'I don't want to marry either of them, I want to go to America. Stefano says that's his dream, too, but I don't think he's serious enough to make the effort to do it.'

Shortly after, Rain was able to judge the suitors. Stefano came first, on a pretext, and hung about Rosalia like a drowsy wasp. He was ponderous, the only notable thing about him being a slight cast in one eye.

When he ran out of excuses to linger and went away, Rosalia sighed. 'But he's my brother's friend and the family expects it. What can I do?'

Rain resisted offering easy encouragement, talking about freedom or independence. Rosalia and her family lived by different rules and Rain did not understand them.

The meal was set out on makeshift tables beneath an awning in the courtyard. Hungry and rubbing aching backs, figures streamed from the vineyard. The talk was all about the quantity of the grapes, the quality of the wine they would make, the kindness of the saints in providing exactly the correct weather for a good harvest.

And then a light motorcycle came leaping along the dusty track bringing Giuseppe, slim-hipped in blue jeans, freed from duties on his father's land. He was cheerfully welcomed because of his reputation as a fast worker. Stefano glowered.

'You see?' Rosalia said to Rain when they were once again in the kitchen together, the meal over. 'What can I do?'

Her colour was high. The men had squabbled, people had laughed, Rosalia had been upset and hidden. 'If I tell one of them that I won't marry him, it'll be assumed I'm accepting the other and then it'll be very difficult to avoid doing so. My brother would be disgraced if people thought I'd broken a promise to marry.'

All Rain could offer was: 'Then you must think of a way of dealing with Giuseppe and Stefano simultaneously. Killing two birds with one stone.'

That evening, when the sun was down and the workers had puttered home in their battered vans, Rain asked Maria about Rosalia. They were sitting alone in the courtyard, oil lamps spreading soft light over rough-hewn benches and the geraniums. Maria tilted honey-coloured wine into their glasses before saying: 'I'm sure her brother cares for her but in his mind the best thing for a woman is to be settled into marriage at the earliest opportunity. Rosalia's speaking up for herself but it'll be another generation before a woman in that family is allowed to *act* for herself. Girls like that are aware of the modern world, a window has opened up for them. But that's not enough, they want a door to let them into it.'

'America?' Rain wondered.

'She can't get there without her brother's help, his money.' Maria flapped at a moth attracted to the wine. 'Freedom is relative. Not so many years ago village girls were made to live their lives in the home, avoiding contact with men.'

In the village a clock clamoured. Maria said: 'I'll tell you what will happen. Rosalia will weaken. Everyone knows about Giuseppe and Stefano so other young men are already deterred. Rosalia will make her choice and marry. And you can come back here in three or four years, Rain, and she'll be among the people scrabbling in the dust of one vineyard or another and you won't recognize her.'

Next day Giuseppe and Stefano clashed. The motorcycle announced Giuseppe's arrival late in the morning. Stefano slipped out of the vineyard to meet him and there was a brief but furious scene. Then Stefano stamped back to work.

Rain, renewing her efforts among the vines, watched him from beneath the brim of her straw hat. He handled the grapes and the *runcuneddu* mechanically, cutting the ties that secured the branches, hunting the fruit, tossing grapes into a plastic bucket, dragging the bucket to the next vine, cutting the ties . . . He moved automatically and his eyes glittered with rage.

And then he was ahead of Rain; yet another of the practised helpers who'd left her behind. She flopped a cluster of grapes into her bucket and stretched to appease complaining muscles. With no trouble at all, she persuaded herself she was lagging so badly that she might as well walk up to the house for a cool drink.

As she neared it, Rosalia stumbled into the doorway, screaming. Rain ran to her, pulled her out of the way. On the kitchen floor she found Giuseppe. He was lying face down, unmoving.

Rosalia's screams were answered by shouts from the vineyard as her family hurried to help her. They all crowded into the kitchen. Someone turned Giuseppe over. There was blood on the tiles.

Suddenly all movement and sound stopped. The silence was frightening. People were figures in a tableau, staring at the dead face of the young man and the terrible stain on his blue shirt.

'As I remember it,' Rain told Holly Chase, 'we remained like that until the police came and took Stefano away. I know that can't be true. Presumably Rosalia described how she walked into the kitchen, after setting the tables outside, and found him dead. And I'm sure that by the time the police arrived we'd looked for the weapon – not one of the sickle-shaped knives, of course, but something with a straight blade long enough to pierce the heart.'

Holly asked whether Stefano had owned up. Rain said not. 'He admitted there'd been a row. He'd tackled Giuseppe because Rosalia had complained that Giuseppe was pestering her. Apparently Giuseppe had been outraged and claimed Rosalia had asked him to tell Stefano to leave her alone.'

'Rosalia provoked that quarrel.' Holly popped the final inch of *grissini* into her mouth. 'Do you think she imagined it would end in death?'

Rain studied the confident Italian woman across the

restaurant, then averted her eyes when the woman glanced up. Rain said: 'Stefano insisted he left Giuseppe alive adjusting the brakes on his motorbike. Nobody else admitted seeing Giuseppe. The police examined everybody's knives and made Maria check the ones in the kitchen. Only one was missing, and that belonged to a ten-year-old boy who said he'd lost it earlier that morning. It was the kind that could have killed Giuseppe. The police searched, everybody searched, but the weapon wasn't found.'

After the body was taken away, those with the heart for it returned to work among the vines because the harvest waits for no one's grief. Rosalia stayed near the house, comforted by a flurry of aunts and cousins all coaxing her to let someone take her home.

That evening Maria drove Rain down into the suffocating heat of Palermo. Added to Rain's luggage was a bag of melons. Maria promised: 'That's only a stopgap souvenir. You'll get a proper memento when our wine's made.'

'It's a delicious stopgap.'

And Maria admitted that it had been Rosalia's idea. 'I always give visitors something from the farm but today's drama put it out of my head. Rosalia remembered and brought me that bagful. She liked you.'

Rain set the bag on her terrace and forgot it for a day. Then she tipped out the melons to choose the ripest to eat. She was surprised to see that the end of one of them had been lopped off. Its flesh was damaged. Slicing the melon, she discovered the murder weapon thrust into the cavity with the seeds.

Holly gasped. '*Rosalia* killed Giuseppe?'

'I've suspected it ever since I cut open the melon.'

'What did you do?' Holly's voice dropped to a conspiratorial whisper.

'Hid the knife in another melon, threw it away, went back to studying baroque. Stefano wasn't held because there was no evidence against him. Don't forget, most of those who heard the distant quarrel were members of his family.

Giuseppe was the outsider. There was no proof how that knife got where I found it.'

The waiter brought their food. Rain forked a piece of melon, deliberately letting its scent enliven her memories. Then, prodded by Holly, she rounded off her tale. 'The family settled on the story that Giuseppe was killed by an intruder he disturbed in the house. Rosalia's brother capitulated and sent her to America within weeks. My feeling is he knew the truth and wanted her out of the way to prevent the story leaking out.'

'*Omerta*,' said Holly, cutting her ham. 'Silence. Everybody kept quiet, some because they believed the murderer was Stefano, and you and the brother because you believed it was Rosalia. She trusted her family to protect both of them and she knew you sympathized with her so she trusted you too.' She paused before adding, ironically: 'Mustn't it be wonderful to know that people will always protect you?'

Rain, recalling Maria's words about tangles of loyalties and duties, said: 'I expect there was a price to pay.'

Sensing herself watched, the woman at the other table looked across. As her eyes met Rain's, there was the faintest tightening of her features. Then her gaze slid to the fork in Rain's hand. The woman gave a tiny, confessing smile. Rain ate the piece of melon.

On their way out of the restaurant, she and Holly had to pass close to that table. Rosalia smiled the kind of greeting she would smile at any acquaintance rediscovered and she detained Rain with a polite word or two. Then she said: 'Perhaps you remember my husband?'

Rain looked down into the face of a prematurely aged man with a cast in his eye. She could hear Rosalia saying something about her husband taking her to Europe for a holiday, taking a break from the business he owned in New York. But Rain barely listened.

Holly Chase contained her laughter until she and Rain emerged into the street. Then she gave way. 'Now we know the price of silence,' she shouted above the racket of London traffic. 'Marriage to Stefano!'

Rain was still stupefied. 'And all these years I'd assumed she'd got away with it. Two birds with one stone.'

'Near miss,' laughed Holly, hailing a taxi which skimmed by ignoring her.

A HOUSE IS NOT A HOME

Martin Edwards

'She's turning her back on a fortune,' said Jim Crusoe. 'It doesn't make sense!'

'So where do I come in?' asked Harry Devlin, although he had a sinking feeling that he could guess.

His partner gestured towards the leaning tower of buff folders on top of Harry's filing cabinet. 'You specialize in lost causes, don't you? I thought you might like to try convincing the silly old girl she should accept Quixall's money before he thinks better of it.'

'I'd find it easier to make the Mersey part in the middle than persuade Gwen Vandrau to change her mind. And if I don't serve this writ before five o'clock the negligence claim will be so high we won't have a business to come back to tomorrow.'

None the less, he was intrigued. Who was Quixall and why was he so anxious to buy Gwen out? And for that matter, why was Gwen so reluctant to sell? When Jim urged him at least to come in and say hello he did not hesitate in pushing his legal pad aside and following his partner next door.

Mrs Vandrau sat on the client's side of the desk, back straight, arms folded and lips pursed. She acknowledged Harry's arrival with a curt nod. By her standards he regarded it as an effusive welcome.

'Hello, Gwen. I gather someone's made you an offer you can't refuse – but you've refused it.'

'You know me. You know what I'm like.'

Harry did. Gwen had told him a little about her life; he was a good listener and he sensed she'd seldom spoken to anyone else about her past. She'd been born in Bootle, a docker's daughter in the days when shipwork was short and labour cheap. At seventeen, she'd caught the eye of a Toxteth night-club owner named Mitch Vandrau and when she became pregnant he had broken the habit of a lifetime by doing the decent thing. But their marriage was fated not to last: he had disappeared from the scene during the war, doing a runner with a girl who worked in his bar, so the story went. Gwen had been left with three kids under school age and sole responsibility for the upkeep of a rambling old house. She'd never bothered with another man and having toughed it out on her own for half a century she saw no need in her old age to start cultivating charm. Yet Harry admired her fighting spirit and even her unwillingness to make the smallest concession to social graces made him smile inside.

'I gather you've seen off that rowdy devil next door since we last met?'

Gwen made a noise which conveyed her opinion of her former neighbour. 'Good riddance to bad rubbish.'

Harry had first acted for her a couple of years earlier. The middle-aged bachelor who lived in the house beside hers had nourished an obscure passion for the music of the late Jim Reeves. He would play it all day and through much of the night. When her complaints, forcefully expressed, had achieved nothing, Gwen had called the police. But they had done little except have a quiet word with the culprit and that word was soon drowned out by the distant drums of which the crooner sang. So she'd come to Harry for advice about her legal remedies and he had obtained a court order to prevent any repetition of the nuisance. The judge, a jazz fan who hated country ballads and fancied himself as a wit, had been at pains to reassure Gwen.

'Mark my words, Mrs Vandrau, if your neighbour offends again, "He'll Have To Go".'

Harry had laughed dutifully whilst Gwen's face remained frozen in its habitual frown. He suspected that even in her younger days she had had more lines than Merseyrail, but seeing her again today he was disturbed by the dark shadows around her eyes and the sunken cheeks which made her seem so much frailer than before.

Knowing there was no point in asking after her health, he said briskly, 'Let's talk business. Jim tells me you have the chance to sell your place in Lovelady Lane for thirty thousand more than the going rate. Is that right?'

'You know what they say about a fool and his money.'

'But you're not letting Quixall part with the cash.'

'Where's he got it from? That's what I'd like to know. He's no more than a back-street scallywag.'

Harry glanced at Jim, who inclined his head. 'What do we know of the would-be purchaser?'

'Not much, except that the estate agent stresses he's good for the money. I'm not disagreeing with what Gwen says about him. But maybe he's simply a rough diamond.'

Gwen brushed a grey hair out of her eye and gave another snort of disgust. 'I don't care who or what he is. He's not having my house.'

'Why is he so set on it?' Harry asked his partner.

'According to the agent, he was born in Lovelady Lane. Reckons he has a sentimental attachment to the area and wants to move back home.'

'I never heard such codswallop in all my days,' Gwen said with a sniff of contempt. 'The moment I first saw the fellow I knew he was up to no good. Walking round, sizing up the house and the grounds. He must think I was born yesterday. I should have chased him off then without more ado.'

'She didn't offer him any encouragement,' said Jim. 'Even though he made her a handsome offer on the spot. But he prised the name of her solicitors out of her and the agent came on the phone to me stressing how keen Quixall is to buy and how willing he is to pay a premium for the privilege. And, incidentally, upping the offer by another fifteen thousand. Enough to buy a nice little bungalow by the coast and have a nest egg in the bank as well.'

'I don't want a nice little bungalow,' said Gwen with a lifetime's scorn for bourgeois respectability.

'But the money will . . .'

'Listen. I've lived in that house for fifty-five years and it suits me. I don't care if it is run down. It will see me out, that's for sure.'

'So you're not prepared to consider moving in any circumstances?' Harry asked.

Gwen shook her head. 'Not at any price. That's my final word.'

Harry exchanged glances with his partner. 'Thank God at least for a client who doesn't beat about the bush. I don't think we can take this conversation any further, can we? It's been good to see you, love, but I can understand that after that length of time another house wouldn't seem like home. If you're happy where you are, that's the end of the matter. Jim will phone the agent himself and say thanks but no thanks.'

After Gwen had marched out, he said, 'What do you reckon Quixall is really after?'

'Development, I expect. The name rings a bell. I have a feeling that a couple of brothers called Quixall used to have a building yard out in Dingle. Didn't one of them go down for grievous bodily harm a while ago? Anyway, maybe the idea is to convert the house into flats. Gwen's right to scoff at the idea of sentimental attachment.'

'The area she lives in is on the up and up, isn't it? If Quixall is in the building game, he must have seen a profit for the taking.'

'Sure, but my point is this. Even allowing for any potential it may have the whole building sounds to be in a dreadful state of repair. Dry rot, wet rot, you name it. Gwen readily admits to problems which would give any surveyor cardiac arrest. It's crazy. Quixall was taking all the commercial risk. At least his offer gave her the chance of buying somewhere decent that would suit a woman of her age far better.'

Harry shook his head. 'His mistake was to set his heart on a house belonging to Gwen Vandrau. When she says that's

that, you can take her at her word. There's no room for any
further discussion.'

But he was wrong, for the following week Gwen came
through to him on the phone.

'Changed your mind about selling up, love? I don't believe
it!'

'I've changed nothing. But the day after I came to see you a
young woman was parked outside my gate waiting for me.
Said she was from the council. She showed me a card, said
something about social services and – environmental health,
is it? Said they had to keep an eye on senior citizens in the
area, that's what we pay our taxes for. I said I didn't want
anyone keeping an eye on me, but she kept insisting.'

'Did you let her in?'

'What d'you take me for? Of course I didn't let her in. Give
those people an inch and they take a yard.'

Harry had to restrain a chuckle. Gwen had never been one
of life's inch-givers. 'Did she say anything about the house?'

'She said they had the right to inspect it. To make sure it
was fit for human habitation. I said of course it's fit for
human sodding habitation, what did she think I was doing
here? She just shook her head and muttered something
about compulsory purchase. In the end I slammed the door
on her and that was that. She went away with her tail
between her legs.'

'And you'd like us to drop her a line, tell her to mind her
own business?'

'I'm not bothered about a slip of a girl whatever official
papers she waves. But a couple of days later a second feller
knocked on my door. A real plug-ugly. Said his name was
Quixall and he'd come on behalf of his brother. I told him to
forget it, I wasn't moving. But he said he and his brother
weren't the sort of men to take no for an answer.'

Harry felt a chill. If he hadn't known Gwen better, he
would have sworn there was a tremor in her voice. 'Go on.'

'When I told him they'd have to get used to this no, he
laughed at me. Said I was a stubborn old cow and I'd see

sense in the end. I wasn't standing for that. I let him have a few choice words and he didn't like it.'

Harry could picture the scene. Despite his anxiety on Gwen's behalf he was amused. The bully boy no doubt believed that ailing old women should be seen and not heard, be frightened and not foul-mouthed. If anyone could convince him he was mistaken, it would be Gwen.

'So what did he say?'

'That I'd be hearing from him.'

He could tell there was more to come. 'And?'

'You know the thunderstorm we had last night?'

'I won't forget it in a hurry. I got soaked to the skin in the time it took me to run from the office to my car.'

'My front porch was awash hours after the rain finally stopped.'

'A downpour like that, it's not surprising.'

'Listen,' she snapped. 'It's never happened before. Never. I soon found the reason. Someone had shoved a block of concrete in the drain.'

'Quixall's brother?'

'Who else? So I thought I'd better have a word with you.'

'Quite right. Look, give me twenty minutes and I'll be ringing your bell.'

'Wait a minute,' she said swiftly. 'I just wanted to know what I should do. I don't want to be paying fancy fees for the privilege of having you coming round here swallowing my tea and guzzling my biscuits.'

'Don't worry, you make such good tea and biscuits, I'll waive any fees. How's that for a deal?'

'You're like the offer to buy me out,' she complained. 'Too good to be true. I've heard enough about deals in the last few days to last me a lifetime.'

'I'll see you soon.'

Rapidly, he told Jim what had happened. 'Who were the estate agents acting for Quixall?'

'Hywel Yorath and Associates. Not the most reputable firm in Liverpool.'

'You said it. I last crossed Yorath's path outside the

magistrates court six months ago. He was being prosecuted for a property misdescription. A hazard of the job, he called it.'

'He's not careful about the company he keeps, isn't Yorath,' agreed Jim. 'The story goes that he's in thick with that well-known public servant, Alan Agriwallah.'

Harry winced. 'Who is as fine an advertisement for Liverpool politics as Crippen was for the medical profession.'

'You're insulting Crippen, even if Agriwallah's voters do think he can do no wrong. But supposing the Quixalls are engaged in a frolic of their own, I still don't like the sound of everything that's been happening to Gwen. What do you intend to do?'

'First things first. I need to see how she is. She may be as strong as the average stevedore, but she is seventy-five. I'd offer to hold her hand for a while, but she'd only put me in an arm-lock for my cheek.'

On his way to Lovelady Lane, Harry thought about her story. It sounded as though the Quixalls were engaged in a classic winkling exercise. First, the nice-as-pie approach. Easy money on offer and every prospect of a happy ending. If that failed, the velvet glove would come off. Harry recalled acting for a couple whose landlord thought nothing of introducing a few rats into his own property to persuade the tenants to vacate so that he could sell for a fat profit. What worried him now was the possibility that Alan Agriwallah might be involved. In this city he was the biggest rat of all.

What were the Quixalls after? Jim's theory was logical, yet Harry could not see how redeveloping a house bought so expensively could generate enough profit to justify putting the screws on Gwen. Of all the old ladies in the world they had to pick the one most likely to fight. His greatest fear was that at her age it might be a fight to the death.

Was any home worth such a price? Harry didn't find it an easy question to answer. He had no hang-ups about any building: for him, home was his native town. Born and bred in Liverpool, he had heard over the years the hoarse screams of hundreds of paper sellers proclaiming the latest news of the city's crime and corruption, its riots and redundancies. Liverpudlians were no strangers to adversity, but they seldom succumbed for long to self-pity and Harry knew of no other place whose people had such humour and heart. He had never lived anywhere else and had never wanted to. He could at least understand why Gwen wished to stay put, why she could not contemplate ending her life in any place other than the one she regarded as home.

Lovelady Lane wound between sandstone walls for three-quarters of a mile leading from high-rise hells to the fringe of Merseyside's green and pleasant. As he left the urban ghetto behind, most of the houses he passed were pre-war family homes. Gwen's stood almost at the end of the lane before it reached a T-junction with a recently extended dual carriageway.

He parked at the gate and studied the house. A rambling redbrick Victorian edifice, it had probably stood in isolation a century ago in the midst of an agricultural plain. The house next door, where the Jim Reeves fan had lived, was smaller and more modern with grounds half the size of Gwen's. There was a double gate at the side of her place, but no garage. A weed-choked path led up to the front door and a wide, well-worn dirt track curved around the building and out of sight.

An idea occurred to him and, instead of walking up the path, he followed the track. It went alongside a couple of out-buildings at the rear of the house and skirted the back garden, a jungle of nettles and long grass whose drabness was relieved only by the vivid splashes of colour from a couple of flowering cherry trees in full bloom. Fifty yards behind the house the track passed through a five-barred gate into a large paddock. Harry surveyed the scene. As far as he could tell the paddock was boxed in by other properties. An idea began to form in his mind.

Satisfied, he retraced his steps and hurried towards the front door. It opened before he could press the bell to reveal Gwen's suspicious face.

'What d'you think you're doing, snooping round the back like that? I almost took you for that fellow Quixall. You should be more careful, I was about to take a pot shot at you.'

Harry stared at what she was holding, scarcely able to credit the evidence of his eyes. 'Is that a rifle in your hand?'

'You bet it is. I need to protect myself.'

'For God's sake. Even if that gun isn't loaded, put it down.'

He followed her into a hall as cold and gloomy as an underground cavern. It would not have surprised him to see stalactites hanging from the ceiling. The furniture was old and dark, the carpet worn and patterned in a fifties style. Damp patches discoloured the walls and a musty smell hung in the air. She turned and looked him in the eye.

'It's loaded, all right. Oiled and ready for firing.'

He looked at the hunched figure in front of him. She seemed smaller than before, as if the stresses and strains of the last few days had shrunk her.

'Listen, your name isn't Annie Oakley. Where did you get that thing from?'

With a mutinous glare, she led him into a sitting room and laid the gun on a gateleg table. 'It's one of the few things Mitch left me, apart from the kids, the house and a pile of debts. He was keen on shooting. And he ran a night-club, remember. Even all those years ago, that was a dangerous game. He reckoned it might come in handy one day – for protection. I started thinking this afternoon that he might have had the right idea.'

'Forget it. This is Huyton, not *High Noon*.'

'You've not told me why you were poking your nose round my back garden.'

Harry sat next to her on a faded sofa which felt as though it lacked any springs. 'I was having a look at your paddock.'

Her heavy eyebrows lifted. 'Since when have you been interested in paddocks? Besides, it isn't even mine.'

'No?' Perhaps his guess had been wrong. 'Then who owns it?'

'A farmer named Hinks. Most of his land is on the other

side of the new dual carriageway. Mind, the paddock's not been much use to him ever since they widened the road.'

'I see.' And he thought he did. 'I presume the farmer has a right of way over your track?'

'Of course, he couldn't get to the field any other way.' She spoke as if to a backward child.

'So there's no other access?'

'No. Why do you want to know?'

He ignored the question. 'May I use your phone?'

She stared at him. 'Please yourself. It's in the kitchen.'

He found the farmer's number and got through to Mrs Hinks. Introducing himself as a property developer, he said, 'I gather your husband owns the paddock off Lovelady Lane. I was wondering if he'd be prepared to consider . . .'

'You're too late,' the woman said. 'He signed a contract of sale only last week.'

Harry made an anguished sound. 'Don't tell me that Alan Agriwallah has beaten me to it!'

The woman became cautious. 'I don't think I can say . . .'

But she had already told him as much as he needed to know. His next call was to Agriwallah's constituency office.

'He's out on business at the moment,' a breathless girl informed him. 'But his surgery's at four this afternoon if you want to catch him then. Shall I book you in?'

'The name's Harry Devlin and it's about a housing problem.'

'And the address?'

'Lovelady Lane.'

'But that's not part of Alan's ward!' She sounded outraged. Her boss prided himself on representing the under-privileged, not the private home owners of Lovelady Lane.

'Tell him I'm calling on behalf of Mrs Gwendoline Vandrau. I think he'll be willing to see me.'

As he put the phone down, a deafening explosion came from the sitting room. It sounded almost as if Gwen had fired her rifle through the window. He raced next door and found her backed up against the wall, her face white. The gun was still sitting innocently on the table. Shards of glass covered the floor and in the middle of them sat a fat half-brick with jagged edges.

'Are you all right?'

'Yes.' Her voice was hoarse with shock. 'I was on my way out to make you that cup of tea you made so much fuss about. How all that glass missed me, I'll never know.'

Harry moved to the shattered window, crunching bits of the old cobwebbed panes underfoot. There was no sign of the person who had thrown the brick. Turning to face her, he said, 'One of your married daughters lives in Wirral, doesn't she? Why don't you go and stay with her? At least until all this is sorted out.'

Gwen folded her arms. For all her recent suffering, she would still have made the most belligerent bulldog seem like a soft touch. 'And let them win?'

'It need only be for a few days.'

'I can't leave here.'

Harry told himself she was an old woman, tired and unwell. He must be patient. 'Of course you can.'

'Not on your life!'

'It could be your life next time,' said Harry quietly. 'The people you're dealing with mean business. The brick was a warning, but next time you may not be so lucky.'

'Lucky!' She glared at him. 'This is my house and no one is going to drive me out of it. I live in Liverpool, not Chicago.'

'For all you and I know, love, Chicago's safer than Liverpool these days. You're better out of the firing line.'

She pointed to the rifle. 'If there's any firing to be done, I can do it. Mitch taught me how to use that thing.'

'Gwen, be serious. I know an Englishwoman's home is her castle, but you can't—'

'I am being serious,' she said, looking him in the eye. 'You don't understand. This was my home when I was on my own with three squealing infants. I've lived here since I was a young woman who thought she was in love and I'll die here, sooner or later. If it has to be sooner because of these thugs, so be it. It may be the best way – the doctor's given me some bad news lately. But I'm not moving out. Not for anyone.'

'Let me call the police, then.'

Her expression was withering. 'Much good they'll do. No, if you want to do something for me, speak to this Quixall. Tell him that the only way I'm going out of here is feet first.'

She strode over to her favourite armchair, brushed the glass from it with an arthritic hand, sat down and closed her eyes. The discussion, Harry realized, was over.

'I need to speak to some people,' he said. 'I'll be back soon. In the meantime, I want you to promise me one thing – that you won't do anything foolish.'

But Gwen Vandrau's eyes remained shut. Harry gazed at her for a moment, reluctant affection mingling with anxiety and exasperation, before walking out and heading for his car.

He stopped at a phone box down the road and called Jim to explain what had happened.

'I suppose the farmer would only have a right of way for agricultural purposes?'

Jim agreed. 'The terms will be written into Gwen's deeds. The paddock won't have been worth much to him on that basis. Now that the European Community is ordering farmers to let so much land lie fallow, Hinks will probably have been glad of the chance to sell. He'll know that the local authority won't allow him to build on it.'

'But if the buyer owns Gwen's property as well and has a pal on the council's planning committee?'

'A different story altogether. It's not what you own, it's what you know. So you reckon Alan Agriwallah is mixed up in this?'

'Up to his neck. One last thing. Will you call the police? Speak to someone, put them in the picture as far as you need to. Ask them to keep an eye on Gwen's place. I wouldn't like anything to happen to her before I speak to Agriwallah.'

'You've got no evidence at all against him.'

'Evidence is for the courts. This is just a chat, man to man.'

'Careful, Harry. He's dangerous to cross. Besides, what do you propose to say to him?'

'I'll think of something.'

But Harry hadn't, even by the time he walked into

Agriwallah's surgery. He'd been waiting in a small room on the ground floor of a welfare rights centre in a back street of the inner city. The place was packed with people. One or two stank of drink or dirt; all had a whiff of terminal despair. Yet for those drowning in debt and without a job or a home they could call their own, Alan Agriwallah offered a chance of confronting the odds. If anyone could fight for them, it would be the man everyone in the city knew as AA. His face gazed down from posters pinned to all four walls. It was the face of a strong and swarthy man whose left fist was clenched in the salute that had been his trade mark for the past fifteen years. He may have been the son of an Indian seaman and a Dock Road whore but these days everyone in the Town Hall danced to his tune. For the voters who had made his council seat the safest in England AA meant more than hope. He was a god.

Yet Harry knew he had another side. In pubs and clubs throughout the city, people muttered about AA's limousine lifestyle and the security corps he'd recruited from the ranks of the unemployed. Now and then an investigative journalist set out to uncover the truth behind the rumours of twisted arms and crooked deals. But somehow the story always ended up on a spike.

How to challenge such a man on his own home ground? How to accuse him of conspiracy and worse? Harry was still wrestling with this dilemma when he heard his name called and made his way into the inner sanctum.

The man behind the desk didn't ask him to sit down. He considered Harry with a care calculated to induce unease. One thing no one ever suggested was that Alan Agriwallah was a fool.

'I've heard of you, Mr Devlin. They say you're a good brief, though too often your heart rules your head.'

On television or the radio Agriwallah favoured the snappy sound bite in a strong Scouse accent. In private his tone was more measured, crisp yet polite.

'And you'll have recognized the name of my client, Mrs Vandrau?'

'Can't say I did. But you're a busy man and, even if you charge less than other sharks, I'll pay you the compliment of expecting that you're not here to waste time. Which is why I asked you in ahead of my constituents waiting outside who have far more pressing personal problems. So what can I do for you?'

'Two small-time builders, brothers called Quixall, are trying to winkle Gwen Vandrau out of her home. They have their eye on developing a paddock behind the house and they need the access.'

'Sorry to hear it. She should contact her local councillor. To say nothing of the police.'

'Trouble is, the Quixalls seem to have friends in high places. Or more accurately, one friend in a very high place. I believe that it's you.'

Agriwallah's face was a mask. 'What makes you think that?'

'You're hand in glove with Yorath, their estate agent. And only someone with clout at the Town Hall could tee up a swift visit from environmental health to pile on the pressure when money didn't talk. I expect you explained there was an old dear out in Lovelady Lane you'd promised to keep an eye on, even though it's not your political patch. Did you shed a few crocodile tears about her not knowing what was best for her and living somewhere unfit for an old woman on her own? After Gwen sent the girl off with a flea in her ear, you called in the heavy mob. Blocking her drains, shoving a brick through her window.'

Agriwallah fingered an election leaflet headed ACTION NOT WORDS. 'Surely you know your law? I could sue you for slander.'

'I'd love you to. Though it wouldn't be as lucrative as this deal. The land's large enough for three or four executive detacheds. Too pricey for your constituents, but never mind. If you move fast, you'll be able to stitch up the planning side so as to lift the agricultural use condition on both paddock and access track.'

'And why should I be in such a hurry?'

'I don't know much about politics, though I know what I don't like. Aren't there elections next month? Afterwards, they usually play musical chairs with the various committees. It might take time to push your scheme through then and there's too much money at stake for you to tolerate delay.'

Agriwallah walked up to Harry and seized him by the shoulder. 'Just what do you want?'

Harry stood his ground. 'Gwen Vandrau is an old woman. I also think she's sick and it may be terminal. She wants to stay in her home and that's her right. I want you to call your thugs off her.'

He sensed Agriwallah's mind was working fast. The councillor relaxed his grip and looked at his watch. 'I could make life rough for you if I wished. I'm not without influence in this city and I don't like being badmouthed by a brief who ought to know better. But I'll make allowances for the fact that you're concerned about this client of yours. I've no idea what you're talking about, of course, but if people are bothering the woman, maybe you'd better get a move on back to her place. The kind of people you're talking about don't hang around. At this very moment they may be conducting – direct negotiations with her.'

Harry walked to the door, then turned. 'I don't want her threatened again.'

Agriwallah gave an irritable flip of the hand. 'Then why don't you get a move on instead of wasting my time?'

Knowing better than to push his luck, Harry retraced his path through the waiting room. Another name was called and a bare-legged woman with two small children rose to her feet. She looked as though she'd been invited into the grotto by Father Christmas. And in a sense she had, for Alan Agriwallah had the power to make dreams come true.

As well as to change lives, reflected Harry, for better or worse. He hoped he'd read Agriwallah's thoughts aright. Like a true politician, Agriwallah had calculated his options in less than a minute and decided to step back from the scam at Lovelady Lane. He'd even given a coded warning that the nastier Quixall was due to pay Gwen a return visit any time now.

Harry didn't deceive himself. There had been no sentiment in Agriwallah's reaction. No one wrote off lightly the kind of money he must have hoped to make through fixing things for the developers with the people in planning. But with local polls in the offing he couldn't risk Harry making waves over the next few weeks. There was talk that he was looking for a safe seat in Parliament come the next general election. He wouldn't dare blot his copybook now. That would give the Party apparatchiks in London who hated provincial upstarts a cast-iron excuse to scratch his name from the shortlist.

Quarter of an hour later, Harry was back in Lovelady Lane. Outside Gwen's gate he saw an unmarked van. Was Quixall here already? There was no sign yet of the police Jim had called. The front door was ajar. He raced up the path, but before he was halfway to the house a muffled sound stopped him in his tracks.

'Gwen! For God's sake don't fire again! I've talked to the man who's behind the Quixalls. He's seen sense and you're not going to be bothered any more!'

The only reply was a dreadful moan. As he watched, a big man with a broken nose staggered out of the unlit hall. He was clutching his stomach, but he would have needed three hands to cover the dark patch which stained his bright blue shellsuit.

Gwen Vandrau appeared in the doorway. The rifle was in her hand. Her expression was exultant, yet half-crazed.

'I told you no one would get me out of here alive!'

Quixall sank to the ground. His blood started to dribble down the path.

'Give the gun to me, Gwen.'

Harry began to move forward, but she waved him back with the rifle. Then she lifted it again.

'It'd be kinder to finish him off.'

'No, Gwen, listen to me. Put the gun down. You don't know what you're doing.'

'Of course I do.' A dreamy look came into her dark eyes.

'Look what I did with the other two. Much as I wanted them to suffer, I put them out of their misery.'

'What are you talking about?'

But, with a sudden sick feeling, Harry realized he knew.

'Mitch and that fancy tart of his, of course. He thought he could kick me out of here and install her in my place.'

'You shot them both?'

'And buried them in the garden. You saw the cherry trees flowering out at the back? Prettier than gravestones, I've always thought. But you understand now why I could never leave?'

'Yes, of course.'

Harry edged forward, trying not to attract her attention. She seemed even to have forgotten about the thug stretched out in front of her as her mind reached back over the past fifty years.

'Mitch was the only man I ever loved, but when he said he was leaving me, I told him to forget it, I'd never let him go. I said I'd see him in hell first. And maybe I will.'

He was within three or four yards of her, calculating when he should make his move. In the distance he heard a police siren and at the same time she noticed he was almost within reach. Once again she raised the rifle.

Harry shut his eyes. The last thing he saw was Gwen's lips, parting in a lovely smile that made her look seventeen rather than seventy-five. He'd never seen her happy before. Then he heard the gun go off and the shock of the explosion threw him to the ground.

After a few moments he lifted his head a fraction and opened his eyes to a sight that made him retch. She must have put the gun in her mouth before firing, for her head had been shattered beyond recognition. She was lying only a few feet away in the shadow of her house, the tumbledown old place that for half a century had been not so much her home as her prison.

PAWN SACRIFICE

Chaz Brenchley

Tell you a story.

No, two. I'll tell you two. Work it out for yourselves, which one is more real, which you want to believe.

Either way, it doesn't really matter. Either way, a boy died; and either way, it was my own sweet effin' fault.

Robbie was my friend. It wasn't one of the world's great friendships, maybe; we weren't best mates, we didn't live in each other's pockets. Hadn't even known each other that long, I suppose, except by sight. We were in the same class at school, but we'd only been talking for a couple of years.

If you'd asked him, mind, he would've said that differently. I've got too many friends, but he never ever had enough. Maybe I was the closest for a while there, maybe he'd have said yes, I was his best mate, who else was there better? But he still didn't live in my pocket, didn't even try to. He always gave me space; which is one reason why it worked so well, I guess. For me, at any rate. If he wanted more, he never pushed for it.

Maybe I should have offered more. God knows, he needed it. Robbie's home life was nightmare stuff, the original family from hell. The way he told it, his real mum had him at sixteen, never meaning to; only that she wouldn't let herself believe she really was pregnant, until it was too late to do anything about it. No surprise, the father fucked off, good and quick. Robbie said he'd never met him, didn't even know his name.

His mum married someone else fast, but that didn't work either; and when he was six, she just got out of it. Dumped them both, and disappeared.

And then his stepfather got married again, and that's who Robbie lived with: a man and a woman, neither one of them his own blood, neither one wanting him around. He was nervous, he was wary, he was dead difficult to be with sometimes; but no blame to him for that, and maybe I should have done more.

Except that in the end I did; in the end I made a great change in his life, and it killed him, whatever way you look at it. Come right down to basics and it's all my fault.

The other thing about Robbie, what started it all off, was that he fluked out just once; in his genes. He wasn't clever and he wasn't strong. It's hard to think of him as lucky any way at all; but in this one way he was; he had lucky bones, incredibly lucky skin. If he wasn't good at anything himself, he was still stupidly good to look at.

To tell truth, I hadn't noticed. We were friends; I'd seen him around every school day for years; I'd never looked at him that way, never thought to do it. I mean, you just don't, right? I noticed when he finally started shaving, maybe a year behind most of us, but that was it. I wasn't conscious of his face, outside of that. Or his body, either.

It was the girls who woke me up. Say it's their fault, if you like, say they started it, really. You won't persuade me, but Christ, I'd like you to try.

I was checking some prints in the school dark-room after classes when there was a skitter of knuckles on the door, and some breathy giggles the other side of it.

'Yeah? Come in, it's safe . . . '

And in they came, two girls from the year below us. I knew their names, I knew what one of them felt like in a disco's bright darkness; so I winked at her for old times' sake, nodded at the other and turned back to what I was doing. I figured they'd just come to collect some work of their own, there were always people in and out that time of day.

But they only stood there, and one of them giggled again. So I looked up; and Emma, that's the one I'd dated for a couple of months the year before, she said,

'Tonio, you hang around with Robbie a lot, don't you?'

'Not a lot,' I said, instantly defensive, the way you do.

'Ah, come on. You know what I mean. I've seen you together, and not just in school, either.'

'OK, sure. He lives close, we do things sometimes. Why?'

'Well, Sharl and me, we were wondering . . . ' They looked at each other, not to have to look at me, and Charlene creased herself giggling. 'I mean, I remember you take pictures all the time, right? Anyone you're with, you've always got that camera going. So,' all in a rush now, just to get it out, 'have you got any pictures of Robbie you could let us have? Good ones, like? We'd pay you for the paper and stuff, I know that costs . . . '

And I could see what it had cost her to do the asking, she was blushing like fire under the strip-light; and I was grinning, starting to giggle internally myself. Remembered pleasure made me swallow that down in a spasm of generosity, but it was a near thing.

'Yeah,' I said, as neutral as I could. 'Not here, they're at home, but I've got a load of portraits I was working on in the summer; some of those are Robbie. And there's a pile of snaps. Look, I'll sort some out, shall I? Bring them in on Monday, you can have a look through, see what you want?'

'Yeah, great. Thanks, Tone. See you, then . . . ' And they were backing towards the door already, moving like they were chained together, Charlene fumbling mutely behind Emma for the handle.

They were halfway out when Emma looked back at me doubtfully, chewing her lip.

'What?' I said.

'Just don't tell him, right?'

'Promise,' I said. That didn't help much, judging by her

face; but no surprise there. She'd met my promises before, she knew what they were worth.

'I'll kill you,' she said. 'If you do. I mean it, I'll bloody *kill* you.'

I did my best to look terrified. She scowled, and slammed the door on her way out.

When I'd finally quit laughing, I sat still – right there where I was, on the floor now, after sliding all the way down the wall and utterly out of control – and thought about it; and yeah, I could see their point. Could have kicked myself, really, for not having seen it sooner. Robbie's hair was as dark as mine, but his eyes were blue, and nothing of his home life showed in his face. Fine cheekbones, clear skin: I should know, I'd spent hours lighting them, practising to be Richard Avedon or Cartier-Bresson. And never a spot yet, though he was near enough sixteen now. If I'd thought about it at all before, it was only with envy, and a mean prayer that such unfairness shouldn't last.

Now I thought about it differently; and about the body below the face, that I'd seen often enough in the showers and the changing-rooms.

And yes, I could understand those girls, no trouble. He might not be clever and he might not be strong, he might have a lousy life and no friends better than me; but just that one way, he was lucky beyond measure.

Robbie was *beautiful*.

And yes, of course I told him about the girls and what they wanted. How not? That's what friends are for, to put you in the way of advantage.

We were round at my place, as usual. I almost never went to his house; he didn't like anyone to see how he lived, or the people he lived with.

When he came round, I had pictures of him all over my bed; so of course he asked what I was up to. He was meant to.

'Sorting out some photos for your fan-club,' I told him. 'I could be on to a good thing here, I reckon.'

'Unh?'

'The girls', I said, 'are queueing up.'

He didn't believe me, till I said I was getting paid. Then he knew it was serious.

'So what should I do, what d'you think, Tonio?' he demanded, suddenly urgent. 'Christ, I never . . .'

'Well, you don't have to do anything. But they won't. I wasn't even supposed to tell you, right? So you do nothing, they stick the pics up on their walls or whatever with all their other pretty boys, and nothing happens. Or the other option, you could ask one of 'em out.'

'Er – which one?'

I grinned. 'Which do you fancy?'

He shrugged, looked down at his feet, screwed one heel into the carpet. 'I dunno. Either one, I suppose. I mean, I don't . . .' *Help me, Tonio*, his body-language was saying.

'OK, look, go with Emma, then, yeah? If you're really not bothered. Her friend giggles too much. And Emma's good, she's happy company.'

'Emma. Right. So how do I do it, then?'

'You ask her, that's all. Get her alone sometime and ask her. No hurry, leave it till the time feels right. Go see a movie, that's always safe. You can't make a prat of yourself at a movie. But make an effort, yeah? Get some new clothes, get a good haircut, take her to McDonalds after. She'll offer to go Dutch, but don't let her. Girls like being paid for.'

That stilled him, for a second; then, squirming more than ever, 'I can't. You know I can't; I've got no money.'

'Oh, yeah. That. I've got a way you can make some money, if you want to. If it's important enough.'

This was important enough. I'd been sure it would be. 'How?' he demanded, suddenly desperate, forgetting even to be wary.

'Easy.' I smiled at him, nice and relaxed and oh so casual. 'Just by having your picture took, that's all. Doesn't hurt a bit. I do it all the time. How do you think I paid for all these cameras?'

*

My parents knew that I worked for Simon, of course; they had to. Only thing was, they thought I just helped out in the dark-room and cleaned up in the studio, ran errands, stuff like that. I did do all of that, but that wasn't what had paid for the cameras.

Like the girls, Simon had an eye for pretty boys and an insatiable appetite. He'd asked me to scout for him before. 'That school you go to, Tonio, so many kids, there must be others like you, yes? Attractive lads who wouldn't mind taking their knickers down for cash? Be careful, of course; if we get caught, it's trouble for both of us, and the well dries up. But anyone you bring me that I can use, I'll pay you a commission.'

I'd never brought him anyone before, though I'd eyeballed a few. I couldn't be sure how they'd react, and the risk wasn't worth it. I was on safe ground with Robbie, though, that much was certain; and I was pretty sure he'd say what he did eventually say, which was yes. He'd never had any money; all I had to do was provide him with the need, and the girls had gifted me with that.

I took him in with me that same afternoon, and watched Simon's face light up.

'Hallo, son. New worker for me, are you? Excellent, excellent. Tone's explained it, has he? What it involves, the work?'

Robbie nodded tightly.

'And you're willing?'

Another nod.

'That's great. Terrific. Just relax, son, no one's going to hurt you. No one's going to touch you, come to that,' in defiance of his own arm round Robbie's shoulders, nice and friendly and welcoming. 'Just a few photos, that's all; and no one you know will ever get to see them, I promise you that. And I keep my promises, Tonio will have told you. We'll take it easy, this first session: bare feet and an open shirt, perhaps, let the dog see the rabbit, but leave the trousers on, yes? You'll be happier? And you can watch Tone working first, that'll calm your butterflies. Right little pro, our Tone. Skin-Tone I call him, eh?'

A nudge and a wink, and he sent me off with his eyes, no stronger message needed.

I changed in the props room, came back in a bathrobe to find Simon kicking a pile of cushions into a corner, draping red satin sheets down the walls. Bog-standard stuff, this was, and he probably didn't even need it; but this was for Robbie's sake, obviously, not his own.

Robbie himself was sitting in a corner, hunched around a coffee, uptight but not looking miserable, not sorry he'd come. I gave him a grin, slipped the bathrobe off and tossed it aside, casual as anything. *Make it look piss-easy*, that was the unspoken order, and that's what I did. Half an hour rolling around on the cushions being sultry and Italian; I could do it in my sleep. And Simon didn't even curse me out when I got a fit of the giggles halfway through, he only chuckled like the laid-back taskmaster he was making out to be, and told me to take my time. When you're ready, he said. First time I'd heard that since my own first time.

Very unprofessional, the giggles. I guess it was just having Robbie there. I wasn't used to any kind of audience, let alone someone from my other life. But they did no harm that day.

No giggles later, when Robbie stood up. Simon took him as he was to start with, just a pretty teenager in cheap clothes stood against the white studio wall. But then he wanted a country look, Simon said; so I took Robbie into the props room and sorted him out a big check shirt and a baggier pair of jeans.

'Leave the shirt unbuttoned, right, just hanging loose. You'll want a belt in the jeans, here, something big and chunky. Bare feet, these people think that's dead sexy. Oh, and no underwear. OK?'

He hesitated, then nodded briefly.

'Don't worry, it's just in case. The most he'll want today is the belt undone and the top couple of buttons on the flies. Just a glimpse of your pubes, that's all. Like he says, it's a teaser. Let the dog see the rabbit. He may not even ask for that much. But you'd feel a right prat if he did, and all we saw was the elastic in your Marks and Sparks kex. I mean, wouldn't you?'

I thumped him on the shoulder, and left him to get changed in private.

Everyone got what they wanted, that first time. I got some extra money and a friend to work with; Robbie got his new clothes, his haircut and a bit later his first date with Emma; Simon got fresh meat for his little publications, and I guess that meant his customers got what they wanted too.

Not a smart operation, Simon's business. He really didn't have the market sussed at all. He was a good enough photographer, but that's where his talent dried up. What his customers got in their plain brown envelopes – and I know this exactly, because I wasn't just a star, I stuffed 'em – what they got every month was a couple of glossy black-and-white prints and a dozen stapled sheets out of the photocopier, more pictures and some letters badly typed.

I don't know what Simon charged for the service, but it must have been too much for what he was providing. I don't know where he found his customers, either, how they got in touch. I used to picture them sometimes: sad old men in raincoats, mostly; living in bedsits and smoking roll-ups, sitting at their windows watching schoolboys on the street. Simon did offer to put me in touch with someone once, 'Sit on his knee for half an hour, kid, he'll give you half his pension,' but, Christ, I wasn't having that. Pictures, yeah, no problem; but I wasn't available for rent. I wasn't that desperate.

Robbie might've been. Desperate for money, or just desperate for something that felt like affection: either way, he might've done it if I'd offered him the option. I could've got a commission on that, too; but the one thing I couldn't do, I couldn't rent out my friend. Couldn't have lived with that.

So we settled for what we had, both of us, what we could get from Simon. We took our kex off, we smiled and sulked to order, we posed with whatever he brought in for toys; and that's as far as we went, until one day he offered us the chance to go a hell of a lot further.

All the way to Holland, we could go if we fancied it, he said.

'I've got contacts, see. International contacts. And there's this publisher, big glossy stuff he does, full colour, not like mine; and he's interested in you two. Wants you to go over, do a session for him . . . '

Listening, I thought it wasn't quite like that. I thought probably Simon had offered the guy some of his own stuff, but it hadn't been good enough; so for Simon this was very much second best, get the commission if he couldn't get the work. I thought I could hear his teeth gritting quietly as he told us.

'What d'you reckon?' I said to Robbie. I knew what I reckoned already. I reckoned a weekend in Holland, two pretty boys on the town with cash in their pockets. Street cafés and beer and maybe a bit of dope, and seeing if we couldn't smuggle a couple of girls back to the hotel bedroom, that's what I reckoned.

'I dunno,' he said, not looking at Simon, not looking at me. 'Have to think about it, yeah?'

'It's good money,' Simon said. 'Pay for your trip over, easy, and enough left to have some fun with after.'

Right. Cafés, beer, dope and girls. Simon's mind worked pretty much the same way mine did, though for him it might've been boys instead of girls. I'd never been sure about that, whether this was just work for him or pleasure also. Whether he was his own most appreciative customer . . .

But Robbie wouldn't commit himself, didn't want to talk about it any more. I signalled Simon to leave it; I'd do the inquisition bit later, on the way home. Robbie would talk to me, but only when we were alone.

When we were, when he did, it was the same old problem.

'Where am I going to get the money from to get to Holland? It's impossible.'

We wouldn't do it on what Simon paid us, that was for sure. Besides, all Robbie's earnings went on Emma, so far as I could see.

'We'll be paid when we get there,' I pointed out.

'Yeah, but that's no help, is it? Can't see Simon giving us a lend, can you?'

No, I couldn't. Not even to get his commission. He wouldn't trust us to pay him back again. And quite right too. He might be bigger than us, he was a big guy behind the thrusting gut; but we had a good hold over Simon and he knew it. Wasn't us would go to jail if we snivelled to the cops about how he'd been misusing us.

'What about you, then?' Robbie asked. 'You going to go, or what?'

I shrugged. 'Want to. But I dunno, don't fancy it on my own . . .'

'Can you do the cash, then, have you got that much?'

'No, but I can get it.'

'How?'

'My uncle,' I said.

'What, he'll lend it, you mean?'

'No. Well, not like you mean.' My uncle knew everyone, pretty much, and everything that went on. Which meant he knew me as well as anyone else, and he knew what my promises were worth. 'But he's a pawnbroker, see? And I've got all my cameras, he'll give us the cash on them.'

He wasn't supposed to do it, of course. You're not allowed to pawn to kids. But he was my uncle, and I'd been pledging stuff with him since I was twelve. He just dealt with me in person, in the back office where no one coming in could see us, and put a fake name on the ticket.

And charged me an extra five per cent for the privilege, naturally. We're that kind of family.

'You haven't got anything you could pledge?' I suggested. 'Doesn't have to be jewels, like, anything saleable would do. Camera, stereo, he's dead happy with electric gear . . .'

Robbie just shook his head and walked on a bit faster, his feet telling me, *that's enough, I don't want to talk about this any more.*

Fair enough. I shut up, hurried up, gave him a twisted grin as I caught up and asked if he was shagging Emma yet.

*

A couple of days later I made him come into a travel agent with me to find out about boats to Holland.

No need to go down south, the woman told us; or no further than Hull. There were overnight ferries, fourteen hours each way with an on-board disco and duty-free booze if anyone would sell it to us. Cheap train tickets from Newcastle, and she could fix us up a room at the other end, best deal in town, she said . . .

'Brilliant, eh?' I said to Robbie outside the shop.

He shrugged. 'Pointless, more like. What's the use dragging me along? I said, I can't come.'

'Oh, yeah. Right. You said that, didn't you?'

But I still talked about it. I really laid it on thick, how much fun we'd have if we both went together. I spent more time than normal just hanging out with him, rubbing it well in what a good friend I was and how he didn't have many others, or any others worth talking of. Not that I ever said that, but I didn't need to. There just wasn't anyone else offering to spend time with him.

So it was no great surprise when he turned up at my place with a backpack full of gear.

'Look, Tonio, could you take this to your uncle, could you? Please? See what he says?'

'You coming after all, then?' As we were private, I rewarded him with a quick hug, and just grinned wider when he pushed me fiercely away.

'I dunno. Depends, doesn't it? What he'll give us, like? Might not be enough.'

I took the backpack off him, undid the straps and peered inside.

After a minute, 'That'll be enough,' I said softly; and then, 'Wow,' tipping it all out on to my bed in a heavy blaze of colour and refracted light.

'Jesus, don't . . . '

'It's all right, no one ever comes in here.' Not without knocking, anyway; and I could flick the duvet over the loot in half a second. Done it before, when I needed to.

Even so he was nervous, fidgeting with the black-out blinds I'd made to be sure no aerial spy could see in, then standing with his back to the door against some eruptive relative of mine. Time lapsed again, with both of us just looking; and then, 'They're not,' he said, 'they're not *real*, you know?'

'They look real enough to me.' And felt real too, cool and hard and heavy in my hand, sharp edges and smooth curves: necklaces and brooches all of one pattern, emeralds set in woven gold.

Robbie shook his head. 'They're all fakes. That's why, I mean, they might be worth nothing . . . '

'Don't you believe it.' I used to help my uncle at weekends for pocket-money, before I discovered Simon. Cleaning and dusting mostly, fetching and carrying and putting away, but I'd listened and I'd learned. Information is crucial, and pawnshops are full of it. 'People pay a lot, to look like they can afford diamonds. The clever ones say what you said, they say, "Of course they're not real, you know. All copies," and then they talk about insurance, and whoever's listening goes away thinking they've got the real ones in the bank. And it's all bullshit, but it does work. So yeah, my uncle'll take these as a pledge. He'll be glad to.'

Robbie grunted and slumped against the door, more relieved than he wanted me to know. 'You'll . . . you'll sort it out, will you, then?'

'Yeah. Of course I will.' And I'd take a commission, too. A small one, off both of them. Fair's fair.

'Put 'em back in the bag, then.'

'No, not yet. I've got an idea.'

'For God's sake, Tonio . . . '

I looked up at him and he was all tension again, tight as a wire. I grinned, said, 'Relax, will you? What are you so edgy about, whose are they?' They weren't his, that went without saying. And would go on the price, too. My uncle wasn't stupid.

'I got 'em from a box in Alice's wardrobe,' he muttered. Alice was his stepmother, or his stepfather's wife, or whatever. Was I surprised? I was not. 'They've been there a couple of years now. She never wears them or anything, but she'd kill me if she knew I'd took 'em . . . '

He hadn't actually answered my question, whose they were. Robbie didn't like lying, but sometimes he didn't like telling the truth either, even to me. *They're not hers* was implicit, understood. She pinched them from somewhere, or else her husband did; no one had offered the right price for them yet, so they sat in the bottom of Alice's wardrobe and Robbie was just praying she wouldn't check up until they were back home again. He didn't get beaten up much any more, now he was older, but he surely would for this. This was bonebreaker material, if he got caught.

But, 'I've got this idea,' I said again. 'This guy in Rotterdam, he wants photos, right? That's what we're going over for. That means he's in the market. And I take photos, yeah?'

'So?'

'So take your T-shirt off, and let me dress you up a bit,' I said, draping a long shining chain round his neck like a teaser. They might not want Simon's stuff in Holland, but, 'I reckon we can sell them a whole feature, see. Even if the quality's not what they're used to, that'll be part of the turn-on, just two boys romping around and taking photos of each other. We can make it look deliberately amateur, even – like you and me really have got a thing going, like that, yeah? So take your shirt off, and we'll use this stuff for toys. Just to give them a taster, sell the idea. Let the dog see the rabbit.'

This wasn't the same as posing for Simon, obviously. This time it was a friend behind the camera, and Robbie was dead uncomfortable to start with, awkward and unsmiling, no use at all. I'd been expecting that, though. It's why I hadn't even suggested him stripping off any further. But I put some music on, opened the window behind the blinds and got out this joint I'd been saving. Soon I had him giggling, and after that it was easy for both of us. In the end he stripped down of his own accord, and I got some great pictures.

'Just a boy playing with his family jewels,' I said, grinning.

That finished him off altogether, and we didn't get any more work done that day; but I figured we had enough. I couldn't risk taking the films into school to process, or to Simon's, not with this. There was a dark-room at the local community centre, though, and I could hire time there. It'd be worth it, I thought. Store the stuff there, too; they had lockers with good security. Safer than home. Kids snoop, and so do parents.

My uncle had held my cameras before; he took them with no more than a nod, and a quick once-over to be sure I wasn't conning him with knackered gear.

Then I gave him Robbie's backpack, 'For a friend, yeah? But we'll use the same name,' and watched with interest as he drew the pieces out one by one.

He checked them by touch, and then again with the jeweller's loupe he always carries in his waistcoat pocket. A traditional man, my uncle; and a careful one.

'And your friend wants, what, the same as yourself?'

'Yeah, that's all. We're going on holiday, see. Soon as we get out of school. He got these off an aunt or something, I dunno. He didn't know what they're worth, but I said they'd cover this, easy . . . '

'Fair enough. And he understands about the interest, he can manage that?'

'Yeah. We'll both be working over the holidays. No bother.'

He nodded. He wasn't really worried about the interest; if he didn't get it, he'd just keep the pledges. He'd done that to me once, early on, when I didn't really believe that he would. Since then I'd been dead careful, never pledging anything I valued unless I was certain of buying it back. A good lesson to learn, my uncle called it.

And on the same principle of never confusing business with family relationships, I asked for my small commission on Robbie's loan, and got it.

A few days before we left for Rotterdam, I gave Robbie a present.

'These are for Emma,' I said, shoving a fat packet of photos into his hands. I'd spent half a day trawling through two years-worth of work and printing off the best. 'Free, this time. I figure they'll keep her going while you're away.'

He flicked through them, saw endless snaps of himself, and shoved them aside again, as I'd been sure that he would. He had no vanity, Robbie; he really didn't understand the fuss the girls made over him. He enjoyed it, sure, he was learning to use it, but he still didn't understand it.

'So why didn't you give them to her yourself?' he asked. It was the last week of term, and we'd bumped into each other half a dozen times at least.

I sighed. 'She's going to be *grateful*, Robbie man. Right? She's going to be dead chuffed. She's going to sleep with these under her pillow. Why waste all that gratitude on me? It's no use to me. It'll be dead good for you.'

He nodded slowly, catching on at last. Robbie's problem, deep down, was that he was just too nice for the sex war thing. Too nice for the world, come to that.

Too nice, or too stupid. One or the other. I'm not sure it really mattered in the end. He needed me, that much I was sure of.

'And don't forget to give them to her, either. Right?' Robbie was a great one for not doing things straight away, and then having them slip out of his mind. The few times I'd seen his room, it reminded me of his mind: dead messy, stacked high with rubbish he hadn't got around to dealing with, and no hope of finding what you wanted when you wanted it.

Luckily, he had me to organize things for him; so we went to Rotterdam, courtesy of Simon's arrangements and my uncle's cash. We went for a weekend and stayed for a week, because the guy Simon had sent us to see was dead accommodating. After the first shoot, he decided he wanted us for a second day; and when I showed him my own pics of Robbie and explained my idea, he found us a room in a smarter hotel and paid for them himself.

'Two English boys enjoying my beautiful city,' he said.

'You take pictures of each other everywhere. Yes? Good sexy pictures. With clothes, I guess; and then without clothes, back at the hotel. On the beds, in the showers, like that.'

'Terrific,' I said. 'Um, only one problem – I had to pawn all my cameras, to get over here . . . '

He laughed, and lent me a couple of cameras of his own.

Tucked a few packets of condoms into our pockets and introduced us to some girls, too, once he'd worked out what we liked. I never could quite figure out if they were professionals, if they were working for him; but either way, whether they did it for money or fun, they were dead good to us. Robbie was a bit uncertain at first, he had this loyalty thing towards Emma, and he looked like making a big guilt trip out of little Sadie; but I just told him he had to practise, or Emma'd go looking for someone more experienced. That was enough, so long as I said it again, every morning, before the girls dragged us off to see some more sights and take some more pictures, as risqué as we could get away with in public.

Next day we travelled back, our generous employer even came to say goodbye and settle the hotel bill in person, he was so pleased with the work we'd done. He gave us a stiffened envelope full of prints, as well: told us we could keep them for ourselves or hand them on to Simon as a freebie, whatever we chose.

'Simon, then,' I said automatically. 'He'll appreciate them.' We had a rule about this, we kept nothing dodgy at home. 'Unless you want to give a couple to Emma, Robs?'

He blushed, I grinned. And thought about the packetful of pics I'd passed on to her already through him, that he'd barely glanced through, he was so unconcerned; and I only grinned wider, no bad conscience to bother me. No conscience at all, some people reckoned.

That wasn't fair, or at least I didn't think so. But I did go through that envelope on the sly and take out the pictures of me, just in case; and I did let my friend take that envelope and pack it away in his bag. If one of us was going to get caught by Customs, better let it be him.

I slipped some dope into his jacket pocket, too. Same reasoning.

Customs didn't bother us, so I quietly retrieved my dope on the train while Robbie was in the loo. And walked him home from the station and said goodnight, good holiday, we'll do that again; and gave him a parting punch on the shoulder, said I'd see him tomorrow, headed off with my bag swinging on my shoulder and happy memories in my head. Didn't bother to look back, didn't think to wave.

The only way I saw Robbie the next day was in a snapshot on the telly, the local news that evening. Ironically, it was one of my own pictures; but I wouldn't be asking for a fee. Not this time.

The telly wasn't telling me anything I didn't know already. I'd had the police around that afternoon, a man in plain clothes and a woman in uniform. They'd told me plenty: more than they thought they were telling me, and a lot more than I wanted to hear.

Robbie was dead, they said. Robbie had been found that morning, hanging from the light-fitting in his bedroom. Cold and stiff, they said.

On his bed, they said, there were half a dozen pornographic photographs, Robbie posing naked for the camera.

He and I had just been away together, they understood; and what they wanted from me was any light that I might be able to throw on the circumstances of Robbie's death.

Take your time, they said.

Oh, they were kind, they were considerate. They knew all about shock, and cups of tea, and patience. But they didn't know how my mind was buzzing, what depth of shock I was dealing with here; and they didn't know how much else they were telling me with their concern, their questions.

Yes, I told them, Robbie did that. Posed for pictures. For a man in Newcastle, I told them, I didn't know his name. Sometimes, when Robbie and I were supposed to be together, I'd been covering for him while he went off to work. Yes, of course I'd felt bad, of course I'd known it was wrong. And illegal, yes, that too. But he was my friend, wasn't he?

It had been preying on his mind too, I told them, worrying at his conscience. Making him ill. But it was like an addiction with him, I said; it wasn't just the money, though he needed that, God knew. He was hooked, he got some kind of kick out of it. That's why I'd taken him on holiday, I said: to get him away from temptation, and try to talk some sense into him.

We'd had a good time, though it was still much on his mind; but then when we came back it must have felt like walking into a known and familiar trap, I said, and feeling it close around him. He might have stayed awake half the night, fretting and uncertain, the same problems facing him and nothing solved, nothing different; and in the end, I supposed, it was simply too much for him to handle . . .

They asked if he only posed for money, or if it went further or deeper than that: did he have sexual experiences with men, did I know? Or did he want to?

I said I didn't think he was a rent-boy, though he might not have told me if he was. I said he had a girlfriend, Emma, they ought to talk to her; but so far as I knew he wasn't sleeping with her, so she might just have been a cover. Mostly I thought he was just very confused about things, I said.

Mmm, they said. The reason they were asking, this could have been a desperate suicide or a cry for help; or it could simply have been an accident, the noose like the photographs, only meant to heighten his private pleasure. Except that he'd made it too well, and he slipped off the bed and strangled.

I didn't understand, I said. So the woman talked to me about auto-erotic experimentation, and I shook my head at her; and the man told me that hanged men always had a hard-on. And I nodded my understanding, and shrugged, and didn't say any more.

That's the public story, that's what everyone reported. Just a muddled kid who died, who killed himself by mischance or intent. The inquest said suicide, driven by guilt and misery;

the tabloids speculated, and warned parents about the perils of pornography. Don't give your kids too much privacy, they said, snoop and pry and ask questions that they don't want to answer . . .

My parents didn't need telling, they were doing that already. They never believed the gullible-innocent act, not from me. I think it was them tipped the police off, to raid Simon's home and studio; but luckily he was way ahead of them there, there was nothing left to find.

Still, I couldn't really go on working for him. I went back to my uncle, to dogsbody for him instead.

And that's the other story; that's where it hinges, with my uncle.

Pawnbrokers know too much about too many people, it's inherent in the job. That's why they mostly choose not to live near where they work; some secrets you just don't want to know about your friends. It's bad for friendship and it's bad for the business.

But they know about property too. That's inherent also. They know about Rolex watches and designer suits, they know about carriage clocks and christening dresses; they know what's antique and what's repro, what's real and what's fake.

They know about gold and about jewellery, and the good ones know a fair bit of history too. Where things have come from, and where they belong.

What's hot, and what's not.

Robbie never understood that, but I think probably the people he lived with, they understood it all too well. They knew how much knowledge a pawnbroker holds in his hands, about things and people both, and how they fit together; and they knew that so much knowledge could be dangerous.

Was dangerous, to them.

*

This is what happened, what I reckon happened, this is the other story: that they went snooping through Robbie's room while we were away, the same way he snooped through theirs when they were out. It's how that family worked; which is why it's odd that Robbie never made connections. He knew that knowledge counted more than anything, he had the proof of it in his own life. That's how he kept out of trouble, by knowing the things they never told him. He just never thought to spread that understanding wider, I guess. He didn't realize what knowledge he was giving away when he brought that stuff for my uncle.

Anyway they snooped, I reckon, and they found those photos I gave him for Emma, that I bet he'd forgotten to pass on. Snooping through those, they'd have turned up the ones I slipped in for a giggle, a couple of Robbie posing with the jewellery, dressed up like the Queen of Sheba in emeralds and jeans.

And then they would have dashed through to their own room, and rummaged in the wardrobe, and found the box empty and the jewels gone.

They would have thought that he'd sold them, that he was off with me, living it up on the proceeds.

So they waited for him, they would have waited all that time; while I walked him home, while we stood outside chatting in the street they would have been in the front room sitting and listening, waiting.

And then I said goodnight and left him, and Robbie went inside and met their anger.

And being stupid, and not understanding, Robbie died.

If I'd been there, if I'd only gone in with him for a cup of tea and a smoke, everything would have been different; but Robbie didn't like people to come in.

So I left him, and he went in alone. And he wouldn't have thought to lie, to say yes, you're right, I found the stuff and I sold it.

He'd have told them the truth. It's in the pawn, he would've said. But I've got the money, he would've said, thinking he was saving his skin. I can get it back tomorrow, he would've said, I've got the money here; but too late already, no tomorrows for Robbie, not now.

Because the pawn meant the pawnbroker, the man who knew. And whether he was honest or whether he was bent, either way the pawnbroker meant trouble.

My uncle knew it wasn't costume jewellery, soon as he touched it. Sooner.

Hell, I was pretty sure myself. But if it was genuine it was worth thousands; which was why Robbie was so sure it couldn't be, of course, because he didn't believe his step-father and Alice were in that league at all.

Which they weren't, really. Shoplifting and petty burglary, that was more their scene. This must've been a fluke; they didn't even know what to do with the stuff after, where to fence it. So they kept it in a box in the wardrobe.

It must've been sheer rage that drove them to kill Robbie, rage or revenge. His death couldn't do them any good, they couldn't rescue anything. Too late now. They'd have been wiser to kill my uncle if they could have managed it. Killing Robbie only made it worse, though I could see how it would have felt good at the time. Especially when they rigged him up to make it look so natural, with those photos in his bag like a gift from God to give him a reason. That would have felt excellent, I thought. Until my uncle got in touch.

I wondered if he'd been round to see them yet. I didn't think he'd do this on the telephone, but I did think he'd take precautions. Like a gun in his pocket, maybe. I knew he kept a gun.

Very polite he'd be, and not at all dishonest. I have these pieces, he'd tell them, and they're stolen property, I should take them to the police with all the information I have, how they came to my possession . . .

I wasn't sure what he'd do then, whether he'd let them redeem the stuff – for its true value, of course, or rather more; certainly not for what he'd advanced against it – or whether he'd just keep it all and take a regular bribe to keep quiet. Probably the first if they could fund it, if they could raise a mortgage on the house or whatever; but if not, then certainly the second. He's not a charitable man, my uncle. That's the chief lesson I've learned from him, that advantage should never be wasted.

My uncle might still have the jewellery, or he might not; but me, I still had the photos of Robbie wearing it. Safely locked away, down the community centre where my parents couldn't snoop. Those pictures were deadly. They'd killed Robbie already, and they could kill me, too, if I wasn't careful.

Stepfather and wife, I thought they'd still be waiting, in that house. Waiting and wondering, were they going to hear from the guy with the negatives or were they not, had they got away with it . . . ?

Oh, they'd hear, right enough. Down the phone, most likely. I didn't have my uncle's pride, or Robbie's foolishness. And I didn't have a gun, either. But they'd hear, and they'd pay, and I'd promise; and some day, when I thought they'd paid enough, they'd find out what my promises were worth.

A MORNING FOR REMEMBERING

Robert E. Skinner

I woke up a little hung over that morning. I'd been drinking hard since '42, so there wasn't much new about that. I started drinking to forget something, but I was just drinking out of habit by then. I wondered if the whiskey was getting to me, though, because I kept forgetting little things, like my cap and my ticket book, and had to keep going into the house after them. Looking back on it, it's funny how I began that day forgetting things.

When I pulled up at my partner's house, it was obvious by the way he bounded out that he'd been timing me to see if I'd be late. Dick Fletcher had only been on the force for about a year, but already he was bucking for the chief's job. He was always early and could quote the traffic regulations by heart.

His equipment was in a constant state of high readiness, as if he expected a surprise inspection at any moment. His badge, and shoes, and the patent leather bill of his cap sparkled like an Ipana smile. Jutting from his spit-shined holster was the ivory grip of a large .44 Special Colt revolver. He was the only man in our district who carried that much iron, and I don't think he realized how silly he looked. But his tragic flaw was that he didn't really give a damn about what the rest of us thought.

'Hey, Harry,' he said when he got close enough to see my face. 'You don't look so good this morning. Too much beer last night, huh?' The cocky little bastard's voice reached out and shook you to make sure you were paying attention to him.

'It's just my age, Dickie,' I said.

The kid frowned at me. He hated being called Dickie and he knew I knew it. I usually called him by his last name, but I felt tired, sick and mean that morning. The milk of human kindness had curdled in me when I woke up to the sickening heat of an early New Orleans spring morning.

The radio crackled, interrupting us, and the voice of Bert Dennis, the dispatcher, came over the loudspeaker.

'Car Four, come in Car Four.'

Before I could get to the mike, Fletcher had snatched it from its clip on the dashboard.

'Car Four, go ahead,' he barked.

'Why, hello, Dickie,' Bert said in an amused voice. 'We got us a domestic disturbance at eight-one-six Lakeview Drive. See the woman, over.'

Fletcher flushed to the roots of his blond crewcut. He knew that Bert was making fun of him over the open police band, but he'd rather have died than rise to the bait. He rogered the call and reached for the switch to the siren, but I grabbed his hand and shook my head. 'Leave it off,' I said. I didn't want to tell him how bad my hangover was. He'd have gotten too much satisfaction out of it.

'But there could be a homicide in progress,' he protested.

'Blowing that thing ain't gonna stop any murders,' I said. 'Besides, we're only about six blocks away from there now.' It was already eighty-thirty a.m. and everybody in the Lakeview section had gone to work in downtown New Orleans. Our part of town was as quiet as the pause that follows a lame joke.

When we pulled up at the address Bert had given us, I saw an elderly lady standing on the front porch of a two-storey brick cottage. She was pressing a white lace handkerchief up to her mouth. I thought she was frightened until I got closer and saw the happy gleam in her small, dark shoe-button eyes.

'Oh, Officer, I'm so glad you're here,' she said in a breathless, high-pitched voice. 'They're just a'screamin' and a'cursin' and a'throwin' pots and pans over there like crazy people.' She shivered with excitement and a smile of unadulterated glee bent her withered lips. Her skin had a high flush that I knew had nothing to do with the early-morning heat.

'Thank you for calling us, Mrs . . . '

'Mrs Peletier. Mrs Charles Anthony Peletier. I've lived here for forty years and never have seen the like of those folks. Why, they've like scairt me to death sometimes.' She pressed her handkerchief up to her smiling mouth again.

In the silence I heard the sound of dishes breaking in the house next door. This began to be accompanied by wet-sounding slaps that confused me until I looked over at Fletcher. He had his blackjack looped over his right wrist and was slapping it against his left palm almost in counterpoint to the muted crashes from next door. His eyes were blinking rapidly from excitement and maybe from fear. I'd warned him often enough about the danger of intervening in domestic disturbances.

'You won't need that,' I said.

He looked at me, his brows knitted fiercely, but I continued to watch him until he stopped slapping his palm and slid the sap back into his pocket.

The house next door had been a pretty little place once, but everything about it suggested the occupants had long ago lost interest in it. The paint was chipped and peeling, and slats were missing here and there from the picket fence. An overpowering coalition of various types of Southern weeds had attacked and defeated the few plants in the flowerbeds.

A cheap tin mailbox had lost one of the screws holding it next to the door and it hung crazily askew. I reached over, shoved it upright and read the dirty white card in the slot. It read 'Mr and Mrs Jerry Peret.' For a second the sidewalk tilted beneath my feet and the sound of my breath roared through my ears.

'Aw, Jesus,' I said out loud.

'What did you say?' Fletcher asked in an urgent voice.

The door was already open a crack so, motioning him to stand clear, I pushed it wide. 'Police department,' I said loudly. 'Anybody home?' No one answered, but the sound of dishes breaking continued to come from the rear of the house. I went in first and motioned Fletcher to follow.

The place was a mess, with broken lamps, torn magazines, shattered records, and dirty laundry spread all over the floor and the old-fashioned horsehair sofa and chairs. The coffee table was upset and the contents of a whiskey bottle had spilled on the cheap braided rug.

Over in one corner, a big cabinet Philco radio hummed, and I could just make out the voice of Rosemary Clooney singing 'C'mon 'a my House' as I went over to switch it off. Now, in addition to the occasional sounds of dishes breaking, I could dimly hear a woman crying quietly but insistently.

Fletcher stood behind me, his breath coming out in harsh rasps. I glanced over and saw that he had his hand on the butt of his big revolver. I caught a glimpse of a bed through an open door to the right, so I walked over softly and looked through it. Jerry was sprawled atop the unmade bed. The years hadn't been good to him. Once, he'd been a tall, good-looking guy with a full head of blond hair, big shoulders and an infectious laugh. I almost didn't recognize him now.

His hair had eroded back to the middle of his skull, leaving behind an artificially high forehead that was pasty and beaded with a light sweat. His bloated stomach swelled up from the rest of his body like a huge, disgusting growth. The clothing he wore was shabby, and stained with what smelled like a mixture of liquor and urine. His mouth was open, and periodically a sound came from it that reminded me of someone rubbing a file across a wooden chair leg.

Seeing that Jerry wasn't likely to move soon, I motioned for Fletcher to follow me to the back. As we picked our way through the debris, the sound of the sobbing got louder until we reached the kitchen. A woman in a pink housecoat, her hair in curlers, sat in the middle of a pile of spilled garbage and broken crockery. She was in the act of throwing a piece of broken dinner plate against the opposite wall. A few of her curlers had come loose and locks of hair straggled here and there. Although it had been a long time she still seemed much the same as I remembered. I felt a strange twisting inside when I looked at her.

'Hello, Annie,' I said.

The sound of her name startled her, and her sobs broke off for a moment. She glanced up, saw my face, and tried to smile. 'Why, hello, Harry. I . . . ' her voice trailed off as the crying fit took control of her again.

I went over and gently helped her up. Her robe and the coat of her pink flannel pajamas were torn, and I could see that she still had the light freckling on her chest and the tops of her breasts. Before I sat her down in the one kitchen chair that was still upright, I pulled the robe closed over the torn pajama top, and lifted her hand up to hold it together.

'I'm sorry to have you see me like this, Harry,' she said finally, rubbing the tears out of her eyes with her free hand. I saw that she'd caught a slap or a fist in her right eye because the skin around it was red and beginning to swell.

'Don't worry about that, Annie.' I took off my cap and laid it on the counter. 'Did he hurt you very much?'

'I've been hurt worse,' she said in a low voice.

I saw that Dick had a slightly dazed look on his face as he probably wondered how I knew this woman. To rescue himself from his own confusion, he took out his pad and pencil. 'Why don't you tell us what happened?'

'Nothing much,' she said with forced casualness. 'I'm married to a bum who likes to go out for a drink and then show up three weeks later with a full beard and a tattoo on his chest. After eight years of waiting up all hours for him to come in from God-knows-where, something in me went crazy. When he got in this morning about seven-thirty, I was waiting for him.'

For a long, anguished moment, there was no sound in the room except the harsh scratching of Dick's pencil on his pad.

'I heard from Mama that you'd married Jerry,' I said, breaking the silence. 'I'm sorry it hasn't worked out, Annie.'

'What the fuck is this, Harry?' Fletcher finally asked. He looked from one to the other of us, more confused than ever. I didn't feel much like helping him get over it just then.

'Did he give you that black eye?' I asked Annie.

'That one and some others too,' she said. 'But I asked for this one.'

'How's that?' Dick said, his pencil working furiously again.

'I called him a lying, cheating sonofabitch, then I tried to beat his damned brains out with that baseball bat.' She nodded at the bat lying in the corner. 'If I'd been a little quicker, I'd have done it too,' she said, a touch ruefully.

Dick looked up at me, startled. I don't think he'd ever heard a woman use that kind of language before. I could have enjoyed the stupid expression on his face if we'd been anywhere else but Annie's airless little kitchen.

'How long's he been passed out in the bedroom?' I asked.

'I guess it's been about a half-hour now. I wasn't paying a lot of attention to him at the time.' She leaned an elbow on the kitchen table and rested her head on the palm of her hand. The skin on her face sagged with weariness and, for a moment, she looked far older than her thirty years. Seeing that she was talked out for the time being, I told Fletcher to stay with her and walked into the bedroom.

I took out my nightstick and prodded Jerry gently in the ribs with it.

'Hey, Jerry. Jerry. Snap out of it, pal. Wake up and talk to me.'

'Umph,' he groaned.

'Come on, boy. I know it feels bad, but you've got to talk to me.' I tapped him again, not quite so gently this time.

'Who . . . who is it?' he grumbled.

'It's the law, brother,' I said in a voice loud enough to penetrate his fog. 'You've wrecked your house and beat up your wife. Now I want you to wake up and talk to me.'

With an effort that I could feel in my own head and back, Jerry dragged his lumpy body into an upright position, then swung his legs over the edge of the bed. His joints cracked and popped with the effort.

Jerry held his head in his hands for a moment, then reached into the pocket of his jacket, and worried loose a pint bottle of Old Overholt rye with about two drinks left in it. He worked the cork out of the neck, tipped it up and swallowed the contents in one long gurgle. When he was through, he dropped the empty bottle on the rug and sighed heavily.

'Feel better now?' I asked.

He looked over and peered at me with eyes that were still puffy and a little stuck together with the slime of sleep. After a moment of intense regard, he began to recognize me.

'You.' He laughed mirthlessly. 'Yes, it would be you, wouldn't it?'

'It's nice seeing you again, too, Jerry. I won't ask you how things have been.' I hung my nightstick back in my belt and leaned up against the wall across from the bed.

'So you're a cop now, huh?' Jerry observed with a lopsided grin. 'That's just too damn priceless for words, Harry.'

'Why's that, Jerry?'

'For ten years, every time things got a little rough, I'd have to hear from Annie about how perfect you were. When we got married, I had a good job over at the shipyard making big money. I bought her everything under the sun, but I was no better than a draft dodger in her book. You were off in the navy being a hero. And now, here you are a goddamned cop. Shee-it, boy, that's rich.' He stopped talking suddenly and pressed his hands to the sides of his head, almost as if he were trying to push two halves of a split melon back together. His breath came out in short pants, like those of a winded dog.

'Did you have to black her eye, Jerry?' I asked when he finally had his breath back.

'What the hell do you know about it, man?' he asked with a sneer. 'How can you know what it's like to live with a woman who's on you and on you all the time? A woman who's always wanting something from you, and always wanting something you ain't got. After a while you just want her to shut up.'

'So you hit her. What do you weigh, Jerry? About two-thirty? And you're over six feet, so you've got a foot in height and a hundred and twenty pounds on her. You didn't have to beat her up, you could have just left the house.'

'Fuck you, Jack,' he sneered. 'I wish I'd hit her harder. I wish to Christ I'd killed her.'

The shock of his words brought me off the wall too fast and Jerry jumped back on the bed, probably thinking I was going to smack him. I wasn't, but I didn't mind him thinking it a bit.

'I'm going to go back and talk to Annie for a few minutes, Jerry. If you know what's good for you, you'll just sit there and not move till I come back, OK?' I stared at him until he nodded grudgingly, then I left the room.

Annie had been at work with a broom and dustpan in the kitchen while I'd been gone. She had cleaned up most of the mess and opened the windows, and a cooling breeze rustled the red-and-white checked curtains.

Before I reached the door I noticed the welcome smell of coffee and chicory. Over on the gas stove a cheap aluminum percolator burbled happily as brown splashes hit the top of the little glass bulb in the lid. Squatting on his haunches, Dick was backstopping a dustpan while Annie swept debris into it. I guessed from the high flush on his face that he was trying hard not to look at her breasts through the torn robe and pajamas.

'Dick, go out front and put handcuffs on Jerry. We're gonna have to take him down to the station for assault.'

He stared at me with resentment in his eyes, gave me a quick nod and left the room.

'Want some coffee?' Annie asked as she began taking the rollers from her hair. Her black eye had swelled almost completely shut, but didn't seem to be bothering her.

'Yeah, I could use some,' I said. I found a couple of unbroken cups in a cupboard and filled both of them. The rising steam felt good against my face and the smell almost made me forget why I was there. We'd shared many cups of coffee in the old days, before the war.

'I don't know if you want to press any charges against him, Annie, but I'm going to take him out of here anyway,' I said to fill up the quiet hanging in the room. 'He told me a minute ago that he wished he'd killed you, so the two of you need to be away from each other for a while.'

She said nothing but continued removing the rollers until she had them all out. Her silence had a chilly edge and I put down the cup and leaned back against the counter and waited. She rummaged around until she found her purse on the floor, then took out a brush and began to use it on her hair. She watched me intently throughout the whole process.

'How come you stopped writing, Harry?' she asked finally.

'I'm not much good at letter writing. Besides, I don't know what I'd have said,' I answered.

'Cut the crap,' she said. 'You wrote me for six months and then you stopped. No explanations. Before, you talked a lot about marriage. Maybe you don't remember.'

'I remember,' I said after a long pause. She'd finished combing her hair and with it back in place, I had a rush of memory to the night we'd lost our virginity to each other in the back seat of my brother's old Plymouth. I felt a little sick, remembering how wonderful that had been.

'What do you imagine I thought when I didn't hear from you, Harry?' She shoved her hands deep in the pockets of her robe, careless of the knowledge that it gaped alarmingly in front.

'I don't know,' I said without much conviction.

'Well, I'll tell you, then. I figured that I'd been played for a fool. That's a pretty lousy way to feel for ten years. I'm sick and tired of feeling that way, Harry. I want you to explain where the hell you've been.' Her one good eye was dark and hot, and sparks seemed to jump from it as she folded her arms in a posture of impatient waiting.

'What difference does it make after all this time?' I wondered aloud.

'You can't be that mean or that stupid,' she said. 'Time doesn't make something like this go away.'

I walked over to the open window and stood in the breeze coming from it. 'I guess I got scared, Annie,' I said after a long pause. 'I was on convoy patrol for the first year of my enlistment. Every week I watched ships blow up, sink without any warning, the crews drowned or burned to death. After a while it was hard not to imagine that one day it would probably happen to me.' I paused and turned around to meet her gaze. 'I figured it would be a mistake to make you wait for something that might not happen.'

'Why are you men so dumb, Harry?' she asked, her voice filled with anger and pain. 'You think it didn't hurt just as bad when you stopped writing and coming home?'

Without any warning she jumped up and rushed to me with startling speed, and hammered my chest with her small fists. I was feeling too numb by then to do anything but stand and take it.

'You jerk,' she cried. 'Even if you'd been killed in the war at least I'd have had something good to remember.' As her anger subsided, she stopped hitting me and grabbed the front of my shirt. 'Instead, you left me with nothing. So I ended up marrying a man I didn't care about and made both of us miserable for ten years.' She paused and pulled us closer together, whispering, 'I've been a rotten bitch, Harry, but it's partly your fault.'

It's funny how you can close a door in your life and do such a good job of ignoring it that self-deception becomes a new reality. It can work well for so long – maybe even for ever – but God help you if somebody opens that door and turns on the light. I had a sick heaviness in my chest, and the room suddenly seemed too bright for my eyes.

'I . . . I'm sorry, Annie,' I said, my voice trembling just a little.

'I know,' she replied softly, all her anger spent.

'Annie,' I said after a long moment, 'is it too late?'

'Oh Christ, Harry,' she sighed. 'I don't know. Don't ask me that now.'

When I could no longer stand the silence that had fallen over the room, I forced myself to remember what I was supposed to be doing there. 'I have to get Jerry down to the station, Annie. Do you want to see him before we go?'

She nodded and walked with me out to the living room. Fletcher stood in the middle with Jerry towering over him. I saw that he'd cuffed Jerry's hands in front of him and had hold of the chain with his left hand. He knew better than to control a prisoner that way. He was just showing Jerry how much contempt he had for him. I guessed he was also making up for his earlier confusion. He'd felt small, and I knew from experience that that brought out the meanness in him.

'He's ready to come along peaceful, aren't you, Peret?' Fletcher said with a smirk. 'He'll be a good boy now.'

'Knock it off,' I said, my voice thick with anger at this needless cruelty. Fletcher shut up but the smirk stayed on his face. I promised myself I'd kick the shit out of him when we got off duty that afternoon.

Jerry's countenance was expressionless throughout this interchange, but his eyes never left Annie's bruised face. His huge shoulders were bunched at his neck, and his whole attitude was that of someone anticipating a blow.

'Jerry, I don't want you to come back here,' Annie said quietly. 'We aren't doing each other any good and I think it's time we just called it quits. If it means anything to you, I'd like to tell you that I'm sorry. It's all my fault, really.'

Annie's face was drawn and grainy with sorrow and lack of sleep, but she looked at him calmly.

Jerry looked at Annie, at me, then back to Annie again. His huge body seemed to shrink in on itself, and his face contorted with an unspoken anguish. As I watched, a single tear rolled down his fat cheek.

Fletcher got in the back of the patrol car with Jerry, and after a last glance at Annie standing on the porch, I started the engine and quickly pulled away from the kerb.

'She make a play for you, Harry?' Jerry asked as we drove down the street. 'She's got a thing for uniforms. I'll bet that cop suit reminds her of the navy uniform you used to wear. Same color and all.'

'Put a lid on it, you fucking loser,' I heard Fletcher snarl. Jerry ignored him.

'I don't think she cared all that much for uniforms until she realized I wasn't wearing one,' Jerry went on. 'Once she noticed that, she began to notice other things about me. Things that reminded her I wasn't you.'

'What are you talking about, Jerry?' I asked. 'You think I wanted to get drafted and risk getting my ass shot off? You got to stay here, make good money in the shipyard, and live with a real nice girl who fed you home-cooked meals every night. I'd have traded with you in a minute.'

'She'd have traded me for you, too, buddy. It wouldn't have taken as long as a minute, either.' He got quiet, and I thought he'd wound himself down. But then he started talking again, and something in his voice had changed. He stopped trying to rag me, and began talking in a flat, terrible voice from which all the emotions had been leached away.

'You know, women are really funny people,' he said. 'I thought she'd be grateful to me for being there when you left. I really did. But the problem was, you were never really gone, Harry. It was like you were always sitting in the room, or standing at the foot of the bed.'

'I'm real sorry, Jerry,' I said. 'I thought she'd forget me when I went away. When I heard she'd married you, I stayed in the navy for a second enlistment just to keep from coming back here.'

'But you're back now, and she knows it,' he said. 'And I'm nothing but a useless drunk who's beat her up. That don't leave me with a whole lot, does it?'

He fell silent after that, but about a block from the station, I heard gagging noises come from the back seat.

'Holy shit,' Fletcher said. 'I think he's gonna puke. Quick, pull over.'

I pulled the car to the kerb as quickly as I could and got out to help, but as I walked around the front end to get to Jerry's door, I saw him begin to struggle with Fletcher. Jerry was out of shape, but he still outweighed the boy by a good seventy-five pounds. Just as I wrenched open the door I heard a deep-throated roar from inside the car, and the àcrid smell of cordite hit me in the face. Jesus, I thought, he didn't cuff him from behind. Of all the stupid rookie tricks.

Jerry pulled Fletcher's body away from him, and I could see blood on the front of the boy's uniform. Fletcher's face was white and his eyes had rolled up into his head. Jerry sat there with a queer expression on his face, the ivory-handled Colt all bloody and clutched between his cuffed hands.

A numbness spread down my face and throughout the rest of my body. Everything seemed to be moving at a very slow speed. I had my gun out, but my hand didn't seem to know what to do with it.

'Jerry, you dumb bastard,' I heard myself say. 'You were only going in for drunk and disorderly and simple assault. You'd have served sixty days at most. Now you've gone and shot a cop. You've shot a cop.' My voice sounded high-pitched and hysterical in my ears. 'Put the gun down and get out of the car. Do it now or I'll shoot you.' I'd never shot anybody before in my life. My body trembled like I had St Vitus's Dance.

Jerry looked sadly at the bloodstained gun in his hands, then at me. Tears were running down his face.

'I didn't meant to hurt him,' he said in a voice that almost broke into a sob. 'It wasn't at all what I meant to do.'

'Put the gun down and get out of the car,' I screamed, but he acted like he couldn't hear me.

'I bet you'd have even done this right,' he said reflectively. 'You wouldn't have fucked it up like this.' Then he shoved the barrel of the pistol under his chin.

I don't remember anything after that until the district captain and the other cars arrived. I was sitting on the ground with Dick, my thumb plugged in the hole in his chest to keep him from suffocating before the ambulance got there. 'What happened?' the captain kept saying, his voice loud and brittle on the quiet, peaceful street.

Dick didn't die, but he wasn't the same man any more. That thirty-six inches of spring steel that runs up a cop's backbone was gone. He quit and got a job landscaping the shady yards of the rich people who live on St Charles Avenue. Sometimes I see him walking a little beagle dog in Audubon Park.

After a time, Annie and I began to see each other again. We've had some nice moments, but I can tell that things aren't quite the same. A lot of water's gone under the bridge since I went away in '42.

I think I know now how Jerry must have felt. In the small hours of the morning when everything is still, and all I can hear is the regular sound of Annie's breathing, I find I can never quite ignore Jerry's presence, somewhere there near the foot of the bed.

THE WRONG REASONS

John Malcolm

They attacked me in the alleyway at the back of George's shop in Camden Passage. There were two of them. The bigger one sported a frayed handlebar moustache and wore a dark blue donkey jacket splashed with brown paint; probably a builder's labourer. The smaller one, in a grubby sweater, had thin ratty hair and a more vicious expression, as though working himself up into a rage about something. He lashed out at me first when, hearing their steps behind me, I turned to meet them.

I ducked instinctively and the blow missed the centre of my face, where it might have done new damage – my nose has been broken for many years – and hit the right forehead bone, sort of at the corner, making me see stars and his knuckles crack. I lurched away from him, glimpsing, in between flashes from the galaxy, the big man aim a punch at my stomach with a large red fist. I dropped my left shoulder and brought my arm across my waist just in time to block a pistol-blow that shunted me back into the brick wall to one side. Shock first numbed me, then the old adrenalin made me react quickly, almost with elation. I hadn't got myself into a good punch-up for ages.

A solid support makes a good start for self-defence, provided you don't let yourself get pinned to it. The alleyway was narrow, restricting their access to me, making them interfere with each other. The wall at my back gave me the return leverage I needed. The small savage man came lunging in for his second try at my face, his eyes not watching below, so I blocked his arm and brought my right knee hard up into his groin. Then I half-fielded another punch from the big fellow, getting a thud in the ribs that hurt, and chopped the smaller one down on the back of his neck with my right fist as he doubled up with a gasp of agony. The downward hammer of my bunched fist on to the soft anvil of his neck made him buckle at the knees. He staggered down against the opposite wall of the alley, dropping to the ground where, after a swift side-step, I kicked him hard underneath. There was a deep, satisfying grunt as I made solid contact. I now had the big man all to myself.

He clouted me in the ribs again, bloody hard.

My head stung with a painful stabbing feeling that told me I was going to have a big bruise and a lumpy swelling above my right eye. My thumped ribs made me wheeze. I felt slightly sick and hot. I was getting into a splendid temper.

The big man was much too slow. He swung at my face this time but I had space to jerk back, steady myself as the swing missed, then bring my right foot up in a full-blown kick to where it hurts most. When it comes to a brawl, fists on arms are not nearly as effective as well-shod feet on legs. He staggered and cried out, but he still bunched a fist to hit me again, bulking large in the centre of the alley-space. His blow lost force, almost certainly drained by painful difficulties down below.

A good trier, if nothing else.

I straight-lefted him under the point of the jaw to set him up, then right-hooked him with real hostility to the side of his face. He hit me a smack on the cheekbone with his craggy red knuckles and I punched him in the stomach, got a right to his nose and jumped back so that he missed his next swing entirely. The scraggy moustache started to turn pink under his nostrils. His eyes betrayed panic. I kicked him on the knee, a real purler of a kick, the welt of my leather brogue catching the bone on the inner side. He shrieked, grabbed the knee with both hands and staggered back against the wall, the leg half-cocked up as he clung to it.

'Jesus!' he shouted. 'Oh, Jesus Christ!'

I had him now and my blood was up. The smaller man was making wet globbery noises where he curled up crooked on the dirty asphalt of the alleyway. The big man had his mouth open in awful pain, heaving for breath. It would be dead easy to break his jaw. I was really getting going now; as angry as a singed snake. I pulled my right fist back ready to do him real murder.

But he'd seen it coming.

'Enough!' he yelled out, still on one leg. 'Enough! I've had enough! Can you not see that? Mother of God!'

Fist poised, I stopped, blinking. Irish, I thought. Definitely Irish. North London is full of them. About a million or so at the last count.

I lowered the fist and caught my breath. My head swam a bit.

'You lousy mugger,' I panted. 'I ought to smash you to bits.'

I glanced up the alley as I spoke. The narrow entrance, with part of the shop bridging it, was empty. Beyond, the bustle of Islington's Upper Street life could be sensed rather than seen. They must have watched me try the front door of George's shop, curse to find it closed and followed me into the alley as a perfect place to have a go at me, invisible from the passage.

'Mugger?' he protested, still stooping to grip the knee tightly in his big red hands. 'Me a mugger? Never. I told that fool O'Gorman' – he jerked his head towards the smaller man – 'that you'd do us a bit of no good at all. Not at all. Look at him, I said. Will you look at that nose? That's a hard man, I said.' He screwed up his face to catch his breath for a moment, then peered up at me. 'But O'Gorman said not. He's too well dressed, he said. Wouldn't have it but that we had to go through with it. The bloody fool. I'm in bloody agony. I'll never walk again.'

'Go through with it? Through with what? What the hell are you on about? You mean you wanted to duff me up? Why? What for?'

He ignored the questions. Gingerly he was trying to straighten out the stricken leg, putting the foot delicately down to the ground and wincing. A cry came from him as he tried his weight on it.

'Will you look at that now? How in hell will I be clocking on this afternoon with a leg like this? Punches and kicks; I said you were either a boxer or a rugby player but O'Gorman there, he hasn't the brains to listen. Which is it?'

'Rugby,' I said.

'I thought so. The kicks would be from that.' He levered himself carefully upright using the wall for purchase. 'Jesus, you've a kick like a mule. Forward, I suppose, from the build of you?'

'Front row.' My head was clearing. The fight, clearly, was over.

'Front row! Front row! The worst of the lot. Dear Heaven, what I'll do to O'Gorman when he gets up doesn't bear thinking about. He sets us up against a front row man. With ribs of iron and a head made of solid granite. Can you believe the eejit? Can you?'

'There were two of you. And you had the element of surprise.'

'Fat lot of good that turned out to be. Look at O'Gorman. Just look at him. You've destroyed him entirely.'

'Serve the little bugger right.'

His voice turned reproachful. 'It's not a very nice thing, is it, to kick a man when he's down?'

'Oh really? What would you have done?'

'Nothing like that.' He sounded quite put out. 'Nothing like that at all. That's a nasty type of business. I'm surprised that a gentleman like yourself kicks a man that way. I'm very disappointed.'

I frowned at him. 'You haven't done much of this sort of thing, have you?'

'Indeed not. I should never have let O'Gorman talk me into it. We're a respectable family, mine.'

'Where from?'

'Ireland.' His voice turned irritable as he caressed the knee tenderly. 'Can you not tell that?'

'Of course I can. I meant where in Ireland?'

'Cork. From Cork, I am. And wish I'd never left.'

'Building trade?'

'What else would there be for someone like me? And there's little enough work here, God knows. Now you've put me out for the duration, surely.'

'No I haven't. Keep rubbing. The knee'll be swollen a bit but you'll be able to hop about shortly.'

'Hop about? Hop about? What bloody use is that to a man carrying hodfuls of bricks up a bloody ladder, I ask you?'

'Should have thought of that, shouldn't you?' I turned to bend over the smaller man, O'Gorman apparently, still writhing on the dirty floor of the alley. 'Can you get up?'

His reply was unprintable. Vivid, explicit and very personal but absolutely unprintable.

'He's a bad lot, that O'Gorman,' the big man said, shuffling carefully on to both feet. 'I should never have listened to him.'

'What was the deal?'

'Oh, now, I shouldn't be telling you. That wouldn't do at all.'

I bunched my right fist and moved towards him. His red-tinged moustache prickled in consternation.

'You wouldn't?'

'Just watch me.'

'Oh dear. You're a hard man, sir. A very hard man. I told him so. But he wouldn't listen. It was twenty quid for each of us. To put you out of action, like. Nothing serious, you understand. I wouldn't have any of the ugly stuff. Just, well, just slow you down, you know? For an hour or so.'

'Just slow me down?'

'Sure.' He tried to smile appealingly, wincing as his split lip moved and fresh redness emerged among the stained yellow-brown fibres of the droopy moustache. 'Nothing personal at all, I assure you. A matter of business, entirely. And funds are short, d'you see, just now; these are hard times. Awful hard it is, just now.'

'Who paid you?'

'Ah, well, he hasn't, like. It was payment by results you see. A man O'Gorman was dealing with. Said you'd be here any moment. Provided you were, er, held up like, we'd get the divvy. There'll be nothing now. Nothing at all. And I've lost me day's work into the bargain, unless this knee eases directly.'

I stared down at O'Gorman, who was getting himself back on to all fours, groaning and uttering soft obscenities. I poked him in the ribs with the cap of my right brogue. 'Who was it? The man who hired you?'

His reply got worse. Much worse. I hadn't heard that sort of language since I played in a scratch side against the Royal Artillery. No, I tell a lie; the Household Cavalry were more inventive than the Gunners. There's something about horses that brings out the most foul curses imaginable; those cavaliers gave an entirely new insight into the phrase 'swearing like a trooper'.

Horses: I stared at the big Irishman realizing I didn't need to pound out the answer from either of them. Not that I would; hitting helpless men who've surrendered isn't really my style. I knew already who'd set this up; it was George.

'It was George, wasn't it?' I said to the big fellow. 'The owner of this shop? I said I'd meet him here before we went to the sale. And he's gone on ahead, paying you to delay me so he can bid for the Munnings on his own. The dirty, underhand, crooked bastard. I'll kill him for this.'

'Ah, now, sir. I don't know the man at all, it was O'Gorman here's contact, I wouldn't go jumping to conclusions now – '

'I don't have to. No one else would want to stop me today. We were off to the auction sale together so as not to bid each other up. But that greedy pig MacWilliams has decided he wants the bloody painting for himself. I might have known.'

Technically of course, George and I had been going to set up a ring, which is illegal. But you tell me why two colleagues or friends should want to bid against each other at auction and I'll believe you've never had a friend. Not that

George MacWilliams was a friend. He was the local King of the Ring, a dealer so elevated in the Islington hierarchy that I had to square him before going to bid for a Munnings of cows and a horse at Zimmerman's Rooms, where a corker had come up for sale. I was bidding on behalf of White's Art Fund, which I run for the investment arm of White's Bank. We own a considerable Munnings collection and this would be an adornment to it. Surprisingly, it had not gone to Christerby's, as one might expect, because the vendor was said to be local, a bookie in difficulties who could rely on the North London horse racing community to bid solidly for it. George tipped me off as he sometimes did about things like that, usually in return for a fee when he wasn't interested himself. Our relationship was entirely about money. Nothing else. So if George had suddenly found a cash buyer, which was quite on the cards, he wouldn't want me horning in. Paying forty quid to a couple of strong men to slow me down, knock me out of the bidding, would be a small price compared with the extra profit he'd get. I ground my teeth in fury. I was already delayed by these two, more than marginally, but come hell or high water I was going to get to that sale, now.

'You're lucky,' I said. 'I'm in a hurry. So there'll be no further repercussions. No police or anything. OK?'

'Ah.' The big man nodded. 'You're a kind man, sir. A very kind man after all. We are both deeply injured enough as it is.'

His big eyes looked at me with unmistakable, mournful appeal. The charmless, ferrety O'Gorman was half-upright now, leaning against the wall, mouth open to suck in air noisily. They were a harrowing sight; humanity at the bottom of its barrel.

'For God's sake,' I said, getting out my wallet. 'You're hopeless, both of you. Buy yourselves a drink. And leave this sort of thing to the professionals. Otherwise you'll get seriously hurt.'

I handed the big Cork man a twenty pound note. Under the drooping moustache his jaw dropped, making him wince once again.

'And there was me', he said, amazement coming to his eye as I turned to walk out of the alleyway, 'thinking that there's not a gentleman left in England.'

And he put an arm under the hapless O'Gorman, helping him to his feet.

Don't ask me why I gave him the money. For all the wrong reasons, I expect. Because he was so hopeless. Because I believed him when he said he wouldn't have kicked me if I were down. Because he was desperate and far from home. Or perhaps because I remembered rugger tours of Ireland, Cork especially, where the hospitality and the talk were so marvellous that I could still recall them with a smile. Or perhaps because I felt guilty about the kicks; they certainly weren't the action of a gentleman. But in a brawl like that, kicks are the most effective measures. It's no good being a gentleman if you're down, with broken bones, at the mercy of a thug. Or perhaps I gave him the money because of a reprehensible, patronizing attitude to an Irish labourer, or some such claptrap. Please yourselves; motives get too complex for me.

I got to the auction rooms and slipped into the toilets to clean my face and tidy up. There was a red mark on my forehead and a bump on my cheekbone that was going to turn from yellow-red to grey-blue, but they weren't too noticeable. I straightened my tie, dabbed my face with cold water and went cautiously to stand at the back of the gallery, hearing the drone of the auctioneer taking bids. Just in time; as the hammer dropped on a brown winter landscape by Rowland Hilder, the Munnings was placed up on the easel ready for the next lot. I glanced round quickly, my heart starting to pound.

George MacWilliams was towards the back, not far from me, where he normally would be. He hadn't seen me because he was staring forward at the painting. The trade always hang out towards the back, except for those gentlemen dealers who'll have nothing to do with the ring and whose names are famous enough for them to bid in splendid isolation at the front or to the side. I was standing behind several of the lesser fry, the type who like to mill about on foot, coming and going about their mysterious businesses at intervals and chatting, to the irritation of the seated audience who want to concentrate. Around me were roughish trade types in anoraks and windcheaters, divided by the odd suited individual and a horsy man in a check Harris tweed jacket, betting-shop regulars with their newspapers open at today's runners and odds, a brown-coated porter and a woman with a shopping bag from MacFisheries; that's an old bag, I thought, never mind the woman.

'Lot one hundred and thirty seven,' the auctioneer announced. 'An oil painting. On the easel here. By Sir Alfred Munnings, President of the Royal Academy. An interesting lot, this. A fine example. Cows and a grey horse by a stream in an orchard. Probably painted before the First War, around 1913. The location suggested is Zennor in Cornwall.'

Someone had been doing their research. Munnings' paintings before his second marriage in 1920 are his best – even his second wife said that – because instead of turning out all those master of foxhound potboilers and wealthy men on costly hunters for extravagant sums of money, he was still painting what came naturally to a country boy. The one-eyed Norwich artist was almost part of the Newlyn School then, at least closely involved with it, but Zennor is on the north coast of Cornwall, near St Ives. Munnings used to follow the hunt on Zennor Hill.

'I'll take ten thousand to start,' said the auctioneer briskly, trying to make it sound like sixpence.

I sensed, rather than saw, a movement from a man near me and, glancing sideways, followed the direction of the movement towards a fat sweatered fellow parked against the side wall further forward to my right. He nodded so slightly back that the motion was almost imperceptible and turned his head towards the centre of the hall as he repeated the nod.

'I have ten thousand,' the auctioneer said happily. 'Twelve? Twelve it is. Fourteen?'

The cow in the foreground of the painting looked right. It

should have been a cross between a Friesian and a Jersey
with a white marking on the forehead, a black neck and the
shoulder shot with dun colour. Behind her shoulder there
was a broad band of white. Munnings said that the cow was
one of the most perfect models to paint. He bought it for
fourteen pounds and got the landlord of the Lamorna Inn,
Mr Jory, to train her to be led on a halter.

Bloody certain George MacWilliams' dirty tricks weren't
going to keep me from this one.

'Twenty thousand,' the auctioneer burbled cheerfully,
trying to hold back his elation at the way the bidding had
proceeded during my thoughts. 'Twenty-five? Thank you,
sir. It's at the back now, at twenty-five.'

So, with my signal, I'd come into the running.

And the fat sweatered fellow gave someone else the
faintest nod and the hint of a wink.

'Thirty thousand.' The auctioneer made his tone more
serious. At this altitude, a statesmanlike gravitas is expected.

I nodded back to him.

The horse would be Grey Tick, a favourite of the painter's,
one he used to paint with Ned, his stable boy, on top,
sometimes wearing a scarlet coat, white cord breeches and
top boots. Ned, in various clothes, and Grey Tick are in
Munnings collections all over the world, from Norwich to
Newcastle, from America to Australia. But here the grey
mare was just a background figure; the cow was under apple
trees, with dappled light and a fresh stream adding to her
own natural camouflage. Another cow grazed near her.

'I have thirty-five thousand at the back.' The auctioneer
glanced away from me towards the middle of the hall.

To George MacWilliams, of course.

Well, if there was one thing for certain, trying to stop me
from getting to the auction like that had only stiffened my
resolve now that I was here. I hadn't had a chance to preview
the painting, but if George was up to tricks like violence to
stop me, then he must be pretty certain the thing was kosher.
Greedy bastard.

'Forty thousand.' The auctioneer raised his eyebrows back in my direction.

I'd even told George that a good early Munnings like that would go to well over sixty, maybe well over seventy thousand, even in today's markets when everyone is so cautious, and even though it wasn't a full-blown hunting scene or a racecourse like Newmarket with jockeys in colours – the ones that fetch the big money. There aren't that many early examples about and Munnings has always been a rich man's painter. The fact that it was more of a quiet study without a human figure in it wouldn't detract from its market-ability; it was a charming scene.

I nodded back.

'Forty-five thousand.' The auctioneer was becoming almost plummy. This must be the best lot he'd had for a while.

George would only get a finder's commission from me if he wasn't acting as principal. A couple of thousand, maybe, depending on the final hammer price.

Munnings is not popular at the Royal Academy, of course. His views on modern art were, to say the least, regressive. And put in the language of troopers. The evil O'Gorman could have taken lessons from Munnings. But the character opinion of fellow-artists has never affected the price of paintings much.

The fat sweatered fellow's expression, I suddenly noticed despite the drumming that was starting in my heart, had gone watcful. No, not watchful; smoothly tense. He was looking into the hall again. At MacWilliams, I would guess. Something was wrong, I suddenly thought, something wasn't quite right. I'd got here, I was bidding, I'd foiled the bastard, dealing those two useless heavies real strife, yet that sweatered man wasn't in the least disconcerted. In fact, he looked almost pleased.

'Fifty thousand. In the hall here.'

Those two useless heavies. They really were bloody useless. Utter tyros. I didn't have any illusions about my competence in that direction; there was no cause for self-congratulation about seeing them off.

So what would be the purpose of making an abortive attempt to stop me getting to the sale?

I nodded back, almost mechanically. My mind was running off at a tangent.

'Fifty-five thousand,' the auctioneer called. A shuffle and a sigh moved through the seated audience and the people standing round me. One or two turned in my direction to look at me speculatively.

The effect would be to make me all the more determined to get that lot, that's what the attack would be.

Anyone who knew me would know that.

So had George MacWilliams got two useless muggers to have a go, knowing that I'd see them off easily and rush in here determined to bid to the death?

That was too clever to be true, surely?

Or had he told them to pull the fight anyway, make sure to lose?

No, not those two. They were trying.

Weren't they?

'Sixty thousand.' The auctioneer's voice had changed. A note of real attention had got into it as he took the bid from the hall.

The cow was supposed to have a large pattern of black and dun, with more white on her quarters. I couldn't see that from the back. A dappled, splashy, impressionistic painting is much easier to fake than a smooth, precise one, especially if period. I was at auction. No catalogue description to hand. No comebacks for me, or at least very difficult ones to make stick. George was going through a bad time like everyone else, including a builder's labourer too decent to be a fighting man but desperate for funds. I could just imagine George picking those two.

'Tim'll crucify them,' he'd probably grinned to his henchmen. 'Tim's a terror in a bundle. He'll thump those two Micks silly and come tearing into the rooms, raring to buy.'

And wouldn't it be great to put one over the city slicker? To rip off the White's Art Fund man, Mr Clever Dick? What joy in the pubs tonight!

The Wrong Reasons

161

'It's against you at the back.'

The auctioneer's anxious voice cut into my thoughts. This was the crucial bid. If I went to sixty-five thousand, I'd be left holding that painting. MacWilliams had judged this precisely. Now was the time for him to drop out.

Between sixty and seventy thousand; he'd never take the next jump. I knew instinctively that he had run me up as far as he dared.

'It's still against you at the back.'

The auctioneer's voice had changed tone. He was peering at me tensely over his spectacles.

Could it be that the auctioneer was in on the scam too? He'd said 'at the back' from the beginning; was he tipping George off? Or was I getting paranoid?

Over on the far wall, MacWilliams' fat, sweatered lookout was staring at me like a man hypnotized. As I looked towards him he quickly dropped his eyes.

Surely I was being set up. Or was I? My heart thumped in my ribs. The Munnings, if genuine, was within my grasp. I'd never get it if I let it go now. The rooms had gone silent, utterly silent. Even the old woman with the MacFisheries bag was staring at me. I thought of the big Cork man in pain against the wall, his moustache reddened, his mournful eyes looking at me, hurt and reproachful.

'Are you all done at sixty thousand?' The auctioneer had picked up his gavel, holding it poised, but he was still staring at me.

Zimmerman's Rooms, Islington, not Christerby's.

MacWilliams territory.

A set-up.

I'd never seen a Munnings of cows and horses together before. Not that it was impossible. But it was something someone knocking up a pastiche based on genuine paintings might not be able to resist.

That fight, if genuine, was a hell of a risk. The Irishmen might have been better, I might not have been in good nick, a chance blow might have concussed me. It was too big a chance to take.

Then the Cork man's voice came to me.

'*I'm very disappointed –* '

And then he handled me so well.

I stood frozen to stone.

They'd been paid to lose the fight. I knew it now, I just knew it. And how superior I'd been, dropping them twenty quid.

The surprise in his face as he put O'Gorman back on his feet.

An unexpected bonus.

The auctioneer's eyebrows were about to meet his hairline as he stared at me expectantly. Shaking my head, I put my hands in my pockets and stepped back to indicate I was out. No more bidding from me. The auctioneer's expression congealed in dismay.

The Cork man in pain, looking at me, making me feel guilty.

'*I'm very disappointed –* '

The Cork man hadn't expected any nasty stuff. What he and O'Gorman had been told to go for was a well-dressed city toff, perhaps not an easy mark, one who'd fight hard, but inside the Queensberry rules. Not anything too difficult. Not a crutch-kicking bastard with a penchant for punch-ups. No wonder he was disappointed. He'd packed up much too quickly; no more personal damage for him, not for a mere twenty pounds. The only consolation, one that made me glad, was that, contrary to what he'd claimed, almost certainly he and his mate O'Gorman had been paid in advance. They knew they weren't going to delay me for very long; just long enough to get me wound up, fighting to buy that Munnings.

Or rather that non-Munnings.

'*All done then, at sixty thousand?*'

The auctioneer's voice was petulant with regret. He brought the hammer down reluctantly, as though working against coil-spring resistance, not with a bang but with a sad tap on the desk in front of him. A sort of rustle swept through the people, both seated and standing, around me.

As I turned away, the old biddy with the MacFisheries bag grinned a huge toothless grin at me and winked broadly. I grinned and winked back. She knew; she obviously knew; probably half of them must have known. They probably even knew who George had induced to paint the bloody thing.

'Sixty thousand,' the auctioneer moaned to his clerk desolately. 'MacWilliams.'

In the main body of the hall, amongst the chairs, my opponent had stood up and turned to stare at me, white-faced.

'Congratulations, George,' I called out. 'Congratulations on your purchase.'

The old biddy cackled loudly, swirling the MacFisheries bag.

Then I too started to laugh, relief making me shake almost uncontrollably. I had to turn and walk out of the rooms, laughing so much that, as I went along the pavement among the market stalls of Islington, people must have thought I was another bruised North London loony, well over the top from drink or noxious substances. I didn't care what they thought. I was still chuckling when I got to the tube station to head back to my office.

Mr Jory's cow and Grey Tick together; a collector's item indeed. I'd had a narrow, narrow escape.

I was glad I'd given the Cork man that twenty pound note.

Even for all the wrong reasons.

BRACE YOURSELF

Russell James

Patterson lets the gun dangle from his hand. You can see he doesn't know how to carry the thing. He lets it trail beside his leg, the barrel inches from his ankles. Occasionally he uses the gun to move wet undergrowth aside. You wouldn't be surprised to see mud on the end of the barrel. You know that Patterson is the kind of man who has rarely *seen* a gun, let alone carried one.

Look at his clothes. Jeans, denim jeans. They absorb water from the bushes and retain moisture. Jeans are the last thing to wear when tramping through damp woodlands. Patterson also wears black wellingtons and a brown tweed jacket. Under the jacket he wears a navy wool jumper. It is a big jumper. His jacket has been forced over it, and looks tight across his shoulders. His arms move stiffly.

He should not be here.

Fenner knew that the moment he saw him. Patterson had slewed his green Montego to a halt behind Fenner's Jag on the gravel before the house. He had heaved his large body out of the car and marched across the path with his engine still running. Obviously he realized that he couldn't park it at the foot of the steps. He wanted instructions. He looked like a tradesman who should have driven round to the back. Fenner waited for Leighton to tell him so.

But he didn't.

Leighton greeted Patterson by name. He was not effusive

about it, but not hostile either. 'Glad you found us, Patterson,' he said. 'Decent journey?'

'Bit of a grind. Roadworks on the motorway.'

'Michael Patterson,' Leighton said. 'Barry Fenner. Another guest.'

Fenner eyed him with interest. 'Patterson, eh?'

The man nodded. 'Good to meet yer.'

'How do you do?'

Fenner made no move to shake hands with Patterson. He and Leighton were at the top of the wide stone steps; Patterson on the gravel below. Fenner – thin, aesthetically drawn, pale blond hair – wore a light grey suit. Patterson – dark haired, large and awkward – wore shirt and slacks. A vivid tie hung loosely round his neck. His shirt was unbuttoned, too small at the collar. One side of the shirt had become untucked from his trousers. Squinting up at the two men on the top of the steps, Patterson fumbled in his shirt pocket for a pair of spectacles. He put them on and said, 'That's better.'

Leighton smiled. 'You can switch your engine off,' he said. 'I'll have someone move the car when they've brought in your luggage. Just leave the key inside.'

'Right.'

As Patterson turned back towards his car, Fenner glanced at his host, expecting some sign of his reaction – a conspiratorial wink, perhaps. But John Leighton's face retained its customary polite expression. Fenner studied him openly. Leighton's dark hair seemed a little thinner than when they had last met. Perhaps it was the afternoon sunlight, glaring on to Leighton's black hair, showing how each strand had been flattened into submission with water, brush and comb. Leighton looked older today. But people don't age gradually, Fenner knew. He had read somewhere that every cell in the human body dies and is replaced within a space of seven years, so that before any decade was out one became an entirely different person. Ageing sounded a gradual process, yet Leighton seemed to have aged an entire seven years in this last month. Cells seemed to be dying on his skin. It was as if he had reached his fortieth birthday and turned off the switch.

He seemed thinner too.

Ahead of the others in the wet undergrowth, John Leighton bites his lip. A flicker of anxiety crosses his face. But he hides it. In his Barbour jacket and plus-fours he looks less thin than he did yesterday. He looks wiry; quite tough in fact. He stands with feet planted firmly apart, his legs warmly encased in leather-lined Le Chameau boots. He has neat Habicht binoculars slung loose around his neck, and he carries a boxlock Holland and Holland Cavalier shotgun in his hand. Two dogs stand patiently beside him, panting in the dewy air. Leighton is boss.

'There's another car coming. Would you like to pop up to your room?'

The tone of Leighton's voice told Fenner not to wait with him on the steps. It underlined whose house this was, whose guests, whose weekend. It said that Leighton wished to greet his guests alone.

Fenner shrugged. He had no wish to linger at the top of these cold steps, grinning aimlessly while Leighton shook hands and prattled to each new visitor. It was dull enough talking to Leighton, let alone to his wretched guests. He went inside.

Alone, John Leighton blinked in the strong low sunlight. Rattling towards the house along the tarmac drive beneath the trees came a battered Land Rover. Harriet Henderson. Leighton hoped she had not brought her dogs with her. She bred the things – made money from it, apparently. He had had to speak to her once, when she had tried to sell dogs at his dinner table. Leighton had never known whether she sold dogs as a pastime, or whether she needed extra money. He couldn't tell. Harriet always wore the same old clothes, drove the same old car – not that that meant anything. Families with money did not flaunt it. The Hendersons and Leightons had been neighbours for two hundred years.

Admittedly, most of the Hendersons had moved away now – had married badly, died, that sort of thing. Harriet was virtually the only one left. She rode to hounds, of course, appeared at the odd gymkhana, but little else. Nevertheless, the Hendersons were part of the countryside around here.

Whereas Fenner . . . Where had he come from? One could not be sure about Barry Fenner's background. A London man; that was written in every vein of him. Smart suits, smart car, smart attitudes. When Fenner had come down last time – when was it, three weekends ago? – he had tried to impress Emily with high-faluting talk of negotiable securities, insider deals. Perhaps she *was* impressed. All Leighton knew was that when he brought the conversation round to include a couple of items from his own diminishing portfolio, the chap grew suddenly evasive – as if he had been delivering lines from a speech he had rehearsed, and he could not leave his script. He had floundered. He couldn't improvise. Surprising, that. You'd have expected a chap like Fenner to be quicker-witted.

Mind you, Leighton thought, as Harriet's muddy Land Rover came out from under the trees and on to his gravel forecourt, if Fenner *had* been a stockbroker he could have done us good. Our shares are languishing, to put it mildly. They are withering on the bough. The trouble is, of course, that I don't understand the things. Investment is like a card game that I don't play. If you play it right, you might win. But for every winner there is someone else like me. There has to be.

Leighton put a smile on his face while Harriet clambered down from her driving seat. He rested it again when, with a brisk wave, she stomped round to the back of her vehicle and began to rummage for her luggage. Leighton's Maltese footman dithered around her, but she brushed him away.

When the footman glanced anxiously to the top of the steps he saw that Leighton was staring at the sky, apparently taking no notice.

But Leighton was thinking that 'footman' was a ridiculous word. What did it mean? A man who waited on foot. How else should a servant wait – on a horse? Leighton wondered whether other people still used the term. Was there a more

modern word? No doubt in London, where Fenner came
from, they used some foreign name – if people in London
kept footmen nowadays. Fenner wouldn't, that was sure.
But out here in the Cotswolds there was less urgency to use
the latest word, to do the latest thing. Families maintained
tradition here.

For half the people here this weekend that was why they
came. Once or twice a year they forsook their elegant city
residences for this brief plunge into country life. They would
rediscover the reality of a rural lifestyle – the fact that the real
countryside neither smelt nor felt like the immaculate pages
of their country life magazines – that the grass was uneven,
that fields were muddy, that old houses were damp and
grubby in the corners. The guests would eat the kind of
hearty meals they would never order in London restaurants.
They would wear old clothes. They would get up early on a
Sunday morning to tramp the woodlands with a shotgun in
their hands.

Harriet clumped up the steps, smiling at him. She had an
old leather carry-all in her hand and the Maltese footman at
her heels. 'I've brought a frock,' she said.

'I'm relieved.' Leighton kissed her on the cheek, and found
that her skin tasted faintly of dog. 'Would you like a room
where you can change before dinner?'

'Sounds better than changing in the hall,' she said. 'But if
your rooms are full of grockles, I can use a bathroom.'

'Certainly not. Wouldn't hear of it. Besides, you'll need
somewhere to sit. We don't eat till eight.'

'You know me, John. Just plonk me in the library with a
glass of Scotch. Many coming?'

'About twenty, I think.'

Most of the party have followed Leighton to the clearing in
the wood. They have a sharp, early morning look about
them. Cheeks are red, eyes are bright. One or two, Leighton
notices, seem out of breath. Just from walking. Perhaps last
night's dinner disagreed with them.

Leighton is surprised to see Barry Fenner out of breath.

The man is lean, fit, in his middle thirties, yet he does look tired. Perhaps he drank too much wine with his dinner. Perhaps he ate too much. Leighton clucks his tongue.

While the hunters stumble to a halt among tree stumps and strands of bramble, Fenner stands aloof. His face is paler than usual. His hair glistens like wet straw. But Fenner isn't tired, or unwell. It is just a little early in the day.

Harriet is chatting to Michael Patterson. The lady and the peasant, Leighton thinks. What can they talk about? Even in her shapeless Barbour and tweeds, Harriet's breeding shows, while Patterson looms over her in his cheap jacket, hopelessly out of place. Harriet behaves like royalty – minor royalty, mildly famous. She is like a duchess in a factory, chatting politely with a workman; effortlessly, meaninglessly. Soon, when the duchess sweeps away to the next stop on her itinerary, the workers will recall how she paused to pass the day. No side on her, they'll say. She spoke to us like we were all the same. A proper lady, that one is.

Harriet is the sort of woman I should have married, Leighton thinks – if she hadn't been so damned ugly. Face like an Airedale. Body like a pug.

While Emily, when we married, seemed to have everything: fine looks, exquisite body – family and fortune, as the Victorians used to say. Leighton smiled ruefully. Perhaps a fortune was overstating the case, but Emily had had money. In their first years together she had spent it generously. Helped rebuild the stable block, converted a row of cottages, replenished furniture. Even the crystal glasses they had drunk from last night were an import of hers. Soon after their honeymoon, Emily had dragged John off to a man in Chipping Campden. A craftsman – an artist, really. Emily had commissioned a full set of his handmade glasses. Three dozen of everything. Was it three, or four? Could it really have been four dozen?

Leighton shakes his head at the memory of their first years together, when she danced through his dusty old house like a fairy queen dispensing magic. With her money she had transformed old pieces of furniture; stripped and polished,

they gleamed in the halls. Some things even disappeared. All
those yards of stair carpet, for instance, worn thin where
they turned each step, fraying along the sides. Vanished.
Replaced. Emily had scattered her money like fairy's silver
dust shimmering in beams of sunlight through the dark
interior of his house.

When he married her, John was only half in love. Deeper
passions came later, seeping slowly into the core of him,
until it seemed sometimes that they were corroding his soul.

No one would have seen that yesterday. Most of the arriving
guests came up the stone steps to Leighton's greeting, and
were led into the house to meet his wife. The few that she
didn't meet then were soon sought out by her, to be
welcomed, to be put at ease. Together with her husband,
Emily and John Leighton made an elegant couple – good-
looking and courteous, perfect hosts. Emily stood beside
John in their grand reception hall, delightfully relaxed in the
only day-dress she had bought this year, beautifully poised
on the fine woollen carpet she had bought twelve years
before. She and the carpet had hardly aged at all.

Each guest was greeted as a special friend, as if Emily was
honoured they had condescended to visit. But half the
people who came were John's business contacts: two estate
agents, a garage owner, the bank manager, a supplier of
feedstuffs and fertilizer. Emily smiled at each of them,
squeezed their hands warmly, touched the wives on the arm.
John, meanwhile, seemed distant, as if behind his polite
smile he was calculating the seating plan for dinner, the
number of plates.

He must have been thinking of something else.

Barry Fenner unpacked in his usual bedroom. Presumably
the Leightons put him in this room to help him feel at home.
It was his fourth visit, and each time he slept here. Nothing
changed between his visits except the flowers in his vase.
Fresh flowers every time. Fresh sheets and fresh flowers.

Despite his familiarity with the room, Feller felt odd in Leighton's house. He did not belong. In his time, Fenner had slept in many bedrooms, under many roofs. He had slept in hotels, flats and houses. He had slept under canvas and on a boat. Once, coming back from America, he had slept on a plane. Or he had tried to. Normally he prided himself on his cat-like ability to snatch sleep anywhere. But not in a plane. And not, for some reason, in this house.

As he hung up his suit, Fenner shrugged. No, he would not sleep easily in Leighton's house. The thought of John Leighton in his own unspecified bedroom somewhere along the corridor put Fenner slightly on edge. As in an aeroplane, he could not relax.

Fenner shook his head. Here he was in the familiar bedroom, greeted by his host and hostess, accepted by the staff. Here he would sleep the night. Here he was in the same room he had been in before. Some of the guests he might have met before. Everyone would be relaxed. This was a fine place for a spot of fun.

Though he would have to be careful.

Well, these upper-class prats have something to sneer at now, haven't they? These stupid jeans. Bloody soaking. I stand out like a brown ale at a vicar's tea party. All right, I'm not one of them. No way I could have pretended that I was. But I didn't have to dress like Charlie Chaplin.

Patterson pulls the steel-rimmed spectacles off his nose and cleans the lenses with his cuff. The damp woodland air seems attracted to the glass. Every hundred yards his spectacles mist over and obscure his view. If anyone is watching, the spectacles will symbolize how out of place Patterson is. But nobody is watching him. They are too polite.

Or if they *are* watching, it doesn't show.

Fenner sank into a bath deep with hot water. He stroked himself. On his lean body the blond hairs stood up in the water, waving like fronds of delicate yellow seaweed. When he sat up to reach for soap, a small wave rushed to fill the space he vacated. When he sank down again, clutching the slippery tablet, the water thrashed. Some sloshed over the side of the tub.

While he rubbed soap around his neck, Fenner smiled. It was only Leighton's carpet. It would easily dry out. To Fenner it seemed faintly provincial to have carpet in a bathroom. He preferred tiles. Carpet might be warmer to the feet, but that only mattered in cold bathrooms. The sort of people who would lay carpets rather than heat their bathrooms were middle class. The working class, after all, couldn't afford carpet in the first place. Certainly not in the bathroom, where it might get wet. Though from what Fenner had seen of working-class families on the television, that hardly rang true. They were more casual with their possessions than were the middle class. Fenner sniffed. What possessions the working class did have were not *worth* preserving – that was the truth of it. Where the rich could afford to be careless, the poor just did not care. Only the middle class cared about their things.

Fenner changed position in the bath, deliberately clumsily, and more water splashed over the side. Did Leighton have middle-class habits? It hardly seemed likely: his family went back for centuries. The beautiful Emily? She was well born herself. Yet one of them had acquired this middle-class liking for carpet beside the bath.

Fenner rocked forward and stood up. A swell of soapy water flung itself at the far end of the tub like a storm wave against a wall, then crashed down and rushed back along the bath, swirling past his pale legs to the other end. But with Fenner standing, the mean level of water had subsided. It did not spill over on to the floor.

When Fenner stepped out of the bath he stood dripping on the carpet. He dried slowly, paddling the wet woollen pile into a swampy mess at his feet. He regretted that he didn't smoke. Then he could have dropped a lighted cigarette and ground it into the floor.

Why was he thinking like this? He could cripple Leighton if he wanted to. If he ever opened his mouth about this weekend – if he told the truth, or even part of it – it would be the end for

Mr Leighton. Quite literally the end. Leighton had so much to lose. The house and land, passed down through generations of his family, would have to be sold. He would lose Emily, and she would keep the children.

Fenner wiped steam off the bathroom mirror and grinned at his reflection. That didn't bear thinking about, did it?

The sky is lightening. Weak sunlight filters low between the trees. On another brighter morning, this sunlight would seem sharp and piercing, bleaching the sides of the tree trunks, dazzling the sportsmen's eyes. This morning's feebler light is preferable. If a bird rises between the low hazy sun and the ends of their gun barrels, the hunters will not be blinded. They will stare the sun full in the face yet keep their aim.

Patterson is not used to early rising. If he ever wakes early in London he lies heavily in bed, blearily aware of cars taking people to work, children to school. When the rush hour has passed and the car noise has faded, Patterson's tired face emerges from the bed clothes, and he thinks about his breakfast.

Where's my coffee? he asks his room.

But sometimes even Patterson must rise early. He grumbles, but when it matters he can be punctual. Take this morning, for example. To shoot partridges you get up early. God knows why. The wretched birds flit around the fields all day long. They won't fly away. But this is how the hunting classes like it: they feel better if they suffer too.

Poor bloody partridges. What have they ever done?

At least they didn't eat partridge last night for dinner. To eat game in the evening and then to trek out next day to bag more is like topping up your larder. You must set out at dawn with the larder shelves empty, track down your quarry and bring the prize home. You can't expect to be welcomed home a hero if your larder is already stocked. You have to pretend you searched out these choice delicacies, that you outwitted and killed them, then brought them home. If all you catch is more of the same meat that you ate yesterday, you might as well have gone to a butcher's shop.

Emily had intended the night before the shoot to be an Italian evening. Game pie and hunters' soup were scheduled for *tomorrow* night after the day's exertions in the wild. For the first night roast beef would be boring, and every French dish that Emily knew deteriorated when bulked up into a canteen casserole. Cold buffet was out of the question. Pies sink and turn leathery. Some guests object to fish.

There was no fresh pasta, only dried.

How the shop in Cirencester could have run out of pasta was beyond her comprehension. Apparently the machine had broken down. A machine! In Italy, peasant women made pasta with just their fingers and a rolling pin. They didn't use a machine.

Fortunately, the butcher at the corner of the market place had prime condition lamb. Where fresh lamb came from in autumn was a question Emily didn't ask.

Crown roast of lamb with paper coronets. End of season mint sauce. Three varieties of potato. Exotic vegetables – of an Italian inclination.

For dinner parties the Leightons' house came into its own. Its panelled dining room was created for large numbers. In the centre stood a huge oak table. Around that table were hide-backed chairs. Behind the chairs and before the long serving tables lining the walls was a wide corridor for the staff to move in. Village girls in Laura Ashley cotton swept along with dishes of food. The butler had ensured that they all knew what to do.

Patterson sat admiring the large oak table. He gripped its top between thumb and fingers to gauge its thickness, then slipped his hand underneath to see whether it remained the same thickness or was simply panel board bulked out at the rim. He pushed his hand forward as far beneath the table as it would go, until the inside of his elbow came up against the rim. All the way in, the wood felt one solid piece. There were several sections – vast slabs of dark oak bolted together. But each slab, he thought, would need a house this big to squeeze through the dining room door.

From time to time he glanced at the horsy-looking woman beside him, watching how she ate. Patterson's table manners did not come naturally. He had no social poise. No matter how he tried to hold the heavy silver cutlery in his fists, he could not relax at it. As he watched the other diners ripping into their crown roast of lamb, he thought it might be easier if he gave up trying to eat nicely and just ate. That was what the others seemed to do. They didn't manipulate their cutlery. They didn't even keep their mouths shut while they chewed. Bad manners looked all right on them.

Patterson realized that he had been placed at the low end of the table, away from family and friends. Obviously Leighton had not mixed the classes in his seating plan. Guests that Leighton would not normally dine with had been seated furthest away. But at least everyone shared the same large table. Here at the bottom end Patterson was tucked away beside a thin farmer and the horsy woman who hardly spoke. Beyond her was a businessman in a suit.

At the far end John Leighton sat beside his wife. Shouldn't she be down at my end? Well, she wasn't. Host and hostess sat side by side among their friends, laughing and talking, enjoying their meal. Whatever they were saying was drowned in the jabber along both sides of the dark table. John Leighton chatted to a thin, regal matron with grey swept-back hair. Mrs Leighton shared a joke with that blond prat who Patterson had met on arrival – the man who drove the Jag.

Fenner smiled at Emily's witticism and glanced down along the table. He saw Patterson watching him. His smile froze.

Because Fenner did not look away, Patterson stared back.

Beneath a tall plane tree, Fenner pauses to wait for stragglers. Several men are out of breath. Their feet catch in low brambles. But Fenner is feeling fitter now: up to the mark.

Among the stragglers he sees Michael Patterson stumbling
along morosely, eyes fixed on the ground. The man looks so
out of place. He is perspiring, and now the stupid great oaf
has pulled off those pathetic spectacles and is rubbing them
dry on a dirty white handkerchief. Why did he agree to
come? He obviously hates it here.

Presumably the thought of a weekend among the nobs was
too good to miss. See how the other half lives. Perhaps
Patterson thought that some of the polish would rub off on
him. Perhaps he thought he would make new business
contacts. Whatever he thought, he'd be badly disappointed.
That was for sure.

He must have feared it would be this way. He could not
have *wanted* to come. Leighton must have been extra-
ordinarily persuasive.

A similar thought had occurred, idly, to Harriet Henderson
at dinner.

'What do you do exactly – back at home, I mean?'

'I'm self-employed.'

'At what – may I ask?'

'I'm in the removal business.'

'Oh.'

Oh, I see. He's in removals. I've never met one of those.
Though since our family hasn't moved house for two
hundred years, I don't suppose I would have done. But
neither have the Leightons. They can't be moving now, can
they?

No, quite impossible. Anyway, they'd hardly invite the
removal man to dinner. So why is he here? Unless he *paid* for
this weekend. But John told me specifically that he wouldn't
sink to that: filling the house with *nouveaux* who have paid to
join a shoot. I can't see his objections, myself: damn good
money, quickly made. Just wish I had the land. God, six
weekends a year, and you hardly have to mix with them. It's
easier than breeding dogs.

'Have you known John long?'

'John?'

'John Leighton.'

'Oh. No, not very long.'

Clearly. Well, I think you paid for this, my man. I think John is introducing selected punters, to try out on the rest of us. What a cheek. He could at least keep them separate from his friends.

Harriet studied the other diners. This man next to me in the pale suit and loud tie. Middle class. Two more at least are businessmen. Nothing unusual in that, I suppose. There always have to be *some* commercial people – the bank manager, stockbrokers, people that you owe favours to, people you want in your debt. It must be so with Mr Patterson. Perhaps John is having trouble with some tenants and wants Patterson to move them out. It could be that.

He still seems an odd sort of man to invite on a shooting party. Perhaps John owes him a favour – though I can't imagine what. He hates being in someone's debt.

Emily was wondering the same. That large person sitting beside Harriet seemed a most unsuitable man. Though nowadays John had peculiar business colleagues. Perhaps he had fallen into some kind of sordid mess with this man – borrowed money from him or something. It was possible. Anything was possible. Recently he had been distracted, absent.

But they both had. They were growing apart.

Outwardly affable and enjoying his meal, John Leighton, from the corner of his eye, could not help watching Michael Patterson. It was the way the man handled his cutlery. It had not occurred to Leighton that anyone nowadays could be so inept. Yet it was not from carelessness. Anyone could see that Patterson ate with enormous care. He was painstaking in his handling of knife and fork. Beside him, Harriet Henderson stabbed at her meat using only her fork in the American style. Yet she did it elegantly. Five hundred years of breeding, of course. God knows who Patterson's antecedents were.

It had been obvious from the start that this man Patterson was an uncultured type, yet somehow up in London he had had a kind of style. A rough diamond, as it were. When Leighton had asked him down for the weekend he hadn't realized that Patterson would be such a misfit. He didn't want the man to stand out like this. People might comment on it, especially afterwards. Why did Leighton invite the man, someone might ask.

Leighton glanced at Barry Fenner. He caught that half smile which kept appearing on Fenner's face – that supercilious, confident smile that in repose was becoming his usual expression. When Leighton had first been introduced to Fenner, he had seemed distant and polite – though Fenner's eyes, Leighton remembered, gave him away. They didn't smile. There was nothing soft below his charm.

There wouldn't be, Leighton thought.

Now, not only did Fenner wear that infuriating half smile, but he was bending his blond head again towards Emily. He was almost flirting with her. Leighton flushed. We'll have none of that. If Fenner thinks I can't say anything to him, he's mistaken. I will not stand for that.

He has stopped it now. Just as well. But it wasn't because he saw me watching him. He and Emily had some momentary togetherness over a joke. I over-reacted. Because I'm on edge. I couldn't really cause a fuss at my own dinner table. Not with all these people here.

But Fenner had better not exchange any more glances with Emily.

I think John saw that look, Emily thought. I saw his colour rise. How quickly he gets angry nowadays. So easily aroused – to anger, that is.

For a few seconds she sat with eyes cast down, a wistful expression on her face as the plates were cleared away. The slight intrusion of serving girls leaning between the diners allowed everyone to break their earlier conversations and begin anew. Emily turned and leant across to ask Mrs

Battheson about her camellias. A dull but undemanding monologue. Mrs B could ramble on for hours.

'Our camellias', Emily said, 'are quite hopeless. The soil is limy here, you see.'

'Oh, you can overcome that, my dear. No problem at all. Let me tell you how to do it. Shall I?'

Drone on, you bat. Will this meal never end?

Dessert had barely been scraped from the bowls when Emily rose abruptly to her feet.

'Shall we retire, ladies? While the men cut their revolting cigars.'

Several women glanced at their husbands. Others clambered dutifully to their feet. Harriet Henderson declared that she would stay to take a brandy. It was the best part of the meal.

'Of course, Harriet, you must do as you like. If anyone else wants to join Harriet, do please feel free. Though I'm afraid the men will fill the room with smoke.'

'So will I,' said Harriet. 'I like a good cigar.'

Patterson watched, amused, as each of the ladies with varying degrees of willingness pushed back their chairs and followed Emily from the room.

'Good for you,' he murmured, leaning towards Harriet. He was glad to see someone flout house rules. That Leighton woman was too used to having things her own way. Several women had not expected to leave the table. One had been eating her dessert. Mrs Leighton had caught them all on the hop, and had loved doing so. She behaved as if it were still perfectly normal for ladies to sail out of the room and wait somewhere while their men dug into liqueurs. People did things *her* way at Nob Hall.

And I wasn't the only one surprised. A woman up there was goggle-eyed, as if she'd just found out that she'd come to the wrong party but it was too late to back out. *She* didn't know that nobs behaved like this either. She thought all that had gone out with World War Two.

Mind you, I bet it's only local rules: this is how the

Leightons behave. But just because it's how they do
things here in Gloucestershire doesn't make it right. I
mean, put that woman in a public bar in Catford, then see
how she'd cope. She'd be as much a lemon there as I am
here.

Home is best.

Their pause among the trees becomes a wait. The dogs lie
down. John Leighton confers with his beaters, one of whom
wets his finger and holds it in the air. He and Leighton stare
irritably at the damp grey sky.

Harriet finds herself close to Mr Patterson, and she asks
him how he finds the day. He smiles at her. She is still the
only person who will talk to him from choice.

'Is it your first time out?' she asks.

'Does it show?'

'You'll soon get the hang. Once you see the birds rise, once
you've fired a round or two, it will all seem different. You
won't forget this day. Carry home a brace of birds, and you
carry the memory with you. At odd times you'll find yourself
thinking back to this cool damp morning, to the smell of wet
leaves, the stalk to kill. This is something you'll remember to
the end of your days.'

'Dare say you're right.'

'And you won't feel the cold when the shooting begins,
though I'm glad we had that snort of brandy before we left.
You like a drop of brandy, don't you, Mr P?'

Last night at dinner, most of the ladies had left in a flurry of
female rising, a rustling of silk and satin, an invisible,
unavoidable cloud of expensive perfumes – the women, that
is, who submitted to Emily's half-command, with the exception of Harriet, and a fishlike old soak enmeshed halfway up
the table. Then John Leighton had told his staff – the
permanent retainers and the hired help from the village – to
serve port, brandy and a choice of cigars.

Patterson ignored the port. During the meal he had sipped
without interest at the wines, as if drinking brown ale. But

when the brandy arrived, he poured a glass and raised it towards Harriet. 'Happy days.'

'Bottoms up.'

'D'you want a drop more? You couldn't drown a fly in that.'

'This is quite all right.'

'Go on, have a taste of it. It's what you stayed for, after all.'

Patterson doubled the small quantity at the bottom of Harriet's brandy balloon. 'That's better,' he said. 'It was only a dirty glass before.'

Harriet raised her drink. 'We needn't wait till everyone's filled their glass.'

'No?'

'This is an informal affair.'

'Could have fooled me.'

Patterson lifted his glass in a large hairy hand and clinked it against Harriet's. 'Here's *to* yer,' he said.

They both drank. As they returned their glasses to the table, Patterson winked.

'A fine Cognac,' said Harriet.

Patterson paused for a moment, then leant closer to whisper. 'Yeah, very nice, but it's not Cognac.'

'Not Cognac?' She tried to match Patterson's discreetly low tone, but surprise would not let her. Harriet rarely spoke quietly.

'No, it's Armagnac. It's a brandy – you know, French and all that – but it's not technically Cognac. Armagnac. Different region. Just as good.'

'Armagnac?' Several people were listening to them now.

'Yeah. Made by Salas, I should think.'

The surprise had left Harriet's face. In the world of dog breeding she often found expertise to lie in the least likely of people. That this unprepossessing hulk of a man could tell Armagnac from Cognac was quite plainly true. It would be foolish to doubt him.

'Do you collect Armagnacs – do you specialize?'

'I used to run a pub.'

*

Fenner, rummaging beneath his silk pyjamas in the bottom
of his suitcase, took out his flask. Funny thing, Patterson
knowing the difference between Cognac and Armagnac.
Fenner unscrewed the silver lid and sniffed at the contents.
Was this Cognac or Armagnac? Fenner had assumed it was
Cognac, because brandy always was. But Patterson had
made him wonder. Which was he drinking?

He should ask Patterson.

Fenner replaced the lid on his flask without taking a drink,
and considered his pyjamas. Would he need them tonight?
He placed them on the bed.

For a moment Fenner stood undecided in the centre of the
room. At the back of his mouth he could still taste his dinner:
charred lamb and mint sauce. He took off his tie.

After he had dropped it like a dead snake upon his bed,
Fenner closed the almost empty suitcase. He lifted it down
and slid it across the carpet to the corner of the room.
Waiting in that corner was the other item of his luggage: a
fleece-lined, soft leather gun slip, zipped, with carry handles
and shoulder straps.

Fenner picked up the bag, unzipped it, and took out his
shotgun. It was an AYA 53 sidelock, with 28-inch chopper-
lump English ribbed barrels and a walnut stock. The gun was
hand-finished with traditional game chokings, a gold-plated
interior and an action decorated with foliate scrollwork. It
had cost a good deal of money. On the shoot tomorrow
morning there would almost certainly be other AYAs, but
they would be Countrymen, not the prestigious 53. Fenner
checked the gun over, weighing it in his hands. It was empty
and clean. In the soft leather gun slip, snug and protected in
a separate compartment, were three dozen cartridges. There
was also a full 12-bore cleaning kit – the mop, the brush, the
jag and bronze, some oil, a duster and the three-piece set of
rods. Fenner ignored them.

From an inner pocket in the fleece lining he took out a
small red-and-white striped rag. It was attached to a piece of
cord with a small weight at the other end. Fenner cocked the
hammer on his gun, dropped the smooth little weight into

the back of one chamber, and let it slip through to the other end of the barrel. Where it emerged he pulled it to drag the cleansing rag through. He repeated this with the other barrel. Then he held the gun with the butt pointed to the electric light on the ceiling, and squinted up inside each barrel. Both were spotlessly clean. He lowered the gun. With the chambers empty, Fenner cocked the gun and fired. He listened to the action. He rested his cheek against the cold metal and sniffed at the oil.

That should do it, he thought.

Fenner replaced the gun carefully in its slip and laid it on the floor. Then he went to the bathroom and cleaned his teeth. Vigorously.

John Leighton's teeth had been worrying him for some time. Two of his crowns had worked loose. He had noticed the change in the first one some weeks ago. While he ate the crown behaved itself, but when he cleaned his teeth it rocked slightly under the toothbrush. Now a second one was wobbling. Leighton had the uncomfortable feeling that below the unstable crowns his natural teeth were decomposing. He would have to visit his dentist. With luck he might be able to have both crowns adjusted and refitted. There should be no need for false teeth. He was still young. Fairly young.

He climbed into bed and picked up a book. It was a finely bound Folio edition of *Undertones of War* by Edmund Blunden. There were pictures, grey and depressing. The words made no sense.

Leighton tossed the book down beside him on the bed. He knew what was wrong. He was trying not to think about tomorrow, but the more he tried to avoid the thought, the more strongly it returned. It would not be suppressed. Leighton was reminded of his recent visit to Lake Orta: he had been to Milan in an unsuccessful attempt to sell some horses, and had spent a further consolatory day on Lake Orta. While standing at the peaceful lakeside he had wanted to photograph a particular effect of sunlight rippling across the clear waters. For his intended composition, a small wooden jetty formed an excellent foreground. It had just the right air of Italian neglect. But every time Leighton prepared to take the photograph someone would walk in his way. The people interrupting his shot were not tourists – they lived there. Tourists don't go to Lake Orta. But although these people lived on the lakeside – there was an old lady, two fishermen, an angular man in a suit – they jarred in Leighton's landscape. He did not want them. They did not belong in the picture he was trying to create. Yet they were indigenous. Leighton wanted to create an idealized landscape, sunlight and nature, peaceful cold water, but these intruders would slip into his frame. One of the fishermen saw Leighton standing there fiddling impatiently with his camera, but instead of withdrawing from view, the man tapped his companion on the arm, pointed at Leighton, and grinned at him posing for the snap.

Leighton abandoned his photograph.

Here in the quiet bedroom the thought of tomorrow stuck in the forefront of Leighton's mind as solidly as had that fisherman on the lakeside. The thought grinned at him mockingly. Leighton picked up his book again. He turned the pages without looking at them. He knew he would not sleep. It was ridiculous. After all, it wasn't as if he was going to do the job himself: he would simply be there on hand to see it done.

Leighton knew that the reason the thought kept returning to him was that he was worried something might go wrong. It shouldn't, of course. He had paid well enough. But it might. The main thing, if that did happen, was to make absolutely certain – by the way he reacted, by where he positioned himself – that nothing could be linked back to him. If there *was* a blunder – some accident, in the true sense of the word – he must dissociate himself entirely. That should not be difficult. He had only to behave as the others did – displaying shock or outrage as the accident merited – and he could leave the mess to sort itself out.

Leighton shook his head at the prospect. There must be no

mistake: the consequences were too appalling to contemplate. There must not and there would not be any
mistake. He had engaged a professional, after all.

Fenner had decided to wear his silk pyjamas. He had
brought them, they suited him, and he liked the feel of silk to
sleep in. Later in the night he could take them off.

Patterson wore old-fashioned striped pyjamas tied with a
cord around his belly. In his own bed at home he preferred to
sleep naked, unencumbered by folds of flannel around his
crotch. But he had an image of country houses as being large,
cold and draughty, with uncomfortable beds and central
heating that didn't work. He had brought the pyjamas to
keep warm. Besides, he couldn't be sure what the toilet
arrangements might be. On the one hand, the house might
be like a posh hotel, where every bedroom had its own
bathroom – a basin, at any rate – or the rooms might share
facilities down the hall. Knowing the way that British hotels
compared to foreign ones, Patterson did not expect a private
bathroom. And if he was going to have to traipse along the
corridor for his last midnight pee, he would need warm
pyjamas. A dressing gown as well. But in his neat little
suitcase there wasn't room for a dressing gown. He hadn't
wanted to bring the big case – the one he took on holiday –
because it wouldn't look right for just a weekend. The
overnight one should see him through.
   Snug and secure in the bulky pyjamas, Patterson felt
comfortable in the bed. A good-sized one, as it turned out.
Private bathroom after all. I bet in some of these old houses
they wouldn't have put the en-suites in: spoil the character,
they'd have said. None of that nonsense here.
   Patterson lay contentedly on his back, reading *The Sporting
Life*. Now, here was real sport: horses, dogs and football –
not this daft business of popping shotguns at unarmed birds.
Shooting game wasn't sport to Michael Patterson. Not that
he knew much about it. Shooting parties on country estates

wasn't the kind of thing he was invited to. But there had to be a first time for everything. Funny the things life threw up.

After a few minutes, Patterson finished his paper and dropped it on the floor beside the bed. He switched off the light. Warm in his belly was an afterglow of brandy. Two glasses of wine he'd had, then the large Armagnac. Moderation, that's the key. Just enough to guarantee a restful night.

John Leighton tossed restlessly beneath his blankets. It might be October, and a fairly miserable one at that, yet the room seemed so hot tonight, close and shut in. Emily had said it was because he would persist in having blankets on his bed. She preferred a duvet. But on those occasions – few enough nowadays – when he did pass a night with his wife beneath her duvet, he found her feather-filled covering more claustrophobic than his blankets. A duvet might feel light and airy, but it trapped the heat. He didn't like the things.

Perhaps I should pop along to visit Emily? I'd better not. It's after midnight: she's probably asleep. I suspect that at this time of night she would not welcome my advances. It's hardly a month since that night when I tapped on her door at midnight, and she wouldn't let me in. She called through the door that I had only come because I couldn't sleep; that I only wanted her as a sedative.

What a thing to say! It wasn't true. I love my wife. I've tried to tell her, in my way. But a chap doesn't say such things – not an Englishman. You show your feelings in the things you do and in the way you behave. A woman can tell.

She could tell once. In our early days – just the two of us here, without children – Emily could tell then. I loved her, and she loved me. We both knew it. No one had to say the words.

But that night a month ago, when I bleated through her locked bedroom door that I loved her, she didn't believe me. Didn't believe me! How could she say that? Her own feelings may have cooled, but to impute the same to mine is unfair.

Have her feelings cooled? I suppose they have. I cannot hide from it. Perhaps it's just a phase. Women go through phases at Emily's age, don't they – when approaching forty?

Or does the menopause come later, when they are older? I'm not sure. It is not the kind of thing that I would know about. But without Emily, there is no one I can ask.

It was not the menopause that troubled Emily. The symptoms were unlikely to creep up on her for another ten years, and she certainly would not anticipate them. She sat with her ivory satin négligé draped about her fine shoulders, the matching ivory nightie chaste upon her breast, and she brushed her hair. Softly, she smiled into the mirror. To while away the dragging minutes, Emily had taken a leisurely bath, lying neck-deep in warm scented water, the bathroom shimmering with steam. Moist warm air pervaded her bedroom. Emily checked her watch.

She paused, with the hairbrush in her hand. Perhaps her hair was too long when she wore it down? At dinner she had worn it elaborately styled. Such pretence. Wouldn't it be better to admit her age, to succumb to simpler styles? So much time now devoted to her appearance: wearing contact lenses instead of glasses, because they might spoil her looks or leave a mark across her nose. Was all this necessary? No need for modesty: her looks were good, her carriage fine. Ah, that was it: her carriage fine. The description of a mature woman. Mature. She looked mature. She even sounded mature. For much of the time Emily spoke with her voice little above a murmur, attractively husky, seldom raised. One could so easily sound strident.

When she had married John Leighton a dozen years ago, he had seemed dashing, rich, considerate: what more could a girl desire? And in truth he *was* dashing – as far as any husband could be, after the honeymoon had waned. He was less rich than she had thought, but there were assets he could sell if the need arose. He remained considerate.

Throughout their twelve years together John had hardly changed. But Emily had. Living in the country had made her dull. Increasingly in recent years Emily found that she ordered John around. She caught an occasional bossiness in her voice – the tone that an actress might use to portray a memsahib in India. Isolated here in John's big house, high in the Gloucestershire hills, was a little like living in the colonies. Emily dreaded that she might become like one of those bored colonial wives in Maugham or Paul Scott. (Though she never read Paul Scott, she had seen his *Raj Quartet* on TV.) She thought how terrible Scott's women were. She could not end up like that.

As she raised her hairbrush once again to her tumbling hair, she heard the gentle rap of a man's fingernails at her bedroom door. Emily rose from her dressing table, slipped across the room and turned the handle. The door had not been locked.

When Barry Fenner came in, his only words before he kissed her were, 'Hello again, my sweet.'

'Any moment now,' Harriet whispers. They are at the edge of the woodlands. Unsuspecting birds prowl the fields: ungainly, without the energy to lift fat bodies off the ground.

'You go ahead,' Patterson mutters in her ear. 'I'm not used to this. Don't want to distract you.'

Harriet turns to smile in his face. 'You won't. Just follow me.'

Harriet gives another encouraging smile, then turns to peer across the field. Among the last thinning trees, two beaters have moved forward. This will be the third volley of the morning. It will be the last.

Everyone is eager to make this broad green field a cornucopia. Pheasants and partridges strut about the rough grass like chickens in a farmyard: like chickens, they have only recently been released from the hutches they were reared in.

Slightly ahead of the shooting party, where everyone can see him, John Leighton holds position. He bites his lip. A few yards off, Barry Fenner smiles in anticipation. He sees the clumsy Patterson frowning at his shotgun as if he has picked it up for the first time in his life. He sees Harriet leaving Patterson. He sees her drift forward with the others through the trees. Then he follows.

As the silent hunters raise their shotguns, the two beaters rush forward on to the edge of the large damp field. Birds rise, squawking, into the sky. Several large birds cannot lift themselves off the meadow. They run in panic as if they have forgotten how to use their wings. From a dozen shotguns comes a blast of gunfire. Birds and feathers fall from the sky.

Patterson waits four yards behind the party. Fenner has this time placed himself a yard apart from his companions. As the hunters blast a second time into the flock of partridges screaming above the grass, Patterson empties a single shell into Fenner's back.

No one sees him fall. He does not cry out. Patterson swiftly breaks open his gun, slips a fresh cartridge into the chamber to replace the one he used, then closes the gun and flicks the safety on. Gliding forward to rejoin the others, Patterson lets his face reassemble into the mild perplexed expression it has worn all morning.

'Someone's down!' a man's voice calls.

The birds fly shrieking. Two last shots ring out. Slowly, people turn and glance around. As they begin to scramble through the undergrowth to the fallen Fenner, Michael Patterson squints down at his gun. Two cartridges lie unused in the chambers. I haven't fired my gun yet, he might say. It wouldn't work. Someone will spot that he still has the safety on.

'I think he's dead.'

By now most of the party is crowded round the body. Fenner is lying motionless on his front. In the centre of his back a dark red stain spreads damply around the torn hole in his green jacket.

'You don't think—'

'Of course he's dead,' snaps Harriet.

'Oh my God,' John Leighton says without emotion. 'Oh dear, oh dear. It's a terrible tragedy, I'm afraid.'

He thinks of Emily, and of how he'll break it to her. 'I have bad news,' he'll say. 'One of our guests has met with an accident. You must brace yourself, my dear.'

DR BUD, CA

Michael Z. Lewin

'I can't get over what a *beautiful* residence decision you made here,' Dr Bud said.

'I'm so pleased you like it,' Mr Mallory said.

'It's how old?'

'Oh, only late Victorian.'

'Victorian . . . Wow! That's hundreds of years old, right?'

'About a hundred, yes.'

'A hundred years old,' Dr Bud said. 'Back home I have a patient in my rebirthing class who is ninety-two, but Victorian . . . That seems so much . . . so much older, you know?'

'A patient, sir?'

'Well, I qualified as a dermatologist,' Dr Bud said, 'but right from the start I had no intention of being culturally impeded by my training. I'm into quite a few redirections so now I'm only a dermatologist by day.'

'And what might you be by night?' Mr Mallory asked.

'Ha ha, that's a good one,' Dr Bud said. 'I always heard how dry you Brits are and you sure do live up to it.'

Mr Mallory redirected himself. 'How long are you planning to be with us, doctor? The note I saw by your reservation indicated you were uncertain when you booked.'

'The person I spoke to . . . She was very helpful and knowledgeable, by the way. Was that your significant other?'

'My . . . ah, my wife. Yes.'

'Well, she said it didn't matter if I didn't make up my mind until the impulse took me.'

'It's not vital, no.'

'Ah, "vital". Not "vital". That was the word she used too. You must be on a very harmonious and resonant wavelength, the two of you. You've been married a long time, I bet. Am I right?'

'Thirty-two years,' Mr Mallory felt forced to admit.

'Oh, well done,' Dr Bud said. 'Congratulations. I doubt I'll ever even dream of that. In this day and age it's nearly a record. I bet you don't have any friends who have been married longer than that, do you?'

'I'm sure there are still many, many people with long marriages.'

'And modest with it. I do envy you. My own first wife took off after twenty-eight months. I say first not because I have a second one yet, but because I believe in an optimistic attitude to life and relationships.'

'So you aren't yet certain about your length of stay?' Mr Mallory said.

'I'm just going to stay here as long as it takes. You have plenty of room at this time of year. That's what Ms Mallory said. Or did she keep her maiden name? Not that I'm prying about whether she was a maiden.'

'We do have only one other guest at the moment,' Mr Mallory said. 'And it is normally a quiet season for us.'

'All the Americans have gone home by now, right?'

'We do enjoy the company of many visitors from abroad, happily.'

'I know. That's how I got your phone number. Friends of mine stayed here two years ago and when they heard I was looking for somewhere in England to restore my inner harmony they said they had just the place. The Rohrmanns? Do you remember them? Chuck and Sophie? Fabulous couple. Fabulous.'

'I'm not sure that I do. But I don't have the best memory for names.'

'Sea salt,' Dr Bud said.

'Pardon?'

'For the memory. Tops up your trace elements.'

'I'll try to remember that.'

'*Remember!* Ha ha! You guys are a hoot.'

Mr Mallory said, 'Would you . . . care to see your room now?'

'Yeah, good idea,' Dr Bud said. 'It's going to be an important space for me. To tell you the truth, why I'm in England is that I've had a prolonged emo-psychic displacement following the non-equal cessation of a major long-term-oriented relationship.'

'Oh.'

'What I need to do is work as hard as I can to get in touch with myself.'

'My headmaster said it makes you go blind,' Mr Mallory said.

'What?'

'But he may have got it wrong, of course. Would you care to step this way?'

Dr Bud did not return to the lobby until after nine, and when he did he found Mr and Mrs Mallory watching television behind the door marked 'Private'.

'Oh, there you are,' Dr Bud said,

Mr Mallory rose. 'Is there some problem?'

But Mrs Mallory patted the cushion beside her on the settee and said, 'Sit down. I've heard so much about you. Turn the television off, Geoffrey.'

Mr Mallory sat down again and by remote control silenced the television sound while leaving the picture.

'I've been hunting everywhere for your other guest,' Dr Bud said. 'In case he or she might want someone to talk to or go for a walk with. It's such a beautiful night. When I came out of my trance I was nearly overcome just looking out the window.'

'Alas,' Mrs Mallory said, 'Mr Baker always stays out past midnight when he's with us. He's a salesman, and he entertains. He's been with us many times and we know his routine. Then when he does return he goes straight to bed.'

'Might you like a walk? Or Mr Mallory? He told me about your marriage by the way. Congratulations!'

A quick look from Mrs Mallory was answered by her husband's shrug. She said, 'There's always Andrew. He loves to go out.'

'Andrew?' Dr Bud said.

'But it depends how you feel about animals.'

'I feel they have every right to co-exist with us in their natural state. As far as humans are concerned, might does not make right, in my opinion.'

'So you don't approve of pets?'

'Animal companions?' Dr Bud said. 'Oh, I try to keep an objective view about situations of inter-species relationship which can be mutually beneficial.'

'What she's asking is whether you fancy walking the dog,' Mr Mallory said without turning from the television screen.

The dog – Andrew – was more interested in running than in walking and controlling him – it – took more physical than psychic strength. The longer the outing went on, the more Dr Bud marvelled at Andrew's energy. He began to muse upon whether Andrew might, in fact, be morbidly hyperactive.

Dr Bud's attempts at one-on-one communication with Andrew were not well received. The dog did not bite, but neither would it remain forehead-to-forehead with Dr Bud long enough for the two creatures to share bio-electrical interaction.

Nevertheless Dr Bud began to formulate a therapeutic plan for Andrew, because the longer he remained on the restraining end of the extendable lead, the more certain he was that Andrew was not in a peaceful relationship with his environment.

'I warned you he was quite a handful,' Mr Mallory said when Dr Bud returned, forehead glistening with perspiration.

'I'd like to get to know him better,' Dr Bud said. 'I sense his inner-caninity is out of balance, and I'd enjoy the opportunity of seeing if I can restore some of his equipoise. There'll be no charge.'

Mr Mallory said, 'Have a word with Betty in the morning. He's her creature.'

Dr Bud felt that the casual ownership concept was a clue to Andrew's restlessness but he felt too tired to engage Mr Mallory immediately, so he smiled and waved good night.

Dr Bud rose at six-thirty with the brain-brightness of re-newed purpose. At seven-thirty, confirmed in his existence by fifty minutes meditation and ten minutes wash and shave, he descended to the guest-house dining room.

'Good morning!' Betty Mallory said. 'Will you have some breakfast?'

'I will indeed,' Dr Bud said. 'But first will you hug me?'

'Pardon?'

'More than food I need to start each day with a good hug.'

'Oh,' Betty Mallory said. 'All right then.'

For a minute by the watch Dr Bud hugged her and cooed and chortled. She did her best.

When it was over she said, 'Now, what would you like to eat?'

But as Dr Bud considered his options, his concentration was interrupted by heavy footsteps behind him.

'Mornin',' said a round middle-aged man whose shirt parted below the button and above the belt to reveal his navel. The man touched Dr Bud on the shoulder, but passed by to give Mrs Mallory a wet kiss on the lips. 'How you doin' this a.m., Betty, love? Got your pan hot and ready for me?'

'Ready as ever,' Mrs Mallory said as the man released her and pinched a buttock.

'Let's see. Three eggs, scrambled. Fried bread. Black pudding. Fried mushrooms. Grilled tomatoes. Make it two of those big sausages I like. And four rounds of toast, don't spare the butter. Got it?'

'Got it,' Mrs Mallory said.

'I'll get it one of these days,' the man said, winking and pinching Mrs Mallory's other buttock. He turned to Dr Bud. 'They may hold out for a while, but nobody resists me forever. Persistence. It's the secret of my success. Winthrop Baker. How d'you do?'

It was just then that Mr Mallory entered the kitchen from the back garden. He was obviously upset. 'Andrew's dead,' Mr Mallory said. 'He's been strangled.'

Saying that it was a matter of respect for Andrew's departed life-force, Dr Bud remained at the guest-house all day. But in truth he was too upset to do anything else.

His upset began to melt into anger as time passed and no policeman appeared. Cops are cops, national boundaries notwithstanding, Dr Bud thought. Now if it had been a *man* strangled, they'd have fallen over themselves to get here when they'd been rung. But because it was 'only' a dog . . . However, Dr Bud knew himself well enough to know that his anger was not one of the constructive forces in the universe. With colonic irrigation not at present a practical option, Dr Bud sat – cross-legged, eyes open, and totally still – on the 'private' sitting room floor.

The law did not, in fact, arrive until late in the afternoon, and even then the young constable who did appear confided that she was only able to investigate the crime because other criminal activity in the city was slack.

'Did anyone have anything against Andrew?' WPC Vanda Graff asked the Mallorys.

Mr Mallory recalled slighting comments from a neighbour up the hill, comments muttered one afternoon as he passed the neighbour, Andrew straining at his lead. 'And I don't even know the man,' Mr Mallory said. 'He moved in about five years ago and those were the first words we ever exchanged.'

'Exchanged?' WPC Graff said. 'Does that mean you spoke to him as well?'

'I told him to mind his own business,' Mr Mallory admitted. 'It was only a week ago, only a few days after we got Andrew, and now *this*.'

'It does seem quite a concidence,' WPC Graff said. 'I'll have a word with your neighbour.'

'Good,' Mr Mallory said.

'I can't think of anybody who had a grievance against Andrew,' Betty Mallory said. 'I've racked my brain all day long, but I can't think of a single person.'

Dr Bud said, 'Mmmmmmmmmmm.'

'What was that?' WPC Graff said.

'Mmmmmmmmmmmm.'

The constable looked at the two guest-house proprietors. 'Is he a hippie or something?'

'American,' Mrs Mallory said.

'Dermatologist,' Mr Mallory said. 'By day.'

'Ah.'

And just then Dr Bud rose from his cross-legged position on the floor. He blinked his eyes three times and he said, 'If I were you, I'd look in the bedroom of Winthrop Baker.'

'You would?' WPC Graff said.

'I would.'

'And why would that be, sir?'

'To find what you seek,' Dr Bud said.

Andrew's collar was discovered beneath Baker's clean underpants.

At first WPC Graff suspected that Dr Bud had put it there himself. Fortunately for Dr Bud, WPC Graff handled the collar with textbook care and the forensic laboratory found clear fingerprints on it belonging to Winthrop Baker. Confronted with the evidence Baker confessed.

His story was that from childhood he had suffered from an uncontrollable fear of dogs. His occupation as a salesman required that he treat life with bluff and bluster, but whenever confronted by a dog – especially a large one – he went weak at the knees.

Throughout his sales area he had discovered congenial guest-houses where the owners were dogless. Then, between his last visit and this, to his dismay the Mallorys had acquired Andrew.

But by the time he discovered the change in circumstances he had already checked in and, as always, he had a tight schedule and a strict routine. Besides, he liked the guest-house. He liked the Mallorys. The ancient city always pro-vided him with good business. What *was* he to do? With so few options, he could think of only one solution. And he took it.

WPC Graff's investigation, however, revealed that Baker had committed similar crimes before. Not only was he afraid of dogs, he had an irrational compulsion to rid the world of them.

Baker was taken away in handcuffs, begging for the chance to submit to therapy.

WPC Graff would only say, 'That's for the judge to decide.'

When it was all over the Mallorys went straight to Dr Bud. 'But how did you know?' they both asked.

'Life', Dr Bud said, 'is all about finding a way to stay in harmony with nature. Winthrop Baker was obviously a disturbed person.'

'He was?' Mr Mallory said.

'Oh yes. Obviously.' Dr Bud turned to Betty. 'But you knew that, didn't you, Ms Mallory?'

But Mrs Mallory shook her head.

'Think of that breakfast he ordered! "Three eggs, scrambled. Fried bread. Black pudding. Fried mushrooms. Grilled tomatoes. Make it two of those big sausages I like. And four rounds of toast, don't spare the butter."'

'What about it?' Mrs Mallory said.

'All the cholesterol. All the calories. It's a clear cry for help. Virtually a suicide attempt. Where I come from if someone went to a hotel and ordered a breakfast like that the waitress would play for time while the owner phoned for the town counsellor.'

Mr and Mrs Mallory stared at their guest. They looked at each other.

'Would you like to meditate with me?' Dr Bud said. 'We can do it right here. Come on. Each of you, give me a hand. Close your eyes.'

Despite themselves, the Mallorys each gave Dr Bud a hand.

FITTING UP STANLEY

Howard Douglas

It was a lovely plan, really it was. I'd got it all worked out. Everything was in place. Just a couple of hours' work and I could get Stan put away for a year or two leaving me with a clear run at his Janice. Of course, as it turned out maybe I'd planned it all a bit too careful. No room for contingencies. No room for manoeuvre if something should go wrong. And something did go wrong. Something bad.

I'm a villain. I don't deny it. I always have been. There's a lot of it about down our way. Villainy. I come from south of the river, south-east that is, and I stick to what I know – Bermondsey, Deptford, even out as far as Lee Green. Anywhere with a SE postcode. Keep to your own patch I always say. Keep it local and keep it small.

See, I've never gone for the big stuff. Nothing like banks or post offices. I've always stuck to the small job. Small to medium, but a lot of it. Working at the small end of the market you've got to do a lot to make a living at it. Cars, private houses and lock-ups generally. Maybe a factory office once in a while, but that's all. You don't want to stir it up too much. Do a bank and the filth are all over the shop asking questions and generally getting in everybody's way and annoying the locals. Eventually someone gets hassled too much and loses his rag and drops your name down someone's shell-like and there you are. Or there you aren't, so to speak.

But turn over a handful of nice posh detached houses a couple of times a week and nobody gives a monkey's.

Me, I've never been caught. Never. Never had my collar felt. Not once. Most villains have done some time, usually a few months on remand and then a suspended year, eighteen months. But it all counts. Your name's in the frame, your prints are on file and when Bill gets his lazy fat arse kicked by someone upstairs, he'll come looking for you. Because you're known. But not me. They never came looking for me. Nobody knew me because I hadn't been caught before, therefore I never get caught. It sounds stupid, but that's the way it works.

In general that is. Of course, if that's what happened every time no new villains would ever get nicked. It's that first pull that you have to avoid. My first was all a mistake. A big mistake.

I don't know how Janice and me got started. I'd known her for some time as Stan's wife. Stan was just one of the blokes down the pub. One of the boys. We weren't what you might call mates. We knew each other, even bought each other a pint or two from time to time, but that was all. I didn't see that much of Stan. Nobody did, not even Janice.

In fact, nobody really knew Stan very well. You see, he just wasn't around very much. He's a villain just the same as me except he's always getting caught. He gets caught because he's careless. And stupid. He's always leaving clues like bleeding great signposts and he likes to hold on to the goods for too long instead of getting shot of them. Because he's a known villain the Bill is always sniffing around and his house is usually chock full of gear.

I know we always knock them (you know the jokes: Question: what wears a blue uniform and has an IQ of 200: Answer: the Metropolitan Police!) but your average copper isn't dim. When he wants a few extra results on his sheet he'll go trawling round the likes of Stan until he scores. I reckon Stan was top of the list round our way. He always had a juicy something in the cupboard under the stairs just waiting for the filth to find. The local nick must have loved him.

Stan the Man he likes to be called round the pubs and clubs. Trouble is he don't spend enough time round the pubs and clubs for anyone to know him well enough to call him anything. I think even Janice had trouble remembering his name sometimes.

Janice was a tasty little piece. Small and foxy, blonde hair cut short, bright red lipstick and legs in black stockings that went up to her armpits. She was married to Stan but by this time she'd just about had enough of him being in and out of Her Majesty's lodgings and was casting her eye about for a bit of comfort. I was well pleased that her eye settled on me.

When Stan got himself banged up for a series of burglaries last year me and Janice had a bit of a fling. I've always got a bit of bees to put around and Janice liked being treated. She paid her way in her own fashion and I reckon I got the best end of the bargain. Money you can get anywhere but what Janice had to offer you don't find just everywhere. She had it and she knew it and she liked nothing better than to share it with someone who caught her fancy. She really fancied me. I don't think it was just the money.

We lived together for a while in her house. I must say it added a bit of spice being in Stan's bed. Very nice it was and we both felt it hard when Stan came out and I had to move back to my mum's flat. To start with it weren't too bad as we both assumed it would only be temporary and Stan would soon be back inside. But that's not how it turned out.

Either Stan had changed his MO or his luck had finally come through because he stayed around. A fortnight went by and Janice and I were beginning to think he'd gone straight or something. Of course he hadn't. He was still turning up down the pub with dodgy goods he wanted to shift. In the past he would have been lifted as soon as he hit the street with a bent VCR under his coat but not now. He was ducking and diving all over the shop with a car full of brown goods and a pocket full of readies and the law just looked the other way.

By the end of the month I was getting desperate. I missed Janice and thought about her all the time. Yes, phone calls are all very well but talking about doing it when you haven't got a chance of doing it and all the while some other greasy git is doing it is somewhat frustrating.

I even wrote her a few, what you might call, love letters, full of me telling her what I would like to do to her if Stan wasn't around. Basically I wrote about what we'd already been up to and told her how I wanted more of the same with variations. Looking back, I think those letters were a bit of a mistake.

My mind was all how's-your-father. I wasn't sleeping too well. I didn't eat. It got so bad that I was beginning to get careless in my work. I nearly got caught daydreaming through the Albermarle Estate with three camcorders in a holdall and a selection of other people's plastic in my pocket and I walked straight into a couple of woodentops looking greedy for a pull. I legged it through the underground car park and, there and then, decided that something had to be done and that something was Stan the Man.

Stanley had to go back inside. It was that, or him and me would have to sort it out face to face and Stanley was a big man. Big and mean. Violent too. I didn't reckon standing up in front of Stan and telling him I was after his Janice. Not if I didn't want to walk with a stick for the rest of my natural. No, the safest thing was to get Stanley safely tucked up in a nice cell away from society in general, and me and Janice in particular.

One lunchtime I was down the pub having a quiet drink with a geezer called Trevor something. Trevor is not the sort of bloke I would normally choose to drink with. In fact, I had been having a quiet drink on my own, dreaming about Janice taking her clothes off, when this Trevor had come in and interrupted Janice just as she was getting to the interesting bit. The bit where she'd take out the silk tie of mine that she'd taken a shine to and put her hands through the bars at the head of the bed with the silk across her wrists waiting to be tied and her body spread out creamy white, hot and inviting.

Trevor asked me what I was drinking and I near bit his head off. Trevor's not such a bad bloke – he bought me a drink and we had a moan about Charlton AFC and then I bought him one and we were getting well into how the country's going to the dogs when the door opened and Stan the Man walked in.

Now I didn't choke on my drink or make a rush for the door like you might think. If I even suspected that Stan knew I'd been up his missus I'd have been out of there like a shot. But I knew that Stan didn't have a clue. Luckily I hadn't said anything to Trevor as he'd like as not make some witty comment that would get my head caved in. Trevor finished his pint and bought another round including Stan in.

Stan was on Scotch which meant he was feeling chipper. He looked full of himself. Perhaps it was the effect of spending a whole five weeks in the open air. He seemed a bit jumpy and soon let us into the secret that he was planning a little excursion that night.

Talking too much in the wrong company was another of Stan's foibles and a contributing factor to his long list of previous. Everybody knew that Trevor wasn't averse to grassing if he could earn a few drinks for himself. You didn't hold it against him, you just kept your business to yourself when he was around. Never tell anyone anything is the rule. I know that Stan himself was as straight as a die but I wouldn't tell him what I was up to. Not just about Janice, I mean.

Stan was full of little hints and asides, talking a lot but not actually saying much. We found out that he was going to be out during the night and he would come back with a few tasty items. It could have involved him going down the curry house for a takeaway but in that company it meant he had some drum cased out and would be in, out and away like a sailor on shore leave. Casually I asked him how long a job it would be. At that moment my only thought was the chance of a quick one with Janice.

Stan savoured his whisky and said he'd be back home in the early hours. He puffed himself up and made some remark about his missus keeping the bed warm for him. I don't rate blokes who make smutty remarks about their women and this little comment and the little leer and the thought of him climbing in beside Janice made my mind up.

'I'll have you,' I thought to myself and started to work out how I could have him in one sense while having Janice in another.

I don't remember what we talked about after that as I was thinking about nothing except how I was going to put one over on Stan. It had to be something subtle. Something that would leave me well out of it. It was a puzzler. I didn't have any idea until Stan knocked back his one-for-the-road and, clapping us on the shoulders and calling out to the guvnor, went into the street. I watched his shadow pass across the old-fashioned frosted glass in the window and then he'd gone. I haven't seen him since.

Trevor said something about straining the greens and went out the back and then I saw the answer. On the stool next to Trevor's, where Stan had propped his fat arse, was the midday edition of the *Standard* and folded inside was Stan's fags, lighter and a little billfold. And all covered in Stan the Man's dabs.

I reckoned I'd got him. When Trevor came back I'd finished my drink and had Stan's stuff in my jacket pocket. I felt well pleased. If all went OK I could get Stan set up and have time for a slow one with Janice before midnight. I said my goodbyes and then, I couldn't help it, I said something along the lines of thinking of paying Stan's missus a visit as he was going to be out.

Trevor said that chance would be a fine thing and called up another pint. I went home.

So this was the plan: If Stan couldn't get caught by his own efforts I would give him a hand. Stan had told a known nark that he was about to be up to no good that night. I knew that Trevor would not be slow in coming forward if he thought the boys in blue might be in the market for a bit of gen. I had a nice little gaff lined up that was just the sort of place that would interest Stan. It had an alarm that wouldn't give me any trouble but would make Stan nervous – he didn't like electrics and his touch would be shaky after a handful of whiskies. All I was going to do was a little breaking and entering, made a little bit more tricky as I'd have to be as clumsy as Stan, nick a few items and leave Stan's wallet and snout in plain view. This might seem a bit too obvious but Stan had once legged it when an alarm went off forgetting he'd left his car round the corner with the keys in the ignition. Rumour has it that he got done for parking on a bus route without lights as well as the usual perm any eight from eleven from the felonies in the Theft Act.

I went home and watched TV until it got dark. I had a quick poke around in Stan's wallet with the end of a biro. The driving licence and income support giro both had his name and address in lovely clear printing. There was a little passport photo of Janice but she was squinting into the camera and had her clothes on so I left it. I had a bath, shaved and put on some clean duds. It was the sprauncest I'd ever gone out on a job. I thought of giving Janice a ring to give her time to work herself up for later but Stan hadn't said when he'd be leaving so I thought better of it. I left the flat in high spirits.

The job was a doddle. Some cheap-jack alarm system not much more use than those dummy ones they put on them houses you never dream of blagging. I mean, if they can't afford a proper alarm there won't be much inside worth having away. I'm a dab hand with locks and the back door would have given me no problems at all but I knew Stan was no expert. I'd brought a small square of carpet along and put it up against the glass in the door and punched the pane out. After three goes that is. The first time I didn't hit it nearly hard enough. I punched it again and the glass cracked and I split my knuckle open. The third time the glass went but so did another knuckle. I hoped it was going to be worth it.

The most difficult bit was deciding where to put the wallet and fags. First I put them on top of the television and then moved them to the kitchen. Then I had the idea of putting them on the window sill just inside the front door as if Stan had lit up a fag just before he left. I took the video, a camera and some jewellery. I left a couple of nice cut-glass decanters with silver handles and a lovely little oil painting with the idea of maybe coming back to get them at a later date. Stan wouldn't even have noticed them. As a final Stanleyesque touch I set the alarm off as I closed the front door.

I'd left my motor round the corner and within twenty minutes I was round by Stan's lock-up garage. Two minutes work on his puny Woolworths padlock and I was inside and tucking the goods away in a tea-chest against the back wall which would be an obvious place to look and therefore an obvious place for Stan to hide stuff. Ten minutes more and I'm outside Janice's.

All the lights were on but there was no answer to the doorbell. Stan's security at home was almost as good as the Mickey Mouse effort at his lock-up so half a minute with my plastic-coated Borough of Southwark library card and the latch was back and me inside.

Villainy affects everybody in different ways. The funny thing is that I'm as cool as a cucumber while I'm out on a job. A lot of boys lose it completely as soon as they've broken in, especially in flats where there's generally only one way in or out. They don't talk about it much but some villains don't get much further than just inside the back door before the old sphincter starts blowing kisses and then, if they've got any sense, they ought to back out and try again somewhere else when the old pump has stopped hammering away at their ribs. There's an old joke about the risk involved in being up to no good: when do you know when you're scared? When you find out that adrenalin is brown! Ask any of your friends who've had their drum turned over and, like as not, they can tell you whether chummy was nervous and what colour his adrenalin was. Wouldn't surprise me if the law haven't got a file of sphincter prints somewhere.

As I said, I'm generally OK when I'm actually lifting the gear but, like this time, the moment I'm back indoors safe and sound I get the shakes. Only for a minute or so, but I come over all hot and sweaty and I have to sit down or lean against a wall. Either that or I'd fall down. It's like a bad dose of the flu and for a few moments I can hardly breathe let alone speak. I don't mind admitting it. It's much better that it happens afterwards rather than halfway up a ladder carrying an armful of Georgian silver.

At that moment, as I'm leaning with my back against the front door, the bell goes. It made me jump and, thinking it was Stan come back, I was set to do a runner out through the back door when the flap on the letterbox was pushed up and someone said, 'Come on, Stanley. Open up.'

Well, if it wasn't Stan it could only be the Bill who would probably have someone waiting outside the back door anyway, so I fumbled with the lock and opened the door and found a big beefy geezer who seemed disappointed that I wasn't Stan. He introduced himself as DI Morris. He had a sergeant with him as well.

My shakes were subsiding but I was still sweating and I knew my face would be red. Morris gave me a funny look. He asked me who I was.

I didn't bother mentioning my name and said I was a friend of the family. By this time Morris and his sergeant were well inside the hallway. I was in no condition to stand on my rights, in fact I was having trouble standing at all. Morris motioned to the sergeant who went up the stairs and disappeared somewhere.

I was most impressed with the success of my plan. Not much more than half an hour after me setting Stanley up and here was London's finest in full cry.

The sergeant wasn't long. He came back to the head of the stairs and signalled the inspector to follow. It was amazing, they didn't seem to speak; it was all gestures and nods and winks. Morris grabbed my arm, not too gently.

Me and the inspector traipsed upstairs and into the bedroom. Janice's bedroom. Suddenly I stopped shaking. My sweat felt cold across my shoulders.

Across the bed lay Janice. Lovely Janice. Lovely, dead Janice. It was obvious what had happened, you didn't need to be Sherlock Holmes to work out she'd been knocked about and then strangled. The bruises on her white cheek and the silk tie, my silk tie, knotted around her neck were all the evidence anyone would need. Strewn across her and the bed and down on to the carpet was a scatter of ragged confetti. I looked at a piece on the carpet at my feet. It was a small fragment from one of my letters to Janice. One of the letters where I'd described my almost indescribable desires.

The sergeant went off to find a phone. Morris felt Janice's cheek with the back of his hand. He said she was still warm and called me a bastard. He wouldn't let me feel how warm she was. He asked me why I'd done it. I wasn't thinking straight. I felt a tear roll out of my eye. I said I didn't know.

That was it really. It looked to me like Stan had found the letters or the tie and had confronted Janice and then in a fit of jealousy had topped her. She'd once told me that he'd never hit her but she'd always known that one day he would.

Of course, Stan had the perfect alibi. I'd made sure of that. He was done for the burglary and, the bloody fool that he was, asked for fourteen others to be taken into consideration – including the gaff he actually did himself that night. The judge took his bereavement into consideration and awarded the smallest sentence he could – suspended. Stan didn't spend more than a couple of nights inside.

Me? What could I say? It all fitted. Trevor told the jury that I knew Stan would be out and he'd remembered me saying I was going round to 'see to' Janice. It was my tie round her neck and I had bruised knuckles. Then there were the letters. I didn't argue. I couldn't be bothered. Janice wasn't there any more and, as I said, Stan's a big, mean, violent bloke. I'm safer in here.

MANGROVE MAMA

Janwillem van de Wetering

Jamy is kind of foolish but I didn't think that he would kill his girlfriend Mangrove Mama. Still, Jamy said he did, staring at me with his twelve-year-old eyes. Jamy is close to forty, but spiritually retarded. He killed, he said, Mangrove Mama by kicking her in her pregnant belly. Unintentionally of course. He just happened to be emotionally upset at the time, and stoned on cocaine somewhat.

Circumstances have inadvertently come about making me Guardian of this Key. This Key is Egret Key, Florida, temporary heaven for the wealthy. Why me? I think a Guardian was needed and I looked like I could fill the vacancy. Nobody, of course, except soliciting TV preachers and fighting mullahs, ever dares look angels in the face, but if Nobody runs into me, Nobody might confuse this kindly and harmless old codger with that of an incarnate venerable power.

Hi! Jannie is the name. I was born in the Netherlands town of Rotterdam, emigrated along with my parents, made out OK as a small-time real estate tycoon in Boston.

Long years ago I retired here, on my acre estate facing Egret Cove and, on the horizon, Eagle Island. I came with my dear wife, who never liked me but got used to me, but she died, and my dear parrot, who never got used to me but learned to like me.

Lately Parrot no longer screeches when we meet but snuggles up on my shoulder, probes and nibbles my ear and gently, ever so gently, does his piped-down imitation of the neighbor's dog yapping.

'Arf arf arf,' Parrot goes softly, then pants: 'huh huh huh,' then breathes in sharply. I stiffen in fear, for a parrot's close-by screech easily punctures human ears, but no, Parrot's final chorus is a melodious 'arf arf arf' again.

Parrot was into his doggie act while drunken Jamy again admitted to doing away with long-legged highbreasted beautiful Mangrove Mama, mother of his unborn child.

'That's not good, Jamy,' I agreed, pouring bourbon. We had dined on chewy stone crabs, served with butter and French bread, followed by fluffy Key lime pie and Cuban coffee. We puffed Dominican cigars. 'Then what happened?' I asked.

Then, Jamy explained, Bad George, his skipper, and Sopwith, his servant, shouted 'Oooh' and 'Aaaah'.

The scene? Eagle Island, where Jamy resides in a look-alike T'ang Dynasty Buddhist temple, partly raised above a lagoon. Dolphins dally while Jamy dines. All of Eagle Island – after Jamy, three years back, had it razed of any wildlife – was arranged by Zen architect 'Goldy' Yamamoto for a cool million or two. The resulting luxury is grossly overdone, even along fabulous Key standards.

I avoid Eagle Island now. Its human refabrication looks distasteful to me. Inside the building an endless expanse of pastel-colored walls surround furniture carved out of elephant tusks upholstered with snow-tiger skins. Jamy runs a wooden-spoked 1920 Lincoln convertible on his few miles of hot-topped highway. The temple's drive is lined with helicopter-transported, elegantly peeling mahogany trees, ever-blossoming frangipani, and a carefully guided banyan hedge, doubling yearly in size. Jamy's marina is decorated by a row of symmetrically placed traveller palms; fan-shaped trees waving welcomes. Lifesize plastic pelicans, herons, ospreys, even – damn the dear boy's soul – bald eagles perch on curved gates and flared roofs. An Olympic swimming pool is walled in by giant mirrors, the nine-hole golf link is freshened by piped-in dollar-a-gallon water. Servant Sopwith climbs the coconut palm grove to pick giant nuts that might smash Jamy's dear head, when he hammocks down underneath, composing poetry:

. . . one evening, dancing in Mallory Square meeting my luv, luv, LUVVV . . .

Leatherbound copies of the completed poem, handprinted on parchment, will be distributed to select recipients some day soon. That includes me. Oh, Jamy is indeed a dear boy, though irritating at the best of times. If I could show you his Yamamoto kitchen, with walls lined by stainless steel counters and floors of genuine marble, complete with a display of culinary machinery (kept spotless by Sopwith), including a cakery and a puddingery . . . and what does Jamy normally have for dinner? A TV tray, zipped in by Bad George on the speedboat. No wonder Jamy likes to drop in at my place, and if I happen to be broiling fresh snapper, or another fine marine-deli Egret Cove provides during my daily outing in the rowboat, well now, seeing that Jamy considers himself to be a friend, he may sit down and dig in vigorously.

I'm stuck here in my old house, bought long before the Keys became fashionable. I dread the growl of Jamy's powerboat covering the distance between Eagle Island and my shore in mere minutes. I never have time to get away. I fear Jamy's repetitive monologues, leaving headaches for Parrot to smoothe away with more 'arf-arf huh-huh arf,' but I almost forgave Jamy when he presented me with his murder.

How exciting. Kicked Mangrove Mama in the belly, did he now? And in the presence of mutinous slave Sopwith and jealous former pal Bad George?

Aha!

If my fellow Keysians project divine qualities on to my humble presence I may as well use that free glory. Besides, I enjoy manipulating the multitude, and I suddenly saw, while Jamy sobbed and slobbered, a chance to work some things out.

So what have we here? I tell you what we have here: a delightful set of circumstances, pointing toward planetary improvement.

Let me provide some background here.

Before our Florida Keys became a maddening, over-

populated, tourist-trappy bozo-bonanza, Eagle Island was
one of many raised mangrove swamps that attracts birds.
Weren't the silvergray pelicans, that its wilderness supported, a great sight as they delicately glided about, before
noisily nosediving for their daily fish? White herons dis-
played themselves too, and slate colored egrets, some
iridescent ibises, a charming bunch of little sandpipers and,
of course, the lone turkey vulture on everlasting patrol, but I
was mainly fascinated by a pair of bald eagles. Bald eagles are
spectacular beings, rare, an endangered species.

Jamy shot those two eagles.

How do I know? Because he told me, at another after-
dinner session, also bourbon-related.

I believe the eagle-murder as Suspect was properly moti-
vated that time. Killing harmless wildlife is what self-centered
dear boys do, especially when they are rich and extra-damned
by prolonged parental absence during early formative
years.

What proper motivation?

Vanity. Jamy originally bought Eagle Island to show off.
He wasn't contented with sharing a regular Key with other
happy folks, no, he needed an entire island all to himself.
Then 'Goldy' Yamamoto meets Jamy in a Key West strip joint
and Yamamoto turns out to be a specialist in architecting
antique Chinese surroundings. A contract is signed forth-
with, but before bulldozers dash out of landing craft to shred
the island's flora, our conspirators check out the area and
observe nesting eagles.

Nesting eagles interfere with the granting of building
permits.

Jamy, sniffed full of cocaine, boards his super speedboat,
shoulders his twelve gauge automatic, zooms out on Egret
Cove and blasts two rare eagles – nine foot wingspan,
immaculate white heads and tails, beautiful specimens
indeed. Didn't I watch and admire them many a morning,
roosting so quietly on their nest tucked high in the
mangroves?

BLAM! BLAM!

Jamy shoots the ibises and the pelicans too, for good measure.

Zen architect Yamamoto submits his plans to Egret Key's planning board. I was away at the time. My fellow members saw no reason to refuse the request. They checked the island but there were no endangered life forms around – nobody but ducks and cormorants, both still plentiful species.

You wonder how I could feed Jamy my fine dinners after he told me what he did to beautiful birds?

Sages stay cool.

Permit me more outline of background.

Jamy's father made millions in oil, skin, highrise and other Texanias of the highflying days. Jamy's mother, meanwhile, was made by macho men.

Jamy himself decorated his handsome head with a garland of bluebonnets, dropped out of everything and surfaced in our capital, Key West. Like that most independent little city itself, 'the unwanted child seemed to welcome parental neglect'.

I surmise he was happy here during these footloose years. In spite of all bad habits Jamy is still attractive today; in his youth he was surely stunning. He met Mangrove Mama, a perfect mate, an unmatched package of Lorelei-like sex. There were other members of the tribe: gangling Bad George, peddling dope, and nerdy Sopwith, attracted to serving German gents. We are talking flower children here, latter-day hippies, making a dollar if they had to, mostly hanging out in far-out space, drunk, doped, no need for sense.

  . . . *One evening, dancing in Mallory Square* . . .

Jamy, part time kitchenscrape, pimped a bit on waitress Mangrove Mama hooking lone tourists on the side. A good time, no doubt, was had by all.

Another sunset comes along and sees our gang dancing again to guitars strummed by Cuban and Haitian refugees, with New York poets going crazy on bongos.

The same sunset, a short while earlier, saw Jamy's dad having a terminal heart attack in his 1958 white Cadillac (only eight thousand instant collectors' items sold). The car careens

wildly between San Antonio and Austin, slips off the highway, projectiles through a row of model homes. Salesmen
and their customers jump off balconies and hurt themselves.
Jamy Sr. is dead throughout the rampage.

The same sunset, a less short while earlier, filtering
through plastic blinds in a Montana motel, saw Jamy's mom,
a wispy woman, squeezed away by an over-enthusiastic
trucker.

Orphan Jamy is rich.

Now what does he do?

For a while Jamy gets going on the togetherness idea. He
shares his fortune. Mama immediately crashes the Jaguar
Jamy buys her as a token of communal bondage. Sopwith
pulls a four cylinder Honda motorcycle over on himself while
trying to be Early Marlon Brando. Bad George, in his role as
Popeye, loses a pricy yacht off Bimini due to gusting wind
and open portholes. All together they wreck a mansion by
knocking down supporting walls to create undivided space.
Eager to economize, Bad George and Sopwith use communal
funds to buy a used school bus. While restoring the rust-
bucket, fifty gallons of old gas are drained into a city sewer.
Better burn that dirty gas. A dropped match causes bad
explosions. The city presents a bill for new concrete. In none
of the above calamities was any insurance taken out. Jamy,
while settling claims, protests, not so much about accumu-
lated losses but because nobody pays respect. He dismantles
the commune.

Not having learned to sit still yet he rushes into more
trouble.

Jamy is buying properties to impress others, who are
impressed until the closings. Jamy is also stood up by dates.
His dates think he is crazy. They're mostly women he meets
in bars. Jamy tells them what properties he owns, scribbling
additions of bonds, shares, warrants, bullion, cash reserves
in foreign currencies on napkins. He invites his new found
partners for rides on the *Queen Elizabeth* and Concorde. They
don't show up at appointed places. He can't figure why.

Mangrove Mama is having a hard time too. She is in her

addictive stage. Trading sex for drugs doesn't work for her. She is raped in a van and dumped on a beach. A disturbed lover tosses her clothes out of a window of a not good hotel. There are other bizarre events that she doesn't remember too well but policemen keep showing to ask odd questions. To escape incomprehensible hassle Mama finds a canoe and paddles between the outer Keys where an abandoned cocaine cruiser offers refuge. She starts living on seaweed and raw fish.

Bad George crews on a flying transport of Mexican marijuana. The old crate crashes in the Everglades. He is ambulanced to jail.

Sopwith is riding blue rented bicycles with lone male Germans again but no tourist wants to keep him. Sopwith branches into gardening, feeding heavy palm fronds into noisy chippers. He cheats on his hours and keeps getting fired.

Now, really, don't we agree that these children need a Guardian's help?

Except for Mangrove Mama, blonde Lorelei siren gone wild and canoeing about Egret Cove, I haven't met any of these kids yet. Mama and I get on good. I take out gourmet lunches to her cruiser at times.

Now we get the goings-on on Eagle Island. I discover, to my grief and fury, that the eagles have disappeared. The island is stripped of its mangroves, Yamamoto builds his infernal temple mansion, Jamy moves in.

Jamy and I meet on the cove, where I yell at him when his powerboat's wake nearly overturns my dinghy. The dear boy's profuse apologies instigate my wining and dining the scoundrel.

Mostly unemployed Sopwith and paroled Bad George are gardening for me at the time and Jamy meets them on the premises. He hires them away respectively as the butler and captain, assuring his former friends that there will be no more Mr Nice Guy.

Sopwith drops in occasionally to complain about his master keeping him and Bad George at long arms' lengths. I hear about Mangrove Mama also trying to re-establish her relationship with Jamy but only succeeding in staying occasional nights.

So much for history. I hope I succeeded in sketching out relevant lines of cause and effect. Now let's see where they cross each other. Maybe their meeting points will indicate a more pleasant picture than that of Mangrove Mama's bleeding corpse.

I tipped the bottle again and handed out more cigars. Key lime pie rested easily on glowingly digesting stone crabs. I could feel Parrot's little dry feet moving about on my shoulder. 'Arf arf,' the bird murmured sleepily. Another lovely evening under the palm trees enjoyed by friends.

'Kicked Mangrove Mama to death, eh?' I asked. 'Now run that by me again, Jamy. Keep nothing back.'

Jamy got up, postured and gestured. There he stood again at the scene of the crime, at the side of his lagoon, and there Mama's begging sharp fingers plucked annoyingly at his sleeve. She wanted to stay the night. He didn't want her to stay the night. He wanted to listen to New Age compact discs on the sound system that Bad George installed and that Sopwith explained.

'Arf arf huh-huh-huh . . .'

Dear Parrot.

'And then you kicked Mama?' I asked.

Jamy said he remembered pushing Mama, watching her fall, seeing lots of blood on the floor.

'But did you *kick* her?'

Jamy couldn't recall. Bad George claimed Jamy kicked her, and Sopwith likewise, so surely Jamy kicked Mama. Here we had two sober witnesses and Jamy, the perpetrator, brimful of coke.

'You were woozy, dear boy?'

Jamy admitting to having sniffed away for a while, preparing proper reception of New Age jazz on his new CDs.

'You remember pushing Mama?'

He did.

'You don't remember kicking her?'

He did not. Sure? Sure. He did remember the blood, though, lots of blood, coming from underneath Mama, who was losing her baby because Jamy had kicked her. Jamy's baby. So said Sopwith and Bad George, later.

'Mama had told you she was pregnant?'

She had not.

'So how could she lose the baby? Your baby? Why *your* baby?'

Jamy said he had been sleeping with Mama at times.

I said that Mama is over forty now. Forty-year-old women are known to get pregnant sometimes, but what with Mama's frugal lifestyle, canoeing about all day, living on seaweed and raw fish . . .

'Have you ever made any woman pregnant?' I asked.

He said that, ah, now that I mentioned it, ah, no . . .

'Now Mama dies,' I said. 'We have her on your marble tiles next to the lagoon in the Zen lounge, and she dies.'

No, no, Jamy said I got that wrong. Mama was alive then, but very sick, bleeding, and he was stoned, quite incapable of dealing with the situation. However, Bad George and Sopwith were sober and able, so he ordered them to take Mama to Key West hospital to get her fixed up. Bad George said hospitals don't take in single women that bleed, not without money. Jamy shelled out money.

'How much?'

A thousand dollars, Jamy said. While he got the cash Bad George and Sopwith wrapped Mama up in a blanket, lowered her into the powerboat – off shoots the rescue party into the dark night. The speedboat planes on the small waves of Egret Cove, the roar of its twin outboards recedes in the black expanse.

'You stayed home, Jamy?'

Yep, he said. Jamy hates blood and he hates suffering women. There were still the new CDs to listen to. While Mangrove Mama got fixed up by modern medicine Jamy planned to relax on the intake of smooth wide-spaced New Age sounds, cresting his spiritual energy, to be telepathized to Mama so that she would get better pronto. She didn't get better pronto. She died before she reached the hospital's shore. Bad George and Sopwith brought the body back, still wrapped securely in the bloody blanket. Mama's long blonde hair hung out at one end and her dead feet at the other. An unbearable sight, which made Jamy switch off his sound equipment.

'Where's the body, Jamy?' I asked, but I had to go on hold. Jamy was off in alcoholickies. He shuffled around my chair, flailing his arms, wailing his lament. How he loved Mangrove Mama, Jamy lamented, how he wished to make repairs, to her, to all, to everything. The world was going to wreck and ruin, and he had been playing with his millions, adding to destructive waste and pollution, adding to the ozone hole – while he could have been another Saint Jean-Jacques Cousteau, captaining a Greenpeace cruiser with Mama as his mate, torpedoing Japanese whaling vessels, or flying a glider plane on solar energy, patrolling Russian nuclear waste sites that interfere with the supply of chanterelle mushrooms that could feed New York bag-ladies.

'Yes,' I said, 'yes.'

While helping Parrot, who had had enough, too, into his cage – the tired little thing almost dropped off my hand – I switched to analysis.

Was it the French novelist Stendhal who said that successful businessmen make good philosophers for they dare to see things clearly? Money makers see what goes on, rather than what they would like to see go on, and profit by accepting bad truths.

What would I like to see go on? Justice, of course. Let's have Jamy in irons, pulling weeds at the side of the road, while a sadistic wad-chewing southern guard gestures with a shotgun.

While another rich fool lolls about Eagle Island. Jamy, no-good slob, miserable halfwit, look at him blabbermouthing away . . .

Egret Key's Guardian forces himself to stay calm, benevolent, benignly detached, while he works harder on himself.

Yes, even angels are tempted, but I wasn't about to join Lucifer. Not until the move suited me, that is.

'Did you throw the corpse into the sea?' I asked. My breathing became a tad irregular. This was the question on which my solution hinged.

'Had Mama buried,' Jamy sobbed.

'Where, dear boy?'

'On Bad George's Pissing Rock,' Jamy sobbed.

Better, much better. The little clump of riprap, overgrown by poisonous Florida holly and acid-dripping cottonwood trees, is about halfway between Eagle Island and my house. We named it after Bad George began using it for sanitary stops, interrupting his ferrying across the Cove.

'Let's go have a look,' I said.

Jamy, worn out by his groveling, slept on my walnut floor. I poured out my watering can's contents. He whimpered but got up.

Parrot woke. 'Arf?'

'No, you stay home, little friend.' I found a spade, dragged Jamy to my dock and dumped him into the rowboat. Jamy clawed my knees. 'Please, Jannie, let Mangrove Mama be.'

He stayed in the boat, slumped over, head in hands, while I dug. Bad George and Sopwith had done a good job, she was six feet under rocks and rubble, but she wasn't Mangrove Mama. I thought I recognized the old girl. On the far side of Egret Cove an ever-changing colony of squatters exists on a flotilla of dying vessels. This woman once lifted a bottle at me as I rowed by, while suggesting a carnal meeting. I constructed a theory that fitted all the facts. Drunk again, she fell in and drowned. Her body bobbed about that fateful night and drifted afoul of Bad George, Sopwith and Mangrove Mama's ship.

My flashlight revealed Mangrove Mama's blonde locks, cleverly braided into the dead woman's matted hair. Who had gone to such grisly trouble? Mama was supposedly ill. Squeamish Sopwith? While Bad George stood over him, raising a threatening fist? I had to smile as I imagined the scene: the lapping of the waves, owls hooting, the flutter of bats' wings, eerie sounds that accompany Sopwith's feeble protest. His squeak sounds like Stan Laurel's thin crying, and Bad George, who sports a bowler hat and who has put on weight, is the pathetic introvert's unrelenting Oliver Hardy. Mangrove Mama stars as the beautiful woman that paired comics need to use for contrast.

I bowed to the dead body, shoveled the rubble back, stamped the grave tight again, got back in my dinghy.

'How is Mama?' Jamy asked.

'Just fine,' I said. We rowed to my house in silence. I put Jamy up in the guest room. The next morning, while watching me eat breakfast, Jamy stirred in his cloud of cigarette smoke and suggested that I should hold his hand while he gave himself up to the sheriff.

'No need,' I said. 'I can save you, dear boy, on certain conditions.'

Jamy, properly awed, whispered, 'You can bring Mangrove Mama back to life?'

'Why not?' Egret Key's Sage asked his unenlightened disciple.

A glimmer of hope made the blood in Jamy's eyes glow.

As I said, my neighbors credit me with certain powers. It's this infernal New Age. We have all sorts of rich self-appointed spiritualists here and the general trend is to force growth of soul. Most seekers on this shore aim for Buddhahood so in order to flavor the general quest I profess to be into Tao.

Taoists, apart from walking the nameless road named Tao, perform tricks. Local legend points at my pool that 'magically mirrors the spirit', my age-old hibiscus tree, 'a set-off point for jumping astrally into space'; my barbecue rack, 'alchemic instrument for preparing invisibility potions'. My age is guessed at one hundred plus. Being born in Europe I am credited with remembering World War One and the Belgian freedom struggle. I will, if pressed, confirm that I studied Tantric Lamaism with the Tsarist spy Gurdjieff in Kum Bum Monastery, Tibet. On a recent Smithsonian-sponsored visit to New Guinea I acquired a skull drum that accompanies my full-moon Penobscot Indian dances. I often chant Dutch children's rhymes and I can juggle telephone books in the W. C. Fields manner. No wonder Jamy wanted to believe me.

'Jamy,' I said, 'you did foully, egotistically and ignorantly, which are three sides of the same coin, murder a pair of magnificent eagles, at least four endangered pelicans and a rare group of ibises in order to take over their island. You are a true tyrant ape. I can give you Mangrove Mama again but must insist on your speedy evolution.'

Jamy drooled and mumbled.

'OK?'

'OK,' Jamy whispered.

'Well now,' the Guardian said, while stroking white whiskers, while flashing steel-blue eyes, 'you will have Mama back, to love and cherish. You and our karmic brethren, Sopwith and Bad George, plus the muse to be revived by me, will together realize your true purpose and assist Saint Jean-Jacques Cousteau. After . . . '

'Arf?' asked Parrot from his cage.

'Yes?' asked Jamy from his hell.

' . . . you see the authorities,' I said from my cloud, 'and tell them you want to restore a bird sanctuary for endangered species and that you require permission to wreck your eyesore house. Personally oversee burning your building, blasting your driveway, exploding your marina. Transfer Eagle Island to Egret Key Wetlands Conserving Society and authorize me, its chairman, to have it legalized as a nature reserve forever.' I pointed at the door. 'Dear boy, do that now!'

Jamy folded his hands. 'And you will bring Mama back to me?'

I said I would do that small thing.

I released Parrot. Together we watched Jamy being reborn, at the beginning of a busy day. Jamy, once he knows what it is he knows, knows how to get it going.

I rowed out to locate Mama. She hid at first but I had brought lunch and its good smells made her canoe float out from between mangrove roots.

'So our little plan won't work,' she said after she had worked herself to the bottom of my hamper.

'It's working very well,' I said. 'How's the bleeding, Mama?'

She blushed under her woman-of-the-islands tan. 'A female complaint, Jannie. I'm of a certain age now, this granola life doesn't balance things out. It's either all or nothing.'

I blushed too. 'No pregnancy gone wrong?'

'No,' she said.

'It all just happened?' I asked. 'You didn't find the old lady's dead body first, anchored it somewhere, then produced it at the right moment to set up your lover within a blackmail scheme?'

It all just happened again, Mangrove Mama cried, like everything always just happened. First she happened to collapse, bleeding, then the drunken woman's body banged the boat, then the blackmail plan blundered along.

'All is well,' I said, 'Jamy loves you.'

I sang: *'One night, dancing in Mallory Square . . .'*

I pointed at her short hair. 'Looks attractive.'

Mama kept on crying.

'No need,' I said. 'Wait here some more. The prognosis is good.'

That evening me and Bad George and Sopwith watched the fireworks on Eagle Island from my seawall.

'I'd like to help out there,' Bad George said, 'but Jamy will be mad at me, I think?'

'Bad George,' I murmured. 'Fussing with the dead old lady and telling lies for money is not quite what your Scout Master had in mind.'

Bad George bowed his fat head and Sopwith did the Stan Laurel squeak again. They wanted to know when the sheriff was coming to pick them up.

'Angels don't squeal on pals,' I said, 'but there will have to be some changes.'

Mangroves have taken over the island again.

Jamy returned from detox the other day. The white coats did a good job. The patient even quit smoking. Mangrove Mama helps him in restoring an old schooner. Bad George and Sopwith are on the job too, and the gang attends a Coast Guard navigation course. Whoever passes the exam first will be the *Saint Cousteau*'s captain and take the vessel out on patrol, pursuing polluters, liberating whales from loose floating nets.

Jamy says I can come along and watch.

Patiently waiting I admire an eagle soaring above the Cove, gliding down every now and then to check out the island. I installed, near the location where 'Goldy' Yamamoto's Ch'an temple once raised its roof, a wooden wheel on a post. It hasn't yet met with the bird's approval.

HOLLOW POINT

O'Neil De Noux

'Pay attention, this is important!' Lieutenant Rob Mason said, and then waited for everyone to settle down.

LaStanza watched his lieutenant shift the ever-present cigarette from one side of his mouth to the other. Mason, sporting a fresh Marine Corps-style haircut, looked worn-out as he stood at the front of the Homicide Squad room. Wearing his burgundy sport coat over his usual white shirt, striped tie and black pants, he looked older than his forty-five years. The Homicide Pressure Cooker was responsible for that. Lately LaStanza had noticed a gray hair or two sprouting in his own dark hair and, worse, in his moustache.

The clock above Mason's head read 8:00 p.m. sharp. Just below the clock hung the unofficial logo of the New Orleans Police Homicide Divison, a surreal drawing of a vulture perched above an NOPD star-and-crescent badge.

'All right,' Mason said. 'You all have a copy of the mug shot of Casey Aloysius. Now, for those not aware of what's happened, let me run it down to you.'

Jesus! LaStanza thought. Whoever hadn't heard must have been on Mars.

'Six years ago, Casey Aloysius was sent to Angola for raping a ten-year-old girl. Through the benevolence and infinite wisdom of our illustrious parole board, Aloysius was released three days ago. He caught the first bus to New Orleans, stole a car, drove directly to the victim's house where he kidnapped her and took her to the same abandoned garage on Tchoupitoulas Street where he raped her six years ago. He chained her hands to a wall and raped her repeatedly for over six hours.' Mason began to rub his neck. 'She was raped anally, vaginally and orally. Aloysius taunted her, laughed at her, beat the hell out of her and told her he was punishing her for turning him in.'

Every time he heard the story, LaStanza's stomach twisted.

Mason continued, 'Then he left her there, chained to the wall like an animal.'

Mason skipped the part where the two little boys found her, curiously entering the garage because they thought they heard a puppy whimpering. He also left out the fact that the girl, struggling for life, told the story through lips so swollen she could barely move them.

'Fuckin' parole board!' someone shouted from the back of the room.

'Fuckin' ass-holes!' another detective snarled.

'Cocksuckers!'

'How's the little girl?' someone finally asked.

Mason shrugged and said, 'According to her doctors, she'll be all right.'

Yeah. Right! LaStanza thought. *She'll be just fine!*

LaStanza looked at the mug shot of Aloysius that had been passed out to everyone. It wasn't a particularly evil face, albeit ugly as hell. Casey Aloysius had a lean, ruddy face with wide-set eyes, a hook nose and a cue-ball head, completely bald. Turning the picture over, LaStanza looked at the information printed on the back. Under the man's name, bureau of identification number and arrest information was the following personal data:

White Male
DOB: 10/31/34
HT: 6'1"
WR: 200'
EYES: Blue
HAIR: Bald

LaStanza noticed the son-of-a-bitch had just had a birthday when Mason finished his speech with, 'Now, you know your assignments. For God's sake, be careful.'

'Careful? The fuck-head better be careful!' someone shouted.

'The fuckin' parole board better be careful!'

'Hey, Sarge, you have their names and addresses up there?'

Several of the men bragged how they were gonna personally save the state some money by finishing off Aloysius.

'God, I'd *love* to fuckin' blow him away,' a fresh-faced robbery detective said as he stood and stretched.

LaStanza looked around the room. Besides himself, only his burly sergeant, Mark Land, and Lieutenant Mason had ever shot anyone. Leaning forward, LaStanza withdrew his weapon from the holster on his hip. He opened the cylinder of his stainless steel, snub-nosed Smith & Wesson .357 magnum revolver and rechecked to make sure he had magnum rounds in it, 125 grain semi-jacketed hollow points. He closed the cylinder and checked his speed loaders.

He saw his partner approaching. Jodie Kintyre, dressed like LaStanza in a gray pull-over shirt and black jeans, had her own .357 magnum snub-nose holstered on her hip. She looked even thinner than normal in black. Shaking her page-boy blonde hair as she arrived, she said, in a motherly voice, 'You carrying hot loads?'

He nodded yes. 'Want some?'

She shook her head no. Following department regulations, Jodie always carried .38 rounds in her weapon.

Fuck regulations! LaStanza thought as he rose and tucked the mug shot in his clipboard. Before leaving, he had one more thing to tell his partner. 'Remember, never split up.'

She was grinning at him now. He had told her all that before, when he broke her into Homicide. Partners never split up. Whatever happens to you better happen to your partner.

On their way out they passed LaStanza's old partner. Paul Snowood – better known as Country-Ass because the crazy bastard always wore western clothes and spoke with a hillbilly accent, even though he was from Bell Chasse, a suburb of

New Orleans – was sitting on one of the rear desks. He was showing off his Glock 17, his new extra special fuckin' NATO gun. He had named it after Elvis's ex-wife.

'Ole Priscilla here carries twenty rounds,' Snowood explained to three curious juvenile detectives. 'She fires as sweet as a jackrabbit runnin' through a thicket.'

LaStanza patted Country-Ass on the shoulder as he passed and said, 'Safest place is to stand directly in front of old Priscilla, when the rounds start flying.'

The juvenile detectives roared and fell away from Country-Ass. LaStanza led the way out of the door and down to the police garage. Before climbing in their car he and Jodie put on bullet-proof vests, black turtleshell-looking vests with the word 'POLICE' stenciled in front and back in large white letters.

A perfect target, LaStanza thought.

Snowood called out as he walked by, 'I better see two heads in that car on your stake-out.' The same juvenile detective started laughing again, even louder.

'*3120 to 3124*,' Mason called on the radio.

LaStanza reached into their unmarked gray LTD, picked up his portable and answered.

'*10-19 the office*,' Mason said.

'*10-4.*'

Jodie shrugged and led the way back up to Homicide. Mason, now in his narrow office at the rear of the squad room, was standing between two detectives from the Rape Squad. Commonly called 'the models', Detectives Sharon Mehan and Donna Meehan were tall thin blondes with hair worn in the same long curly style. As soon as the models were partnered up, the rest of the Rape Squad started calling them by the number of the letter 'E' in their names. Mehan became One-E; and Meehan, Two-E, for obvious reasons.

They were impeccably dressed, usually in tight skirts, and their well-polished nails always sported wild colors and were never chipped. That evening they wore similar outfits, only One-E's was tan, while Two-E wore a navy blue version of the skirt-suit outfit.

Mason cleared his throat as soon as LaStanza and Jodie had squeezed into the room. 'Um, Kintyre. You've been requested to go along for the formal statement from the victim.' He took a deep drag from his cigarette, let out half of the smoke and added, 'The victim knows you.'

Jodie looked at LaStanza and shrugged.

'Her name's June Holmes,' Two-E said, shifting her weight from one spiked heel to the other. 'She says she lived near you back when you used to live on Laurel Street.'

Jodie shook her head.

'Well, she remembers you. Her mama and your mama were friends.'

'Oh.' Jodie looked back at LaStanza. 'Mrs Holmes. I remember her.'

LaStanza and Jodie followed the models down to their cars and over to Mercy Hospital and up to Room 313, where a prim nurse with steely-gray hair worn in a bun was waiting.

Two minutes later La Stanza found himself in a private room. Since he was the only male present, he tried to blend in with the wall. Besides the models and Jodie and the nurse, the victim's aunt and mother were there huddled around the lone bed. LaStanza stood just inside the doorway as the models let Jodie move in and greet the victim. All LaStanza could see of the girl was a splash of dark brown hair above a wide forehead and her milky-white left arm with its IV attachments.

The victim's mother and aunt looked like twins, salt-and-pepper hair worn short, wide bodies in shapeless dresses with little flowers on them, and faces filled with sadness, eyes red from too many tears.

'We're going to take your formal statement now,' Two-E said. 'We've got a tape recorder, OK?'

'OK,' the girl answered in a voice surprisingly strong.

LaStanza could see Jodie holding the girl's hand now as Two-E began with, 'This is a voluntary statement of June Marie Holmes, white female, date of birth June 6, 1969 . . . '

LaStanza backed up against the wall and tried to escape the smell. The room smelled like a funeral parlor. Scented with roses and disinfectant and something that resembled hairspray. He glanced around until he found two vases of roses along the dark side of the room. He hated that smell. It always reminded him of his brother's funeral.

Finishing the introductory questions, Two-E asked June Holmes to tell, in her own words, what had happened the day before yesterday.

'I was at home,' June's voice quivered over the word home for a moment, 'and somebody knocked at the front door.' Her voice never quivered again. 'And when I answered it, it was him. He grabbed me, shoved his hand over my mouth and dragged me out to his car. It was Casey Aloysius, the man who raped me six years ago and went to jail. It was him. He tied me up, and drove me to that garage, the one full of those oil barrels. He cut my clothes off with big scissors and dragged me to these chains.'

Two-E interrupted, 'Please describe your clothes.'

'Huh? Oh. An orange top. Long sleeves. Some blue sweat pants. A white bra. White panties. White socks and blue running shoes. Nikes. That's all.'

'OK. Please continue,' Two-E said in a voice that sounded well-rehearsed.

'He put chains around my hands and started slapping me. I closed my eyes and tried not to cry. Then he raped me . . . '

June began to describe, in chilling detail, exactly what the man did to her body, to different parts of her body. LaStanza felt his stomach twisting again and wished he could just melt into the wall. As June chronicled, in a high voice that was strong and determined, the attacks on her body, LaStanza squirmed.

He began to stare at his feet. Then his radio blared out in a loud beep tone. He immediately made for the door, turning the volume down.

'*Headquarters to all units. Signal 34S on police. Signal 108. Magazine and Napoleon Avenue. Units respond.*'

Dammit!

A policeman shot. An officer needs assistance call. And he was in a hospital hallway, miles away, LaStanza thought as he moved down the hall and turned his radio up.

The first unit to arrive at the scene was Unit 220, who screamed for an ambulance. *'We've got an officer down and another in foot pursuit up Napoleon!'*

LaStanza was pacing now. He thought he heard Mason's voice but wasn't sure. So many voices came on the air, they drowned each other out. Typical police stupidity. Then he heard 220 again. *'Can you copy a script on the perpetrator?'*

'10-4,' Headquarters answered.

'White male,' whoever 220 was went on, *'about fifty, dark clothing, bald-headed, about six feet, two hundred pounds. Got a nine millimeter, blue steel.'*

LaStanza felt icy tingles along his spine. He sat heavily in one of the green plastic upholstered chairs in the hall. He didn't have to say it aloud. He knew someone would on the radio. A heartbeat later, Mason did.

'Headquarters, that sounds like wanted subject Casey Aloysius. He's wanted for a 44 and a 42 by the bureau.' That was Mason's voice all right, telling them their perpetrator was wanted for aggravated kidnapping and aggravated rape. LaStanza leaned back in the chair. His knees were bouncing now. He wanted to get over there – so fuckin' badly!

'How'd he get a damn nine millimeter?' a voice asked.

'Don't the parole board issue them to parolees?'

Headquarters cut off the chatter. *'We've got officers in foot pursuit!'*

The yakking died down until after the foot pursuer advised he'd lost the perpetrator. About two million voices tried to get on the air at once, asking where the perpetrator was last seen, asking the condition of the officer who was shot, asking for the crime lab, asking for ranking officers, asking for detectives.

LaStanza turned his radio down and eased back into the room. It looked as if Two-E was finishing up. He tried to get Jodie's attention, but his partner had her back to him. He stood against the wall and waited. Two-E seemed to drag it on, asking again if June was positive the man who'd raped her was the same man who'd raped her six years ago.

'Yes. It was Casey Aloysius. He even showed me his new tattoos.'

'What were they?'

'One was a snake. On his chest. And he had the letter "C" in his right hand and an "A" in his left hand.' June's voice seemed stronger. Her mother and aunt were now sitting on the two chairs on the other side of the bed. Jodie was still holding June's hand.

Two-E asked, 'Is there anything you wish to add to this statement?'

'No,' June answered.

LaStanza heard the tape recorder click off. He cleared his throat and said, 'Jodie, we gotta run. There's a 34S on police.'

'Damn!' Jodie turned to him and crinkled up her round nose. Moving slightly, she allowed LaStanza his first good look at June Holmes' face. The top of the sixteen-year-old's head was wrapped in thick white bandages. So was her jaw. Her right eye was blue and swollen shut and covered with some sort of salve. Her lips protruded in hideous mounds of puffy redness. Her left eye stared right at him.

LaStanza took a step forward and winked at June. She blinked back and he swore he saw a hesitant smile on her pained lips. So he said, 'I'm Detective LaStanza. I'm Jodie's partner.'

June nodded slowly.

He wanted to tell her something like, 'I'm the one who's gonna get the bastard.' He wanted to say that so badly, to say anything to make that little girl know how much he wanted to get the son-of-a-bitch!

Five minutes later, he was pushing the LTD for all it could give him, Jodie hanging on to the arm rest and her seat belt. They made it to Napoleon Avenue in eleven minutes, siren screeching, blue light flashing through the dark New Orleans night. He blew through every red light along the way.

He killed the siren a few blocks away and rode the brake to an even halt behind one of the marked units stopped in the street. Before they got out, Jodie grabbed his arm and said, 'What the hell was all that about?'

'Anger,' he told her. She didn't respond. They'd been partners long enough for her to realize LaStanza's famous temper was better focused on inanimate objects, like his briefcase thrown across the squad room, and his trash can careening off walls, and the accelerator of their LTD jammed to the floorboard.

They found Mason standing next to a pool of blood on the sidewalk about thirty feet up Napoleon from Magazine, along the uptown side of the avenue. His tie loosened, his jacket obviously in his car, he was staring at the blood, a cigarette dangling precariously from his mouth, another cigarette in his left hand.

'Say, what it is?' LaStanza said, using his old Sixth District lingo.

'Typical cluster fuck,' Mason said in disgust. 'It's Aloysius all right. Second District patrolman ID'd him already. He was a 107 down by Tchoupitoulas.' A suspicious person. 'A two-man unit responded. He beat feet. They split up. He got the drop on a patrolman named Matt Hanchon. Know him?'

'Vaguely. How is he?' LaStanza asked.

'He'll pull through.'

LaStanza looked at his partner and could see she knew what he was about to say.

So she beat him to it. 'I know. Never split up.'

'You got it.' Turning back to Mason, LaStanza was about to ask what they could do when someone went ballistic on the radio.

'Suspect on foot on Carondelet, crossing Euterpe.'

'Can't be him,' LaStanza said. 'How'd he get that far?' Backing away quickly toward the LTD, he called back to Jodie, 'Come on!'

They were pulling out on Magazine when the same voice broke through the radio chatter with, *'Suspect crossing Terpsichore . . . '*

'Cocksucker'll stick out in that neighborhood!' LaStanza said. Any white boy would stand out easily in that particular area of town, an area LaStanza was very familiar with, his old police district, the Bloody Sixth.

'Suspect lost on Terpsichore . . . '

'I thought he crossed Terpsichore?' Jodie said as La Stanza

ran the red light at Magazine and Jackson Avenue, turning up Jackson.

Jodie clicked on her radio and asked which direction on Terpsichore. Nobody answered.

LaStanza punched the accelerator and didn't ease up until they slid to a grinding halt behind a beat-up Oldsmobile waiting for the light on St Charles Avenue. They didn't stop again until LaStanza made a sharp right on Simon Bolivar. Then he slowed the LTD to a creep.

'He's in the project,' someone shouted.

'Suspect entered the Melpomene Projects, Headquarters.'

'10-4.' Headquarters repeated the information, probably on all channels.

'Stone fuckin' nuts!' LaStanza said, accelerating the LTD. 'Stupid white boy's gonna hide in the projects.' He glanced over at his partner and saw she was focused directly ahead. Her eyes narrowed, she gripped the dashboard with both hands. He had to chuckle to himself. He wasn't the best driver. He *had* run over a stop sign once in a marked police car, but it *had* been raining.

They were the second unit to pull up in front of the Melpomene high-rise, an ugly multi-storied tenement painted vomit yellow, the tallest eye-sore on a street of eye-sores. Parking next to a rusted dumpster that smelled like rotten shrimp, LaStanza and Jodie climbed out and watched several patrolmen race toward the front of the high-rise.

'Hold up a second,' LaStanza told his partner. He motioned her over. Jodie's nose was crinkled from the dumpster stench. 'Let's walk around here,' he said, leading the way across the sidewalk and around the uptown side of the high-rise. He noted two patrolmen guarding the front door, their weapons out in the ready position.

LaStanza unsnapped his holster, but left his magnum in its place, content to move cautiously with his hand on the grip. Jodie walked next to him, her hand also on her weapon. Rounding the building, she said, 'What are all these people doing out?'

LaStanza had to snicker. She might be a helluva Homicide dick, but Jodie didn't know the projects.

'It's always like this. Day or night. They got nothin' better to do.'

A skinny black woman in an orange robe, standing next to three black men in assorted shades of dark clothing, called out to the passing detectives in a cocky voice, 'What y'all lookin' for?'

'A bald-headed white boy with a gun.'

'Say what?'

LaStanza and Jodie continued past the small group. LaStanza turned and added, 'He's one of them skinheads. You know, a Klansman.'

'Fuck!' two of the men said in unison, moving off in different directions quickly.

'The word'll be out in two minutes,' LaStanza told Jodie as they moved past another group, mostly children this time. 'Aloysius makes it outta here alive, I'll spring for supper.'

'Occifer. Occifer!'

LaStanza looked up at a group of teenagers on a low balcony of the high-rise. One of the girls, in a tight turquoise jumpsuit, leaned over the railing. In a teasing voice she repeated, 'Occifer! Is that your wife wit' ya'?'

'Naw, I like black women.'

At least they laughed. One of the boys called LaStanza a silly ass. Another said he liked Jodie's ass and all that blonde hair. LaStanza called back as he walked away, 'Hey, we're looking for a white boy, a skinhead with a gun. He's one of them Nazi bastards.'

'Shit!'

By the time they reached the scattered tenements behind the high-rise, LaStanza had passed the word to three more groups. One, a gathering of teenage boys all wearing LA Raiders jackets, spread out in an angry mood.

'Now this is something you don't see all the time,' LaStanza told his especially quiet partner, nodding to several cops walking around with project residents, all searching together.

'Shouldn't we be looking?' Jodie finally spoke.

'Naw. They know the area better. Let's get back to the unit.'

Might as well make sure Aloysius didn't double back on them. As soon as they stepped on to Simon Bolivar, after working their way through the ever-growing crowd in front of the high-rise, they climbed in the LTD and moved it across the wide street, to get as far away from the dead shrimp dumpster as possible.

'It stinks over here too,' Jodie said, squirming in her seat as they set up directly across from the high-rise. LaStanza watched a lean, pitch black street dog loping along the neutral ground in the center of Simon Bolivar. The dog was scoping out the crowd.

'Ruff! Ruff!' LaStanza called out to the dog, which stopped, bent its front legs, lowered its head and looked around cautiously. When LaStanza ruffed again, the dog saw him, barked and loped off in a cocky gait.

'It always stinks around here. Isn't it nice?' He grinned at Jodie, which brought a smile to her face.

'You Sixers think you're something, huh? Like you worked above-and-beyond-the-call-of-duty.'

'We did.' LaStanza cocked his head and let his tongue dangle out.

'Jerk off.' Jodie leaned back and began to relax. He could see her shoulders loosening. She wouldn't look at him, and he knew why. She didn't want to laugh.

'Just tell me when you give up,' she said. 'I'm thinking about what you can buy me for dinner.'

Yeah, right! If they didn't come up with Aloysius, he had to spring for supper. LaStanza looked back at the Melpomene. It looked like a parade across the street. He expected someone to walk up any minute with a shopping cart and start selling candy apples and cotton candy.

Two hours later, when the search was called off, Jodie stretched and said, 'I'll let you off easy. How about the Camellia Grill?'

LaStanza could use a good burger, a good onion burger.

He felt anti-social. Actually, he felt angry as hell. He'd been thinking about June Holmes' face, about the split lip and the closed eye, about hands chained to a wall and how did Mason put it? 'Aloysius taunted her, laughed at her, telling her he was punishing her for turning him in.'

The rotten mother-fucker! LaStanza felt his steam rising as he pulled away from the kerb, made a U-turn on Simon Bolivar and moved slowly back to Magazine Street to take the long way to the Camellia Grill. By the time they arrived on Carrollton Avenue, in front of the converted ante-bellum house that was now the most famous grill in town, LaStanza's blood had cooled. His mind had already played out several scenarios concerning the demise of Casey Aloysius. In each scenario, LaStanza blew the bastard's diseased brain right out of the fucker's cranium. He could do it. Easily.

The following evening, at 7:55 p.m., LaStanza was back at his desk, his feet propped up next to his gray Smith-Corona typewriter. LaStanza wore a black pull-over shirt and black jeans this evening. Jodie had on another gray pull-over and faded blue jeans. Paul Snowood, clad in one of those John Wayne blue cavalry shirts, brass buttons and all, and a pair of faded jeans, along with gray snake-skin boots, was seated at his own desk directly across from LaStanza. Spitting mouthfuls of brown saliva into a Styrofoam cup, Snowood was explaining the benefits of smokeless tobacco to some of the patrolmen assembled for the meeting.

'Your lungs last longer,' Snowood said.

'But your lip'll fall off,' LaStanza injected.

Both patrolmen had sour looks on their face, especially when Snowood spat another gob into the cup.

The room was extra stuffy with all the bodies. There were more uniforms that evening, mixed in with the dicks; and more guns than a goddam Ku Klux Klan picnic on Martin Luther King Day. LaStanza turned away from his old partner, only to focus his eyes on another police apparition.

The black face of his old friend from the Sixth – a man named for the street where the Sixth District Station was

located – Felicity Jones leaned against the coffee table. Fel
wore a pair of shiny black satin-like pants and a form fitting
gray T-shirt with white lettering stenciled on front that read:
'IT'S GOOD TO FIND A HARD MAN!'

When Fel noticed LaStanza looking his way, he called out,
'Say man, mind if I pay your wife a visit tonight?'

'Naw,' LaStanza answered. He pulled out his house keys
and tossed them across the room to Fel who caught them.

Grinning broadly, Fel told the men around him, mostly
patrolmen, 'You ever see this boy's wife. Oh, man. Prettiest
white girl you ever seen.'

Calling back to LaStanza, Fel said, 'You sure it's OK I visit
your wife?'

'Sure, go ahead,' LaStanza said.

Some of the guys laughed. Some kept quiet, looking
around to see if they were joking. Jodie, who'd eased up next
to LaStanza, poked him in the ribs with her bony finger.

'You should be ashamed of yourself, talking about Lizette
like that,' she said in a harsh whisper.

When Mason came out of the lieutenant's office, Fel
tossed the keys back to LaStanza. The chatter in the room
died away quickly as Mason took his position beneath the
star-and-crescent badge with the vulture perched atop.

'All right,' Mason started. 'We got some new information
concerning Aloysius.' There was no need to re-introduce
Aloysius to this group. Shoot a cop in New Orleans and
you've got everyone's attention.

'Last night,' Mason began, 'two Second District patrolmen
stumbled on Aloysius. They thought he was sleeping off a
drunk along Tchoupitoulas Street. He started running. They
pursued and split up and he got the drop on one. Officer
Matt Hanchon was shot twice in the stomach. Aloysius got
away. How the fuck he got a hold of a nine millimeter is
beyond any of us.'

'The parole board issues them to parolees,' someone in the
back of the room said.

Mason's face remained stoic. 'Aloysius was last seen
running through the Melpomene Housing Project.'

'He's dead.'

'I wouldn't count on it,' Mason responded to the cat call. 'We've expanded our stake-outs to everyone who ever knew Aloysius. So y'all should have your assignments. Let's keep on our toes. And for God's sake . . . be careful.'

Down by their LTD, LaStanza and Jodie donned their bullet-proof vests again. Snowood stopped by and offered to help Jodie. 'You sure you don't need me to tuck that in?' he drawled.

'Get lost.'

'I like them jeans,' Snowood said to Jodie's rear end.

Fel Jones stopped his prowl car on the way out of the police garage next to LaStanza and pointed to Jodie and said, 'Why come you get all the pretty white girls?'

LaStanza wasn't about to answer that one.

Jodie stepped over and kicked the side of Fel's LTD, leaving a nice dent in the front quarter-panel.

'Dammit,' Fel said, accelerating the hell out of there.

LaStanza smiled and joined her in the LTD. Jodie remained quiet as LaStanza drove directly to St Claude Avenue, parking a half block on the uptown side of the house where Casey Aloysius had grown up with his Aunt Anne. Parking against the kerb, LaStanza flashed his lights to signal to the unmarked unit parked on the downtown side of the house that they were relieved. He watched them pull away quickly.

The 4200 block of St Claude Avenue, just across from the Fifth District police station, was in a perpetually dark section of town. Jammed against the Industrial Canal, this dingy area of tired buildings and pot-holed streets always seemed slick with oil. It was a greasy tract, an industrial area that was dying on the vine of new Republicanism. What LaStanza hated most was the canal itself, an ugly, eye-sore of a concrete ditch that connected the Mississippi to Lake Pontchartrain. It always smelled like dead fish and tar.

At least it's a cool night, LaStanza thought, as he rolled down his window and hunkered behind the steering wheel. A breeze filtered into the car, scented with the aroma of speckled trout well lubricated with motor oil.

'Um,' Jodie said, tapping the seat.

LaStanza eased the front seat back, allowing his partner to stretch out her long legs. She was a couple of inches taller than him, all of it in her legs.

After a few minutes, Jodie said, 'How'd we manage such a plush assignment?'

'Suits me fine,' LaStanza said. 'Let someone else catch the fucker. My luck, I'll have to shoot him.' He didn't have to add that he was snakebitten. He had enough bad luck to prove it. New Orleans was not the wild west, but you'd never know by the way Snowood dressed and LaStanza shot people.

He expected her to remind him that the new superintendent of police had personally warned LaStanza, labeling him 'unstable' with a 'penchant for violence that was unacceptable'. Involved in five police shootings, LaStanza had killed two men. Needless to say, five Grand Juries found all shootings justified. LaStanza knew, everyone knew, the new superintendent was lying in the gap for him, just waiting.

LaStanza leaned his head against the door jamb and set in for a long wait. The traffic on Rampart was fairly steady, mostly beat-up cars, interlaced by the occasional smoke-belching bus. There were people along the street also, some sitting on the front stoops of old wooden houses, some standing on corners or in front of the neighborhood barroom across Rampart down by Mazant Street.

LaStanza's mind went into surveillance mode, watching for every movement on the street and in the street, along with keeping a wary eye on the aunt's house. Stucco in construction, painted a dull gray, Aloysius's Aunt Anne lived in a one-storey house, with a roof that leaned precariously to the left, as if a good wind could blow it over. Lights were on in the house, so LaStanza figured it wasn't abandoned.

If I have to shoot the bastard, I will.

There was no hesitation in LaStanza's mind. Not like the first time he shot someone. He didn't even know he could shoot someone. He remembered how cold it was on that particular Tuesday. It was a day all policemen in New Orleans despised. It was Mardi Gras.

Assigned to parade duty on St Charles Avenue on Mardi
Gras morning with his first partner Stan-the-Man Smith – the
most conceited, obnoxious, opinionated, show-off policeman
on earth – LaStanza was nearing the end of his rookie year as
a patrolman. He didn't hear the gunshots two and a half
blocks away at Lee Circle. At Mardi Gras, it would be hard to
hear a cannon go off a block away.

He had no idea until two policemen ran past them in a big
hurry. Stan immediately followed with LaStanza close
behind. Off to the races LaStanza quickly overtook the
leaders, raising his revolver high as the others had, shouting,
'Police! Move! Police! Move! Move! Move!'

They were nearly bowled over by the mob of people
rushing away from Lee Circle. LaStanza slipped to one side
and ran up the slope along the base of the tall pillar
supporting the statue of Robert E. Lee that stood, arms
folded, defiantly facing north. LaStanza found two cops
trying to stop the bleeding from a belly wound on a third
patrolman who was sprawled on his back on the grassy
slope. Their hands were covered in blood.

LaStanza looked at the wounded cop's face and saw it was
pallid, saw death crossing the man's face. The man's eyes
began to glaze over. Stan arrived in time to pull LaStanza
aside as a patrol car careened up the embankment and slid to
a halt a few feet from their wounded comrade. The cop and
his two attendants were hustled into the car and wheeled off,
siren whooping, blue lights flashing, up Howard Avenue
toward Charity Hospital.

Looking back at St Charles Avenue, LaStanza thought of
an old Errol Flynn movie. The cavalry was coming. There
was a wall of blue coming toward Lee Circle, night sticks
waving in the air as the long snake-like line of policemen
wormed its way to them.

A description of the perpetrator was quickly dispatched by
a lieutenant who had materialized as if from nowhere. 'White
Male . . . six feet . . . black hair and beard . . . wearing
a navy pea-coat . . . carrying a large caliber blue steel
revolver.'

That was enough for Stan, who hustled LaStanza away from the multitude of angry cops. At the bottom of the circle, LaStanza looked up St Charles Avenue at a kaleidoscope of colors, people shoulder to shoulder for miles. He thought, *You could hide an elephant in that crowd.*

How could they find one man in a pea-coat, carrying a blue steel revolver? How could they find the man with murder in his eyes? *He could be anywhere*, La Stanza thought. *He could have just melted into the crowd or hid in any nearby bar, or ran away along the deserted streets on either side of St Charles Avenue.*

It was Stan who decided they should move away from the crowd and check the surrounding streets. As they left, the roar of the crowd slowly diminished. It was then LaStanza noticed the fog that slithered along the unoccupied streets. The further they moved from the crowd, the less the noise, the foggier it became. It was like moving through a fine, wet mist that gave the streets an eerie, surreal look. The fog brushed across LaStanza's face, nearly covering his feet as he and his partner moved along the quiet streets.

In the distance the crowd was a dull roar now. Their portable radios repeated the perpetrator's description. *'White Male . . . about six feet . . . black hair and beard . . . wearing a navy pea-coat . . . large caliber blue steel revolver . . . consider armed and dangerous . . . wanted for a 34S on police.'*

LaStanza turned his radio down. No need to telegraph their presence. He remembered thinking after, again and again, as he replayed that morning, how things happen so quickly. Things happen so quickly that you can only act. There's no time to think. No time for anything but survival.

They approached two alleys in a warehouse district. Stan took one and LaStanza the other. From the moment LaStanza started down the alley, it was as if the world held its breath. Moving slowly and purposefully, over pavement damp with dew and mist, LaStanza noticed the silence. It was as if he was suddenly the last person on earth. It was as if he were on a movie set and the director had just shouted, 'QUIET on the set. This is a take!'

LaStanza checked a doorway on the left and was about to

move across to the other side of the alley when he heard the
sounds of footsteps slapping, directly ahead of him, in his
alley. Turning to his left, he spotted the man running right at
him. The man wore a navy pea-coat. The man had black hair
and a beard. The man had something in his right hand. It
was a blue steel revolver. Then everything seemed to shift
into slow motion.

LaStanza started to shout, 'Police! Freeze!' But his mouth
wouldn't work. A noise came out of his mouth, a squeaky,
raspy noise. The man, still rushing forward, raised his gun.

'Police!' LaStanza shouted in a voice that sounded like a
whisper in a hurricane. He cupped his revolver in the palm
of his left hand, his right hand squeezing the black rubber
grips on the new four inch barreled, stainless steel, Smith &
Wesson .357 magnum. In one movement he bent his knees
slightly, pulled back the hammer, aimed at the center of the
man's chest and fired just as the man fired.

The gun erupted in his hands. His bullet struck the man
squarely in the chest. The man stumbled, looked down at his
chest for a moment before collapsing straight down on the
wet pavement. LaStanza could feel something now. He
could feel his heart thundering in his ears. He waited. One.
Two. Three.

The man did not move; the revolver was a good two feet
from his hand now. LaStanza moved and stood over the
man, who was lying on his back. He looked up at LaStanza
and they both knew, in that instant, that LaStanza had killed
him. In that instant there was truly no one else in the world
except the man and the policeman who'd killed him.
LaStanza watched the man's life slip away.

A million people celebrated a few blocks away. Doctors
frantically worked on a policeman who would die shortly in
Charity Hospital's Emergency Room. Children shouted for
throws along boulevards crowded with people who knew
nothing of what had happened at Lee Circle. One cop's
family that was celebrating on Canal Street would discover
later that the mother was a widow and the two sons would
never see their father again except in a casket. Women on

Bourbon Street exposed their breasts for beads. Men cheered in response. It was not even nine o'clock in the morning and LaStanza had killed a man.

And Stan-the-Man was in the wrong alley.

When Stan arrived he went ballistic, screaming and jumping around, slamming LaStanza on the back. 'You killed the mother-fucker! You fuckin' got him! Jesus fuckin' Christ! You really got him!'

LaStanza searched until he found the mark on the ware-house wall where the man's bullet had struck after it passed over his head. Later the Homicide detectives would locate the pellet. They gave it to LaStanza as a keepsake after the Grand Jury hearing.

'You know,' Jodie said, interrupting the quiet, 'sometimes Fel can be as annoying as Snowood.'

Fel Jones never bothered LaStanza. He was too good a friend. They had worked the Sixth together. But he figured something was bugging Jodie. She could usually blow off the sexist shit with ease. One of the reasons they got along so well was because LaStanza *never* pulled that sexist bullshit on his partner.

'He sure likes your wife.' Jodie prodded him now.

LaStanza smiled. 'He keeps trying to catch her naked in our jacuzzi.' That opened Jodie's eyes wide. He could hear her gulp.

'I'm surprised he hasn't,' LaStanza said.

'You serious?'

'You know I can't keep clothes on the girl.'

Jodie shook her head.

LaStanza readjusted himself, trying to get comfortable, when a movement caught his eye just beyond the aunt's house. He had to blink. It was Aloysius! The man's moon white face and the bald head were clear under the dim street light. LaStanza could even see the blue semi-automatic pistol tucked in the waistband of the man's pants. Aloysius walked out from between two houses and came right for them.

LaStanza touched Jodie's hand before withdrawing his magnum. Sinking lower he gently cracked open his door and waited. Aloysius stopped just before reaching his aunt's house, stopped in his tracks and looked around. He inched backward, turned and then bolted.

Fuckin' unmarked LTD stuck out like a goddam bus!

LaStanza jumped out and closed fast on Aloysius before the man ducked back between the same two houses. Pumping hard, LaStanza heard his partner following. Stopping, he pressed himself against the wall of the house where Aloysius had turned. He heard the rustle of a chain-link fence and peeked in time to spot the bald-headed bastard jump off the fence and stumble across the back yard.

LaStanza rushed down the side of the house, his partner hugging the wall of the other house. He jumped the fence easily and crouched a few feet beyond, looking for Aloysius. He heard the chain-link fence rattle as Jodie climbed over behind him. Clearing the rear of the houses, he caught a flash of Aloysius jumping another fence. The son-of-a-bitch was heading for Poland Avenue!

By the time they reached Poland, the bastard was nowhere in sight. LaStanza strained to hear as he peered up and down the avenue and its narrow neutral ground. After several long seconds he told Jodie she'd better call in. He knew his partner would have her radio still clipped to her belt. LaStanza's was back in their car.

'3126 – Headquarters.'

'Go ahead, 3126.'

'We're in foot pursuit – Headquarters . . .'

LaStanza saw Aloysius racing up the narrow bridge over the Industrial Canal.

'There!' LaStanza bolted for the bridge. He could hear his partner following, still talking on the radio, calling for backup.

Nearing the top of the bridge, Jodie yelled, 'Slow down!'

LaStanza wasn't about to slow down. Aloysius was running like a madman. Turning his head, LaStanza called back, 'Keep me in sight!'

There was no way Aloysius was going to outrun LaStanza. No way. A miler in high school, LaStanza loved to run. He'd even worn his new Nikes.

Aloysius disappeared just over the crest of the bridge. LaStanza increased his pace and discovered, when he reached the top of the bridge, that the son-of-a-bitch was gone. It took a couple of seconds to realize there was a stairway to the right. He rushed to the top of the steps and caught sight of the bald head as Aloysius turned right and raced down the street below, back toward the levee.

LaStanza sped down the concrete steps, taking them three at a time, trying his best to keep Aloysius in sight. Stumbling, he turned his right ankle and tumbled down the last steps to the ground. He looked up just in time to catch Aloysius ducking behind one of the dumpsters sitting at the end of the street, along the base of the levee.

Cupping his magnum in the standard two-handed police stance, LaStanza cocked his .357, and started down the street, hugging the cement support wall of the bridge. He heard Jodie starting down the steps as he peered through the dim light. He watched for any movement.

It was even darker on the lower side of the Industrial Canal. Most of the streetlights didn't work, especially those along the narrow one-lane street that ran alongside the bridge, down to the levee that kept the canal from flooding the city. In the distance, LaStanza heard the faint echo of sirens over the pounding of his own heartbeat.

Sweat moved slowly down LaStanza's temples as he inched his way along the wall. His hands were sweaty too. He squeezed the black rubber grips of his revolver. Dampness made them sticky. Aloysius had to be behind the dumpsters, unless he was crawling up the levee. It was too dark to see from that distance. If the bastard jumped the levee, he could go either way, to the left down to the river or to the right to pass beneath the bridge and disappear along the streets on the other side, or even to double back across the bridge.

Jodie came up behind LaStanza, said in a breathless voice, 'Where is he?'

LaStanza nodded to the dumpsters as he continued forward. The sirens were closing now. A whiff of putrid air belched across the levee from the canal right. A second later, when a passing tug blew its horn, both detectives jumped.

'Jesus!' Jodie said, going down on her knees.

LaStanza stopped moving and crouched. Leaning back, he told his partner to keep close. He kept watching the dumpsters for any movement, and led the way to the tunnels that allowed Sister Street to pass beneath the bridge. He crossed the first tunnel opening and then the second. Stopping, he tapped the inner wall and told Jodie to wait there.

'Where you going?' Jodie asking in a harsh whisper. She grabbed his arm.

He still couldn't see enough of the levee from there, or the far side of the dumpsters for that matter. He needed to get on the levee.

'I'm going in the shadows,' he said, pointing about fifteen feet away to the darkest area along the bridge wall, at the base of the levee. 'If he tries to jump the levee, I'll cut him off. If he tries to cross Sister Street, I'll cut him off. If he heads this way, we'll both get him.'

'Wait,' she said as she grabbed her radio. The sirens were closing in now.

'*3126 – Headquarters.*'

'*Go ahead.*'

'*We're under the St Claude Bridge. On the lower side, river side.*'

'*10-4.*'

Jodie clipped her radio back to her belt, pressed her right shoulder to the inner wall, her revolver held high. LaStanza nodded and eased his way into the shadows until he could see the outline of the levee's crest. His back to the bridge wall, he spread his legs and waited.

The only way Aloysius could go now was directly away from them and they would still be able to see him. Glancing back at his partner, LaStanza could barely make out her hands and the nose of her revolver peeking out from the tunnel opening.

Turning his head back toward the dumpsters, he saw something move by a tree across Sister Street. He saw Aloysius ease out from behind a tree and raise his gun at

Jodie. Swinging to his left, LaStanza fired before aiming. He saw it strike Aloysius in the side, spinning the man about 360 degrees. LaStanza fired again, striking the man square in the chest. Aloysius stumbled away from the tree, but he wouldn't go down. LaStanza aimed and fired a head shot, snapping the man's head straight back. He saw blood and brain matter rise in a mist behind Aloysius as the man fell to his butt and then sank back to the ground.

The loud echo of the magnum remained in the air, even as Jodie stepped out from the tunnel and turned to him with eyes as large as silver dollars. LaStanza moved toward his partner. He watched her gun hand slowly descend to her side. Her shoulders sank as she opened her mouth and said, 'I didn't see him.'

LaStanza reholstered his revolver and said, 'He didn't see me.'

A second later, a man came rushing up, a tall black man in a pair of overalls. 'Man-o-man!' the man stammered. 'You got him good!'

LaStanza told him to keep away from the body. Then he made the man give him his driver's license.

'My what?'

'Give me your driver's license.'

'But I didn't do nothing.'

'I know. Just give it to me.'

The man shook his head, pulled out his wallet and passed his driver's license to LaStanza, who passed it to his partner.

'Our lieutenant's gonna want you to tell him what you saw,' LaStanza explained. 'That's all.'

'Oh,' the man said in obvious relief.

LaStanza had seen enough witnesses melt into the night to let this one get away.

Overhead a police car screeched to a halt, its siren still blaring. LaStanza heard someone on the radio saying something about shots fired. Sucking in a deep gulp of slick, damp air, he moved over to Aloysius and knelt next to the man.

'I don't see his gun,' Jodie said in a shaky voice.

He could feel her hand now, on his shoulder.

'It's under him,' LaStanza said. He noticed his voice was . . . even and smooth.

'He had a gun,' the black man said. 'I seen his gun!' The man was stammering. 'I thought he done shot this white girl. Man-o-man. That was some good shootin'!'

LaStanza looked around and said, 'I don't know how the fuck he got over here.'

Two patrolmen came rushing down the concrete steps. Jodie, her voice still a little shaky, asked them to secure the area. She sent one around to canvass the houses on Sister Street, in case there were any other witnesses. Then she told the second patrolman to make sure no one messed with the body.

The patrolman glared at the head shot and said, 'Oh, wow!'

Jodie unhooked her radio and called headquarters, asking for Lieutenant Mason and Mark Land and the crime lab and the coroner.

The patrolmen began to bathe Aloysius under a bright flashlight. LaStanza reached up and asked the patrolman for the light. He pointed the light at the dead man's hands. He could see tattoos in the palms. There was a 'C' in the right palm and an 'A' in the other.

He could hear more car doors slamming overhead as cars stopped on the bridge near the steps. LaStanza found three teeth missing from the man's open mouth, along with a faint scar on the man's chin. Moving the light, he checked his handiwork. There was a black hole in the man's sternum, surrounded by a stain of blood. There was another hole in the man's right side, also stained.

LaStanza heard Mark Land descending the stairs, the sergeant's deep voice booming out orders along the way. LaStanza moved the flashlight to Aloysius's forehead where there was another black hole, neat and round, with only a hint of blood around it. Leaning forward, LaStanza looked for the exit wound, which was obscured by a mass of blood, gray skull splinters and gooey-white brain matter streaked in blood.

Standing, he turned and faced Mark. The burly Napolitano sergeant grimaced like an angry grizzly. Behind, Lieutenant Mason stepped up. Mark shook his head and said, 'Don't tell me it was you.'

LaStanza nodded slowly.

'Fuck!'

Mason's tiny eyes were narrowed as he said, 'All right. Button up. You know what to do.' He grabbed Jodie's radio and asked headquarters where the hell the crime lab was.

'Looks like you saved the state some money,' one of the patrolmen said.

'Shut up,' Mark snapped. He was right. Civilians were already gathering across the street.

Naw, LaStanza thought. The Aloysius family was bound to sue. It wouldn't be too difficult finding a fuckin' lawyer in Louisiana to file a suit. Instead of thinking that he and his partner just might be lucky to be alive, he was thinking of another Superintendent's Hearing, another fuckin' Grand Jury, another blast from a ballistic media. He could see it now. 'LaStanza shoots another one.'

Snakebitten!

Stepping back to let Mark Land at the body, LaStanza bumped into Jodie. He looked at her and she was pallid. He grabbed her arm. She looked into his eyes and whispered through shaky lips, 'I didn't see him.'

LaStanza shrugged and looked down at his tennis shoe and scratched the ground. 'That's why God invented partners.'

'Hey,' Mason said, 'you know y'all can't talk now.'

LaStanza let go of her and moved away. He was standing too close to her anyway. Neither said anything, but they continued to watch each other as Mason told Mark to take Jodie to the bureau as soon as the crime lab technician arrived. Jodie's hazel eyes, which always reminded LaStanza of a cat's eyes, slowly lost their roundness, and became catlike. He felt himself shrug again, and saw Jodie let out a long sigh. And it passed between them, there, next to the bridge, in that dark greasy part of town. It passed between their eyes. It was linking, a bonding, a knowledge that no matter what they would ever do for the rest of their lives, they had been with death, had seen death up close, had brushed against it, felt its foul breath in their faces and had defeated it . . . for the moment.

The crime lab technician arrived and took Jodie's gun. He also swabbed her hands for a neutron-activation test, to prove she hadn't fired a weapon. Before leaving, Jodie passed the driver's license of the witness to Mason and looked at LaStanza once again. Her eyes looked tired now and her eyebrows rose like a question mark. He moved over to her, leaned forward and whispered in her ear, 'Wanna fuck?'

She jabbed him in the ribs instinctively. Then he could see a hint of a smile on her lips. That was the best line he could have come up with at the moment. It was more than a joke. From the moment Mason paired up the two, *everyone* was sure they were fucking. And they were so wrong. That's what kept them close. They didn't.

Mason let out a huff. 'Quit talking,' he said through gritted teeth.

'It was personal,' LaStanza answered with a shrug.

Shaking her blonde page-boy once again and trying not to smile, Jodie followed Mark back up the steps.

LaStanza turned his weapon over to the technician, who asked Lieutenant Mason to open the cylinder, while he photographed the bullets and spent casings in the cylinder, before noting their exact position on a crime scene sheet.

Mason closed his eyes and said, 'Magnums!'

After the technician swabbed LaStanza's hands, LaStanza walked Mason through the scene, running the story down to his lieutenant.

'All right,' Mason finally said. 'After Mark takes Jodie's statement, he'll take yours.'

LaStanza knew that. He was thinking he'd better call home. He'd better call Lizette and tell her. She would be all right about it, at first. Only he knew that later, later she would think about what her father had said about him when they became engaged. He called LaStanza 'a violent man. A dangerous man'.

And he'd have to call his mother before she heard it on the news. He knew what her reaction would be. She'd start shaking and let out a faint cry with, 'Oh, no! Not another!' He couldn't call his old man to tell him to break it to his mother. At that time of night, the old man would be sleeping off the day's drunk. Anyway, the old man would just be proud. Retired police captains were usually proud when their sons did well. He'd probably call LaStanza by that damn nickname again . . . *'leopardo piccolo'* – little leopard. What bothered LaStanza was that his father was right. Sometimes he felt just like a little leopard. How did his father put it? 'Pound for pound, nature's most efficient killing machine.'

He spotted Snowood now, walking around with the crime lab technician as the man took photos of the body. Snowood was talking. 'I want an eight by ten close-up of that cocksucker's face.' Country-Ass was assembling a collection of LaStanza kills, the sick bastard.

Snowood snapped when he saw LaStanza. 'I can't believe ole Priscilla's still a virgin and you got to pop another one!'

Yeah. Right! LaStanza was certain . . . if ole Priscilla would have been there, the damn tree would have been murdered, along with the house beyond, and any cars unlucky enough to have been parked down Sister Street.

Mason told Snowood to shut up and take LaStanza to the office. Then he told LaStanza, 'Give me the keys to your unit.'

LaStanza had to tell him they were still in the car.

Snowood led the way back up the steps. Ascending slowly, LaStanza gazed down at the men milling around the body, gazed at the dark mass of blood pooled around the dead man's head, and felt, for a moment, like a leopard in a tree looking down on his kill.

'Unbe-fuckin-lievable,' Snowood said when they reached his car. 'I can't believe you got another one!'

LaStanza shrugged once again and said in a deadpan voice, 'So, what's one more Grand Jury?'

Fel Jones approached from their left. As soon as LaStanza

focused on him, Fel started laughing, grabbed his sides and leaned on the rear fender of Snowood's car. Raising his right index finger, Fel pointed at LaStanza and roared.

LaStanza was about to ask what was so fuckin' funny, but he knew the answer. He was fuckin' funny. And the more he looked at the grown detective in the slick black pants with the T-shirt labeled 'IT'S GOOD TO FIND A HARD MAN!' the more he wanted to laugh too. But he couldn't.

'Who the fuck's laughing up there?' Mark Land's angry voice boomed up at them. LaStanza looked at his watch. It was ten minutes after ten. *Jesus! It happened so fuckin' fast!*

As soon as he sat in the car, LaStanza felt his ankle tightening up. He closed his eyes and thought of Lizette, of her round face, of those full lips and her gold-brown eyes that meant more to him than anything that happened in the lower Ninth Ward.

Snowood started the engine and another thought flashed into LaStanza's mind. He had some powerful talking to do with Jodie. He had to convince her that she didn't make any mistakes that night. If she'd have moved into the shadows, she'd have been the one to shoot the bastard, even if she wasn't a fuckin' leopard. But he knew it wouldn't be easy convincing her.

He had made a mistake that night. He was so sure Aloysius was behind the dumpsters. He was lucky to spot the bald-headed bastard. How did the old police cliché go? Something like, 'It's good to be good, but it's better to be lucky.' He would have to tell Jodie all that.

Cruising back up St Claude, Snowood said he had an idea. 'Why don't we drop on by Mercy and tell that little girl you just blew that fucker's brains out?'

'Naw,' LaStanza said. 'No good unless I got to shoot the whole fuckin' parole board.'

'Yeah, you're right!'

This story is for debb

MIDNIGHT AT THE LOST AND FOUND

Mark Timlin

It all started at a party at Vincent Garibaldi's restaurant near Loughborough Junction. Vinnie's it's called. It's situated about halfway between the railway station and the turning that runs up to the hospital. It was always full of young nurses, which is one of the reasons I started going there. I was in the job then, and Vinnie spotted me right away. He liked having coppers as customers. They drank a lot, and kept the place tidy, so he started giving me free meals. He still does, even though I'm long off the force and run a one-man private investigation firm in Tulse Hill. But I don't take the piss. In fact, before the party I hadn't set foot in the place for six months.

The thrash was all in aid of Vincent's one and only offspring, Vincent Garibaldi Junior, more usually known, at least at home, as Little Vinnie, on the occasion of his engagement to be married to one Claire McCammon. A model, as Big Vinnie told me on the phone when he invited me.

Now I've known Little Vinnie since he'd needed stabilizers on his bike, so naturally I put in an appearance, and even stumped up for a Chinese vase that caught my eye in Harrods one Saturday afternoon, and had it gift wrapped with a big red ribbon on top. Don't ever say I haven't got class.

And besides I was looking forward to seeing Vinnie again.

He's a good man. Kind. A friend. And he knew that I'd do anything for him, any time. No questions asked.

I walked into Vinnie's dead on eight. There was a notice in the window declaring the place closed for the night for a private function.

The walls of the restaurant were white with dark beams set in them every six feet or so, and dotted with framed watercolours of Italian scenery. The tablecloths were red and white checked, and most of the tables had been pushed up against one wall and were covered with platters of food. Elvis was on the stereo system and the place smelt wonderful. I felt like I'd come home after a long and difficult journey.

Inside it was already pretty crowded. An eclectic bunch. Guys in smart suits, from where Little Vinnie worked, I surmised. Some beautiful young women, who the guys in suits were ogling. Model friends of Claire's, I imagined. In fact one of them would probably be Claire herself. Then there were some of Vinnie's old gang. The Italians he'd grown up with in the East End, friends and family both. And finally, a few honoured customers, like myself, who Vinnie had adopted over the years.

Big Vinnie, Little Vinnie, and the Garibaldi matriarch, Maria – Vinnie's missis and Little Vinnie's momma, as she never stopped reminding the world – were sitting in one of the booths holding court. I'd been right about Claire being one of the beautiful young women, as Big Vinnie called her over on my arrival.

She *was* beautiful, although maybe a little older than the teenage super models who were always popping up on TV these days. Her hair was long and dark. Her heart-shaped face was perfectly made-up, her teeth gleamed like she had a personal dentist and, in the little black dress she wore, she was drop-dead gorgeous. I envied Little Vinnie.

Big Vinnie introduced me to her. He described me in such glowing terms and was so profuse in his compliments that I almost blushed. Claire offered me her hand and I shook it. Hers was cool and smooth. Mine, I'm sure, wasn't. I gave her the present, and she put it with some others and thanked me. Little Vinnie nodded. He'd always been cool, had Little Vinnie.

Vincent got up to fetch me a drink. We walked over to the bar together, and he reached for the Jack Daniel's bottle, and I said, 'You went a bit over the top there, Vinnie. I thought for a minute you were going to get out my baby pictures.'

He swung round towards me so fast that the bourbon he'd poured slopped all over his hand. He was as white as a sheet and I said, 'What's the matter? Are you all right?'

'Nick,' he said. 'I've got to talk to you.'

'Talk away.'

'Not here. In private.'

He poured me another drink and one for himself and, taking the bottle, he took me through the kitchen, up the back stairs to the tiny room he called his office, where we'd shared more than one bottle in the past.

He sat behind his desk, and I took the comfortable old chair next to it.

'What's the matter?' I said.

'I don't know how to tell you.'

'Just tell me,' I said. 'Fast or slow, long or short. We've got all night. I'm going nowhere till we get this sorted.'

'It's Claire. You've seen her. A lovely girl. A model like I told you. She's like a daughter to me and Maria already. The daughter we never had.' He hesitated for a long moment. 'There are some photographs of her.'

I was going to say that if she was a model it was a racing certainty, but it didn't seem to be the time for jokes by the look on Vinnie's boat race.

Vinnie squeezed the glass he was holding until I was afraid it would implode from the force. 'Such photos. It was when you mentioned "holiday snaps".'

'Go on,' I said. I was none the wiser.

'I got them through the post. Filth. If Maria was to see them . . . ' He hesitated again. 'He wanted money.'

'He?' I asked.

'Whoever sent the letter.'

It was like pulling teeth but, when I spoke, I spoke gently. 'What letter?' I said.

'The letter that came with the photographs.'

'Blackmail?' I asked.

He looked into my eyes. 'You know?'

'It's pretty obvious. Now tell me exactly what happened from the beginning.'

He sighed, drank a mouthful of JD and asked for one of my cigarettes. I'd never seen Vinnie smoke before.

'Little Vinnie and Claire have been together for over a year,' he explained. 'A month ago he asked her to marry him. She accepted. It was the happiest day of Maria's and my life. Our only son. Our only child. They are to be married next year. I already have your invitation to the reception. It will be here in the restaurant. Just like the party tonight.'

'Thanks Vinnie,' I said.

'It should be a time of rejoicing. Instead . . . '

'Instead?'

'A week after the engagement was announced I received two photographs and a letter.'

'Where?'

He looked puzzled. 'What?' he said.

'Here or at home?' I said.

'Here at the restaurant. If Maria was to see them . . . ' It was the second time he'd said that, and I knew what he meant. I'd seen her moods before.

'What did the letter say?'

'Here,' he said. 'I kept it.' He took a piece of paper from his inside pocket. He held it as if it were contagious. 'You and I are the only ones to have seen it . . . '

'Nobody's going to hear about it from me.'

'I knew I could trust you.' He handed the paper to me. It was typed by an electric typewriter or a word processor on a sheet of A4 bond. It read:

Mr Garibaldi
I am enclosing a few snaps of your daughter-in-law to be.
Nice aren't they?

These pictures and negatives are a wedding gift to you.
But there are others. The rest will cost you £10,000.
I will ring you at your restaurant next Monday at noon.
If you don't want them, I know plenty who will.

It was unsigned. Naturally.

'And he rang?' I asked.

'Yes. He wanted the money in used twenties and tenners,
to be wrapped in newspaper, put in a plastic bag and left in
the unlocked boot of my car in the National Theatre car park
on the following Thursday at eight p.m. I was to leave the car
for at least an hour. He said I'd be watched. If I didn't do
exactly as I was told the photos would be sent to Little
Vinnie's boss and Maria.'

'Did you recognize the voice?'

He shook his head.

'Is Little Vinnie still working at the same place?'

Little Vinnie worked for a city bank. He was a high flyer.
Destined for orbit before he was thirty. I knew that Vinnie
had always dreamed that one day his son and heir would
take over the business. But things had changed. The old
Italian creed of the son following in his father's footsteps had
been washed away. It was tough. But that was the way it
went in the new Britain.

'Yes,' said Vincent. 'Photos like that would make him a
laughing stock. Ruin his career.'

'What? In the city? Christ, Vinnie, they do it with donkeys
up there, don't they?'

'Have you ever seen the place he works in?' he asked.
'They'd do the accounts with quill pens if they could still get
them. It's the only merchant bank in the square mile with a
notice outside that says, "We don't do it with donkeys in this
establishment".'

I was glad he hadn't lost all of his sense of humour.

'Take my word for it, Nick. It would screw up his career
and wreck his marriage before it even took place. Maria
would make sure of that.'

'So you did as you were told?'

'I didn't know what else to do.'

'Police?'

'Are you joking?'

'Why didn't you call me straight away?'

He shrugged. 'I thought I could take care of it myself.'

'Did you receive the photos as promised?'

'Yes. Another dozen.'

'And the negs?'

He nodded again.

'Did you keep them?'

He looked across the room. 'In the safe. No one ever goes in there but me.'

'And now?'

'Another letter.'

'That makes sense. Where is it?'

'In the safe also.'

'Let's take a look.'

'At the photographs too?'

'I'm afraid so. I won't be able to do much unless I do.'

He shook his head sadly, then took a bunch of keys out of his jacket pocket and opened the door of the ancient safe that stood in one corner under the barred window. He took out two large brown envelopes, and a smaller white one, and handed them to me. The first brown envelope was typed by what looked like the same machine as the letter I'd read. It was a piece of cheap stationery sold at thousands of outlets in the UK. It had been postmarked three weeks earlier in London W1. The second one was exactly the same. Same typeface, same postmark, a week or so later. The white envelope was similarly cheap, similarly typed, similarly postmarked, two days ago. I opened the brown envelopes first. Inside were fourteen, glossy, professional looking 10x8 colour prints, and a stack of negatives in little transparent envelopes of their own. They were all of Claire and a dark-haired man with hair long enough to hide his features. Her face was clear enough. She looked a couple of years younger than the woman I'd met downstairs, but not more innocent. Each of the prints was of explicit sex acts. What those two weren't doing to each other wasn't worth doing. I lined the photographs up on Vinnie's desk, much to his distress. 'Sorry Vinnie,' I said. 'I'm not enjoying this.'

And I wasn't. My old friend's eyes were full of tears, and he was wringing his hands together as if he were going to pull them off at the wrists.

'Have you got a magnifying glass?' I asked.

'*Nick*,' he said, and his voice broke with emotion.

'I want to see if the place these were taken can be identified. If you want to go back downstairs, I'll talk to you later.'

'No,' he said. 'I'll stay.'

He found me a magnifying glass in a drawer, and I pulled over the lamp that stood on the corner of the desk and switched it on. I studied the pictures closely. They'd all been taken in the same place. A white painted room with a double bed covered in a white sheet. On the wall behind the bed was a framed poster of a holiday advertisement for Athens. On the table by the bed was a digital clock radio. Using the glass, I could see the display clearly. The photos had been taken between 22.10 and 00.20. I couldn't be sure, but it looked as if they'd all been taken on the same day. Or night. There was an empty glass on the table in the earliest photo, and it was still there in the last. The man was unidentifiable. No tattoos or scars on his body. When his hair hadn't hidden his face for the camera, he'd kept it out of shot. Like I said, Claire hadn't been so coy. She looked like she was half-stoned when the photos had been taken. In one, where the man was putting it to her doggie fashion, her face was looking directly at the camera lens. Her mouth was open in an 'O' of what could have been pleasure or pain, and her eyes were as vacant as a closed down hotel.

When I'd finished studying the photos, I gathered them together and put them back into the envelopes. Then I took another piece of A4 bond from the white envelope and unfolded it. It was typed on the same machine again, and read:

Mr Garibaldi
Thanks for the cash last time.
Sorry, but expenses are mounting. I need another £10,000.
I'll phone next Thursday at noon.
You know what will happen if you don't help me out.

Once again there was no signature.

'Tomorrow's Thursday,' I said. Sometimes the obvious needs stating, just to try and keep hold of normality.

Vinnie nodded again.

'These are pretty explicit,' I said, tapping the envelopes. 'How do you think Little Vinnie would take that?'

He shrugged.

'And how about you?'

'We all make mistakes,' he said. 'She's a wonderful girl. A diamond. She makes Little Vinnie happy. That's all I care about. I don't want him to know anything about this unless he positively has to.'

'You're a good man, Vinnie,' I said. 'But we've got to put a stop to this. You did right telling me.'

'What can you do?'

'Lots. But first I need another drink.'

Vinnie poured me out another large one and I lit a cigarette. 'Well,' I said. 'Some things are obvious.'

He looked surprised. 'What?'

'Don't get excited, Vinnie,' I said. 'Nothing that's going to solve the problem in a flash. Just some elementary facts.'

'Like?'

'Like the blackmailer knows that Little Vinnie and Claire have got engaged. He knows about the restaurant. He knows you and your motor. He knows that Little Vinnie has the kind of job that a scandal could ruin. And most of all he knows that you'll pay. And if you pay once, it's a reasonable assumption that you'll keep on paying until you're white. That's why he kept some photographs back.'

'And how does knowing all that help?'

'I don't know yet. But I know one other thing.'

'What?'

'I'll have to speak to Claire about it.'

'No.'

'I mean it, Vinnie,' I said.

'Why?'

'A load of reasons. She's the only one we know who can identify the geezer in the pictures, and who took them. There was either another person there, or the camera was on a timer.'

'Couldn't we just fix up another drop and you pinch whoever comes to collect the money?'

'Sure we could. Nothing simpler. But what happens if it's just a mug punter the blackmailer's paid to do the gig? A nobody. The blackmailer sees what's occurred, and the photos are all over London in a few hours.'

He sighed again. 'Sure, Nick,' he said. 'You know best.'

'It's the only way, Vinnie. It doesn't give me a good feeling. But at least she should be aware of the mess she's got you in.'

'But not Little Vinnie. He mustn't know.'

'I promise you, Vin. He won't know from me. If Claire gives me a blank, we'll do it your way. But if she's the kind of woman you say she is, she'll understand. And if she isn't. Well, it's better to know now, rather than later.'

'What do you mean?'

'I mean she might be in on the plot.'

'God no. Not that on top of everything else.'

'I'm not saying that she is, Vinnie. But it's best to know, isn't it?'

'I suppose you're right.'

'I know I am. Have you got her number?'

He fetched a little notebook out of one of his pockets, took a restaurant card from another, and copied an address and telephone number on to the back and slid it across the desk to me. 'I'll phone her in the morning,' I said. 'And I'll need those photos and letters.'

'What?'

'You heard, Vinnie.'

'Why?'

'Lots of reasons. Shock value for one. If she knows we've seen them, and you've paid, she'll be much more likely to talk. I want to see her reaction. If she's as horrified about what's happening as I hope she'll be, fine. I won't need to show them to her. I hope I don't. Otherwise I will, just to jog her memory. Either way, she has to know they exist. She was there for God's sake, even if she did look like she'd been dabbling with some serious medication. I want to know who took them, and who's had access to them since.'

'I don't know. What will she think?'

I was going to say that she might think about leaving the lens cap on next time, but I wasn't looking for a slap from one of Vinnie's big hands.

'Quite frankly, Vinnie, I don't give a damn what she thinks,' I said. 'It's you I'm worried about. And one thing's for sure.'

'What?'

'If whoever wrote the letters kept some photos back the first time he put the black on you, he'll do it again this time. He'll keep taking your money till you're skint and sold the house and hocked the restaurant. He'll see you in the poor house, and Maria too. This is the kind of person you're dealing with. So if Claire gets her nose put out of joint by what I'm going to say to her – tough.' I was angrier than I thought I was, so I didn't say more.

'OK, Nick,' Vincent said eventually. 'But don't be too hard on her.'

I continued saying nothing.

'And what shall I do?' he asked after a moment.

'When the blackmailer calls?'.

'Yes.'

'Go along with whatever he says. He thinks he's got you where he wants you. Let him go on thinking that.'

He nodded yet again.

'And can I take the photos?'

Another nod, and he said, 'I'm trusting you, Nick.'

'I appreciate that, Vinnie,' I said. 'I won't let you down.'

'Do I owe you anything?' he asked.

'For what?'

'For helping me.'

'Vinnie. You ever ask me a question like that again and were not friends. Understand!'

He stuck his hand out, and I shook it. 'You sort this out for me,' he said. 'And you need never buy food again.'

'Cheers, Vinnie,' I said, and we went back to the party. But it didn't seem much fun after what I'd heard, and I left pretty soon, without saying goodbye to anyone.

I called the number Vinnie had given me for Claire the next morning at ten. She was in. 'Claire McCammon,' she said when she picked up the phone.

'Hello,' I said. 'It's Nick Sharman here. I met you last night at the party.'

'I remember. Thank you for the vase. It's lovely.'

'Good.'

She paused for a moment. 'So what can I do for you?' she asked.

'I'd like to talk to you.'

'Why?'

'Not on the phone.'

'It sounds serious.'

'It is.'

'Is it to do with Vinnie's father?'

'Yes.'

'Is he ill?'

'No.'

'Does he know you're phoning?

'Yes. Look, can I come and see you?'

There was another pause. 'I suppose so. But I wish you'd tell me why.'

'I will when I see you.'

'When?'

'Today. Now.'

A third, shorter pause. 'All right. I'll be home all day. Do you know the address?'

'Yes. Vinnie gave it to me. And Miss McCammon . . . '

'Yes?'

'Please don't tell your fiancé about this. Just wait until I've spoken to you.'

'It does sound serious. And mysterious.'

'I'm sure it will be all right. I'll be over soon. I'll tell you then.'

When I put the phone down I wondered if she thought I was going to ask her for a date.

She lived in Fulham. I drove over and took the envelopes with me. I hoped I wouldn't have to use them. Her address was in a thirties block. I went up to her floor in an old-fashioned lift that was as slow as it was noisy. She answered my ring immediately, and led me into a warm, airy room with a view of the Fulham Road. The windows were double glazed, and it was very quiet in the flat. She was wearing an old sweat shirt with *Primal Scream* printed on the front in faded letters, and blue jeans. Her feet were bare. She offered me coffee and I accepted. She told me I could smoke. It was all very civilized. But I was about to drop a bomb that might blow her civilized little life into pieces. When she came back with the coffee I was standing by the window watching the people going about their business in the street below. 'Do sit down,' she said.

I sat on a pink sofa, and watched her pour out the coffee. When we'd got a cup each and she was seated in the armchair opposite me, I told her what I'd come to tell. As I talked, her face paled to a dirty grey colour, and her hands shook so much she had to put her coffee cup on the small table next to her, and when she tried to light a cigarette she dropped it twice. I didn't pull any punches. I wanted to know if it was her and an accomplice who had written the letters and made the telephone demands of Vinnie. When I'd finished she said, 'My God, I'd almost forgotten about them.'

'Whoever is blackmailing Vinnie hasn't.'

'Have you seen them?' she asked.

'Yes.'

'My God,' she said again, got up, dropped her cigarette into her coffee cup where it died with a hiss, and ran for the door. I could hear the sound of retching, then silence. If she was putting on an act, she should give up modelling and take up a career on the stage. She came back about five minutes later. She'd regained some of her colour and was carrying a white towel which she used to dab at her lips. The front of her sweat shirt was spotted with water stains. She sat down, lit another cigarette and pulled a face at the taste. 'Poor Vincent,' she said.

'That's exactly my sentiment.'

'I'm not blackmailing him.'

'I believe you.'

'How can I help?'

'Tell me about them.'

'What?'

'You know,' I said.

She took a deep breath. 'I hardly know you,' she said.

'Perhaps I'm the best person to tell then.'

It was that simple. 'All right,' she said.

I took out a notebook.

'You're not going to write anything down.'

'No one will see what I've written. That's a promise. But I need to take notes. Now we can do this my way, or I can leave now and let Vincent Garibaldi pay ten, twenty, thirty, forty thousand quid to some scumbag. Until he has to sell the restaurant and his house, and he and Maria are living in twin cardboard boxes on the Embankment begging twenty pence pieces from strangers. Do you want that?'

She shook her head.

'Right. So tell me.'

And she did. 'It was six years ago. I'd not been in London all that long. I was just a baby. I met a photographer. His name was Damien. Damien Simmons. He's quite well known, or he was. It's the old story.' Her mouth twisted bitterly. 'Young, naive girl. Experienced man in the business. He swept me off my feet. Told me he'd make me a star. I went and lived with him. He was a bastard.' She started to cry gently. I gave her a handkerchief. I always carry one when I'm going to screw someone's life up. 'He was on drugs. Everything. Booze, dope, coke. Smack sometimes. Pills all the time.'

'How old was he?' I asked.

'When I met him? Thirty-five or so. He'd been around.'

'And?'

'And he did what he promised. Broke me into the big time. But there was a price to pay. I became his property. He made me take drugs too.' She looked at me. 'Oh, I know. It's no excuse. I was stupid. But I was so young. He ruled my life. There was money coming in. Big money. We had everything. A beautiful house with a studio. Cars. Clothes. But it couldn't last.'

'How long *did* it last?'

'A year. Eighteen months. But I knew that if I didn't get away I'd be an old woman by the time I was twenty-five. Washed up. Literally.'

'So?'

'So I left. Packed a few thing and ran home as fast as my BMW would take me. And it was mine. Bought out of my own money.'

I didn't argue. It was her story.

'My family comes from Manchester,' she continued. 'I cleaned up my act and got taken on the books of a Manchester agency. Not as glamorous as London maybe, but not far off. It was all happening up there then. Remember? The Happy Mondays. Factory Records. The Hacienda.'

It had hardly been my scene, but I knew, so I nodded.

'All gone now, of course. Like everything goes. Anyway, after a couple of years I heard that Damien had got married and moved to New York. So I came back and did even better down here. Then I met Little Vinnie and the rest you know.'

'Is he still in the States?'

She shook her head. 'No. He came back a couple of years ago.'

'Have you seen him?'

The little colour she'd regained in her face disappeared again. 'God, no. I make sure I don't.'

'Is he still married?'

'Oh yes. Damien knows which side of his bread is buttered.'

'How do you mean?'

'He married a lady.' She saw my look. 'A real Lady. With a capital "L". Daughter of a Lord. Very rich. And I mean very. But the old man hates Damien.'

'How do you know all this if you haven't seen him?'

'Gossip. Modelling is that kind of business.'

'So being married to money, he wouldn't need any extra.'

'Knowing Damien, he always needs extra money.'

'Do you know where he lives?'

'Several places. A house in the country, a flat in town and a studio. And of course the cottage in Provence. And when I say cottage I mean twelve bedrooms.'

I was beginning to like Claire. 'Have you got any?' I asked.

'Any what?'

'Any of the photographs.'

She wouldn't meet my eye.

'Claire. I need to know. I need to know how many were taken.'

'He took thousands of photographs of me.'

'Jesus,' I said.

'But mostly glamour shots. Nothing bad.'

'The ones I saw weren't like that.'

She blushed. 'I know. I remember that session. It was just before I ran away from him. It was the last straw really. He'd been on at me for ages to do some fuck shots.' She paused. 'Sorry, but that's what we call them. That night I gave in. I didn't know what I was doing. I was on dope, wine and Quaaludes.'

'That'll get you every time. Who's in the photos with you?'

'Damien.'

'And who took them?'

'He did. On a timed exposure. I couldn't do what I did in front of anyone else, no matter what I'd had.'

'I see. So only you and he knew about them.'

'As far as I know. Are they something you'd boast about?'

'I wouldn't,' I said. 'But maybe he would. Do you think he's capable of blackmail?'

'He's capable of anything,' she said with such certainty that I believed her.

'Do you know how many photos were taken that night?'

'I don't exactly. It was a long time ago, and I was out of it. Three rolls, I think.'

'How many on a roll?'

'Twenty-four or thirty-six.'

'And Vincent has only fourteen. This could go on for years. How many do you have?'

'I don't know.'

'Are they here?'

'Yes.'

'Can I see them?'

'Why?'

'Not for kicks, Claire,' I said. 'Because I need to.'

She sighed heavily. 'I'll get them,' she said.

Once again she got up and left the room.

She came back carrying a plain white envelope, cardboard backed, A4 size, with 'PHOTOGRAPHS – PLEASE DO NOT BEND' printed in one corner. I opened it. Inside were a sheaf of glossies, twenty in all. Plus a bunch of negatives. They were a mixture as before, except that in two the man had not hidden his face. In one in particular his features came across clear and sharp. He was handsome in a rattish kind of way, and he didn't look a tenth as stoned as Claire. 'Thanks,' I said.

She shrugged.

'I'll need to take these with me.'

'Why?'

'I have my reasons. Trust me. No one, and I mean no one will get a glimpse of them.'

She hesitated. 'I do trust you, Mr Sharman. Vinnie's father has a real love for you. But you have my life there. My life with Little Vinnie. Don't let me down.'

'I won't,' I said.

What I *didn't* say was that if I screwed up she probably wouldn't have a life with Little Vinnie. But I think she knew. That was why she let me have them.

I told her not to worry. I don't think it did much good. I
also told her that as soon as I had any news I'd call. Finally I
told her not to say a word to Little Vinnie, and act as much
like normal as she could. She said that she would, and I left.

I got back to my place around one and called Vincent
Garibaldi Senior on the phone. When he answered, I asked,
'Has he called?'
   'Yes.'
   'And?'
   'The deal as before. Ten thousand in tens and twenties in
my car at the National Theatre car park, Saturday night,
seven o'clock.'
   'Good.'
   'Shall I get the money?'
   'No. I've had an idea about that. Let me sort it out.'
   'Ten grand. Where are you going to get that sort of money
in a hurry?'
   'Let me worry about that.'
   'Suit yourself. Have you seen Claire?'
   'Yes.'
   'Is she all right?'
   'As well as can be expected.'
   'Could she help?' he asked.
   'Yes.'
   'Good.'
   'Are you in the restaurant later?' I asked him.
   'All day.'
   'I'll pass by about six.'
   'I'll see you later then,' he said, and rang off.
   Next I looked up Damien Simmons in the phone book. As
Claire had said, there were two addresses and numbers for
him in London. One appeared to be his home, and the other
his studio. I copied them both down in my notebook.
   After all that I left the flat, got in the motor and headed for
Tooting. I parked on a meter outside a vast gin palace of a
boozer on the main street. I pushed open the doors and
walked in to where another frenetic lunchtime drinking

session was just winding down. The bar was smoky, and the tables were covered with empty glasses and full ashtrays. The big screen TV was tuned into Sky Sport, and the jukebox was pounding out Whitney Houston. The fruit machines were doing great business, and the two pool tables were in use. At the bar, a line of serious drinkers were gazing at their reflections in the mirror behind the optics. The clientele was a rich mixture of the underclass taking their leisure, and spending the DSS's money, and anything they could cop on the black economy. They ranged in age from fifteen to seventy-five. The men seemed to be either toothless and bald, or shell-suited and gymnasium obsessed. The women were mostly blonde, mostly showing too much chest and thigh, and most of them seemed to have OD'd on the sun bed, except for a few ratty old crones who sat together with their milk stouts dissecting the morals of everyone else in the place. I strolled up to the bar, and the barman, a thug in black trousers and waistcoat over a white shirt open almost to the waist, put his cigarette down in an ashtray and walked over.

'What?' he said.

'Is Swanson in?'

'Mr Swanson to you.'

'Is *Mr* Swanson in?' I asked.

'Dunno. Might be.'

'Well, his Roller's outside on a double yellow with a traffic warden making sure nobody nicks the hubcaps. So is he in or not?'

'I'll have to check. Wanna drink?'

'No thanks. I've seen the state of your glasses before.'

The ice cream frowned then picked up the phone and tapped out a number.

When it was answered, he said, 'That geezer Sharman's here.'

Mr Sharman to you, I thought, but said nothing. Discretion being the better part, and all that.

'OK, Guv,' said the barman and put down the dog. 'Go on up,' he said. 'You know the way.'

I did, and I did as he said. I went upstairs and tapped on

the last door in the corridor. 'Come in,' said a deep cockney voice, and I did that too.

Terry Swanson's office was big and plush, befitting his status in the local underworld. It held a huge desk, two upright chairs, a sofa, a cocktail bar and a huge filing cabinet. It also held Terry Swanson, sitting behind the desk on a leather swivel chair. He was about fifty-five, huge, ugly as shit and twice as dirty. He was wearing an immaculate double-breasted suit over a white shirt with a Kray Brothers tie. The suit was too tight, and well out of fashion, only no one dared tell him. In one hand he held a cigar nearly as long as Nelson's column, and in the other a glass of Scotch. The bottle was on the table in front of him.

'Hello, Nick, m'boy,' he said when I walked in. 'How are ya?'

'Fine, Mr Swanson. Never better.' Note I called him 'Mister' to his face.

'So what can I do for you this afternoon? Have a drink, son. Sit down.'

I got a glass from the bar and helped myself to a small one from the bottle.

'So?' said Swanson when I was settled.

'Funny money,' I said.

He sat up in his seat. 'Do what?'

'Funny money,' I repeated. 'Counterfeit.'

'What about it?'

'I need some.'

'And you think I know about that sort of thing?'

'Good chance.'

'What makes you say that?'

I was on tricky ground. 'Word about.'

'About where?'

'The manor.'

'Interesting.'

'I thought so.'

'And why would you want snide dough, Nick? You looking for a career change so late in life?'

'I need some flash, Mr Swanson,' I said. 'It's a little

situation I've got involved in where I don't want to use real money.'

He seemed affronted. 'Not real,' he said. 'What I've got is as good as real. Better. Silver strips and aged by experts. Just ask the mug punters who run offies round here, and the Paki shopkeepers who take it every day. This once great country of ours is run on snide money, Nick. How do you think the government's keeping inflation down? They don't print any more themselves these days. They leave it to people like me.'

'I bet you're sorry Maggie's gone, aren't you?' I said.

'Those were the days, Nick,' he said nostalgically. 'Free enterprise. That's how I made my dough.'

'Literally,' I remarked.

He smiled. 'That's right. I like that. I'll have to tell my old woman that one.'

'So you've got some?' I said.

'You could say that. You could say I was holding certain assets. Yes.'

'Ten grand's worth?'

Swanson sat back and waved his cigar in the air as if ten thousand pounds was nothing much. It probably wasn't to him. 'That how much you want?'

I nodded.

'No problem. Now normally I sell it off at three to one. But as it's you, and it's getting late on a Thursday, I'll give you a special discount. You want ten grand. Give me two and it's yours.'

'Well, actually, Mr Swanson,' I said. 'I don't want to buy it.'

'What *do* you want then? Do you want me to pay you to take it off my hands?' And he smiled evilly.

'I thought I might borrow it for a while,' I ventured. 'Just till Sunday. Early Sunday. Saturday night really.'

He laughed a gravelly laugh. 'Borrow? No such thing, son.' He thought for a moment. 'But you're not a bad lad. You've kept a low 'un for me a couple of times, so I might find my way clear to hire it to you for a couple of days.'

'Like Avis?'

'No, son. Hertz. Number one. See, I've got overheads. Clerical staff to pay. If I just lent it to you, who'd count it when it came back? Anyway, I'd be setting a precedent. A dangerous precedent.' You could see Mr Swanson watched the Open University. 'Before you know it, every little slag round here would be asking for sale or return on the gear. Nothing personal, but you do understand, don't you?'

I nodded. 'How much?' I asked.

'Give me a monkey and the snide's yours till Sunday. But if I don't get it back by closing time, then you'd better be here opening time Monday with the other fifteen hundred, or I'll have to send someone out to find you, and we wouldn't want that, would we?'

I shook my head. No, we definitely didn't want that. I'd seen Swanson's collectors before. *Jurassic Park* wasn't in it. I took out the sum of my worldly goods and counted out five hundred in twenties, and put them on the desk.

'You don't mind if I check this, do you?' he asked. 'There's some very dodgy stuff around at the moment.'

I shook my head.

'Help yourself,' said Swanson. 'Top drawer of the cabinet. There's tens, twenties and fifties in thousand lumps.'

'I'll take half and half, tens and twenties. No one takes fifties in this town any more.'

Swanson smiled. 'Criminal innit?' he said, as he examined my notes.

I went to the filing cabinet and pulled open the top drawer. Inside were bundles of cash in plastic bags. I took out five packets of tens and five packets of twenties and put them on the desk.

'Not much security here,' I said. 'Don't you believe in safes?'

'Who'd rob me?' said Swanson. 'The last bloke who knocked me for a pint downstairs ended up on Tooting Common with his hand nailed to a tree.'

I watched as he checked the snide I'd taken. 'Good job he didn't drink double Scotches, wasn't it?'

'For *him*. No, son. No one robs me round here. My justice is swift and hard. You'd do well to remember that.'

'I will. Got a bag for this lot?'

'What d'you think this is? Fuckin' Sainsbury's? Bung it in your sky.'

I put the bundles of notes into my jacket pockets. 'Thanks, Mr Swanson,' I said. 'See you Sunday.'

'Thank *you*, Nick. A pleasure doing business with you. Come in the afternoon. Bring your bird, or some of the family. There's a right nice atmosphere down here on Sunday afternoons. Complimentary roast potatoes and all.'

'I heard there was nude mud-wrestling in the snug, and Pit Bull fights in the beer garden.' I was feeling bolder now I'd got the cash.

'Always the sense of humour. Now fuck off, and be careful with that dough, or you owe me.'

I nodded, and fucked off like he said, went home and had a beer.

Around six I drove back to Vinnie's. He fed me up with spaghetti and meat balls, and then came and sat at my table. It was still early and the place was practically empty. I'd got the counterfeit cash with me in a carrier bag.

I told Vinnie what had gone on at Claire McCammon's place, and when I'd finished he asked, 'Do you think she was in on the plot?'

'No,' I said. 'I wouldn't stake my life on it, but I'm pretty sure.'

'Thank God for that at least. What now?'

'Now you do exactly what the blackmailer says. You put the cash in the car and the car in the car park. On the top floor. I'll be watching. If Simmons picks up the dough, I'll follow him. I've got a couple of addresses. I've got a pretty good idea where he'll end up. If it's not him, I'll nab whoever it is, there and then, and scare the truth out of him. This is the money you use.' I tapped the carrier. 'Don't get it mixed up with yours, or try and spend it. It ain't exactly kosher.'

'Where did it come from?'

'Contacts. Don't worry about it.'

'If you say so. Aren't you going to see Simmons before Saturday?'

'No. I don't want to frighten him off. I need hard evidence that he's the blackmailer. I want to catch him with the readies. And I want all the photos and negs. If I go and see him now, and he *is* at it, he won't turn up on Saturday. And you and Claire'll know that the pictures still exist. I don't want him to know that anyone else is involved. Stay cool, Vinnie. It's got to be him.'

'How will you know him?'

'I've got a couple of photos.' Then I wished I hadn't said it.

'What kind of photos?'

'You know.'

His face crumpled.

'Sorry, mate,' I said. 'Claire salvaged some when she left him.'

He shook his head. 'I wish I'd just paid up and never got you into this.'

'You'd've never stopped paying.'

'I know, but . . . '

I was getting a bit pissed off after all I'd done. 'Listen,' I said. 'Are you sure you want to go through with this? I can go now if you want, and leave you to deal with it on your own.'

He looked up with misery written all over his face. 'Sorry, Nick. I'm behaving like an ungrateful bastard after you've gone to so much trouble to help. Yes. We go through with it.'

'Good. Now I'm off. I'll check with you on Saturday that there's been no change of plan. You won't see me on the night. So don't go looking. We don't want to spook our friend, do we?'

He shook his head.

I spent Friday and Saturday morning on other business. I called Vinnie at three on Saturday afternoon. He'd heard nothing. I told him to keep calm, and I'd talk to him after it was all over.

I drove up to Waterloo about six. I'd borrowed a Cortina estate off a friend of mine in the motor trade, because my Jaguar was too noticeable to be any good in a tailing situation. The evening was dull, with a light rain that didn't seem to want to settle, but rather hung like a fine mist over London. I dressed in a woollen shirt, jeans and DM's, with my old Burberry on top. I put all the photographs and negatives into one of the brown envelopes which I slipped into the pocket of my coat. I parked in the NT garage, in a space on the ground floor, near the exit to the stairs. Then I took the lift to the top floor and found a niche next to a concrete pillar with a good panoramic view. The only problem was that I might get nicked for loitering with intent. At seven precisely I saw Vinnie's green Mercedes drive up the ramp and park. He got out of the car and walked to the lift without a backward glance. A fair amount of other cars arrived during the next ten minutes, but no one showed any interest in the Merc. At 7.10 precisely, a blue BMW-7 Series came up the ramp and drove slowly round the parking area. The car drew up behind Vinnie's, and a tall, dark-haired man got out. He was an older version of the man in the photos in my pocket. He opened the boot of the Merc, took out a green carrier bag, threw it in the back of the BMW, slammed the boot of the Mercedes, got back into his car and drove off slowly. I legged it for the stairs, and ran down them as fast as I could, and straight to the Cortina. There was a queue at the exit, and the BMW was two cars in front of me when I joined it. I was lucky. But I find you make your own luck in this game.

I saw the BMW turn right outside the car park and fidgeted whilst the driver of the car in front of me paid up. I tossed the geezer in the box a fiver, didn't wait for change, and the tyres of the Ford screeched as I took off in the same direction as the Beemer. I had a pretty good idea which direction he'd take. Both the addresses for Simmons had been in Bayswater, and I caught him at the roundabout on the south side of Westminster Bridge. He was in no rush. He'd had a result. It was the second time, so why should he worry? He'd got away with it once and thought he was golden. I kept the BMW in sight as he weaved through the traffic on Parliament Square and headed for the park. I dropped back and let him show off a bit in Park Lane, but it wasn't difficult keeping his car in sight, even through the rain and the gathering darkness. For my part, I did what I could to avoid him spotting me. I kept as many cars as I could between the Cortina and the BMW, and I kept switching from sidelights to dipped headlights to main beam, but I didn't think he had a clue that I was there. He went straight to the studio address. I'd guessed that he would. Saturday night there'd be no one there, and I imagined he'd kept schtum about his little scheme to the wife. He parked his car outside, and took the money in with him.

I gave him a couple of minutes inside, then walked over and rang the door bell. He answered it.

'Mr Simmons?' I asked.

'Yes.'

'My name's Nick Sharman. I'm a private detective. I wonder if I might have a few minutes of your time?'

'Why?'

'It's a private matter.'

'Obviously. You being a private detective and all.'

What a wit. I knew we weren't going to get on right away. 'It concerns Miss Claire McCammon,' I said.

'Claire. How is she?' he asked coolly.

'Not bad. I wonder if we could talk inside. It's rather damp out here.'

'Talk about what?'

'I think you know.'

'No,' he said.

'Then we'll talk here. It's about some photographs.'

'Photographs?' As if he'd never heard the word.

'Photographs of you and Claire. Do you really want the neighbours to hear about this?'

He looked up and down the street. 'You'd better come in,' he said. 'Go upstairs.'

I did as he said, and climbed a narrow flight into a room furnished in Laura Ashley and dark wood. There was a desk with a phone on top, a couple of armchairs. Several framed prints of good-looking women were on the walls. None of them was Claire.

'So what about these photographs?' said Simmons.

'Don't tell me you don't know,' I replied, and held up the envelope I'd taken from my pocket. 'The photographs in here. Photos of you and Claire McCammon in what used to be called compromising positions. Photos that are being used to blackmail her fiancé's father.'

'Her fiancé's father,' said Simmons. 'So that's it. I heard she'd got engaged.'

What a wanker. 'Don't dick me around, Damien,' I said. 'If you weren't in on this you'd've never let me through the door.'

'All right,' he said resignedly. 'I suppose you're here for the money?'

'That's right,' I said.

'You didn't say you'd come and collect it. I thought you'd phone like last time.'

'What are you talking about?' I said.

'The money of course. The future father-in-law's and mine.'

'Yours?'

'Ten thousand pounds in exchange for the photos. The same as I paid last time. But I warn you. I'm not going to cough up again. This is it. The finish. If you hold any back this time, you can send them to my wife, or her father or whoever. I just don't have any more money. It's all my wife's.'

'You say *you're* being blackmailed too.'

'Of course I am. You know damn well. By you.'

I shook my head slowly.

'Not by you?' he said.

'No.'

'Then what the hell are you doing here?'

'Because you collected the cash that Vincent Garibaldi was

paying for the photos of Claire McCammon and you, that he
left in the boot of his car in Waterloo tonight.'

'That's what I was told to do.'

'By?'

'By a voice on the telephone. A Londoner's voice. Like
yours. You . . . I mean he sent me a letter, some sample
photographs and then called. Once, a few weeks ago, and
then again the other day.'

'Are you winding me up?'

'Like you said before. If I was, I wouldn't've let you in.'

'Yeah, I suppose.'

'So what photos have *you* got?' he asked.

'The ones that were sent to Vincent Garibaldi after he paid
up last time. And some that Claire took when she left you.'

'May I see them?'

I handed him the envelope, and he opened it, took out the
glossies and gave them a squint. Then he held the negs up to
the light and said, 'Shit.'

'What?'

'Some of these are the same as the ones I was sold. They
must've been internegged.'

'Come again?'

'Copied. The bastard sold me copies. Or maybe these are
the copies. I just don't know.'

'And you never sussed?'

'I took them years ago. And I didn't study them too closely
when they were sent to me. I just looked at them quickly,
and burnt them right away.'

'You're a bit of a mug then, aren't you?'

'Jesus. There could be dozens of copies in existence.'

The phone rang all of a sudden, and Simmons jumped. He
picked up the receiver, listened for a moment, then said,
'You . . . Hello. Hello. Oh shit. He's hung up.'

'Who?'

'The bastard blackmailer.'

'What did he say?'

'He told me to leave both lots of money in the same place
as last time.'

'Which was?'

'The Euston NCP at midnight. In a briefcase in the unlocked boot of my car. Park it there, and vanish for half an hour.'

'Show me the money,' I said. I still wasn't sure I believed him.

Simmons went to one of the framed prints on the wall. It was mounted on hinges, and he pulled it open to show the front of a safe. He worked the combination, opened it, and took out a leather briefcase and the bag containing the snide dough. He put them on the table and opened the case to show me ten banded stacks of notes. Each one had £1,000 printed on it in red.

'What shall I do?' he asked.

'Exactly as you were told.'

'But there might be dozens of copies. This could go on forever, and I don't have any more money.'

'Tough.'

'This is insane.'

'Tell you what,' I said. 'Why don't you hire me to get your money back? I'm not exactly earning out of this job at the moment.'

He seemed relieved and said, 'Will you? How much will it cost me?'

'Twenty per cent. Two grand.'

'That's a lot.'

You can't help some fuckers, can you? 'Take it or leave it,' I said. 'But that seems to be the going rate these days.'

He pulled a face. 'All right.'

I reached into the case, took out eight thousand of Simmons' money and gave it to him. I put the other two into my coat pocket, transferred the bent cash from the plastic bag to the case and slammed it shut. 'There you go,' I said. 'Simple. I'll try and get your other ten grand back too. For the same deal. But I can't promise.'

'You're not even going to give it to him?'

'No.'

'But . . . '

'No buts. I did what I said I'd do. I got you your money back, less commish. Now all you've got to do is to drive your car to Euston at midnight, leave it for a bit, then collect it again and go home to the missus. Or whatever you normally do on a Saturday night. So just shut up. I'm beginning to get tired of you.'

'You're as bad as the blackmailer.'

'No, I'm not. Think about it. This way it costs you just two thousand, and I take all the stress.' I looked at my watch. 'We've got some time to kill, I suppose a drink's out of the question?'

As it happens it wasn't, and he broke open a very acceptable brandy and we sat around his place having a few.

At about eleven-thirty we got under way. He took the case and slung it in the boot of the BMW and drove off in the direction of Euston. I followed a few minutes later. When I got to the station I stuck my motor into the NCP and went looking for him. It was parked up empty on the second level, and I found a spot where I could watch it without being seen.

At twelve ten when I'd been waiting for about fifteen minutes, a figure appeared at the door marked 'EXIT' and walked over to the car.

It was Little Vinnie. Just what I'd been dreading. Bastard. I watched him open the boot, take out the case, close the boot again, put the case on the roof of the car, and open it. I walked over towards him, silent in my Doc Martens, and said, 'Hello, Vinnie'.

He jumped at the sound of my voice, looked round and slammed the briefcase shut.

'Mr Sharman,' he said. 'Christ, but you gave me a fright. What are you doing here?'

'You know me. I get around. Firm's car?'

'Yeah.'

'You must be doing well.'

'Can't complain.'

'Working late?'

'Yeah. I've got to get this stuff sent up north, Red Star.' He was quick, I'll give him that.

'I didn't know they were open this late.'

'I dunno. I came on the offchance on the way home from the office.'

'You *are* working late. And on a Saturday too. Come on. I'll walk you. We can get a cup of tea.'

'That's all right.'

'No, come on. The pubs are shut, and I'm not doing anything. I'll carry it for you.'

'You don't have to bother.'

'Yes I do.' I took the case from his hand, and we walked back through the car park exit and up in the lift to the concourse level. The station itself was quiet at that hour, with only a few punters wandering around looking lost, and a geezer mopping the floor and nattering to two coppers. We walked past them to the cafeteria. Vinnie got two cups of tea and we went and sat down. I put the briefcase on the floor next to my seat.

I lit a cigarette and said conversationally, 'Is she in it with you?'

'Do what?'

'Don't fuck about, son. The blackmail. Does Claire know about it?'

'I don't know what you're talking about.'

'Bollocks. The money's in the bleedin' briefcase. *Red Star*. Fuckin' hell. How could you do that to your dad?'

He could see there was no point arguing. 'Oh shit,' he said. 'I had to have the money.'

'Is it dope? Or have you been cooking the books at work?'

'Both. I'm in a mess, Mr Sharman. Even this lot won't bail me out for long.'

'You're joking.'

'Peanuts.'

'Not to your old man. It's his life. Why didn't you just ask for it?'

'And let him know that his precious son who he dotes on can't keep it together? No chance.'

'So you put him through all this.'

'I had no choice.'

'You git. So is the blushing bride in on it too?'

He shook his head. 'No. She doesn't know a thing about it. She's mad about the old man. Loves him.'

'Good job one of you does. So how did you get the evidence?'

'I found it, would you believe? One day when I was in her flat on my own. I was just looking through her stuff.'

'You're a real charmer, aren't you?'

'What does it matter? Anyway, I found the snaps and had the negs copied. Dirty cow. I knew all about this Simmons character from what she'd told me. And that he's married to the daughter of a belted earl or something.'

'And you thought it would be nice to put the black on him, and include your dad as well?'

'I had to. I keep telling you I need the cash. Anyway it'll all be mine one day, when Mum and Dad drop off the perch.'

'I can't believe you.'

'Listen, Mr Sharman. No one has to know about this, do they? I can cut you in for a few bob—'

'Shut up,' I interrupted. 'Shut up now, or by Christ I'll shut you up, you little bastard.'

Then, all of sudden Little Vinnie grabbed the case from off the floor and ran out of the door of the café on to the concourse. I jumped up and ran after him and shouted, 'Vinnie, it's not . . . ' Then I saw the two Old Bill again, still chatting to the cleaner, and so did Little Vinnie, who tried to slow to a walk, but lost his balance on the wet tile flooring and fell on to his back. The briefcase went up into the air, crashed down and burst open, spilling out bundles of money and some loose notes, right at the coppers' feet. One of the constables went to help Vinnie up, whilst the other rescued the cash. He held one of the twenties up to the light and frowned, which was my cue to walk off in the opposite direction.

Poetic justice.

On the upside, Little Vinnie was nicked. Obviously Swanson's notes weren't as good as he'd promised. On the downside, the counterfeit money was gone, but at least I had

Simmons' two grand to pay for it. And on one side or another, I figured I'd better find something else to do on the day that Little Vinnie and Claire were due to get married.